left
drowning

left drowning

a novel by

JESSICA PARK

SKYSCAPE

SKYSCAPE

Text copyright © 2013 Jessica Park

Amazon Publishing
Attn: Amazon Children's Publishing
P.O. Box 400818
Las Vegas, NV 89140
www.amazon.com/amazonchildrenspublishing

Library of Congress Cataloging-in-Publication Data is available upon request.

ISBN-13: 9781477817155 (paperback)
ISBN-10: 1477817158 (paperback)
ISBN-13: 9781477867150 (eBook)
ISBN-10: T/K (eBook)

Editor: Kate Chynoweth

Printed in The United States of America (R)
First edition
10 9 8 7 6 5 4 3 2 1

This book is for everyone who has *survived*. You are not broken.
You can love and be loved, despite what may feel like
the eternally brutal nature of the world.
Even when you're drowning and so far under,
there is always time to reach for someone who will teach
you how to breathe again.

BASELINE

I CATCH MY FOOT ON THE FIRST STEP OUTSIDE OF my dorm and fall unceremoniously onto the concrete. I stay where I am for a moment, thinking that the set of keys digging into my hand should probably hurt more. Not to mention my knees, since they just endured a direct blow. "Awesome," I mumble as I push to a wobbly stand and careen toward the door. I giggle slightly while struggling to fit the key into the lock. The good news here is that if I banged the shit out of myself like I think I just did, I might just feel something tomorrow. *It has to be better than feeling nothing, right? How's that for a goddamn silver lining?* I brace myself against the giant door, steadying myself. Wait, what's less than silver? Iron? Zinc? Could there be a zinc lining?

It takes a few failed attempts at working the lock for me to realize that the key to the house I grew up in near Boston will not, understandably, unlock a dorm in Wisconsin. I finally shove the proper key in the hole and turn the lock. "I've opened the door!" I whisper triumphantly to no one. The thick metal door is unbearably heavy and resists opening fully, so I slam my shoulder hard against the door frame as I try to slither through the narrow opening. *Yet another victory!* I think hazily. The hangover I'm sure to have tomorrow, plus the injuries from smashing into objects, is definitely going to hurt. So continues my endless search for physical feeling, sensation. Anything. Still, even in my decidedly inebriated state, I know that the bruises from a drunken night can hardly be equated with any sort of positive emotional step forward. At least it will be something, though. Something other than numbness. It will be a distraction, and distractions are always welcome.

The stairwell is flooded with hideous fluorescent light. It's empty, although at this time of night, I realize one of my drunken peers might stagger past me with a one-night stand in tow at any minute. I really don't understand how people ever get laid on campus. Anyone who looks even vaguely attractive in a normal setting becomes drastically less appealing on the way back to a dorm room. Beer goggles are no match for atrocious lighting. I lean against the wall on the second-story landing and yank my phone from my pocket. My reflection in the small black screen confirms my suspicion. My already messy curls have popped out of my ponytail so there's a frizzy halo around my head, and even on my dark phone I can see the puffiness under my eyes. I look bananas.

"I look bananas!" I holler, noting the echo of my slurred words. Maybe I always look like this? Not that I care. I don't spend a lot of time in front of the mirror or concerning myself with my appearance in any

left drowning

way, really. I look however I look, and that is that. In the scheme of things, it just doesn't matter. And no one is paying attention. However, I do indeed look bananas.

When I get to my room, I practically fall through the unlocked door. Luckily, I don't have a roommate who might complain about my noisy entrance. She moved out a few days ago—presumably to go live with someone less catatonic—so the double is now all mine. I don't blame the poor girl. If you're going to be trapped on a relatively small campus outside of Madison, Wisconsin, it's best to surround yourself with cheerful people.

I walk through the dark room, stub my toe on what I'm pretty sure is an anthropology textbook, and collapse onto the futon. Oh, the irony of my having replaced my dorm-provided single bed with a full-size futon. Anyone seeing it might imagine I was the type to bring home boys.

But I am a failure in that area. *Add it to the fucking list*, I tell myself. I've lost track of the guys on campus that I've drunkenly led on and then pushed away before anything could happen. The thought of someone's hands on my body makes me want to retch. This is not normal. I understand that. Which is why I always have that moment when I'm drunk and the idea of fun, no-strings sex seems like a bright idea. For God's sake, if I could ever go through with it, I'd be in good company. Plenty of other twenty-one-year-olds were making walks of shame home in the wee hours of the morning. I've heard those supposedly shameful nights retold with plenty of laughs and sordid details.

I can lure a guy in when I want to. Alcohol gives me that. And boys respond, although I have no idea why. It's natural to want to connect with other people, I guess. Except I don't want to. Not really. Which must be why I don't have any real friends. But I drink and play the role, holding out hope that self-fulfilling prophecies exist, and that I might make a connection and feel whole again if I pretend long enough. The act is fun for me initially, yet leaves me even worse off by the end of the night, when reality hits and my intolerable loneliness engulfs me.

I know it's not especially smart to lead guys on and then bolt the minute they try to touch me. But I have my strategies. I often mumble something about being a virgin, a revelation that effectively puts a damper on most guys' interest. Discovering this did sort of amuse me. I'd have thought guys would like the idea of being a girl's first. No pressure to perform acrobatic-style maneuvers and whatnot since I wouldn't know any better. But it seems the generally smart, decent guys at this small liberal college in the middle of Wisconsin's snow tundra don't want the responsibility of deflowering a drunken coed. Go figure. Either way, I make sure nothing physical ever happens, despite my fervent desire to find an escape, however temporary. God knows it wouldn't be fun for me anyway, considering I have the arousal level of a rock.

So I add *frigid* to the list. To that stupid mental inventory I try so hard not to keep. An increasingly large list of all of my flaws. My inadequacies. My failures.

There has to be a list of my successes, too, doesn't there? Or at least my . . . adequacies? I try to focus. All the fucking liquor makes it hard, but I try. This is important.

I'm a not-terrible student.
I shower regularly.
I know a lot about tides.

left drowning

I will eat nearly anything, except for raisins.

Christ. I refocus. I may be drunk, but I can do better.

I have mastered the art of melancholy.

I have my doubts about whether this can even vaguely be considered a "success." I think again, determined to find something I've done that is worth recognition.

I lived.

The laugh that escapes my lips is awful, and the bitter sound echoes throughout my sparse room. "I'm a regular fucking Harry Potter!" I shriek. "Fuck!"

I sit up and kick off my shoes. My phone is still in my hand, and I look dizzily at it.

I never give up on my brother. That at least should go on the "success" list. Without thinking about or planning what to say, I call him.

"Jesus Christ, Blythe. What do you want?" James grumbles.

"Sorry. I woke you, didn't I?"

"Yes, you woke me up. It's three in the morning."

"Is it that late? Well, you're in college, too. Thought you'd just be getting home." I wait, but he says nothing. "How's school? How's the leg? I bet you're getting stronger every day still."

"School is fine, and knock it off with the leg questions, all right? You bring it up every time I talk to you. Enough. It's as good as it's going to get, which is shitty. Stop asking." My brother yawns. "Seriously, just go to bed." The clear irritation, the disgust, in his voice sears through me.

"James, please. I'm sorry." Damn it. I can't disguise the drunken edge to my voice. "We never talk. I wanted to hear your voice. See if you're okay."

He sighs. "Yes. I'm as fine as I can be. You sound like a disaster, though."

"Gee, that's nice."

"Well, you do." James pauses. "Mom and Dad wouldn't like this crap. You know that. Can you just . . .Can we do this another time?"

"I'm so sorry for everything. I need you to know that. To really know that. Things can be better for you. I want—"

"Don't. Not now. Not again. We're not having this fucking conversation again."

"Okay." I stare out the window into the dark. It's late September in the wee hours and although the Wisconsin temperature is still moderate, I know what is coming. Nothing good. The same as it is every year. "Sure thing, James." The ridiculous attempt at conveying a cheerful, nonchalant tone makes my voice crack. "We'll talk soon. Take care, James."

So that went well. Not that I should have expected better. Inebriated middle-of-the-night calls are sort of destined to fail. I know because I've made them before. What's tragic is that after each dumb call to my brother, I resolve that the next one will go more smoothly. However, sober calls during the day aren't any better since they always result in exchanges that are stilted and uncomfortable.

I sigh heavily, then turn on the flashlight app on my phone. I love that not only does it make normal white light, but it lets me select whatever damn color I want. I set the phone down on my bed, and it illuminates part of the room with haunting blue electronic light.

As I stand and shuffle to the small sink, my body feels drained of all its alcohol-fueled energy. It takes a few tries, but I eventually shove my long, messy hair into a knot on the top of my head. A few curls fall from the tie and hang by my face. I can't look at myself because I cannot

left drowning

stomach looking at a girl who has so little hope left. Who is inexcusably weak. I am humiliated by my own inability to do better. I vow to spend at least the next twenty-four hours booze-free.

The water that comes from the tap is ice cold. Minute after minute goes by as I collect handfuls of water and toss them over my face, and I don't stop until there are no more hot tears to wash away.

2

IMPORTANT GESTURES

SIX O'CLOCK ON A SATURDAY MORNING IS NOT exactly my preferred time to wake up. I glare at the clock. Well, there is nothing to be done. I am awake. My choice is either get up and deal with the day or stay in bed and spend the next several hours being sucked into the unpleasant and familiar vortex of racing thoughts, panic, depression, and listlessness that has dominated my life for the last four years. Better to get out of bed. As I blink into the dark, I am again hit with how tired I am and how little fight I have in me.

My lack of fight was clear enough yesterday when I met with my fifth, and presumably final, academic adviser, some woman named Tracey. A woman who seemed to think that reviving my career at this liberal arts college might be easy. She clearly doesn't know who she's dealing with. Or maybe she forgot to factor in that I only have eight months to drag through until graduation.

I take a deep breath and wiggle my toes. At least I am not hungover, since I stayed true to my vow and got through a whole twenty-four hours without drinking. It's a nice change of pace. After that disastrous phone call with my brother two nights ago, I'm filled with regret over what I'm capable of while drunk. Not to mention how horrifying it was to meet with my adviser while dealing with the hangover of a lifetime. I'm quite sure that I left a pool of alcohol-laced sweat on the seat of her office chair. There will be no drinking tonight either.

I turn on the light by my bed and push the sheets down with my feet, again grateful that I do not have a roommate to growl at me for my odd hours. The yellow light shines over my body, and I involuntarily wince as I sit up and see my legs, which are covered in bruises from falling down while wasted two nights before. As a general rule, I give little thought to my appearance, but even I can see that it's not just the bruises that make me look like a mess. My legs and bikini line are in dire need of a good shave. Upon further examination, I accept that I could probably stand to work out once in a while. Surviving on little food and too much beer and tequila is, unsurprisingly, not serving my body well. I tap my feet together and watch my thighs. They're both bony and jiggly, which is not exactly a super-attractive combination.

The shade that covers the one large window in my room retracts with hurricane force when I tug on it, and I flinch at the loud noise it makes. It's still dark outside, but the act of opening the shade seems like something that people—normal people—should do when they get up. It's an important gesture, and for some reason I think that today should possibly be a day of important gestures, if not actual connectedness with the real world. I have already made the decision to get out of bed early, and not drink for another twenty-four hours, and that's better than I've done in a while.

After pulling on jeans and a hoodie, knotting my hair into a twist, and brushing my teeth, I stuff a few things into a backpack and head for the student union. If I hope to make any other important gestures today, I will need coffee.

Although it's normally swarming with students, the union is empty at this hour, save for the unfortunate work-study victim who is behind the register at the café. "Coffee?" he asks.

I nod. "Two, please. Extra large. Black."

He peers behind me.

"Yes, they're both for me."

I tap my fingers rhythmically on the counter as I watch him pour.

"Here you go." He snaps a lid onto the top of each cup and swipes my student ID card.

I thank him and look around the room. Normally I sit by the wall near the emergency exit door, but since the place is so empty today, I decide to sit down in a chair in the center of the room and kick my legs up on the seat of another. The first big sip of coffee is so strong and bitter that it makes me cringe, but I know that by the fourth sip it will go down easier. *Just like shots!* I think.

I check my phone. Still no message from James. Not that I expect one, really, but it is hard not to hope. *Aha*, I think. *There it is again. Hope.* Maybe one night he will call me after a college party, drunk and full of rambling, incoherent questions that symbolize everything that's wrong with our hideously damaged relationship. All of a sudden, I feel like an

left drowning

idiot. Could there be a stupider thing to hope for? What I should want is for the two of us to have a sober, heartfelt conversation in which we work out all of our unspoken issues and wind up the best of friends. The way that we used to be. I grimace to myself. *Like that's gonna happen.* It's probably good that he goes to college in Colorado, far away from me, so that he does not have to deal with me being able to just stop by his dorm anytime I want.

I close my eyes and take a deep breath. *Just get through the day, Blythe. You can fucking do this.* It would have helped if I hadn't woken up at the crack of dawn, thereby making this day longer than necessary. But I'm out of bed, out of my room, I have coffee, and I even have my earphones so that I can listen to NPR. I don't listen to music much. Not anymore. Before—when everything was good—I would spend hours flipping through radio stations, downloading music, and dancing around my room. I'd drive around in my parents' Honda and get lost in music. Music that had heart. That moved me. It used to be fun to feel.

I open up the NPR website and scroll through stories until I settle on a rather disgusting-sounding piece about a former vegan learning to embrace butchering. Just as I near the end of the story and am learning that said former vegan's favorite cut of meat is pig's feet, someone crashes into the seat across from me.

"Hey! You got me a coffee! That was very thoughtful."

Startled, I look up. A scruffy-looking guy in a ripped T-shirt and jeans faces me. He removes a cowboy hat, revealing black hair that is sticking out every which way—although in an admittedly adorable manner—and he has at least three days of good stubble going. Even though they're bloodshot, his eyes are sharply blue. He is a big guy. Not fat, just bulky. Based on his general aroma, I guess he's carrying a fair amount of beer weight. What's most noticeable, however, is the big grin plastered across his face. Well, that and the fact that he is helping himself to the second cup of coffee that I so recently purchased.

He takes a sip. "You know, this really isn't bad coffee. Sure, sure, everyone likes to make a fuss and complain that campus coffee is grotesque sludge, but that's just an excuse to get Mommy and Daddy to fund repeated trips to that overpriced coffee shop down the street. What's it called? Beans, Beans, right? What a dumb name. Not, however, a dumb name for the show that I'm producing, called *Beans, Beans: The Musical*. Since you generously got me this coffee, I shall thank you for your kindness by giving you front-row seats. And backstage passes! Wait until you meet the guy who plays Evil Grinder Number Three. He'll scare the hell out of you in the show, but he's a really good person deep down." He pauses to take a long drink from the cup, and then bangs his fist on the table and grins. "This is hot as shit, huh? Just how I like it."

I blink a few times and wait to see if his one-man show is over. He tips his head to the side and continues looking at me while I try to figure out what to do next.

He leans forward. "Too much?"

Yes, you weirdo, just a bit. But I say nothing.

He sticks out his hand. "I'm Sabin."

"Blythe." I put my hand in his. As much as I'm uncomfortable with physical contact, I feel surprisingly at ease when his big hand engulfs mine. The touch is somehow soothing.

"Blythe, it is my true honor to meet you." He claps his other hand on top of mine, and I still don't pull away. "Now tell me, what are you doing up so early?"

left drowning

"Just . . . I don't know." I wrinkle my forehead. *Who is this guy?* "I couldn't sleep. Why are you up so early?"

"You caught me! In my case the question should be, why am I up so late?"

I smile shyly. "Oh, I see."

We sit without speaking for a few moments, my hand still in his, while he looks at me expectantly. I should take my hand away, but I simply can't. He is too odd and too endearing.

"Aren't you going to ask me why I haven't gone to bed yet? Given our close relationship, I'd think that my whereabouts would be an extremely pressing issue here. Your curiosity should be driving you insane. Was Sabin at an all-night karaoke amusement park? Was he abducted by alien cowboy goats?" He points to the hat on the table and raises an eyebrow. "And subsequently subjected to a humiliating yet arousing strip search? Or did a well-intentioned but inept and drug-addled tattoo artist foul up 'Jesus Loves Me' and forever brand him with 'I Love Cheese'?"

"Oh." Even given this bizarre speech, I feel less uncomfortable than I normally do talking to strangers, although I am still quite lost. "I should have immediately asked those questions. Sorry." I try to get a handle on the situation, wondering if he is trying to flirt with me. It doesn't quite feel like it. "So," I say, "why haven't you?"

"Why haven't I what?"

Good Lord. "Gone to bed yet?"

"Oh! Yes!" He grips my hand tighter and stands, pulling me up with him and then pressing my hand into his chest. "I have met a woman, so technically I have gone to bed already. I just haven't slept. Her name is Chrystle, and she is utterly ethereal. Heart-stoppingly beautiful. And"—he says with a wink—"angelic in the most unangelic way. I am in love."

I can't help but laugh. Especially because he most certainly does not seem to be hitting on me. He is already in love. Or at least lust. "Saved by a good woman?" I offer.

"For now." Another wink. He drops my hand, flops back into his chair, and puts on his cowboy hat again. "So now you know all you need to about me. Let's hear about you, Miss Blythe. You're a freshman?"

"What?" I say too defensively. "No. I'm a senior."

"My apologies. You have that lost lamb way about you. It's sweet. Sitting here alone, a backpack probably full of overpriced textbooks . . . I know the type. Besides, I'm a junior and I haven't seen you around before, I don't think. And you don't seem to know who I am."

"I don't have a backpack full of textbooks. And I'm not really *around* all that much. I'm more about counting the days until graduation at this point." I shrug. That's not entirely true, of course, because it's not as though I have plans I'm looking forward to—but it's one way to explain my lack of engagement with campus life. "Am I supposed to know who you are?"

"If you're not a big fan of the theater scene here, then probably not. When I'm not wooing the lady folk, I'm in the theater department. So you didn't see me in *The Glass Menagerie*? My performance was none too shabby, if I do say so myself. And I directed *A Doll's House* last winter." He waits expectantly. "No? Nothing?"

I stare blankly at him. "Sorry. I don't really . . . go to things."

"I'm hurt. Very hurt. Considering that you and I are close friends now, I expect you to attend each and every performance of mine from now on. Deal?"

left drowning

"We're close friends now?" His shtick is both disarming and amusing.

"We are. Don't you think? This feels right."

"Sure," I say. He is, in fact, onto something. The mood in the room has shifted. *My* mood has shifted.

"So you'll come to see me in *The Importance of Being Earnest*? It opens four weeks from last night."

"Fine. I'll be there." I can tell that it is easier to agree than to try to explain my general aversion to public events. At least sober ones.

"And I, in turn, will attend anything you invite me to."

"That's . . . sweet. I don't expect to have occasion to invite a guest to anything in the foreseeable future, but I'll keep you in mind." The lid on my coffee cup keeps me busy as I avoid looking at Sabin. He has to be as hyperaware of the differences between us as I am. I'm mortified and feel as though being honest about my complete lack of a life looks like a cry for attention. The last thing I want.

"Wait a minute!" Sabin suddenly exclaims. "I have seen you! You funnel beer better than any girl I've ever met!"

"Oh God." I drop my head into my palm.

"I'm friends with a true champ. This is fantastic." He folds his arms across his chest and beams.

"Fantastic, indeed. So, so fantastic," I mutter.

"Listen, new friend Blythe, thank you very much for the coffee, but I have to get back to my dorm and get some sleep." He helps himself to my phone and begins typing, then pulls out his own phone and coaxes me into telling him my number. "There. Now we have each other's digits. What dorm are you in? I'm in Leonard Hall, room 402, if you want to stop by."

"Okay. I'm in Reber. Room 314."

"Cheer up." He leans in and kisses me on the cheek. "You're beautiful when you smile."

And then the whirlwind that is Sabin exits the building, stage right. I shake my head. That was . . . that was . . .

That was kind of nice. In fact, I am noticeably moved.

And then I am crushed—overwhelmed, really—with sadness. That small interaction is the best thing that has happened to me in ages. And how goddamn awful is that?

Of course, this guy has no idea what a mess I am, and he'd probably never have come over to me if he knew that I am such a despondent dope. I sigh. He will find out sooner or later. Probably when he sobers up.

But the encounter has undeniably energized me, and I decide to take what remains of my first coffee—the second one having been polished off by Sabin—and head down to the lake. Today I will be able to say that I did something unexpected. This walk will be my important gesture.

3

THE STONE SKIPPER

I PULL MY SUNGLASSES FROM MY BACKPACK AND start what I'm guessing will be a long walk to the lake. My encounter with Sabin, while somewhat disconcerting, has put me in an uncharacteristically good mood, and motivated me to finally make this first trip down to the water. It is pretty silly that I've never gotten myself to the lake here, especially after my insistence on applying only to colleges near water. True, I haven't ventured down to the lake in over three years, but the whole time I've known it was here. That mattered. Access to water is, despite my generally precarious mood, a stabilizing force for me.

I zip up my sweatshirt against the morning chill but notice the sun is already gaining strength; it will warm up to the sixties in a few hours,

I'm guessing. Being outside feels good. Sunshine is supposed to help depression, after all. Not that I would classify myself as depressed. Sure, I have numerous depressive symptoms, but I think that I have good reason. Anyone in my situation would be depressed, right? And the whole concept of depression is . . . well, depressing. It doesn't seem to take into account that I may damn well be justified in feeling how I do. So what if I'm often in an apathetic haze and spend half my time drinking until I feel numb? It's not like I cry all the time. I think back to my psych textbook and grimace as I think how clearly my symptoms match up to the clinical definition.

Fine, fine. I'm depressed. There. I said it.

What I find interesting, at least from a human-interest standpoint, is that while I am painfully aware of my feelings and symptoms, I'm unable to shake them and move forward. I am stagnant, I guess.

I shake off my lame attempt at self-analysis, put on my earphones, and listen to an NPR news podcast on my phone for the rest of the walk. When I reach the lake, I find a path that takes me through some overgrown brush and lands me by patches of grass and pebbly sand that skirt a small beach area. The lake is stunning, especially at this still-early time of morning. I take off my earphones. It is almost totally quiet except for the occasional lap of water. This appears to be on the less popular side of the lake, but I can see a larger beach area and a few docked boats on the opposite shore.

I sit and wiggle my butt into the sandy ground until I have carved out a comfortable sitting spot. The air is fresh and reviving. I can breathe. Why have I never come here before?

Well, I know why.

The love/hate relationship that I have with water. Well, mostly I

left drowning

love it. Yet it's also a reminder of a past that I'm both clinging to and struggling to outrun. I may not have come to this shoreline yet in my years at Matthews, but I knew it was here and that mattered. I wanted to be able to come here when I felt ready. Apparently I am ready today, because it feels glorious to be here. The light is extraordinary. Photographs and paintings invariably cheapen morning light, but the real-life version can be stupendous. Like it is right now.

Reality is not necessarily my friend—then again, neither are dreams—but this moment, this reality, is beautiful. I am alone without being lonely, for once, staring across the water and watching the sun begin its climb into the clear blue sky.

When I scan the shoreline, though, I see that I am not alone. There is one person.

He stands about ten yards from me, just at the edge of the water, wearing only worn jeans and blue sneakers, no shirt. His profile is silhouetted against the growing light, and I watch him as he stares across the lake. His black hair falls nearly to his shoulders in soft waves. He has to be at least six feet tall, beautifully long and lean. He isn't big like a weight lifter, but he looks incredibly strong.

I'm watching him so intensely that I realize I'm holding my breath. I force myself to inhale and exhale deeply.

Crystal-clear thoughts hit me. *He is confident, he is assured, and he is centered.*

I can't look away.

He looks down and kicks at the ground a few times before bending down and picking up something. Weirdly, I guess what he is going to do before he does it, and I catch myself smiling slightly as he reaches back his arm and skips a rock into the water. I try to count the skips. *One, two, three, four, five* . . . It's hard to see from where I am. He takes a few steps from where he is and then roots in the ground for more rocks. I watch as he skips another. Then another.

He moves smoothly, seamlessly. I know that he's done this before; I can tell by his clean, competent movements and rhythm. He strikes me as free, freer than I am or could be. Again, I catch myself holding my breath as I watch him. I have no idea why I feel so drawn to this stranger. But the feeling is undeniable.

The stone skipper searches the ground again and then reaches into the front pocket of his jeans before sending a stone bouncing across the water. *Smart boy.* He brought his own stash. I know the sort of perfect stone one needs to get the dance of rings to appear on the water's surface. I searched for those same kinds of stones as a kid, although despite my repeated efforts to learn, I never got very good at skipping. This boy, on the other hand, is a master.

I inhale and exhale again, wondering why I feel overwhelmed just by watching him. A thought I don't understand flashes into my consciousness. *He is the past, and the present, and the future.* I shake my head hard. What in the hell is wrong with me? Is this because I didn't drink last night? Maybe I'm going into some kind of bizarre booze withdrawal. I should probably go back to the dorm and crawl into bed. But the lure of watching the stone skipper is too much, and I cannot get myself to leave. I stop fighting my impulse to run and lean back on my elbows for the show.

Twenty minutes later and he is still at it. I like how he takes his time before throwing, the way he assesses the water and rubs each stone in his hand for a few minutes to feel its shape and texture, weighing it in his palm. He pauses after each throw, letting the ripples from each stone fade, allowing the process to have its full beginning, middle, and end.

left drowning

Without full awareness of what I'm doing, I stand up and walk toward him. He must catch sight of me from the corner of his eye, because he turns slightly my way and smiles. From my place in the sand, I'd noticed that his muscular body was hard to ignore, but I hadn't expected his face to be so gorgeous. As I get closer to him, I begin to wish I had stayed away. I want to grimace as I take in the perfect angular lines of his jaw—attractiveness on this level is a bad sign. Anyone this hot is usually a complete creep. I barely care about my own body, and rarely notice someone else's, but a flat stomach and abs like his undeniably appealing.

"Hi," he prompts me.

Oh. I am staring. And not into his eyes. His arms have the most beautiful definition that I've ever seen.

"Sorry. Um . . . Hi." I am fumbling for words, pathetically so, and it only gets worse when I look up. He pushes his hair from his face. His green eyes, framed by strong dark eyebrows, nearly cause my knees to buckle. This is ridiculous. He is just another human being. I take a deep breath and try to look at him critically. After another minute of staring at him, I'm relieved to see that he probably isn't every girl's idea of perfection. He's a little too skinny, maybe, and his nose is slightly crooked. Of course, I actually like that. I see perfection in things that are likely considered imperfections by others.

"Hi," he says again, looking slightly amused.

"I saw you skipping stones," I blurt out. "You're really good."

"Years of practice."

I squirm, curling my toes in my sneakers, wishing yet again that I had just kept my distance. I don't know what I'm doing. "I've . . . I've never been good at that. I used to try as a kid, but my stones always just cannonballed in."

"I've done that plenty of times. You've got to send it off with enough force. But also enough care."

I nod. "Well, sorry to bother you. Just wanted to tell you it was nice to watch." I pause and brazenly reword what I have said. "You, I mean. *You* were nice to watch." I turn to leave, appalled at what I have put out there.

"Hey," he says, stopping me. "Do you want me to help you? I could give you a few tips if you like."

I spin around, aware that trying to resist would be really fucking futile.

"If you don't mind, that would be . . . cool." I cannot think of a better word than *cool* right now because he has rendered me closer to insane than I usually am, and I have no idea why.

"I'm Christopher Shepherd, by the way. Chris. Whatever you like."

"What do you like?"

"Whatever you like." He smiles. "And you are . . . ?"

"I'm Blythe McGuire."

"It's nice to meet a fellow enthusiast." He smiles softly, and I am entranced by how one side of his smile lifts higher than the other. It makes me both unnerved and physically unsteady. "I think I've tapped out the area right here for good stones, but if we walk a bit we should be able to find more."

"Okay."

Chris gestures to the left. "Should we try this way?"

"Yes. If you think so."

"I'm just going to grab my shirt. I'll catch up with you." He backs up.

Under the guise of looking for good stones, I keep my head down

left drowning

as I start to walk because otherwise my eyes will follow him. I find him . . . I don't know. Something. I don't know exactly what, but I do know that I wish I were wearing something besides a shitty sweatshirt, although I have no idea what I could have resurrected from my closet.

I feel him next to me. "What are you doing here so early in the morning?" he asks.

"Sleep issues. What about you?"

"Who'd want to miss this?" Chris waves his hand in the direction of the lake sparkling in the sun. "Damn spectacular."

I glance to the side. He's put on a faded black T-shirt. "Aren't you cold?"

"I like it. Refreshing. Before you got here, I'd been considering stripping down and diving in."

"You were not." I look up. He towers over my five feet four inches.

"I most certainly was." He is grinning at me.

"Now you're risking that I'll brand you an exhibitionist."

Chris kneels down for a moment, picks up a stone, and slips it into his pocket. "What's a little risk now and then, huh?" He rushes past me and turns so that he is walking backward, facing me as he talks. "It makes you feel alive. It brings you crashing into the here and now. Keeps you alert and grounded."

"I have more here and now than I can handle, thank you very much, without skinny-dipping."

"Technically it wouldn't have been skinny-dipping because I was going to keep something on."

An image of Chris in nothing but snug boxer briefs flashes into my head, and it takes me a moment to recover. I try to walk nonchalantly, following the backward path he is making.

"Are you a student?" he asks.

I nod.

"Where?"

"I'm a senior at Matthews," I tell him.

He stops and I nearly crash into him. "Me, too. Why don't I know you?"

It's bad enough that I've had this conversation once already today, but to have it with Chris feels worse.

"I transferred in last year as a junior," he continues, "but I don't think we've ever met. What, do you take all independent studies classes and never leave your dorm room?"

I don't say anything.

"Oh my God, you don't actually do that, do you? I'm sorry. I feel horrible. I was just making a joke."

"What? No! I take real classes. Of course I do." He steps aside as I keep walking, moving past him. This is so embarrassing. Have I really become invisible unless I'm funneling beer at parties? Yes, I accept, I have. It is pretty easy to pass unnoticed when you want to.

Maybe I don't want that anymore.

Chris bounces ahead of me again. "I'm sorry. Sometimes I move a mile a minute and miss things. Miss *people*."

"Maybe there will be some good stones up toward the grass." I move up the slight incline from where we are standing. "I'll go check."

"Oh. Okay." I know he is staring at me. "I'll look in the shallow water."

We spend a few minutes silently collecting stones, and I wonder what sort of excuse I can come up with to leave. Clearly I have botched our entire exchange. It's one that I never should have started in the first

left drowning

place, considering that I'm idiotically out of practice when it comes to basic social interaction. I try to give myself a pep talk. Perhaps this will be like riding the proverbial bike? If I keep going, maybe I'll remember how to behave like a normal person again? I used to be good at this.

"Hey, Blythe," he calls out. "I found a bunch of good ones. Come down and we'll get more, and you can show me what you've got." His voice is deep, masculine, yet I hear compassion and humanity in each word he says. Hearing him relaxes me and undoes my self-consciousness in a way that nothing else has been able to since that one night four years ago.

Four years. Jesus, I have been like this for four fucking years? I start to wonder what I have missed out on. *Who* I have missed out on. I am momentarily furious.

But then I look to the water, to Chris, and his infectious grin meets me. This boy makes it impossible for me to be pulled under. I smile back at him with a real smile. "Yeah? You found more? Okay." I step over the overgrown grass and the half-buried rocks to reach him.

"Shoes off!" he commands.

"What?"

"Shoes off and pants rolled up! We're going to get you in tune with the lake. Good stone skipping is not just about the stone. It's about the water, and it's about you. So, off with your shoes!"

"It's cold!" I protest.

"Baby," he teases as he starts removing his shoes.

"Am not. I'm showing a measure of sanity." The irony that I am saying this is not lost on me.

"There's nothing good to be said about sanity. It's dull. Live a little. Come on."

I try not to smile back as he arches his dark eyebrows playfully.

"Fine," I say, kicking off my sneakers and rolling up my jeans. "To prove I'm not a baby."

"In we go." Chris wades a few feet into the water and turns back to me. "It's really not cold. Promise." He holds out his hand. "Really."

I step forward into the cool water, and the soles of my feet sink into the grainy sand. It's a striking feeling, one I've avoided on purpose for the past four years. Without really thinking, I place my hand into his. My eyes close, and I feel him tighten his fingers around mine. The dark world in my head begins to break into pieces, and flashes of old, forgotten memories break through. I find that I am taking quick, shallow breaths. *Stop it. Stop it!* I instruct myself. I focus on my hand in his, feeling his steady and solid grip. The flashes burst apart as I open my eyes and speak too quickly, hoping to recover from the moment, hoping to cover up my lapse. "You're right. The water isn't so bad."

Chris cocks his head to the side. "You okay?" He squeezes my hand. I nod. "Yes. I am now."

He studies me, more serious now. "Do we know . . ." He can't seem to finish his question.

"What?"

He shakes his head. "No, we haven't met before. It's just . . . Nothing." He slips a smooth stone onto my palm and closes my fingers around it for me. "Show me." Chris steps back.

The water splashes gently around my ankles as I position my body perpendicular to the line of the water. "Now don't laugh at me. It's been a while since I have even attempted this."

"There is no laughing in stone skipping," he says, clearly dramatizing his voice for effect. "This is a very, very somber activity. You may now proceed with your first attempt."

left drowning

I try not to smile at his mock formality as I keep my arm level and fling the stone over the water. It veers off fifteen feet to the right and then shoots through the surface of the water like a bullet.

"Well," Chris says, "what you lack in skill, you make up for with sheer force."

I laugh. "That did not go as I might have hoped, but I appreciate your tact."

"Do a few more. I'll back up in case things go really awry."

"Ha-ha. Very funny. Although that's not a bad idea . . ." I can feel him watching me as I try three more times, managing to get only one stone to produce a sloppy skip. "I'm hopeless, I think."

"No, you're not. Why do you throw like you're a little kid tossing a Frisbee?"

I can't help but laugh again. "Is that what I look like?"

"Well, you sort of throw your arm across your body like this." He smiles and flings his arm out wildly. "See? That's no good."

"Aha. I didn't realize." I think for a second. He is right. As intently as I was watching him before, I hadn't noticed that he doesn't do this.

"Here, try it a different way." Chris moves in and stands behind me. "I see you're right-handed, so you'll want to turn the other way so that your throwing hand is away from the water." His hands touch the top of my arms as he slowly pivots me around, coming to stand so close to me that our shadows become one. As he steps away, his shadow emerges from mine until it is distinct on the sandy ground. I turn to focus and throw my smooth stone.

"It feels awkward," I confess.

"Sure, at first. We're breaking a bad habit. Try again. Let's wade in a bit more. It sounds corny, but you have to sort of unite with the water."

I sigh, doubtful I can do this, but I sidestep a few feet until I feel the water hit the rim of my jeans. I give another attempt.

"Better!" Chris says. "You got two skips. Do another."

I pull a stone from my pocket and aim. This time the stone soars off to the left and does not skip at all. "Ugh. I give up."

"No, you don't." He is behind me again, and I can feel his chest just brush my back. He rests his hands on my shoulders as if to ground me, and I shiver. Not from cold, and not exactly from lust. At least, that's not the only thing making me tremble. "Look out over the water. Zero in on the skyline. Don't think about where you want to hit the water."

I feel him run his hand down my arm until he reaches my wrist, then he lifts up my arm for me. I inhale and exhale slowly.

"Then," he continues, "make the stone hit where the water meets the sky." He pulls my hand in closer to my body until my arm is crossed in front of me, a slow-motion rehearsal for how I will throw. "Be firm and confident. Remember that you're not the boss of this. You and this stone are partners."

"We're partners. Okay."

Chris stays where he is, inches behind me, as I follow his advice.

Three skips.

"Beautiful," he whispers. "Do it again. Listen to your partner."

Four skips.

He lifts my hand an inch higher and puts his mouth by my ear. "Breathe into it."

Seven skips.

Holy shit.

"Did you see that?" I can hardly speak. It is just skipping stones; there is no reason to be so awestruck by what I've done, but I am.

"That was awesome! Really awesome!" Chris squeezes my shoulders. "Just gorgeous. Hey, I bet if you keep at it, you'll be skipping

left drowning

across the entire lake in no time. It's really cool when you skip so far that you lose count. The way the rings move farther and farther out . . ."

Chris continues to talk, but I can barely hear him. I am just staring at the spot where the stone finally broke the surface for the last time, dropping to the bottom of the lake.

"Chris?"

". . . one time I tried to show someone else how to skip, and he completely sucked. You're so much better—"

"Christopher." Without thinking, I lean my head back, resting it just below his shoulder. He is so tall and . . . somehow familiar. I roll my head to the side and take in the sunlight, stronger now, which hits the small ripples in the water and turns them bright white. My vision seems sharper, my thoughts less muted, than just an hour ago. This near stranger is inexplicably giving me more safety and security than anyone else ever has.

"Yeah?"

For no discernible reason, it feels unfathomable not to tell him. "My parents are dead."

He doesn't move away. He doesn't even tense up at my words.

It is the first time I have said this out loud in . . . well, ever. Could it be possible that I have somehow managed never to say this? Yes, I accept, it's true. People from home didn't need to hear it directly from me. They all knew. News like that spreads quickly. And no one at college has needed to know. I say it again. "My parents are dead. They died four years ago in a fire." I step forward, suddenly shocked at how blunt I am being. "Oh God. I'm sorry. I don't know why I just told you that. I'm so sorry. It's not your . . . I shouldn't have . . ."

I wait for him to do what everyone else did after my parents died.

Spout off some conventional words of sympathy. *I'm so sorry. How awful. You poor thing. Terribly sad* . . . I hate all of those words because it means that people will run from me. People always do. Nobody knows what to say after the initial words of supposed comfort. Death and grief make everyone around you vanish because death and grief are intolerable.

But Chris does not run. Instead, he slides his arm around my waist and pulls me in close until my back is tight against his chest. "It's okay. Breathe into it."

"I have a brother. James. He hates me because of it. *I* hate me because of it. I am so tired." I close my eyes and press my cheek into Chris's shirt. His arms cross in front of me and hold me gently while flashes of that night roll over me. Flashes are all that I have. Maybe because I can't or maybe because I don't want the full memory. I can barely stand the pieces. The days immediately before and immediately after don't exist for me either. They are entirely empty, and I prefer to keep it that way. I shudder in Chris's arms. Right now I cannot control what is showing in my head, although I wish I could. The flashes of memory I'm getting now are more vivid and intense than I have ever experienced. I am remembering in a way that I have not before.

Heat. Water. Glass. Dirt. The dock. The dock in the cove. The colors on the patchwork quilt.

I am starting to choke. Why is this happening to me now? Why, when I start to have one vaguely tolerable morning, am I plagued by the past?

His fingers tighten on my arms. "Breathe into it," he says again. His voice helps, his touch helps. "Let it happen. I'm here."

The smell. The pictures on the quilt. Red. Red. Red. Trees. The ladder, the sound, the hero. The hero. My hero.

left drowning

It is enough. I can't take anymore.

Think about the dock, I tell myself, my eyes still closed. *Think about the dock*. This always calms me. I don't know why, but when I picture the dock, it always helps me to stop spiraling. I imagine rowing to it, over and over. I am safe on the dock, and I feel stability and safety there, although I have no idea why.

My eyes open and I feel my breathing slow.

"I think," I say slowly, "that we're out of stones."

"There are always more. You want to keep skipping?"

"Yes."

"Then we will."

BREAKING THE RULES

MY SUNGLASSES DO LITTLE TO BLOCK OUT THE sun's strength, so I shut my eyes. Part of me is scared to do this because I'm totally convinced that he'll be gone when I open them. I test my theory and roll my head to the side for a quick peek. Chris is still there, lying next to me on the sand, both of us on our backs while we talk—or rather, while he talks. I make him do most of the talking since I'm so out of practice. Good thing that Sabin gave me a warm-up this morning.

It takes everything I have to look away from him again, but I don't want to be caught staring. I love his imperfect nose, his full lips, and the way he runs his hands through his black hair every so often, tousling the soft waves. Every time he does this, the muscles in his arm flex slightly and I am further entranced.

More than my undeniable physical attraction to Chris is the fact that I feel something else for him that I can't explain. It's more than a little confusing. I've read countless literary works that detail the longing and ache that characters have for someone they love, and over time, I have developed a strong belief that it's just dramatic bullshit meant to entice readers. Today, however, I understand that it's not bullshit. It's very strange the way my stomach and chest are tight and fluttery and how his presence is so entirely magnetic. While it's a decidedly wonderful feeling, it's also terrible because I know that I am alone in this; there is no way that Chris can possibly feel what I am feeling. I push aside that thought because I'm not exactly in a position to barrel into any serious romantic entanglement anyway, even if he was interested. Which he's not. I can tell by the way he's just lying next to me on the beach, chattering. So I will just enjoy this time with him.

Part of my old self has awoken, and I am going to let this day happen.

Chris has already told me that he's lived "too many places to mention," and that he's majoring in economics and minoring in English lit. We also spent twenty minutes discussing our favorite coffee drinks, a conversation that only cemented how fucking cool he is. How many college students have a French press and a milk frother in their room? One. That's how many.

"My sister has tried to steal the press on more than one occasion. I bought her one, but she claims the coffee mine makes tastes better."

"You have a sister?"

"A sister and two brothers."

"How old?" I ask.

"They're all here at Matthews with me. Estelle and Eric, they're twins, are sophomores, and my brother Sabin is a junior."

"Wait. Sabin?" There couldn't be that many Sabins on a campus this small. "Tall, dark hair, a little . . . wild?"

Chris laughs. "You know him?"

"Just met him this morning. He stole my coffee. Apparently coffee-related thievery runs in your family."

"He's a handful. Best brother you could ask for. Well, he and Eric."

"Sort of funny that you are all at the same school," I say. The air is much warmer now, and I'm about to take off my sweatshirt when I remember that I just have on a T-shirt underneath. One that would show my left arm. I settle for unzipping the sweatshirt and dealing with the heat.

Chris shrugs. "We're pretty close, I guess. The thought of us all being spread across the country at different schools sucked, so here we are."

"How did you end up at Matthews?"

"I saw it on a shirt once. Seemed like a good idea."

I impulsively swat him on the arm, aware of how comfortable I feel doing this. I'm amazed that I don't feel weirder about my freakish behavior earlier, but I don't. It seems Chris can tolerate my eccentricities. "I'm serious!"

He tips his head to me. "So am I."

"That's a weird way to choose a college."

He grins. "We're a weird bunch."

"Your parents must have whopping empty-nest syndrome with all four of you away now, huh?"

"It's just my father at home. My mother died when we were all

left drowning

pretty young. A brain aneurysm. Totally random. No way to see it coming." Chris sits up, and his shadow travels across my stomach. "So we have something in common."

"Dead mothers."

"Yes," he agrees. "Dead mothers."

So he understood what was happening to me while we were standing in the water together. That was the connection that I felt.

"I'm glad that we don't have dead fathers in common," I say. "At least you still have one parent."

He says nothing. I roll onto my side and tuck up my knees, and Chris does the same so that we are facing each other. I don't shy away from studying him, letting my eyes travel over his body. I am relaxed, thoroughly relaxed. And exhausted. I drowsily ask him anything that I can think to ask because I want to keep him talking. His voice is soothing and beautiful, and his face is all I see as I drift off.

I sleep without dreaming, and when I wake up, Chris is still beside me, leaning back onto his elbows and looking out at the water. Slowly I sit up and he smiles at me.

"Hi."

"Hi." I busy myself with brushing sand off my jeans and redoing the knot holding my hair back so that he can't see how embarrassed I am. It's disorienting to have zonked out so completely. "How long was I asleep?"

"A few hours."

"A few what?" Oh my God. "I'm sorry. You didn't have to sit here while I slept. I'm sure you have things to do."

Chris shakes his head. "Why would I want to leave? Beautiful day, happily snoozing girl? Did you sleep well?"

"I did." It's an almost nonexistent occurrence, and I am positive that I slept so peacefully because of Chris. Asking him to sit next to me every night so that I can sleep without nightmares is probably unreasonable. . . .

"Know what?"

"What?"

Chris bounces up so that he is looming above me. "I'm fucking starving."

"Oh. Okay." I squint up at him. He likes to curse, too. "I should probably get going, too."

His hand stretches down to me. "Let's go to lunch. I know a great place. Actually, that's not true. It's not a great place, but it's an interesting place." He picks up my backpack as he grabs my hand and pulls me to standing. "You've got to be hungry, too. It's way past lunchtime and I bet you didn't eat breakfast."

He's right, and I am starving, but I'm hesitant to push this day anymore. The safety that I feel with him by the lake can't possibly hold up if we leave. "I don't know. I have studying to do, and—"

"Nonsense. C'mon." He pulls me forward and then drops my hand as he again walks backward.

Our walk back toward campus is quiet, but not awkward. It's a rare thing to be with another person and not feel an obligation to fill every second with talk. Chris shoves his hands in his pockets and lifts his head into the sunlight as we stroll. Eventually the local businesses come into view, and he points to a blue flag waving in the slight breeze. "Have you eaten here? You must have, of course. Everyone has."

I look up. Artemis Piccola. I shake my head. "Odd name for a restaurant. No. I haven't been here."

left drowning

The truth is that I rarely leave campus. My life follows a direct path from one place to another with virtually no wandering, except for nights that I get drunk enough to want a second party that might have more booze. Dorm to class, class to the cafeteria, back to the dorm, a quick trip to the library when vitally necessary, a stop at the union for coffee. If there's no keg involved, I'm not one to linger or stray. Well, until today. Today I am breaking all the rules.

"What? You've never been here?" Christopher's jaw might as well have fallen open. "Good Lord, girl, we need to fix that right away. This is practically a rite of passage. You certainly can't graduate this spring if you haven't eaten here. C'mon. I'm buying you lunch." He swings open the door and waves me through the entrance.

After grabbing a menu from the rack on the wall, he leads the way through the maze of tables. The way that he moves is clean, almost stealthy, and soon we are sitting at a table buried at the back of the restaurant. The room is all wood and brick with no windows, and it's incredibly dark despite the perfect weather outside. The hard bench that I sit on gives me a good view of the space, but because I have my back to a wall, Christopher has only me to look at. I spend a full minute wishing we were sitting in opposite seats.

He holds the menu in his lap and smiles playfully at me. "So, Miss Blythe, what part of the world would you like to visit today?"

What is he asking me? I assume I am missing out on a joke that most people would get. "I don't . . . I don't know what you mean." I feel incredibly awkward.

"Pick a country. Where would you like to go?"

For God's sake, I barely leave my dorm room on most days, so the idea of foreign travel is not exactly at the top of my fantasies. "Greece?"

"You don't seem very sure about that."

I fidget with the zipper on my sweatshirt. "Greece," I repeat more definitively. "Santorini."

"Pick one more."

My zipper digs into my hand as I pull it up and down. "Brazil."

"Ah. Carnival."

"Yes. Carnival."

He flips open the menu. "I'm not sure if we can get as specific as Santorini, but you never know here at crazy Artemis Piccola." He scans the page in front of him. "Ahhh. Based on your choice of locations, you will be having a gyro followed by the feijoada."

I reach across the table and take the menu from his hands. What kind of place is this? The menu is a freakish collection of dishes that have nothing whatsoever to do with one another. Spicy tuna maki is listed right after vegan lasagna, and the specials are an African curry ("Choice of meat!") and a bacon-mushroom bison burger. I clear my throat. "And where are you going today?"

"Nowhere."

I look up and frown. "Why not? Is the food that horrible?"

Christopher leans back in his chair. "No. I'd rather stay right here with you."

"Oh." I feel heat rise in my cheeks—although I can't quite place the emotion. Excitement? Embarrassment? Whatever the feeling is, it's something I haven't felt in a long time. Feelings this intense make me undeniably nervous. I wonder if there is any chance that they serve liquor here. A shot or five of ouzo to go with my gyro might help me. I glance down. "So something local then. A cheddar cheese omelet and . . . What else? A whole cow? Is that Wisconsin-y enough for you?"

left drowning

"Perfect!" He snatches the menu and makes a rather loud display of snapping his fingers while he calls out, "Waitress! Waitress!" He leans in conspiratorially. "The service here is atrocious."

I cringe as he begins banging his fork against the water glass. And just when I thought he might be perfect.

"Do you have to do that every goddamn fucking time you come in here?" A thin young woman with closely cropped black hair appears at our table. Her voice is level, but the cursing makes her irritation obvious.

"Yes, I do. Otherwise you might ignore me and let me simply pass out at the table from hunger."

She sneers. "If you weren't making such a racket, I'd be more than happy to let you fucking collapse. What do you want?"

"I don't want to hear my little sister say *fucking*, and I do want to introduce you to somebody. Estelle, this is Blythe McGuire. Blythe, this is Estelle. My eternally cursing sister."

Estelle puts her order pad and pen in one hand and reaches out with the other. "Pleasure to meet you. You must have incredible strength of character to be out dining with Christopher."

"It's very nice to meet you," I say, fully aware of my messy hair and baggy sweatshirt. Especially next to Estelle, who is positively stunning. Any woman with hair that short has to be, because high cheekbones and sharp eyes are required to pull it off. Even with no makeup, her features are perfect. She is thin, probably too thin, with a boyish frame that makes her look like a model. I notice a good-sized cross that hangs from her neck, but she wears no other jewelry. Her look is simple and beautiful, and not one that I could ever pull off.

"Are you two hungry?"

Chris starts to order but is interrupted by a booming voice that comes from the entrance. "Christopher Shepherd! Have you stolen my girlfriend already?"

Chris shuts his eyes and laughs. "Go away! Go away!"

Sabin storms his way to our table with the fakest angry look that I've ever seen. "I cannot believe that you have betrayed me like this, my brother. We will duel over this princess, and I shall be victorious."

Chris rolls his eyes. "Hi, Sabin. How are you?"

"How *am* I? How do you think I am? I'm devastated, that's how I am!" He pats Estelle's arm before sliding into my booth and throwing an arm over my shoulder, glaring at his brother. Sabin drops his head onto my shoulder and lets out an exaggerated sob. "When did you get your nasty claws into my best girl? I was not expecting to have been so wronged by both my brother and my true love at once. I must try—no, I *will* win her back, you scoundrel!"

I bite my lip to keep from laughing. "Sabin? As of earlier this morning, weren't you in love with someone else?"

He pulls away. "Was I?"

"Yes. Chrystle, right?"

He slaps his forehead. "How quickly one forgets when caught up in the beauty that is Blythe. Yes! The fair Chrystle. I shall thus return my sights to her and leave you to the clutches of this less-than-dashing knight."

Chris folds his arms in front of him. "Dude, get a grip. And don't date anyone whose name sounds similar to mine. It's creepy."

"Well, shit, I hadn't thought about that. Chris, Chrystle . . ." Sabin pauses and frowns before regaining his theatrical air. "Oh, the tragedy! Clearly I cannot make juicy love to the woman ever again, for I would only

left drowning

think of you, dear brother. And that would be a sin of outlandish and vile proportions."

Estelle taps Sabin's foot lightly with hers. "That's enough. Leave Chris alone. You're wrecking his perfectly nice date with a very tolerant girl."

Sabin swings his head my way again. "My apologies. But I must warn you. While Sir Christopher may have an excess of charm, he will most certainly break your heart." Sabin looks at his brother, serious for the moment. "I guarantee it."

Chris gives him a warning look before his face softens. "Knock it off. Blythe and I are friends having lunch. Stop being hysterical."

I reach for my water glass. "We just kind of ran into each other at the lake. And then we ended up here."

"Whatever you say. So this means that Blythe is fair game again," Sabin teases. "Okay, kids. I'm going to blow this international joint and get a giant pizza from Gianni's all to myself. I must recuperate before this evening's events, which are sure to be tantalizing." He stands. "A pleasure to see you again, Blythe. Don't forget about my show."

"I won't. I promise."

Sabin high-fives Chris and kisses Estelle on the cheek before hurtling out the door.

"I'd apologize for him, but it's just hopeless," Chris says to me as he hands the menu back to Estelle. "So I think that Blythe will have the gyro—"

"Nope, sorry. Didn't you see the sign? Today is Irish food only."

"Again?" Chris groans.

"Anya, the owner, is a fan of themes," Estelle explains to me.

As if on cue, the lights dim and hymnal music blares through the speakers. A flash of light causes me to blink, and as I ease them open again, I find myself just inside the edge of a projected image coming from an old film reel. I peek to the left to see grassy hills and views of an Irish landscape floating across the wall, as well as my face and body.

"Fucking hell," Estelle mutters. "Anya!" she shouts, calling to the older woman behind the projector. "Is this necessary? It's the fifth time this month. And if I have to listen to 'Be Thou My Vision' one more time, I may up and quit!"

"Ambience, my dear. Authenticity!" Anya yells back as she adjusts the bun of hair at the nape of her neck.

"Oh for God's sake, this is bullshit!" Estelle shouts. "I can't even see anything properly."

"I can," Chris says just loudly enough for me to hear. He is watching me.

The bright light from the projector has mostly blinded me, but I know that the pattern of colors is dancing across my face and shirt. I squint until I find Christopher's gaze. I wish he wouldn't look at me, and I also wish that he'd never stop. I inch over in my seat until the images no longer move over me.

Estelle raises her voice to be heard. "So, I guess that it's fucking cream of turnip soup, cabbage, and soda bread for you two."

"Seriously, Estelle, enough with the swearing. I can cuss up a storm, but you're my little sister and I can't take it." Chris raises his chin to the cross that hangs from her neck. "And I thought God didn't approve of swearing. Especially when hymns are playing."

"Like you care what God thinks."

"Like there is a God," he spits back.

Estelle freezes, gripping her order pad.

left drowning

"'Stelle, really. How can you possibly believe for one fucking minute that—" He stops, and I hear him inhale.

Her voice is softer now, barely audible. "Chris."

"Sorry." He touches her arms. Despite the music, I think of the term *deafening silence*. "Estelle, really, I apologize."

She nods. "I'll get your food. And two Killian's. You'll need beer to wash down the atmosphere."

Chris looks down at the table, but I keep my eyes fixed on him while he runs his hands through his hair a few times. The music washes over us as the wall next to me is filled with dark Irish skies.

I wait. Eventually he looks up.

"I feel bad. I shouldn't have said that to her. And I shouldn't have said it in front of you." He fusses with his napkin for a few minutes and then lets out a small laugh.

"What is it?"

He tilts his head to the speaker above us. "Amazing Grace."

I haven't noticed that the music changed.

Chris crumples the napkin in his fist and bites his lip. "Fucking bagpipes."

"Fucking bagpipes," I agree.

"I really shouldn't have. With Estelle. I need to be more respectful. And I'm sorry if you believe—"

"Don't," I say quickly. "Don't apologize. I don't believe." My water glass is steady in my hand as I sip from it, and I take my time setting it down. I move my silverware to another spot on the table, trace the rim of my plate with my finger, and then sit straight up. I wait until his eyes meet mine. "We both know that there is no God."

"No," he agrees. "There is no God. Not for us."

FIGHTER

IT'S NOT EVEN TEN O'CLOCK WHEN I SLIDE out of my clothes and pull a T-shirt from my bureau. This day has tired me out. Pausing before I pull the shirt over my head, I step in front of the full-length mirror. This is not something that I've done in a while, but I'm overwhelmed with the impulse to see my reflection. I'm not sure why. Few women I know, including myself, find it particularly thrilling to look at themselves only in underwear. But now I look at my calves, my thighs, my stomach. Pivoting slightly on my toes, I check out the view from behind.

Huh. Maybe it is the low, flattering lighting from the small lamp by my bed, but I definitely don't look awful. Surprisingly, my body is not so unappealing that I want to burst into tears. Although I don't look great, either. I sit down on the floor and fold my legs in front of me. *Crisscross applesauce.* I examine my face and my hair, almost as if I'm meeting myself for the first time. My hair tumbles from the knot on the top of my head as I pull out the elastic. Unruly curls fall over my shoulders; I'm neither blonde nor brunette, but somewhere in between. I stare into my own eyes. My blue eyes, which even I have to admit are decent. Prettyish. My full cheeks have a slight pink flush from being out in the sun today. Yes, I am not entirely disastrous looking. On the verge, perhaps, but not without the possibility of salvation.

Of course, there is still my arm. I hold out my forearm and peer at the reflected image. The four-inch scar is still jagged despite the surgeon's neat sutures. Maybe a larger hospital would have had a more skilled surgeon, but I don't really mind. I deserve to have a much worse scar than this, all things considered. I uncross my legs and put my feet flat on the floor. Pushing myself up, I slowly come to a stand as I move my hands up the lines of my figure. The skin under my palms tingles and tenses, not used to touch. Even my own. My hands trace over my calves, around to the back of my thighs. I certainly have some extra weight in my legs. Somewhere under my palms has to be muscle and definition, but I can't find it. My fingers skim the curve of my waist. It is the one part of my body that hasn't seemed to gain weight. Everything that I eat or drink hits my legs and ass, but my stomach somehow stays relatively flat. So at least there is that. My touch travels over my stomach, back and forth, and I close my eyes as my hands move to my breasts. I linger for a few moments, suddenly aware of how much I'm enjoying this. One hand moves lower, back across my stomach, under the edge of my underwear.

Okay. Apparently I still have some kind of sex drive.

I stumble to the bed, seemingly drunk on what I'm feeling. As I fall against the rumpled sheets, my free hand moves into my hair while the other moves farther between my legs. A longing and need grow, one that I haven't felt in ages. I rub my fingers slowly over myself while my mind drifts to Chris as I first saw him, his lean body silhouetted against the morning light.

What's a little risk now and then, huh?

I turn my head to the side while my eyes close and I curl up my hips. I take my time, letting my body's reactions lead my fingers to where feels the best. I can't even remember the last time that I've touched myself like this. My thoughts are blurry and wonderful, and the stress and depression that usually lead me have dissipated for now. There is one sensation overwhelming me, one desire in charge, and I surrender easily to this because for once, *for once*, I am seeking and finding something other than self-loathing and pain. My rhythm is soft at first as I find what I like and how I like it, but soon it seems I have unleashed some sort of fiend that's been shackled for far too long. That fiend is demanding, and my body and my unconscious thoughts take over.

Live a little.

My hand presses harder, faster, making the intensity build.

Show me.

Heat overtakes me and I shove down the sheets.

I'd rather stay right here with you.

My breathing picks up.

There is no God. Not for us.

One hand is back in my hair, tightening against my scalp, and my heels dig into the bed as my body tenses. I start to tremble and shake. *Breathe into it.* The sound that comes from my lips surprises me, but the strength of the release makes it impossible to be quiet.

left drowning

I'm smiling, and I turn onto my side and swallow hard as I catch my breath. Holy shit, I needed that. I so, *so* needed that. It occurs to me that what I felt just now was so crazily awesome that I may never leave this bed again. I might just stay here and masturbate all the time, classes be damned. Then I am laughing, almost giddy, because I am persuaded that, to at least some degree, my body is my own again. Perhaps my mind will follow?

What's certain is that I feel better than I have in months. Years, really. I think of Sabin, with his exuberance and charm; and of Estelle, with her enviable physical beauty and her self-assurance. And Chris. Chris with his . . . magnetism. His stability.

I try to coax myself into thinking about something besides Chris. Sure, he stayed with me at the lake, took me to lunch, and walked me back to my dorm—our dorm, as it turns out—before heading to his basement single. So what? I laugh out loud as I confront the truth: There's no way he's lying in bed right now, obsessing over his day with me. Well, or masturbating himself into a frenzy. Today was probably a completely ordinary day in his life. Even if I never speak to him again, I am grateful for this day, this one day when my misery lifted, even if just for a little while.

Later, in the depths of my sleep, I dream. A new, unfamiliar dream this time.

I'm on the shore somewhere. It's a long stretch of pebbly sand, and I dig my toes into the little rocks until it hurts. Until I start to bleed. I look down and wonder why I'm doing this. It occurs to me to look around to see if someone will help me, but the rest of the beach is empty. Miles to the left and right are silent. Still. There is no one to help me, and I am horribly alone.

Then I look in front of me. There is a boy standing on a sun-bleached dock.

I guess that he's about . . . I don't know. Twelve? I can't quite tell. He is wearing swim trunks and a sleeveless shirt. Deeply tanned, the wind in his hair. A beautiful child. Then I see that he is skipping stones. The water is rough, so I can't see if his stones end up making rings. When I try to call to him to ask if he will help me stop digging my bleeding feet farther into what are now shards of rock, I can't make a sound. Nonetheless he turns to me. As if he hears me despite the silence. The peaceful, content look on his face calms me, and I'm able to take a few steps forward and my pain eases. I am no longer alone.

Without warning, fire erupts around him, and the boy is engulfed in leaping flames. I start to choke. I can't move now; I can only watch and scream. I'm confused because he doesn't struggle, he doesn't jump into the water, he doesn't do anything. I watch as his figure fades and then the fire subsides. The dock is now empty, as though he was never there. As though it never happened.

But soon I'm smiling, and I throw my head back, laughing. The boy emerges from the water, unscathed by the fire, and climbs back onto the dock. He puts his hands on hips and looks at me, an unmistakably determined expression on his face.

The boy is a fighter.

He nods once at me, and I nod back with some sort of understanding that I can't identify. I have no explanation for the clear connection between us because we are nothing alike.

He is a fighter. I am not.

And yet, we are unquestionably linked.

left drowning

A LONG WAY TO RUN

THE WORKOUT PLAYLISTS THAT OTHER PEOPLE listen to do not hold a whole lot of appeal, but I continue scrolling through the music app. It seems that the 1980s are a great source of adrenaline for many people—alas, the era of neon leg warmers and stretchy terry headbands doesn't seem to rock my shit.

After settling on a song collection of remixed Top 40 hits that seems slightly less offensive, I start warming up. My neck cracks as I lean over my outstretched leg. Given that I haven't done anything yet and my body is already producing audible noises, this is in all likelihood a very stupid idea. I am probably going to pass out about twenty feet from here. But I continue trying to coax my body into awareness by going through the handful of stretches that I can think to do. Because my calves already hurt after a handful of toe lifts, I do not feel confident.

My goal today is to exercise for forty-five minutes. It just can't be that hard. People do it all the time. The sun is out, the air is cool and sharp, and it is perfect weather for running. When my earbuds are firmly in, I look at the time. It is 8:17 a.m. At two minutes after nine, this will be over and I will have accomplished something.

After only six minutes, I am miserable. Trying to match my pace to the rhythm of the songs has only resulted in a fierce burn ripping through my lungs. Everything about my existence feels uncomfortable. My baggy sweatpants are chafing my thighs and my breasts are jostling uncomfortably since I didn't think to change out of my regular underwire. Clearly, a good sports bra is going to be in order if I plan on doing this again. Which at this point seems unlikely.

I slow down to a stride that feels more natural, even though it's against the beat. The commitment to forty-five minutes has been made, and I am going to honor it, damn it. Even if my outfit sucks and the songs I chose aren't right.

Minute eighteen is not good. I am breathing too hard.

Minute nineteen makes me near suicidal. A sharp cramp stabs continuously on the right side of my waist.

Minute twenty. I stop and drop my head down while I rest my hands on my legs. My breathing evens out quickly enough, and the cramp dissolves. I stand up and put my hands on my waist, assessing the route in front of me. The grass-lined path ahead will take me to the lake. A good destination? Maybe. But I'm feeling too indecisive to move. It's then that I realize what's stopping me in my tracks is not indecision. It's heartache. *It is fucking heartache.* Nonsensical, yet distinct. Today, without Chris, it would just feel lonely to see that rocky shore.

left drowning

Minute twenty-one. I decide to make a new path of my own. If I am not going to run, I am at least going to walk.

So I walk hard for the next eight minutes, mapping out a circular route in my head that will loop me back to the dorm. I'm breathing hard and wanting distraction when I remember that exercising is when people like to "think." I try to relax and see what turns up.

As my legs churn and my heart thumps, I rack my brain, skimming through my life history. Images flash quickly through my mind. My mother chasing after me as I'm boarding the school bus, laughing and frantically waving my lunch box. My dad prepping me for the SATs by flashing index cards at me over breakfast. God, every memory is so tied to them, and it seems impossible to separate the memories from the grief.

My thoughts move to Annie, my mom's best friend, who fought the life insurance company that tried to buy off me and James with a paltry settlement. I have no idea if another lawyer would have brawled the way that Annie did. She made sure my brother's college education and expenses would be paid for. I told her at the time that I didn't care what my fortune amounted to. But Annie got us more than enough.

Annie. Thinking about her is a sore subject for me because it's just another way that I have failed. She is the one person who I can say unequivocally did not run from me and James when my parents died. Annie is the person who went to O'Hare Airport in a nightgown, flew from Chicago to Boston, and then drove over three hours to find us at the hospital in Maine. Annie is the person who drove James and me back to the house where we grew up in Massachusetts, although with our parents dead, the house no longer felt like home in the least. She made the service arrangements and probably dealt with more horrific details than I care to know. She got me dressed for the funeral, and she forced me to eat and even shower when I couldn't handle basic life skills. For three weeks she kept James and me functioning in ways that no one else could have. Then we moved in with Lisa, my mother's sister, and Annie went back to Chicago. After that, I couldn't tolerate hearing her voice on the phone.

Everything about her shredded my heart because she reminded me too much of my mother, and so she reminded me too much of my mother's death. I couldn't handle it. I pushed her away, and even a loyalty like hers could only take so many unreturned phone calls and letters. But even while I was cutting her out of our lives, she continued to fight like hell so that we got the best possible financial result. Lisa eventually dropped her as our family attorney, solidifying the end of that tie. Our new attorney is perfectly good, but he's not Annie.

I start running again as I shake my head, but last only until I catch sight of my dorm, when I slow to a walk. I tuck my phone into the band of my sweatpants and retie my ponytail. Now that the horrid run is over, I admit that I actually feel good. Although my muscles hurt, and I am overall embarrassingly fatigued, I am alert in a way that I love. In fact, as I near the steps to Reber Hall, I wish that I'd sucked it up and kept going for the full forty-five minutes.

The door opens before I reach it, and a stocky blond guy in shorts and a fitted shirt holds open the door for me. "Good day for a run, huh?"

"What?"

"Couldn't ask for better weather." He adjusts the armband that holds his small music player and smiles. "Cool, but not cold. I hate how the cold tightens you up when you run, you know?"

left drowning

He thinks that I'm a runner, like he is, and I feel false even as I embrace the lie. "Oh. Yeah, I hate that. It's really gorgeous out today." I step through the threshold. "You'll have a good run."

"Sweet. Catch you later."

The real runner makes his way down the steps while he rolls his shoulders in circles.

I roll my own shoulders as I climb the wide staircase to my floor. Shoulder rolls. I should have thought of doing those before, but at least I'm doing them now. In fact, I'm going to do more than this. I unlock my door, grab a towel from the top shelf of my closet, fold it in half, and set it on the hard floor. I get on my hands and knees and shift my weight forward. Twenty push-ups can't be that hard. But even modified push-ups (I refuse to think of them as "girl" push-ups) leave my arms shaking by the seventh one. Ten will have to do for today. Now ab crunches. Twenty to the center, ten to each side. I may barf. I stand for lunges—fifteen forward, fifteen back. They are clumsy, shaky lunges, but they are mine.

It is a start. More physical activity than I have even considered in a long time. Not that I have ever been much of an athlete at all, but I've done a number of classes with my friends at the gym back home. *Before.* James is the real athlete of the family. Or he used to be. He is obviously never going to forgive me for ruining that, and I can't blame him. I deserve his hatred.

Stop, stop, stop, I order myself.

My e-mail chimes, and I groan as I roll over to check my phone. I am probably being alerted of an impending disaster that will require the transfer of my bank funds to an exotically named prince. Instead it's from my aunt Lisa, who James and I have lived with for the past four years. Her place has been our home base because the house we grew up in was too full of painful memories of our parents after they died. When we were unwilling to sell it, Lisa rented it out to strangers.

I skim the e-mail in disbelief; it is cluttered with falsely cheerful exclamation points. I ignore the bullshit pleasantries. The e-mail informs me that since James and I are now both in college, we are technically adults, so we "get to move back" into our parents' house. Apparently, the renters' lease is up and Lisa sees the chance to get us out of her hair; that much is clear by the way her e-mail also explains that she's shipped all of our things to our old address. The icing on the cake is that she's going to New Orleans with friends for Thanksgiving and leaving us out of it. So that's that.

I want my mother right now. I want her so desperately that I physically ache to have her hold me, and it's absolutely bullshit that I have no one. In the past, I'd tried to trick myself into thinking that I could connect with Lisa, and that she would fill that maternal void. But Lisa never made much of an effort to conceal her lack of interest in housing her niece and nephew. Maybe James and I were too much of a reminder of her sister, or maybe it was just that Lisa is in her early thirties, single, and with no desire to domesticate her independent life. Or maybe she's just a rotten person.

Still, our "home" is—or was—Lisa's house. It's where both James and I have rooms. Guest rooms. It is by no means a place we love, but it's what we've had.

My legs burn as I walk out of the room. My aunt is a bitch. I have made so many excuses for her near-total indifference to us, but I refuse to do that anymore. Her grief, her loss, also belongs to me and James.

I clomp loudly down the dorm stairwell in the midst of a mental

left drowning

tirade. I'm so sick of Lisa and her craptastically awful attitude. Not that I'm one to be complaining about someone's attitude necessarily, but if my sister had died, I'd be a lot damn nicer to her children. I'd cling to them and smother them with too much love. Instead, Lisa has done the bare minimum. I hit the landing and continue to the basement of the dorm while I fume. It's not like we've been any financial burden to her.

I enter the lowest floor of the dorm and turn left. If the basement numbers correspond to the ones on my floor, his room is directly below mine a few floors down.

Selfish. She's inexcusably selfish. Fuck that. Fuck her.

Without hesitating, I knock on the door. I need help.

7

IT'S JUST PAIN

"HEY, NEIGHBOR." CHRIS SMILES UP AT ME. HE'S
sitting at his desk with a book in one hand and a pencil in the other.

"Hi." Of course, now that I'm here, I feel like an asshole, hit
with the clear understanding that my showing up in this frazzled
state is totally inappropriate. Yet I do not turn and run. The fact that
he is using a pencil distracts me for second, because I find it totally
adorable that in this technological age, he is still a pencil kind of a
guy. "Sorry, you're obviously studying. I didn't mean to interrupt
you. It's just . . ." I struggle to catch my breath, partially from taking
the stairs so fast and partially from my emotion. I put my hands on
my hips and look down.

"What is it?" he asks softly. His voice is calm and patient.

"I tried to go running, and my playlist sucks, and it didn't go well. Every song felt wrong and stupid. *I* felt wrong and stupid. And my aunt is just horrible. And . . ." I look straight into those intoxicating green eyes. "And why can't I get over everything? My parents died four years ago, not a month ago, but it overtakes my entire life. I can't make it stop. I can't be happy. I didn't used to be like this. I used to be vivacious and fun. I used to be *me*. Your mother died, so you know what it's like, yet you manage to have a life. I want a life, too. How do you have that? And . . . and . . . and my playlist sucks."

He waves me into his room "Sit." Chris points at the bed, so I sit and watch as he gets up from his desk smoothly despite the cramped quarters of his single room and moves his chair so he can face me. "Give me your phone."

"What?"

"Give me your phone. Let's see this ineffective playlist of yours."

"Oh. Okay." I pass it over. The back of my hand brushes against his as I slide my phone to him.

Some people describe certain physical connections as being like electricity. Sparks flying. When Chris and I touch, it's different. I think of the feel of water. The way it is when you wade into the ocean and a small wave cascades against you, swirling sand over you and awakening every pore.

Slow motion, I think decidedly. *He can make things happen in slow motion.* The rest of the room grows blurry while Chris stays sharply in focus, and I watch him silently as he taps the screen. He has beautiful hands. Strong, deft, exacting.

Suddenly I notice that he's been talking. ". . . impossible to run to this shit. You need an entirely different tone."

"Hair metal? Oldies? Orchestral?" I suggest with a smile.

"Funny, funny. You're trying to run at the same pace as these songs, I bet."

"Well, yeah."

"You're competing. Don't compete. The music has its own pace, and you have to make yours. Be in charge. Find a zone. A holding space."

"*Holding space?*"

"Give me a few minutes. I'll show you." Chris pushes some papers around on his cluttered desk until he finds a set of earphones to put on. He stays fixed on the screen as he starts scrolling through options, only occasionally pausing to look out the small basement-level window behind me.

I lean back on my hands and wait. Save for the hint of sound that comes from the earphones that Chris has in, it is quiet. He swivels lazily back and forth in the chair, and I like that he is so engaged in whatever music he is listening to because it allows me to look at him closely. To take him in. I try not to squirm. He hasn't shaved in a few days, and it's a good look for him. For *me*. Since he keeps brushing hair from his face, he could probably stand to get a haircut, but I like his gently scruffy look. And the way his hair falls against the back of his neck . . . God, I find the tanned skin between his shirt and his hair almost intoxicating. What would it be like to have that skin under my lips, to slowly inch my mouth across his shoulders, to touch him lightly with my tongue . . .

I've gone insane. At least I am not drooling, though. Or moaning.

"The music has to be the background, the mood. Once you're in that safe place, that holding place, then you run, push your body. You need songs with meaning, and mood, and heart. Not this pop crap."

He has brought me back to the real world, and I shake my head. "I don't know. I don't like meaning. Or mood or heart."

left drowning

Chris kneels in front of me as he takes one earbud out and moves his hand to my ear. I place my hand under his to adjust the fit in my ear, and he pushes back my hair for me. His hand stays on the side of my head as he tilts my face so that I am looking into his eyes. "You need songs that make you feel. Some make you strong, some make you weak. Some build determination, some tear you apart. But you need all of those." Music begins to play. Slow music. Soft and rhythmic, layered. "Run through the pain."

I shake my head again and look past him. "No." I want to concentrate on the tan on the back of his neck instead.

He nods. "Yes. Run through it, feel it, let it happen."

"No," I say more adamantly. "I do that too much already."

"I don't think you do. I think that you dwell on parts of things and then brush them away. Stop fighting it."

"How do you know that?" Damn it. I can feel that familiar sting in my eyes again. It's so easy for my emotions to be played with, flipping erratically from one extreme to the next. Lust, then anger, then pain . . . It is never ending.

And Chris seems to make the extremes much worse. So why did I come to his room?

"You scream it in everything you do. You're holding on to what happened because you think that's all you have."

"It is all I have."

"Find more."

I shake my head. I don't know how to do this.

"Blythe." Chris looks around the room as if trying to find a way to convince me. He thinks for a minute. "Your parents died. Your world fell apart."

I nod.

He puts his hand on my cheek. "You were left drowning."

I nod again.

"And you're struggling to breathe."

I am. It's a constant struggle to stay near the surface. I have just enough air to stop me from totally going under, but not enough to thrive.

"So do it. Breathe. Just breathe." He turns up the volume and strokes my hair.

I want to tell him that the pain of the last four years has taken a toll, and that I'm not sure I can breathe on my own.

"You have the here and now," Chris says. "You have a future. Deal with the past so you can stop looking back. It's just pain."

I sigh heavily and look at him again. "It's just pain," I repeat.

"Yes." He tucks my hair back again, and I catch my breath as heat sears through my body. His touch is incomparable to anything that I have felt before, and this mix of my personal anguish with the intensity of his touch is messing with my head. "Yes, Blythe."

"Just breathe?" I manage with a laugh.

"Pretty much."

"Is that what you did?"

"Yes. I got myself out of hell. I dealt with it and moved on. You can, too."

There is no way to stop myself. I grab the front of his shirt and pull him in until my lips are just before the point of touching his. I want his mouth, I want his taste, and I want to breathe him in. I feel his body tense, but he doesn't pull away.

Neither of us moves.

There is heat here, of that I am sure.

left drowning

Finally, I lean in a bit closer so that my mouth is barely against his. I soften the hand I have on his chest and move my fingertips up and over his shirt, over the collar, until I'm finally touching the back of his neck. His skin is warm and perfect, just as I knew it would be. Chris starts to move his lips against mine, ever so softly, and so I ease in more. His tongue meets mine, and I shiver. The atmosphere in the room is loaded; loaded with my emotion and my fervent, raw, inescapable lust for this person.

I never knew that slow kissing could be so passionate. His tongue isn't halfway down my throat, nor is he clawing at me with his hands. I cannot be wrong in imagining that he's feeling the same way I am.

I'm not, because Chris moves his hand to mine and starts inching his fingertips across the top of my hand and up my arm. He takes out our earphones, quieting the music and leaving only us. The touch of his hand is intense, and I pull my mouth from his because I want to see how he moves. My fingers begin digging into his skin as I watch him touch me, look at me, take me in. I try not to flinch as his fingers travel over the scar on my forearm. I've forgotten that I'm wearing short sleeves. This is definitely a first, because I never, ever forget. And now he is touching my arm as if he doesn't even know the scar is there, making that visible reminder of my past and my guilt about it temporarily invisible.

When his hand reaches my shoulder, he doesn't stop. I close my eyes as he moves to the top of my chest. When he first grazes my breast, I can't help letting a small sound escape my lips. Chris lowers his hand and slides it under my shirt, then under my bra, until his warm hand is on me. Now his breathing becomes ragged.

Oh God, I'm going to scream.

The way he skims the fingers of his other hand over my lower back is making me crazy. So deliberate and steady. He is so controlled. With the hand that's just under my breast, he pushes against me slightly until I pull back enough for him to look me in the eyes. Every part of my body is burning for him. I love the way that his eyes pierce me as his hand moves against me. His face has just the hint of a smile and . . . surprise? I see a touch of confusion, as though he hadn't been expecting this. If he didn't before, I can tell that now he feels the same connection that I felt out by the lake. An all-consuming clarity that there is a magnetic pull between us. At least, I want him to be feeling that.

With both hands, I push his black hair from his face and run my fingers through it and then down his shoulders. I take my time because I want to take in everything that I can about him and absorb all the details of his face. How the curve of his eyebrows is so beautifully arched, how the hint of a sideburn blends into his unshaven cheek, and how he bites his lip as I study him. And more than that, I see both our kinship and our differences: how we both have pasts full of pain, and how he emanates survival in the way that I want to. Right now, I embody failure and surrender, but I see in him the possibility of what I could have.

So his touch is more than just physical touch.

Under my bra, Chris covers my breast with his hand and strokes me slowly with his thumb. I'm not prepared for the powerful ache that surges between my legs as he tightens his fingers around my nipple, and I drop my head back slightly. I arch my back some, pushing my breast against him, wanting more. For a second more, he pinches my nipple, but then moves his hand away. I nearly whimper, but then he leans into me and kisses me again. Harder this time. He tastes like eternity, and healing, and completion.

No one else could ever kiss me like this, of that I am positive.

I could breathe him in forever.

I could fall in love forever.

left drowning

It is impossible to deny that I am clearly starved for physical contact, for sexual contact, but that still doesn't entirely explain how desperately I want to tear off this boy's clothes after I've shied away from everyone else. Never have I been so turned on. I move to the very edge of the bed and drop my hands to Chris's lower back, bringing him against me. He wraps his arms around me and holds me tightly as he presses his waist between my legs. His lips are sealed against mine, his tongue perfect. I cannot get close enough to him, and I want more. I want everything. It doesn't make sense. I barely know him, but this is the most intimate that I have ever been with anyone, physically or emotionally.

Right now, I know that this is right, even though it's baffling. Chris has tapped into the small part of me that still seeks hope. And pleasure.

His mouth moves to my neck, his lips grazing against my skin and his breath heated. The only downside to lifting the back of his shirt is that he has to take his lips from my skin so that I can pull it over his head.

Holy hell, he's gorgeous.

I touch his chest. As I'd seen when we were by the lake, he is all muscle. Lean, and defined, and utterly incomparable. And now I get to have my hands on him. Mesmerized by his body, I follow the lines of his chest muscles with my hand, tracing my fingers across his nipples, down to his abs, and still to the faint trail of hair that leads into his jeans. Then I work my way back up again, aware that I could do this for hours. Chris groans softly. There is no insecurity about what I am doing nagging at me, no doubt about how to touch him. Feeling his body, exploring him, is intuitive. Just having my hands on this boy seems like it could fulfill any lustful craving I have. He is absolutely captivating.

As he kneels in front of me, I lean in and sweep my lips over his chest, touching my tongue to him every now and then. His hands are in my hair, cradling me while I taste his body. Later, when my mouth knows every inch of his muscled chest, I lift my lips to his. He does not hesitate and kisses me again. Weakened, I fall back onto the bed, and he crawls into me, resting his weight against me. My hips press up into him as he kisses his way from my mouth to my breasts, over my shirt and down my stomach.

"Christopher." I can't help murmuring his name, and I have to stop myself from saying it over and over. I feel such relief to have found him.

Then his weight is on me again and he kisses me deeply as he presses his body between my legs. I feel how hard he is, how much he wants me.

But then, without warning, he pushes up on his arms, panting a bit. He touches his cheek to mine, and I can feel that I've lost him. I don't know what I've done wrong, but he is clearly stopping this before it goes any further. The sudden distance between us, the wall, threatens to wreck me. Whatever was there a few seconds ago is gone.

Chris kisses me lightly on the cheek and whispers, "I don't . . . I don't think this is a good idea."

"Oh. Okay." I have no idea what to say or what has happened. And I don't know why he hasn't moved away from me or why he is trembling. So I ask. "Chris. Why are you shaking?"

"I'm not," he says. But he totally is.

I brush my hands up and down his arms, wanting to touch him for as long he'll let me. He drops his head into the crook of my neck as his breathing eases. I am so confused.

He lifts up on his arms. "I'm really supposed to be studying. Whopper geology test on Monday."

I turn my head to the side and face away from him. "Of course. I've got tons to do, also."

The next few minutes are awful. A horribly awkward scene while

left drowning

we extricate ourselves from each other's hold; me muttering an idiotic thank-you for the help with my playlist, and Chris looking apologetic as he yanks on his shirt, only making me feel worse.

After a stupidly casual good-bye, I rush from his room before he can say anything else. The walk from his room up to mine is unforgivingly long. Talk about a walk of shame. I slam the door to my room and fling myself onto the bed.

I sniff. Well, fuck, I certainly don't smell great. That's one problem. Perhaps my stench drove him away? It's not like I planned on stripping off his shirt when I went to his room. I roll over and drop one hand to the floor. A few flights down, Christopher is probably now studying the boring layers of the earth or something, and here I am, all sorts of bewildered.

But, damn, that was hot. Even though I don't know why Chris pulled away, or what I did wrong, that was still hot.

And that is enough to make me smile.

JULY TWENTY-FIRST

"*I'M GOING DOWN TO THE WATER*," BLYTHE CALLS INTO THE HOUSE AND then leans forward on the deck's wooden railing. Even with all the trees, there is still an amazing view of the ocean cove, the water sparkling in the midafternoon light. And she loves that briny smell, especially strong now, at low tide. The stink always makes her younger brother, James, wrinkle his nose, but she breathes it in with pleasure.

"Have fun at the clam graveyard hour!" James shouts. That's what he calls low tide. Blythe's repeated explanations that the smell has nothing to do with dying clams, and that, in fact, the clams are just fine and perfectly alive, does nothing to make him like it any better. Or understand her love for it.

The truth for his sour attitude, she thinks, is that James is still pissed that she was the one to choose their vacation house from the list of possible rentals her parents printed out.

It didn't seem worth being pissy about. It was only for two

weeks, after all. Once the fourteen days were up, Blythe's family would finally be able to move into their new summerhouse in Bar Harbor, a house called The Stone's Throw, where the current owners were taking longer than expected to pack up their things. The delay was a surprise, and put Blythe's parents in an awkward spot; by mid-July, it was virtually impossible to find any place to rent near popular Bar Harbor. That's how they ended up in Chilford, a couple hours south, in an old house.

Luckily, it turned out to be a fine substitute vacation home for the place in Bar Harbor, and they settled in right away.

Blythe knows that fun, easy vacations aren't easy to come by for most families, but hers pulls them off every time. She knows that's mostly because her parents walk that magic line between being involved in her life and giving her space to grow up on her own. Plus, her brother is pretty damn great, too. It seems like she and James should fight more given that she is seventeen and he is fifteen, but they don't. He is levelheaded, disciplined, and reasonable—many things that she is not. But under that cool exterior, he is kind. Truly, incredibly, deeply kind. And miraculously modest, considering that he is the top-ranked soccer player in Massachusetts. She is definitely the more carefree and sillier of the two, but James seems to appreciate that about her. They are a good pair.

"Hey, James! Jamie!" she hollers. "The dying clams want to say hello to you! Come down to the beach with me!"

"What? My God, quit yelling, you nut." Her brother slides open the screen door and puts his hands on his hips. "We're on a relaxing vacation. Soft voices, calm attitudes." He half smiles, and the spark in his eye tells her that he is most definitely in a good mood.

"Come swimming! It's a perfect blue-sky afternoon. There's a dock not too far out that we can swim to."

"I just scarfed down a massive sandwich. Later, okay? I'll have to work off the six pounds of food I ate." He pats his muscled stomach. He is a good-looking kid, Blythe knows, yet so far he has resisted the nearly incessant phone calls and overall interest from swooning girls. Soccer is his priority. "You shouldn't swim that far alone, though," he continues. "Take the boat, and I'll watch you from up here."

"Okay, Mr. Responsible. You can rescue me if I start to drown. I'm no hotshot soccer star, but I can swim well enough." It's true. She is a good swimmer. Her strokes and form might not be pretty by swim team standards, but she is capable of handling herself in even rough ocean water. All of her general athletic failings don't seem to matter in the water. She feels strong in the water, and more than that, she just loves the feeling of buoyancy. Nothing compares to being cradled and moved by the force of the ocean. You just have to be aware of its power. She hears her father's words in her head: Never forget that the current, the tides, the waves . . . they are all smarter than you are. They are in charge. It's your job to listen. Don't ever stop listening.

Her father was right. And so Blythe always listens to what the water tells her. "Fine, fine, stay here. I'll be back in a bit. Wanna do steamers and lobsters for dinner? I saw a guy on the side of the road with a seafood shack. We can cook for Mom and Dad!"

"You got it," he says, smiling. "Have fun."

The path from the house to the shore runs under tall ever-

left drowning

greens and is lined with feathery ferns. Blythe likes the way the leaves tickle her legs and how the rocky terrain makes her take her time getting to the water. She wants to slow down in general while here. This Maine vacation will be the calm before the storm. College applications are ahead of her in the fall, her senior year of high school: SATs and then forms, interviews, and freak-outs. Matthews is her top choice, obviously. Her parents met there, and aside from that cool aspect is the plain truth that it is an excellent college. She doesn't want to go to an overpopulated university where she'd get lost in a sea of students. Frat parties and campus chaos are not her thing. Matthews is going to be her school. It has to. She even has on a frayed Matthews shirt right now. The pale blue lettering is chipped in more places than she can count and the red background is now closer to pink, but she doesn't care how ragged the shirt is. It is her favorite. The Wisconsin winters would suck, obviously, but the beautiful campus and dynamic professors would make up for that. Blythe sort of hates that she will have to put down on her application that both her parents went there, because she wants to get in on her own merit, but she also isn't entirely above using that connection if it can guarantee her an acceptance. If that's what gets her in, then she will just have to validate the shit out of their decision to admit her once she's there.

The thought of all the work that lies ahead of her makes her even more determined to enjoy every minute of the summer. Which is pretty easy to do, considering the house has its own section of private beach. Blythe much prefers this shell-covered shoreline and cold, rough water to the perfectly smooth white sand and warm aqua water at tropical resorts. Maine feels real to her, and much less showy. The boulders that are covered in seaweed, the barnacle-encrusted tide pools, and the salty air that invades every pore of her body; this is what makes Maine special.

She walks to the end of the narrow dock and tosses her things into the old rowboat that is tied up. She throws on the still-damp orange life vest and easily starts rowing out to the square floating dock that rocks with the waves, her boat bouncing playfully in the water. Blythe loves being around people, but she likes her privacy almost as much, and adores how this dock is like her own island in the middle of the cove. She reaches it a few minutes later and clambers on top of it, situating herself on her towel. At three thirty in the afternoon, the sun is still strong, but a slight chill from the cold water blows over her. She has her bathing suit on under her clothes, but she will try to warm up in the sun before she dives into the Atlantic. She kicks off her sneakers and removes her shorts, but keeps on her shirt.

Blythe lies down on her stomach and rests her head on her crossed arms. The sound. Oh, the sound of small waves lapping against the dock is hypnotic, and the sun burning on the back of her legs is nicely tempered by the ocean air. Bliss. The dock rocks under her, and she gives herself up to the will of the ocean, succumbing to the unpredictable rhythm of the water and her daydreams.

After what could be hours or minutes, Blythe isn't sure which, she lifts her head, her contentment broken, but broken by what, she doesn't know. She looks around. The rowboat is

left drowning

still tied to the dock. Nothing is amiss. She shakes her head. Blythe scans the shore to her right and studies the houses. Some are too far back or too shielded by foliage to see, while others are clearly visible.

Movement on the opposite shore makes her look straight ahead. Someone is walking slowly where the water hits the land. She props her chin on her hands. From this distance it is hard to see the figure too clearly, but she guesses that it's a boy about her age. He's tall, with dark hair peeking out from under a baseball hat. He has on tan cargo shorts, and no shirt or shoes. And he is carrying two large metal buckets, one in each hand. She watches as he plods slowly through the sand, wades a few feet through the heavy low-tide mud into the ocean, and then empties the water-filled buckets. He pauses a moment, tips his head back, and stands still. Maybe taking in the spectacular day? Or maybe something else.

The boy leans over and refills each bucket with water. Slowly he stands and brings the pails to his side and begins walking, obviously weary, back down the shoreline where he'd come from. He keeps his arms slightly bent at the elbows, flexing his muscles to keep the buckets from hitting his legs. When he reaches what is likely the end of his property line, he plods back into the water and dumps his buckets again. For ten minutes, Blythe stares entranced as he repeats this ritual over and over. What on earth is he doing? Does he have some sort of compulsive disorder that requires him to repeat mundane acts over and over until his brain is satisfied? Although she would hardly call this activity mundane. Buckets of water are heavy, even for someone with his strong build, and the repetition has to be tiring him out. Perhaps it is some kind of physical conditioning exercise? He could be a sports nut like her brother. She continues staring.

Twenty minutes must go by. His pace remains the same, but his physical pain is easy to see. He has to be hurting. She stands up and brings her hand to shield her eyes.

Ten more minutes.

Stop. You have to stop now. It's too much.

Who knows how long he'd been doing this before she noticed? This is insane. But the boy keeps going, focused and unfailing in his routine. Even when he stumbles and spills half of a bucket, he continues.

Jesus, stop! Blythe pleads silently. Put the buckets down. You're going to pass out. This is crazy.

Finally he pauses, turning his back to her as he looks toward the trees. Holy shit. His back is badly sunburned. If she can tell from this distance, it is definitely bad. It must hurt like hell, or at least it will later. He continues looking toward the trees for a bit, craning his head to the side. Looking for something? Someone? He drops the buckets and leans over, bracing himself with his hands on his legs. Catching his breath, for sure. The boy moves toward the water, looking down as he wades in a few feet. He seems to be shaking his head.

When he raises his head, Blythe finds herself clearly in his sight. She should probably be embarrassed, having been caught staring at this stranger, but she isn't. She takes her hand from her eyes and stays where she is. The boy is looking right at her. His exhaustion, his sadness, his hopelessness, they all travel over the water and rip through her. Something is very wrong here.

left drowning

She lifts her hand and gives him a tentative wave. He returns the gesture.

Blythe cups her hands to her mouth. "Hi."

"Hi, back!"

"Are you . . . okay?"

He puts his hands on his hips and looks off to the side for a second before answering. He calls back, "Yes. I'm fine."

"What are you doing?" She tries to feign curiosity rather than concern. "With the buckets. Are you in training for something?"

She can see him laugh. "Sort of!" he yells.

"You've got a terrible sunburn. You should put on a shirt."

"I'm okay."

"No, really. It's bad."

"I'm gonna be all right. Promise."

"Is that your house? Please just go grab a shirt."

He glances behind him. "I can't. I shouldn't . . . I can't really talk. I'll be fine."

Blythe frowns. "I'll give you mine. I can row it over to you." She crouches down and starts to untie the boat from the dock, but he stops her.

"No! Don't do that!" The alarm in his voice is startling and worrisome. He looks behind him again and then back at her. "Just . . . no. I'm sorry. I'm so sorry."

"Don't be sorry." She can feel her heart pounding as she stands back up.

They stand silently. She can't take her eyes off him. Desperation and exhaustion radiate from this boy. Blythe is afraid to move, afraid he'll drop to his knees if she breaks away. So *she holds their unspoken exchange.* Whatever this is, it isn't forever. It's going to be okay. You're going to be okay. *She is nodding to him.* I'm here. I'm right here.

Finally he says, "I have to keep going."

Blythe is unable to speak for a bit. She doesn't want him to keep going. She doesn't understand what is going on, but everything about this feels off. Dangerous.

She nods. "If you say so. I'm going to stay with you."

"You don't have to."

"I'm going to. I want to."

"Thank you." *She thinks that she hears his voice break. He picks up the metal buckets and begins pointlessly filling them and transporting water from one side of the shore to the other. She knows precisely how hard it is to walk through the heavy wet sand at low tide. Your feet sink in deep, making each step trying and draining. It can be fun if you are digging for clams, even funny when you lose a shoe to the thick sludge. This? Whatever this boy is doing, this is not fun. He only pauses once to slowly take something from the bucket and set it a few feet deeper into the ocean.*

Near tears, Blythe peels off her shirt. She looks around for a solution, since he's made it so clear she should not row to him. Then it hits her: the life vest. She sits down with it. It takes a few minutes, but she manages to tie her Matthews shirt and her water bottle to the vest by using the straps. She moves to the end of the dock, her toes hanging off the edge, getting as close to him as possible. Blythe throws the life vest as far as she can. "The tide is coming in," *she yells.*

The boy looks her way as he walks.

"I'm not leaving you." Now her voice nearly breaks.

He nods again.

Blythe sits down and tucks in her knees to her chest. No, she will not leave him. So for the next hour and a half she stays, willing some of his hurt to come her way. She would take this away from him if she could, somehow share whatever this is. For minutes at a time, she closes her eyes, sending him strength.

This will not break you. This will not break you.

He isn't crying, so she doesn't either. The battle against tears is one she almost loses several times. He is consistent, steady now. Brave. The only time that he stops again is when her life vest reaches him. She holds her breath as he struggles to untie the shirt and water bottle. His hands must be weak and trembling. He clumsily gets the wet shirt over his head, peeks behind him to the trees, and then downs the water. He raises the bottle in her direction as thanks.

Later, when he has completed his . . . goal? job? . . . he suddenly hurls both buckets off to the side, slamming them into sea-worn boulders. The sound echoes across the water, making Blythe flinch. He paces erratically, almost manically, for a minute, and then turns to her and raises both hands into the air, his palms held high, fingers spread.

Blythe raises hers, too, reaching out to him as though she is pressing her hands against his. Then she folds her fingers as if they could fall between his, while he simultaneously does the same. As if he knew she would do this. The boy moves his hands over his heart, and she follows the movement.

Blythe grins.

He just kicked a little ass.

He nods almost imperceptibly and then slowly turns and begins to wearily walk away from the water and back to his house.

The glow Blythe feels from their connection fades once the boy is out of sight, and a new restlessness sets in. She can't relax.

After rowing back and tying up the boat, she takes the path to the house, pausing on its deck for a last look at the cove. One of the deck's lounge chairs beckons, and she falls into it, staring out at the water and feeling exhausted.

A few minutes later, she hears James's steps coming toward her across the creaky wooden deck. "You ready to go? I saw you come back a while ago. What are you doing out here?"

The lounge chair is digging into her back, but she still doesn't move.

"Blythe? You okay? What are you looking at out there?"

"What? Oh yeah." She keeps her focus across the cove. "Just looking at the water. The whole view." She closes her eyes for a moment and then pulls herself away. "Sure, let's go." She stands up.

"You're going to need to put on something over your bathing suit. I'm not letting you drive me around town half dressed. Besides, it's going to get cold soon. You know how the nights are up here." James looks around. "Where's your Matthews shirt?"

"Oh. That. I don't have it . . ."

"What do you mean? You lost it? How could you lose it?" He frowns as he unzips his own sweatshirt and hands it over. "That's your favorite shirt."

left drowning

"Thanks." Blythe slips her arms through the sleeves and struggles with the zipper because her hands are trembling. "It's okay. My shirt . . . found a new home."

"Huh?"

"Nothing." She smiles at him as they head into the house. Being with James makes her feel better. "You know what?"

"What?"

"You're a really good brother. I love you. And I love our family."

James fakes a serious look. "Are you dying? What's wrong with you?"

She laughs. "Shut up. Seriously, we're lucky."

"Does this mean that you'll let me drive?" James swipes the car keys from the counter and dangles them in front of her.

"Hell, no, you're not driving." She snatches the keys from him. "Not only do you not even have a learner's permit, but I wouldn't trust you to get us through that narrow rut that's passing as a driveway."

"Fine, fine," he grumbles. "Let's go get dinner, and hope this roadside seafood shack of yours doesn't sell us clams that land us in the ER."

"That's the spirit!" She holds open the front door.

"Blythe?"

"Yeah?"

He puts one hand on top of her head and messes up her hair. "Even though you won't let me break the law in what is really a minor, minor way, I love you, too."

Blythe sighs. "God damn it. Fine. You can drive. Don't you dare tell Mom and Dad."

8

FINDING AN ALWAYS

CHRIS HAS WORKED SOME SORT OF MAGIC WITH my playlist. Minute eighteen is not so awful. *Running* is not so awful. This is my second full week of going out every day, and even though it's still impossibly hard, I'm not giving up. I feel a little bit stronger with each run.

It's just pain.

I crank up the volume. Chris is right. Competing with music does nothing to help speed or endurance. It would never have occurred to me to run to the slow rhythms he's provided, but it is working. Granted, the lyrics and mood of half the songs are killing me: love, lust, angsty yearning, rage, desire, sadness. But the truth is that I can relate to all of these feelings. It is surprisingly comforting to know that other people in the world suffer like I do. It's a stupidly obvious realization, but I'm starting to understand that it's been hard to see outside of my own pain. Chris and his siblings have survived their mother's death, and that was surely incredibly difficult. Is it harder to lose a parent when you're a little kid or when you're a teenager? I feel a stab of sympathy for Chris. He was so little. His father must have had so much to deal with; not just his own grief, but that of four young children. I wonder if he ever remarried. Maybe I'll ask Chris. Or Sabin, since things are less awkward with him because I have not sexually assaulted him in his own dorm room.

But the point here is that other people have problems and haunted pasts, just as I do. I am not alone. Yes, I have lost both of my parents in a pretty dramatic way, which I generally consider a pretty damn good excuse for total devastation, but . . . Maybe Chris nailed it by saying that I am holding on to the past because I think it's all that I have. And by clinging to my guilt, I get nowhere.

He managed to find something besides hurt, and I can, too.

The music in my ears changes, and I feel the urge to walk for a few minutes.

No, no, no! You are not walking! I yell at myself. *Listen to the music. Toughen up. There are people who have it much worse than you do. Stop being so selfish and . . . and . . . narcissistic. Fuck, the world doesn't revolve around you and your grandiose sense of pain.*

My phone chimes and I look down. A rush of feeling rips through me: it's Chris. He has just sent me more music. Another thirty songs, maybe more. The first new song starts, and while the first line of lyrics nearly breaks my heart, my energy, or at least my motivation, is renewed.

It's just pain.

I am not going to quit. I focus on the music and the words and ignore my body's protests.

I want to fantasize about Chris to distract myself, but since we haven't exactly been cozy since our ill-fated encounter on his bed, I try not to. He's clearly not fantasizing about me. When he's seen me on campus, he hasn't obviously bolted in the other direction, but he hasn't gone out of his way to talk to me, either. It is entirely possible that the connection I felt between us simply doesn't exist. Maybe my reaction to him just stems from not having touched someone or been touched in years. Honestly, the last time I probably had a lot of physical contact with anyone was when I got a whole lot of hugs at my parents' funeral—and that kind of touching is not anything like what went down in Chris's room. So maybe it made sense that I was freaking out.

What I do remember during the first few weeks after my parents died was the near-constant embraces, arm squeezes, and shoulder pats I got from concerned family and friends. It wasn't what I wanted at the time. I remember wanting to swat away everyone who came close to me. I started associating touch with death and grief. I don't know if I actually started rejecting people or if they just stopped trying to console me, but eventually the unwanted affection just petered out. James and I never hug, not anymore, and my aunt has always been so uptight that I'm quite sure she's as frigid as I am. Well, or as I was—these days, things seem to be looking up for me in that department.

I have spent four years without touch and affection and without wanting any, but now there is Christopher Shepherd, the boy who has changed all the rules.

Not that he seems to want me the way that I want him. I've accepted that he probably let us mess around in his room out of pity. Of course,

left drowning

just because he felt sorry for me did not mean that he had to touch me like he did or lie down on top of me with a raging hard-on. At least fooling around with me hadn't sent him into a completely flaccid state. Another small victory.

Whatever. I am trying to look at it as a fun, meaningless make-out session with some pleasant additional groping. Even though it didn't feel meaningless to me. At all. It felt like everything.

Fuck.

I look down at my phone and eye Chris's new playlist. Handpicked songs. I don't know how much to read into what he's chosen to send me, but it's hard not to see it as some kind of affection, even if he's not hanging around me much.

And another big question looms over me: Why didn't he react in the least to my scar? He didn't hesitated at all when he touched it, and he didn't ask about it, either.

I run harder. My breathing is not as uneven as it was on that first run. On today's run, my body is starting to feel smoother and more natural. My dorm comes into view and I check the time. Huh. I have reached the end of my normal route six minutes earlier than I did yesterday, and I'm not ready to keel over. I start to cross the street.

Damn.

I turn around. I have it in me to run for another ten minutes. And the playlist is calling my name. *Chris* is calling my name. Ten more minutes of running will give me ten more minutes to play in my private fantasy world where Chris doesn't pull his body away from mine, and he doesn't stop kissing me, touching my hair, or moving his hand under my shirt. He goes further, feeling every inch of my body.

And so I run in order to stay with him.

9

THE IMPORTANCE OF BEING

WELL, THESE PANTS ARE HIDEOUS, AND THERE IS no way I can be seen in them. I glare in the mirror. My ass might as well have a sign that reads "Proof of Gravity." The material seems to puff unreasonably, causing strange wrinkles and folds that add to what is already not a perfect shape. Angry, I yank them off and throw them to the bottom of my closet. For once, I actually want to look good, and instead I look like utter crap. I put my hands on my ass and squeeze. Stupid fat. Wait a minute . . . There is definitely improvement here. A new firmness. Running is paying off.

Holy shit. These pants are too big. No wonder they look so terrible.

I start digging through my closet. I have to own something less horrible that I can wear to Sabin's play. I locate a pair of inexcusably expensive straight-leg jeans my aunt gave me that I've never really fit into before, and I squirm into them now. A peek in the mirror does not cause gagging, so I keep them on. The good thing about tight pants is that they pack everything in and hold it in place, and these have enough stretch that I can still breathe. My long-forgotten mascara has somehow not caked up, so I darken my eyelashes and then run an equally old tube of pink gloss over my lips.

The knock on the door startles me. I can't remember anyone stopping by my room before. "Who is it?" I quickly reach for the closest shirt from the pile of rejects thrown on the bed. I may be out of practice having visitors, but I know enough not to answer the door in a bra.

"It's Estelle."

"Oh. Come in."

Estelle opens the door. Great. She is decked out in a sleek navy minidress and gorgeous three-inch heels that tie up her calves with a wide ribbon. Her dark hair now has electric pink streaks running through some of the short pieces around her face. Jesus, she looks so hot that even I want to jump her. "Hey. You're going to the play tonight, right? Sabin put us in charge of bringing you, and Chris is going to meet us there. This is our brother Eric."

"Hey." Eric steps out from behind Estelle. Even if I hadn't been told they were twins, it is obvious. He is the shortest of the three brothers, and if it weren't for Estelle's heels, they'd be exactly the same height. Eric has the same strong facial bone structure that she does. They make a perfectly gorgeous pair.

"Good to meet you, Eric."

"So you're a friend of Sabin's?" he asks.

Oh. Sabin *was* been the one to invite me to tonight's play, not Chris. So I am *Sabin's* friend. Am I really friends with either of them, though? True, Sabin has been texting me incessantly about his show: *If you don't show up on Friday night, I'm going to gouge out my eyes with a spork so that gazillions of tears cannot fall and drown the entire campus population.* Chris, however, has been as absent as they come. Yes, he held open the dorm door for me last week and was perfectly friendly in the two seconds that it took him to say, "How's it going?" before rushing off to his class. And he sent me that playlist. But that seems to be the disappointing extent of our relationship.

I nod. "Sort of. I've only met him a few times, but he seems quite insistent that I see his show."

Eric squints at me. "You don't seem like his usual type."

Estelle swats him with her hand. "She's not one of Sabin's conquests. Or Chris's, for that matter. She's a friend."

Eric blushes slightly. "Sorry, I didn't mean anything. Sabe is just . . . a busy guy."

"Ha! Like Chris hasn't had his moments, too?" Estelle adds.

"Well, Sabin seems very nice. And entertaining. Let me just get my shoes." While rummaging through grungy sneakers and clunky black clogs, I vow to do something about my wardrobe. "Sorry, hold on. I don't dress up much. Where did you get your shoes, Estelle?" I ask from the depths of my closet. "They're beautiful."

"Online somewhere. What size are you?"

"I have huge, gross feet. At least an eight and a half."

"Here." Estelle taps my back.

I emerge and try to brush my hair back down with my hands. "What are you doing?"

Estelle has begun an elaborate process of untying the satin ribbons that wrap around her ankle. "Giving you my shoes."

"What? No! You can't do that. What are you going to wear?"

"I have another pair of shoes in my bag. Besides, these will look great on you. Eric, get my other pair, will you?" This is dreadful. Totally embarrassing.

Eric opens Estelle's giant purse and pulls out a pair of teal snakeskin ankle boots with stiletto heels even higher than the ones she's wearing. "Oh, 'Stelle, these are idiotic. I'm not sitting next to you."

"Fuck you. And fine by me. I'm not planning on trying to sit next to you while you're in that boring outfit. For a gay boy, you don't dress all that well. Here, try these on." Estelle holds out the black shoes and smiles. "I'd give you the boots, but based on the clogs you just threw out of your closet, I doubt you can handle the heels."

"I think these are going to be enough for me to handle. This is really cool of you. Thanks." I slip my feet into the heels and then hold the ribbons cluelessly.

"Here, I got you." Eric kneels in front of me. "I've watched my sister do this enough times. Let's cuff these jeans a little to show off the shoes."

"Aha! There's some gay!" Estelle says triumphantly. She purses her lips as she jams a foot into one of her boots. "I bought these on the small side, but it was the last pair they had."

"Are you sure you don't want these back?" I am uncomfortable that she has lent me these shoes, but they really are hot.

Estelle looks up and eyes my feet. "Mother fu—"

"Estelle!" Eric throws up his hands.

She rolls her eyes. "Oh my, golly pie! Better?"

"No, not really."

"Then, motherfuck, those look better on you than they do on me. Keep them. I can't possibly wear them again after seeing them on you." Before I can protest, she is already up and pulling at my shirt. "Are you sure about this shirt, though? I'm not convinced the vintage Coke thing is really working for you."

I look down. This is what I get for not paying attention to what I'd yanked out of the clothing pile. "No, this . . . I'm not wearing this out. I hadn't really figured out what to wear yet."

Estelle whips around and roots through the mess on the bed, surely for far longer than she would have had to if I actually shopped and paid attention to fashion trends. Finally she reaches into her giant bag. "Here. This will be awesome on you. Man, if I had your tits, I'd be wearing this shirt every day." She tosses a pale blue top over to me. "It's freakishly warm tonight for October, and tomorrow we're supposed to get snow, so enjoy the good weather and show off that body."

"Estelle, I can't possibly—"

"Yes, you can," Eric says. "She appears to have twenty-seven outfits in that bag, so take some weight off her shoulder."

"Eric, turn around," Estelle instructs. "You're still a boy."

"Thanks, darling."

I put on her shirt. My scar is totally uncovered, but I decide that I'm not going to let this stop me. No one has complimented me the way these two have, and . . . and . . . and I'm having fun. I feel good. "So what do we think?" I raise my hands up and pose.

Eric turns back around. "Well, Miss Just A Friend, you look great." He winks.

"You do. Damn hottie. Now, let's go. If we're late, Sabin will tear us all a new one." Estelle throws her giant purse over her shoulder and leads the way out.

∼∼∼

I cannot wait for this play to be over. Sabin is fantastic, very spirited and skilled onstage. He is not the problem. The college auditorium, however, seems to be doubling as a sauna. I shift in my seat and fan myself with the program. I know rationally that the temperature is fine in here. Nobody else looks overheated. Estelle, on my right, is the picture of relaxed and cool, and Eric, on her right, hasn't taken his eyes off the stage.

The source of my sweating and discomfort is sitting about four inches away from me on my left. Chris's upper arm has brushed against me no less than fifteen times. Given that I don't have many, or really any, friends, I should be focusing on this play so that I can come up with specific compliments for my new pal Sabin. Instead, it is all I can do to keep looking straight ahead. I realize that if I steal one look at Chris, I might come unglued. Of course, there is no reason to think that he is feeling my presence the way that I feel his. But every time that he laughs at a line from the play or mutters to himself—or, for Christ's sakes, sniffs—I practically shudder with lust.

If I believed in God or was religious to any degree, I might argue that these crazy physical sensations are punishment for masturbating. For masturbating a lot. I think that I may have an addiction. A sex-maniac beast has awoken, and I am a horny mess nearly all the time. I almost feel surprised that I haven't yet grabbed Estelle and shoved my tongue down that beautiful girl's throat. I'd probably get further with Estelle than I did with her brother.

Oh my God. What is wrong with me?

The thing is, while Estelle seems incredibly cool, I am not interested in her. Or Sabin. Or any of the other hundred people in this auditorium. What I want is to feel Chris's arms around me again. I want to go back to that day last month by the lake. Maybe minus the bizarre blurting out that my parents are dead and the flashbacks that left me defenseless in his arms. Or go back to that moment in his room when he pushed my hair out of my face, when his breathing had became ragged. What I wouldn't give to be able to rip off that button-down shirt of his right this second and feel his chest again. . . .

Not that I would know what the hell to do with him if given the opportunity to take off more than his shirt. I hardly have a wealth of experience to work from. It is probably better that nothing else is going to happen between us and that I am alone in this nearly excruciating ache. At least this way he never has to know how inexperienced I really am.

"Excuse me. Can I squeeze past you?" says a bleached-blond guy who stops at our aisle. "Sorry. Hey, Chris, how you doin'? I know, I know. I'm majorly late." He's in a wrinkled shirt and jeans and is noticeably good-looking. He squeezes in front of us to reach the empty seat next to Eric.

"Reliably majorly late," Chris jokes. He leans his head toward me, touching his arm to mine again. "That's Eric's boyfriend, Zachary. You'll like him. Cool kid."

It's hard to think now, but if I don't say anything, then he'll pull away. I come up with an ordinary enough response. "How long have they been dating?"

"Since early last year."

I turn my head a bit. Not enough to meet his eyes, though. My heart is pounding.

left drowning

"It's good that we all like Zach so much," Chris whispers. "I can't imagine one of us dating someone the others didn't approve of."

"You guys watch out for one another," I say.

"Of course. Don't you and your brother?"

"We used to. Not so much anymore."

Chris pauses. "I'm sorry."

I lift my chin to look at him. "It'll get better. Someday. I'm starting to believe that." I am way too close to him, but he is actually engaging me in conversation like nothing is weird between us, and I don't want to lose that.

"Yes. It will."

Although Chris is distracting, I eventually get pulled into Sabin's performance. I may not know a ton about acting, but I do know that I enjoy watching him and that I laugh more than once. I'm disappointed when it's over, partially because I'll have to leave my spot next to Chris, but also because it has been such a pleasure to see my new friend onstage. Applause erupts and I feel Chris looking at me as he stands and starts clapping. I glance at him. Damn, that little crooked smile of his is gorgeous. I rise from my seat and raise my hands above my head, clapping loudly as Sabin runs to center stage and bows. The Shepherd siblings whoop and yell, and their enthusiasm rubs off on me. I clap harder. Chris is screaming Sabin's name, and Estelle starts whistling through her fingers as Eric climbs up on his chair. He reaches for Zach and then Estelle, bringing them up high, too. Estelle's hand finds mine, and I am pulled up to stand on my seat next to her. I look down and hold out a hand to Chris. The rush when he places his hand in mine is nearly too much.

Sabin scans the room and sees us. He points at our group, beaming. His family goes nuts, and although I join in, I am painfully aware of the envy I feel about the obvious bond they have. I have nothing like this with James anymore. He barely feels like my brother, and I imagine that he doesn't think of me as a sister. It isn't normal and it isn't acceptable. I desperately miss him. I will try harder. Harder but without pushing. Whatever that means.

The houselights come on and the auditorium slowly begins to empty. I can feel Chris standing behind me as we wait to move out of the aisle, and it seems to take an eternity before we are all gathered outside the building.

"Where the hell is Sabin?" Estelle asks. "He said he'd be right out after the show."

"Probably figuring out which party to go to. He'll be here," Chris assures her.

I intentionally stand away from Chris and talk with Eric and Zach. I catch him looking at me a few times, but he doesn't make any effort to move closer. Eric and I discover that we are both in the same English class, Love and Madness in Eighteenth- and Nineteenth-Century Literature. It's an elective course that is open to both sophomores and upperclassmen, and it's one of my favorites.

"So who do you prefer?" Eric asks. "The Marquis de Sade or Kate Chopin?"

I laugh. "Well, depends what day you ask me and how masochistic I'm feeling. And you?"

Eric grins. "I see you're a girl after my own heart."

"So, the Marquis de Sade," we say together.

Zach shakes his head and puts his arm around Eric, rubbing his arm to stave off the now-cool October evening. "I think you both could do

left drowning

with a little less madness and a little more love." He kisses Eric's cheek. "But I'll take the mad with the good."

Eric groans but can't help smiling. "That was a tragic pun."

"My loyal fans have congregated, awaiting my arrival!" Sabin blows through the group and lands next to Estelle. He has changed out of his costume into jeans, a T-shirt, and a leather biker jacket, but remnants of makeup still outline his already-dark eyes. He is flushed and buzzing in the afterglow of his performance. Or from the bottle of tequila in his hand. Either way, he is a firestorm of energy. "So? Whaddya think? Whaddya think? Blythe, you go first. Lay it on me. I was terrible, wasn't I? You fell asleep? You were in a near coma and had to be revived with a kiss?" He raises his eyebrows in ridiculous exaggeration. "And I see you've been revived. Hmm. . . ."

"I most certainly did not fall asleep!" I protest. "You were wonderful. Honestly, Sabin, it was a great show."

He beams. "Thank you. That's very kind. Okay, who's next? Who else has endless praise ready to be lavished upon the world's best actor? Anyone? Really? Nothing? I'm crushed."

"You know you were awesome," Estelle says. "Your ego is big enough without us fawning all over you." Then she cups a hand to her mouth and whispers, "But you were fantastic."

The boys toss more deserved praise his way, until even Sabin starts to look humbled. "So, c'mon, everyone. There's a band playing up on the hill, and I've got just the spot to watch them." He starts leading the group across campus, and he has to yell to be heard over the noise of the band's warm-up and the chatter from the theater crowd.

I am frozen in place, unsure what to do. Am I supposed to go with them? Am I invited? Do I even want to go? "I . . . I'm going to head back," I say to no one in particular. "Thank you so much—"

"I heard that! Blythe, get up here!" Sabin calls over his shoulder. "You're not going anywhere, is she, guys? I think she's stuck with us now, right, everyone?"

"Shitting rainbows!" the rest of the group yells.

I scurry up to Sabin and let him throw an arm around my shoulder. "Shitting rainbows? Explain."

"Stupid family joke. Bucking up in the face of tragedy and whatnot." He waves a hand. "I gather you've been there."

Chris has told them all about my parents. Awesome. They are taking me in like the orphan that I am. "Really, I should get back to the dorm and—"

"Shut up," he says teasingly. "I know what you're thinking, and that's not why you're here with us."

We walk for a minute. "Why am I?"

Sabin shrugs. "Does there really have to be an answer to that? Sometimes it's just right. You fit. Jesus, kid, can't you feel it? Don't question everything."

I smile. I do feel it. Belonging. It has been hard to recognize. Even the drama with Chris doesn't change what's here. I hear Chris's voice in my head. *Stop fighting it.* Plus, Sabin has a warm, protective bear-hug hold on me that is irresistible; a big guy with his arm over my shoulders just feels good right now.

"Stop calling me *kid*. I'm older than you are."

"Ooooh, feisty girl! I like it!" His big arm shakes my shoulder and I giggle.

"So where are we going?"

"You'll see."

left drowning

He leads us through the lighted paths between campus department buildings and up a back hill to the most modern building at Matthews. "Welcome to Architecture 101. Have you been here?"

I shake my head. "It looks cool, but we can't go in, right? It's kind of closed."

"We're not going *in*. We're going *on*." As he pulls down the fire escape from the side of the building, the noise seems to echo across the entire campus. "Up we go."

"Sabin!" But he is already starting to climb the ladder. "Sabin!" I yell again.

How I am going to manage this shaky fire escape in Estelle's crazy shoes is beyond me. I look up. Sabin has already reached the roof. *Shit.* I'm not much of a rule breaker, but this is only a minor infraction, so I'm not about to wimp out because of sexy shoes. Tentatively, I start up the first few rungs.

"Need a hand?"

I don't have to look down to know who it is. His voice is unmistakable, because of the sound and because of how my pulse goes fucking crazy.

"I'm perfectly fine," I say and continue up.

I hear Chris and the others talking below, their voices fading as I near the top. Sabin is leaning over the concrete ledge that looks across campus.

He raises the bottle as if toasting me. "You made it, feisty girl!"

I kick a foot out in front of me. "Barely. No thanks to Estelle's shoes." I stand next to him now and take in the view. The campus looks pretty spectacular at night.

"Hey, about before," Sabin starts as he puts his arm around me again, "I really am sorry about your parents. That absolutely sucks."

"Thank you. And I'm sorry you lost your mom. You were really little, huh?"

Sabin nods. "We were."

"I'm glad you've had your father."

He laughs. "You shouldn't be."

"Why? You don't get along?"

Sabin glances behind us. Chris is holding his hand out and helping Estelle up over the edge of the last ladder rung.

"My father's kind of an asshole. Chris makes him out to be worse than he is, but it's just easier not to deal with Dad's crap."

"Oh. Then I'm doubly sorry."

"Not a big deal. We pretty much stay away from him, so it's not much of an issue anymore. We're all good now." He brings the bottle in front of us. "Unscrew, please, madam. I'm not ready to let you go. Chris might snatch you away from me."

I practically snort. "Yeah, right. Hardly." I unscrew the cap on the tequila.

"Don't be so sure." Sabin looks behind us as Chris and Estelle head our way. "Where are Eric and Zach?"

"You know how he feels about being up so high," Estelle says. "I mean, hello, Sabin. How long have you known him?"

"Oh Jesus, what is wrong with me? I totally forgot." Sabin looks solemn for a moment. "I'm an asshole. I'll go after him."

"Don't worry," Chris said. "You know Eric. He doesn't really like big crowds."

Sabin turns to me. "Eric is more of a one-on-one kind of a guy, just so you know. He's the quiet one."

left drowning

"And this whole time I thought it was you."

"Oooooh, nice, Miss Blythe. You're a funny one, I see." He rubs my arm with his hand.

"You cold?" Chris asks me, but I don't turn around. "Do you want my jacket?"

"I'm fine. Thanks." In fact, I am freezing now.

"I got her." Sabin takes his arm from my shoulder and takes off his leather jacket. "You are most definitely chilly."

I look up at him as he holds the jacket while I slip my arms in. We return to face the band, and he tips his head in to me, saying softly so that only I can hear, "A little jealousy never hurt anyone, huh?"

It takes all I have not to smile.

Sabin takes a swig and then tips it my way. "Drink?"

"No, thanks." I continue looking out over the campus lights, keeping my back to Chris. "Tequila and I have a troubled past."

"Ha! Is there any other kind of past?"

I laugh. "Fair enough. Pass it over." I agree to the drink tonight because it's for fun and possibly to calm my nerves, not because I'm trying to block out the world. Even the small sip of tequila burns my throat. "Shit, that's rough." But I take another small drink anyway. "I don't suppose you carry salt and lime with you?"

"I do not. I'm a purist."

"I bet your sister has some in that bag of hers."

"Bet she doesn't."

"Bet she does." I tip my head back and interrupt Chris, who is talking to Estelle. "Estelle, we have a bet going. Do you happen to have a lime and some salt with you?"

"Depends. Who thinks that I don't?"

I turn around. "Sabin."

"Well, let's see here," she says mysteriously. One of the shoulder straps falls as she searches through her oversize purse while Chris and Sabin shake their heads. She looks up and grins. "Catch."

I swipe my hand in front of Sabin's and catch the pass. "One lime," I say with satisfaction.

"Only halfway there," he grumbles.

"And," Estelle continues as she roots farther into her bag, "roughly twenty salt packs from the caf."

"God damn it." Sabin tosses up his hands and starts toward her. "You're gonna pay for this, little sis!"

"Consider them celebratory confetti," she yells as she tosses her handful into the air. Sabin tackles her but she manages to climb onto him and force a piggyback. "Faster!" she commands. Happy squeals echo above us as Sabin starts zigzagging back and forth across the vast rooftop. They collapse in a laughing, tangled heap and stay where they are.

Perfect. Now I have lost my Sabin security blanket, and I am alone with Chris. It's what I want most and least. The college band has finished their sound check and launched into a pretty good cover set, a series of indie and college rock–type songs. At least there is music to fill the quiet between me and Chris. I turn around under the guise of enjoying the lofty view of the stage. Eventually, Chris sidles up to me.

"Hi," he says gently.

I hate how fucking perfect his voice is. While I've now spent countless minutes thinking about him during my runs—and, if I'm honest, alone in bed at night—I don't care for how unnerved and flustered I am getting around him tonight. How can I not, though? I sexually molested him in his room (probably with less skill than he was used to), and then

left drowning

I don't hear anything from him, except for the emotionally loaded play-list.

He loves me, he loves me not, he loves me . . .

"Hi," I say back. "Tequila?"

"Sure, why not? Do a shot with me?" Chris pulls a key chain with a pocketknife from his pants and takes the lime from my hand. "I even caught a few of Estelle's salt packets." He bends down in front of me and cuts the lime on bended knee. I can't help smiling when he holds a lime wedge out to me. "What's so funny?"

Before this night, I hadn't had a drink in a while, and the slugs of tequila that I've already taken have clearly gone to my head, because I start giggling and can't stop.

"Why are you laughing?" he asks, bemused.

"It looks like you're asking me to marry you with a lime."

He grins. "I guess it does. So? Are you taking the lime or not?"

"Yes." I take the wedge from his hand. "I am indescribably moved by your proposal."

"Ah, thank you. I think I can promise that a proposal with a lime is the closest I'll ever come to the institution of marriage."

"So you feel the same way I do," I say.

"If people really love each other, then why bother with all the cer-emony."

"Precisely."

He stands up. "Salt?"

I nod and lick the top of my hand between my thumb and forefin-ger, and Chris sprinkles salt for me. I do the salt/tequila/bite-the-lime routine. I suck on the lime for a second and then say, "It fits perfectly. All that planning was worth it."

"I have an eye for these things." He winks just before he licks and salts his own hand.

It's a good thing that he can't read my thoughts, because watching his tongue sweep over his own hand nearly makes my knees buckle. Apparently I have forgiven his disappearing act over the past few weeks. When we are together, that's easy.

He downs a decent gulp, coughing as soon as he swallows. "God, Sabin drinks some cheap crap." He sucks his lime wedge nearly dry.

"You're not kidding. This stuff is pretty bad." I pause. "Wanna do another one?"

"Totally."

So we do.

After we've both coughed our way through another round of too-big shots, we stand side by side and watch the crowd below us that is progressively getting louder. A group of girls by the front of the stage begins hooting and chanting as someone comes onstage. I squint. "Hey, is that . . . "

Chris follows my gaze. "Yup. That's Sabin. He and Estelle must've gone down the back ladder. I didn't even notice."

We watch as Sabin struts across the stage and waves to the crowd gone wild. "This one's for the newest member of the clan. I love you already, B.!" he yells into the microphone.

"Oh my fucking God." I close my eyes. "What is he doing? He sings?"

"He can do anything."

"I know you're up there, sweet girl." Sabin looks in the direction of the rooftop as he swings a strap over his shoulder and begins to run his fingers over the strings of an acoustic guitar. "No more worrying, okay?"

left drowning

I am both jarred and unspeakably moved by his calling me "sweet girl," and it takes me a moment to recover. When he sings, there is a beautiful, deep rasp in his voice, and I am nearly gutted by what he is singing to me. I don't know what this song was originally intended to be about exactly, but I know what Sabin is telling me. He is telling me to protect my heart, but to love. He is telling me about timing, and dreaming, and surviving. And mostly, he is telling me to abandon my worry. To find joy and to live again.

The tears that fill my eyes are, for the first time, happy ones. I blink them away. Sabin shields his eyes from the lights and peers up to the rooftop. He waves and then does a ridiculous champion-boxer move where he punches the air and then throws both hands up in the air while he takes a victory lap around the stage. He is too much in all sorts of wonderful ways.

"Sabin's a good guy, isn't he?"

"Yes," Chris agrees. "He is. He's incredible."

I keep my eyes on the stage. "You are, too." Tequila is making me brazen with the truth.

Before I have a chance to regret my words, Estelle rescues me. "That's your brother, not mine! And, hey, where's my lime?"

Chris cuts another wedge, this time using the wall instead of going down on bended knee. "I don't know what's wrong with him," he says affectionately.

Estelle takes the bottle with one hand and smooths down her still-perfect hair while she catches her breath from her rushed climb back up the ladder. "Too much to list. But look at him. He's awesome." The shot of tequila makes her wince as much as it did me and Chris. "Lord, this is bad booze. No lime could save us." She takes a spot next to us, and we stand silently watching as Sabin continues his onstage reign. She rubs the cross that hangs around her neck. "I wish Eric had stayed."

"Me, too." Chris rubs her back briefly. "He's with Zach. He's fine."

"I know. I just wish he'd hang with us more. Anyway, Blythe, I'm glad *you* came out. Drink what you want, guys, and then let's go down. Sabin has a spot for us by the stage. I think we're in for a long night."

left drowning

10

THE COURSE OF AN ETERNITY

CHRIS HOLDS OPEN THE DOOR TO OUR DORM.
"After you, ma'am."

"Thank you." I walk by him into the dimly lit entryway. As much fun as I've had tonight, I'm glad to be back here. The crowd, the music, the noise, the talking to so many people . . . It has all been a lot for me, and I'm ready to decompress. The blasting sound from the speakers by the stage has left a good ringing in my ears, and my voice is raw from having to yell over the music. I feel grateful, though, that Sabin was my home base tonight. He let me come back to him as often as I needed to ground myself. When the noise was too much or the social interaction felt overwhelming, he remained my rock. Chris? Chris was more of my risk. Gravitating to him took more bravery, and he could see that the evening was more than I could handle. He must have asked me fifty times if I was all right and if I was having fun. He seems to know me—and knows what to worry about—more than he should. Maybe that was why he'd offered to walk me back after Sabin ran into Chrystle, and Estelle took off with her giant purse after getting a text.

Chris and I pause after stepping into the dorm, knowing it's time to part ways. I'm tired, but I'm not ready to leave him. At least I am clear-headed, since we abandoned that vile tequila on the top of the architecture building hours before. I know that I won't do anything horrifying like throw myself at him. Despite the massive appeal that holds right now.

The staircase to the right leads up to my room, and the one on the left leads down to his. "So, I'll see you around. Thanks for tonight. It was really fun to see Sabin onstage." A quick exit is probably smart, so I start up the stairs.

"Hey, Blythe?"

"Yeah?"

"Where do you think Estelle was going? When she got that text, she sort of took off fast."

I laugh. "Honestly? As her brother, you may not want to know what I think."

"What? Do you think . . . " Chris wrinkles his brow. "Oh no. Really? You think she had a date?"

"Define *date*. But yes, I do."

He shivers. "Yuck. But she's all . . . religiousy and shit. I was hoping that she was morally opposed to . . . stuff."

I try not to smile. "Stuff?" It's funny to see Chris like this, since he is usually so articulate.

left drowning

"I'm not phrasing it any other way."

"Understood."

We linger for a moment by the first-floor landing. Why are good-nights always so uncomfortable?

Some partiers, loud and clearly drunk, stumble through the front door and stagger up the stairs. I finally walk up the first few steps. "It's really late, I guess." I tuck my hands in my back pockets and do what I can to appear casual. "Good night, Christopher."

"Good night, Blythe."

I feel a certain pride in making it back to my room without giving in to the urge to turn around and jump him. It's a positive in an otherwise frustrating situation. The main thing here is that Chris seems to like me well enough as a friend, and having him in my life in any capacity is better than not having him. Plus, it's only because of him and his siblings that I went out tonight with a group of people—a pretty monumental event for me. And it was fun. Truly, honestly fun. All in all, I can't complain.

The light of the moon through my window is bright enough that I don't crash into anything, and I welcome the quiet of my room. I strip down to my underwear and throw on my black cotton robe. It's two in the morning and I should be exhausted, but I'm not. I walk aimlessly around my room, remaking my futon in the dark and tidying the untouched single bed that used to belong to my roommate. There is some laundry that I could put away and a book I've been wanting to read. . . .

Awake and restless, I stand unmoving in the center of my room. I don't want to clean and I don't want to read. This night should not be over, and I am hyperaware of missing Chris. He has grabbed on to my entire core in a way that I cannot shake off tonight, and in a way that I will probably never shake off. Nor would I want to. I turn and face my door as if it's possible that he can feel our connection.

And then there is a knock. It has a hesitant, questioning rhythm, but it shouldn't.

Without saying anything, I open the door and he is there.

Chris steps into me and kicks the door shut behind him. The second it slams, his hands are tight on my hips, and he moves in. Turning me around, he is behind me, pulling me against him hard and crushing his chest into my back. "Blythe," he murmurs. I gasp as he moves his hands roughly over my waist, my stomach, his breath hot in my ear when he pushes the fabric of my robe aside. Going up the back of my thigh, the palm of his hand eases steadily and confidently higher until he has my ass in his hand. Over and over, he strokes me up and down in a sultry rhythm. Chris slides my robe off one shoulder and brushes my hair to the side with his other hand. The feel of his lips on my neck and the top of my shoulder is heaven. When the grip he has on my ass tightens so much that it begins to hurt beautifully for only a fraction of a second, he stops and slowly slips his fingers under the back of my underwear. Over the course of an eternity, he runs his touch just under the edge of the fabric.

I force myself not to grab his hands and move them immediately where I want, and it's torture. But I don't want him to stop, so I let him set the pace. When he's traced his way to the front, I lean my head back into his chest, willing this to never end. His hand moves from my hair, across my collarbone, down my chest, and then slips under the top of my robe. Now he is brushing my breast ever so teasingly, and I am convinced that I have hit my tolerance for standing up straight. My knees are beyond weak, and with the way my legs are starting to shake, I'm not sure how long I can stay like this in the face of so much pleasure.

left drowning

Chris's voice is a low whisper in my ear. "I want to hear you come. I *need* to hear you come."

I tremble and turn around into his arms. Chris backs me up until I am pressed against the door to my room. The way he kisses me with such raw sexual heat just about makes me lose my mind. He takes my hands in his and raises them above my head, pinning them against the door as his kiss deepens even more. The feel of his body starting to grind slowly into mine is getting me dizzy. I cannot think, I can only react. We kiss for what seems forever until he lets go of my hands so that I can finally hold him the way that I want, my hands working over the front of his pants. It's the first time that I've ever touched a guy like this, but my need for him makes it easy. I like feeling him hard under my palm, and I love the way that he presses himself into me a bit. He's not pushy or self-serving, though. He's responsive.

He moves his mouth from mine and lowers his lips to my neck, then works slow kisses down to my breast. The tip of his tongue sweeps over my nipple so painstakingly slowly that I can barely take it. Then my nipple is in his mouth. He sucks on me firmly and decisively until I whimper, and he moves to kiss my mouth again. This time he is gentle, running his tongue over my bottom lip, teasing me with his lips and his taste.

Keeping his body close to mine, he looks down and unties my robe. My hands are now in his hair, and we both watch as he caresses the curve of my breast, moves down my stomach, then to the inside of my thigh. This is the first time anyone has touched me or seen me like this, and I'm surprised that I'm not nervous or self-conscious. There's a reason why: it's Chris. He sweeps his hand over my underwear, just once, making me dig my fingers into his shoulders.

"Christopher." His name is barely audible even to me.

"I want to hear you come," he says again.

Jesus, he is making it impossible to talk, but I want to tell him something. "No one . . . No one has . . . ," I manage.

He pauses for a moment and then lightly trails his fingertips up from my underwear all the way to my face. "No one?"

I smile a little. "Well, no one but me."

He smiles back. Chris holds my face in his hand, kisses me once more, and then presses his cheek against mine. "Will you let me? I have to know how you sound."

All I can do is nod.

He has one hand over my underwear and the other flat against the door by my head when he speaks again. "Tell me if you want me to stop."

"Don't you dare." I will kill him if he stops.

He eases my thighs apart just a bit and barely grazes the back of his hand between my legs. My arousal level has just gone into new territory. I am delirious with lust, but he keeps his pace unhurried and steady, making me want more with every move. Using one finger, he lifts my underwear and holds it to the side. Chris stays still, letting my tension and need mount as he hovers over me.

"Please," I murmur.

So he runs a finger up and down, smoothly and sensuously, over and over.

I whimper again. The sound of his voice drives me crazy, and it is impossibly easy to turn myself over to him. I feel completely safe.

His finger goes against me a bit harder until he is moving in slow circles against my clit and I am groaning in his ear. I am not this loud when I'm alone, but there is no way to control myself with what he is doing to me.

left drowning

"Yes . . . ," he encourages me. "I want to know what feels good for you." His words coax me closer, heightening what already feels so perfect. He adjusts his touch slightly and I put my hands on his shoulders.

"You like that?" he asks me in a murmur.

I groan again in response.

Then my underwear is down—I have no idea how this happens because I am so, so perfectly lost—and his fingers move lower. He parts me open slightly while he goes up and down with the barest hint of movement. "What about this?"

I dig my fingers into his skin.

The sound that I make when the tip of his finger goes inside me is unlike any other I have ever made.

"So that's good, too?" he asks as he eases in a bit more.

"Yes."

He starts to slip his finger in and out, delicately and seductively, luring me closer to orgasm. "You are so wet," he breathes as I start to move reflexively into his hand. "And so hot. God, you feel like velvet." He continues while he also places one finger higher, rubbing my clit again, just where I need it. I can hear my breathing getting faster, my sounds getting louder, and my world getting smaller, until the only thing left is the intensity of us.

"You're close now, aren't you?" he says, moving a little faster, pressing a little harder. I can't talk, but I let myself fall into his words and his touch. "I've been wondering how you would sound like this," he purrs. "From the moment I met you, I've wanted to hear this. And you sound incredible. . . . You *feel* incredible. . . . Come, Blythe, come. . . ."

My body tenses and then I am still for a bit while the sensation climbs to incredible heights. "Oh God . . ."

I half open my eyes as I feel Chris take his cheek from mine so that he is watching me. My vision is blurry, but I know he is staring right into my eyes. "Baby," he whispers. "Look at me. You're so, so close. . . . It's like I've been waiting forever. . . ."

I hold his look as he keeps working his hand against me. I groan and shake into his hold as my orgasm starts to hit. I have never come like this. My pleasure with him is more complete, more layered, more overwhelming than anything that I could give myself. I find that I am saying his name over and over as each wave engulfs me deeper in the beautiful abyss he has created. When it becomes impossible to see, I let my eyes close as he keeps his hand against me, making me shudder again and again.

Then his tongue is against mine, and his arms wrap around my lower back. He kisses me intensely and presses his chest against mine. I can feel how hard he is, and as dizzy and out of it as I am, part of me wonders what is going to happen next and whether or not I'll know what to do.

But I don't need to figure that out because Chris is too busy kissing me and only eventually slowing down until he gives me a final, light kiss and then nestles against me. I can feel him shaking his head back and forth, just slightly. "You are amazing." He moves his hands to my waist and then slips my underwear back up. "You're just . . . You're every-thing."

His words are perfect, but the tone in his voice is not right. Wistful. Apologetic. Maybe even afraid?

I'm still catching my breath, but now I'm waiting for the ball to drop.

"I . . . I should go." He pauses and slips his fingers into my hair, cra-dling the back of my head as he kisses me again quickly. "I need to go."

left drowning

"Wait, what?" I am so lost now. "No. No, you don't have to go."

"Yeah. Yeah, I do," he says gently. "I want you too much."

This I understand because I want him so completely right now that it terrifies me. "So stay."

It seems to take forever for him to answer, and his hands are still playing with my hair, his lips still darting against mine every few seconds. "I can't." He steps back and takes my hand to move me out of the way of the door. "I'd give anything to stay, but I can't. You're stunning, Blythe." He gives me an almost-sad smile. "But I just can't stay. It's too much. *You're* too much."

And before I can figure out what the fuck that means, he is gone.

11

JUDGING THE DISTANCE

I ADJUST THE PILLOW BEHIND MY BACK AND look at Eric, who is sitting on the extra bed in my room. "How long have we been at this studying nonsense?"

He yawns and rubs his head, smoothing down the buzz cut that is just starting to grow out. His head is fuzzy and soft, which I know because I've developed a fondness for rubbing it as though it's some sort of genie lamp. Every time that I do this he yells out, "Three wishes!" I always respond with something like, "Triple D breast implants, a basket of mini alpacas, and a spray can of whipped cream!"

This exchange is less traumatizing for both of us than should I answer: *I wish for parents who are alive, for a brother who doesn't hate me, and for Chris to rip off my clothes and ravish me on a regular basis.*

So, yeah. I go for the amusing wishes instead.

"So," Eric says, grimacing. "Do you think we're ready for this test? I hate essay exams."

"Multiple choice would be worse. I never can pick just one answer. I always want to write in the margin, 'I pick B, but depending on the approach you use to think about the character, D can be correct, too.' You know?"

"Exactly!"

I smile at him. We have become regular study partners for the class we share, and every Saturday for the past month we have met up in my room or the student union in an attempt to stay on top of its demanding assignments. He is warm and easy to hang out with, and fortunately does not look so much like Chris that I can't bear to be around him. But anytime that I see his last name written on anything, my stomach knots up.

The truth is, I have no idea where I stand with Christopher Shepherd. The last time I was alone with him was the night he bolted from my room.

I guess it isn't that surprising. After our first encounter in his room, which was just kissing and minor groping, Chris made himself pretty scarce. Once he'd finger-fucked me up against the door of my room, he became almost invisible.

Christ, if I'd fucked him, he probably would've just vaporized.

Although it seems like he has.

The only guy I do see all the time, besides Eric, is Sabin. He is constantly texting me to check in and hounding me to go to parties with him, despite the fact that I almost always turn him down. Instead, we meet for coffee at least twice a week, and I listen as he rambles on about girls (lots and lots of girls) and acting, and spouts general silliness. I adore him.

I'm also seeing lots of Estelle. She recently coaxed me into a pedicure so extreme that I was scared my soles might bleed when I went running. She'd also dragged me to a salon to have my unmanageable hair cut and highlighted. Although I initially resisted her attack makeover, I admit that I feel better about how I look. My hair now has bright blond streaks running through it, and the curls fall more softly thanks to the good cut. I am starting to look like my former self.

I stare at Eric.

"Why are you smiling at me?" he asks, smiling back at me.

I shrug and then look off to the side. It is stupid.

"What is it?" he prods softly.

I shake my head. "Nothing."

But my inner voice is loud. *You have friends. You have friends again.*

The door to my room flies open, slamming into the doorstop. Estelle steps inside, her knee-high boots tracking snow and water onto the tattered wood floor. "What a stupid fucking bitch! My roommate can just go to hell and fuck the devil for all I care." She storms across the room and sits down in the desk chair. Her hair is damp and glistening, and despite her diatribe, she looks angelic.

"I see it's snowing out," Eric says calmly.

"Yes. It is." Estelle crosses her legs and removes the cashmere scarf from around her neck. She is fuming.

"Damn it," I say. "I wanted to run later. I hadn't even noticed the snow." I lean forward and glare out the window at the wet snow that is falling. The streets have just been fully cleared from the last snowfall yesterday, and now this. The indoor track is fine, and it's probably safer when I run during the dark early-morning hours, but I much prefer running outdoors. The track is smooth and predictable, but I do not like running in circles. Plus, there are other people there. I prefer solitary running, and when I'm at the college gym,

left drowning

there are other students around to see my slow, ungainly style. My new, expensive sneakers, however, will probably last longer without being subjected to the wet, snowy streets.

"How far do you run, anyway?" Estelle asks.

"Oh." I think for a minute. Two playlists isn't really a definitive answer. "I don't know, actually. Probably a few miles. Maybe more."

Estelle tosses up her hands. "I wish my roommate were a runner. Maybe then she'd be too busy to bitch endlessly about my laundry pile. She's an obsessive-compulsive neat freak."

"You are a slob," Eric says.

"Shut up. And she wants to turn on the lights and roll up the shades at ungodly early hours, and she gets bullshit that I might want to sleep past six fucking o'clock in the morning. She barrels around the room intentionally making loud noises until it's impossible for me to sleep even with pillows on my head. I hate her. Why did I get stuck with such a stupid loser?"

"You didn't choose to live with her?" I ask.

"Hell no. I know, I know, you're wondering why I didn't put in for a particular roommate like everyone else. Girls don't like me. Which is fine. I don't like other girls much either. Except for you. You, I like."

"Yeah?"

"Yeah. You're not a moronic bitch."

"I don't think you're a moronic bitch either."

"Good. So the final straw was this morning. Is it unreasonable not to want to wake up to Michael fucking Bublé? It is not! So while she waltzed around the room humming to herself, I did some humming to myself, too."

Eric slams his book shut. "Estelle, you did not!"

"What?" I ask. "What are you talking about?"

Estelle examines her perfectly manicured red nails. "I whipped out my biggest vibrator and turned it up to high."

"Oh my God." I am not sure what else to say.

"She was not happy, let me assure you. And frankly, I wasn't all that thrilled with the results, either. Have you ever tried to masturbate while singing 'It's Beginning to Look a Lot Like Christmas' at the top of your lungs? It's not easy. Plus, I'm not in the stockings-and-tinsel mood yet. It's only November and I refuse to deal with Christmas until after Thanksgiving."

"Of course she was pissed off." Eric is blushing and his sigh echoes throughout the room. "You're not supposed to—"

"Blythe? What do you think?" Estelle crosses her arms.

"I think that I don't want to listen to Michael Bublé's music, but that thinking about him while I masturbate is something to consider. He's not bad looking. That said, I might choose a different method to retaliate against a roommate. One that doesn't, you know, involve a high-speed vibrator."

Estelle taps her foot for a minute and then smirks. "So no anal beads either?"

Oh God. "Probably not," I advise.

Eric has turned nearly purple.

"What am I gonna do?" Estelle clomps from the desk chair over to my futon and throws herself down, resting her head on my legs. "I hate that abominable wench."

"Move in with me," I blurt out.

She rolls over to look up at me. "What?"

"You could move in with me. I have this double to myself. There's no reason that you should be so unhappy." What am I doing? Why can't I stop talking?

"Really? Really?"

"That's awesome of you," Eric says.

"Yes! Yes! I accept your freaking amazing offer! Let's do it now! Let's move me!"

"Now? Like, right now?"

"No time like the present to make positive changes, right? Right?" Estelle is already on her phone. "You're rockin' my world right now, B."

It doesn't take long for Estelle to orchestrate things. It seems like only an hour passes before we've loaded most of her things into a pickup truck. The plan is for Eric and me to head back to my dorm room while she stays behind to clean up. The pickup's wheels skid dangerously as we come to a stop sign.

"Of all the days to move, Estelle has to choose this sloppy one. She couldn't have waited a few days for this weather to clear up?" Eric's cheeks are slightly rosy from the chill, and he turns up the heat.

"Estelle wouldn't be moving for another six months then," I point out. "You know how it is here. Matthews College is a bag of frozen peas in the giant Wisconsin freezer."

"True." Eric checks for traffic and then crosses the intersection. "Thanks for helping us move her stuff out of her dorm room. You didn't have to. You're doing plenty already by letting her move in."

"No problem." It was certainly uncharacteristic of me to invite her to room with me, but I surprisingly don't have a hint of regret. "It's a good thing you have this truck, considering that she lives on the far end of campus. Lugging this shit by hand would've sucked."

"Actually, this is Chris's truck. It may be old as dirt, but it runs great. The rest of us have newer cars, but he said that he wanted to go with something used. Something that has stood the test of time, which he thinks bodes well for the future or something." Eric pats the dashboard. "At least Sabin put in a killer sound system."

"Wait, so all of you have cars?"

"I know. It seems a little excessive, huh?" Eric turns on the wipers. "Chris insisted."

"*Chris* insisted? Wouldn't that be up to your dad?"

"Theoretically. I guess we think of Chris as the head of the household." We turn a corner, and hear a box in the back slide across the truck bed.

"Your father must love that."

"Chris is just much better at handling things. He researched safety and performance and then informed us what we were getting." Eric points ahead. "Hey, is this part of your regular running route? I saw you here one morning."

"Yeah, it is."

"Show me your route and we'll map it out. See how far you're going."

"Why? So I can tell everyone that I run a whopping one and a half miles? Besides, everyone is waiting for us so they can help unload Estelle's stuff."

"They can wait a few more minutes. C'mon. You should know. And now I want to know."

"Okay, well, I usually come out of campus there." I motion to the now snow-topped iron gate by one of the dorms. "And then I go all the way down Stanton Street toward the river and head left."

I watch as Eric resets the odometer to zero. "Here we go!"

"So Chris is an interesting guy, huh? What with making car assignments and whatnot." I brace my elbow against the window frame and lean my head into my hand.

left drowning

Eric glances my way briefly, clearly trying to hide a smile. "Smooth. Is there something going on between you two?"

I clear my throat. "No."

"Oh," he says, shifting gears. "We all thought maybe— "

"Nope," I say, cutting him off. I think about seeing Chris half naked, and the way he pinned me up against the door and made me come in what was by far the most erotic moment of my life. "No, we're just friends. Friendly. He's . . . I don't know . . . He's helped me feel better. But that's it."

"We were hoping it was something more."

I blink a few times and watch the snow. "Maybe I was, too."

"Sorry," Eric says. "So much for Chris settling down."

"He gets around a lot?"

Eric laughs. "Not like Sabin, but he has a past. He's not one for long-term girlfriends, although I keep hoping. If he'd just slow down a bit . . . But Chris is always racing to get to the next thing. The next class, the next project, the next step after graduation, all that sort of stuff."

"Ha! I'm stuck in the past; he's stuck in the future. End of story. What about you?"

"Maybe I'm a here-and-now kind of guy; I have no idea."

"Well, you seem to like Zach a lot. He's the here and now. Plus, he's wicked cute."

"He is wicked cute, isn't he?" Eric pauses. "*Wicked*. Are you from Boston?"

"Not right in Boston, but about a half hour out." I wiggle into the seat. The truck may have a few miles on it, but it's comfortable as hell. "You moved around a lot, right?"

"We're products of about seven different states, I think. I've lost count."

"So where do you feel like you're from?"

"Nowhere. We're from nowhere."

"You can't be from nowhere. Where did you live before you came to college? Where does your dad live now? Oh, turn left here."

"Truthfully, Blythe." Eric turns by the river. "Our father is not a good guy. We don't see him, and we don't talk about him. Wherever he lives is certainly not our home. It's easier like this."

I stare at Eric as he drives, realizing that Sabin told me something similar—although with Sabin, I'd assumed he was being dramatic. I reach out my hand and touch his arm. "I'm sorry."

He nods. "Me, too. But I've got Estelle, Sabin, and Chris. And I have Zach, who I'm crazy about and who tolerates my insane family."

"Make a right onto Hoover Ave., and then bear left and head back to campus up Webber Road. We'll have to double-park outside Reber Hall."

We ride without talking for a bit. The drive is peaceful, the hum of the motor and the bounce of the truck comforting. Finally Eric speaks. "We don't even go home for Thanksgiving. We never go home."

I draw a terrible cartoon of a turkey on the wet window. "Neither am I this year."

"Good," Eric says. "Then we get you for the holiday. There's nothing better than a dorm Thanksgiving. We'll have a good time."

"Okay," I agree. "That's very nice of you."

I continue to direct Eric where to drive until we come to a stop outside my dorm. I almost wish that he would keep driving. Anywhere.

Eric looks toward the steering wheel. "So how far do you think you run?"

"No clue. I mean, I'm slow as shit, but I just run like an idiot until

left drowning

I can't anymore. And I always end up walking part of it, too much of it, even though I hate myself for it. Oh God, is it shorter than I thought? I'm terrible at judging distance." I squeeze my eyes shut. "Tell me, tell me. I can take it."

"Five point three miles."

"I'm sorry, what?"

He laughs. "Five. Point. Three. Miles. That's pretty damn good."

"Oh my God, seriously?" I am shocked. And giddy. I had no idea. "It's not like it's a marathon, but still . . . That's not bad, huh?"

"It's not bad at all. You should be proud. I don't think I could run a quarter of a mile. Good for you!" Eric opens the door. "Stay with the truck, would you, in case anyone needs to move their car or something? I'll start unloading."

I bite my lip. *Holy shit.* Two months of running and I can run over five miles? It is true that I feel stronger, firmer. That I crave the workout. Six days a week sometimes doesn't feel like enough, and the day that I don't run leaves me restless. When I run as far as I can and push myself as hard as possible, my entire body feels it. The ache in my legs, the nausea, the pounding from my heart, and the prickly heat that covers my skin are all addictive. Yes, it is pain, but it is pain with a purpose. Maybe the purpose is to escape, but that escape is letting me heal. I can feel it happening.

A thump on the side of the truck startles me out of my thoughts. I roll down my window. "Hi, Sabin."

"What's happenin', the cakest of all my baby cakes?" Sabin's messy hair blows in the light wind. His leather biker jacket is unzipped, and he has on only a thin white V-necked T-shirt under it. A pair of faded red cargo shorts show off legs that are stuck sockless into unlaced hiking boots.

"Aren't you freezing? It's snowing, you nut!" I lean out the window and wrap my scarf around his neck.

"Awww! You care! But I'm all good, sweets. This is not cold, kid. Negative fifty with the windchill is cold. Today is refreshing. You on truck duty?"

"Yup. You didn't see Eric? He already started taking stuff inside."

"Okay. Stand guard for any suspicious-looking fellows passing by. Oh! Like this guy! Blythe, help me!" Sabin runs off, staggering wildly up and down the sidewalk as Chris approaches, shaking his head and rolling his eyes.

Chris tucks his hands into his jeans and peers into the window. "Hi."

"Hi, back." We haven't spoken in weeks, and I feel like an asshole just sitting in his truck like this.

"Sorry about Sabin. As usual." Before he can say anything else, Sabin tackles him in a bear hug.

"Oh, thank God, it's just my dear brother. I thought you were an obsessed fan. Or a zombie." Sabin kisses Chris on the cheek, noisily and sloppily, and then grabs something of Estelle's from the truck bed. "So, Blythe? Where, pray tell, would you like this?"

I crane my head out the window. "What the fuck is that?"

"It's a two-by-three-foot oil painting of Jesus." Sabin holds the atrocity out to his side as if it were a top prize on a game show. "A stunning portrait, done in shades of neon, and complete with an ornate gold frame. Fancy, yes?"

"That is some ugly, crazy shit." Chris closes his eyes.

"Oh fuck," I say. "Seriously? Is this for real?"

"Estelle makes interesting artistic choices. Regretting your decision yet?"

left drowning

"No, no, of course not." I slump into my seat. "I'm sure this will look striking above the bed."

"I better get this priceless objet d'art out of the snow. Back in a sec." Sabin swooshes from the street to the sidewalk on his boots like he's skiing, and uses the backside of the painting as an umbrella.

I am alone with Chris, and it's hard not to stare at him now that I'm given the opportunity. There is a strong family resemblance between Chris and Sabin, but Sabin is more stocky and burly, and generally more disheveled. Sabin reminds me of a big, messy kid, while Chris has a lean, groomed, and definitely grown-up allure. Chris is put together in a way Sabin isn't. Even when Chris's hair falls into his eyes, as it is doing now, it is perfect. And I know what is under his layers of clothing, how the muscles in his arms and chest are insanely cut and defined. I know how he breathes when he cups my ass in his hand, how he kisses me with that incredible mix of lust and tenderness. . . .

More than those things, I know how he sounds when he talks me down from pain and guides me to safety.

I know too much not to be affected by his presence.

The windshield is nearly covered with snow. I squint my eyes. All the giant flakes cling to one another, and none are able to survive alone.

"Hey, Blythe, listen." Chris leans into the cab of his truck and grabs my hand, but I refuse to look right at him. "About earlier . . . About that night?"

"What? What about it?" I focus on the snowy glass in front of me again. Those damn green eyes of his are too compelling, and I'm afraid they'll make me all weak and pathetic. I have a right to show him how severely irritated I am. How confused I am.

"I'm sorry. That probably shouldn't have happened. And I didn't mean to just . . . to leave the way that I did. It wasn't you. And I'm sorry."

"It wasn't me?" I snap. "That's got to be the goddamn dumbest thing you've ever said to me. You're way too smart to say something like that. Don't be such an asshole."

"Okay, yes. It was you."

"Awesome. That's great to hear."

"No, I don't mean like that. It was just too . . . I don't know."

I finally turn to see his face as he grasps for the right words. Chris looks lost, and I have a hard time not empathizing with that. More than lost, though, he looks scared. Something else that I understand.

Finally he continues. "It was too intense."

Oh. He had felt that, too.

"It's just that . . . I went too far with you, and I shouldn't have. I'm not really boyfriend material."

I glare at him. "That's rather presumptuous of you. Who says I want a boyfriend? Or that I want *you* to be my boyfriend?"

This, I am somewhat surprised to discover, is true. While, yes, I have spent more than enough time fantasizing about Chris, and I can't deny the fierce connection that I feel with him, I haven't really considered the idea of having an actual relationship with him. I've imagined lots of nakedness and dirty talk, yes, but commitment? No. Life is just starting to surprisingly and wonderfully creep back into my screwed-up soul, which means I am hardly equipped at the moment to sort out boyfriend stuff. It's a relief to recognize this.

"Did you ever consider that maybe I'm not girlfriend material?"

Chris strokes his finger over the top of my hand. "Yes, you are. You're outstanding girlfriend material. I'm the one who's all kinds of fucked up. Trust me. You and I are better off as—"

left drowning

"Don't you dare say the F word, or I swear to God I'll pass out."

He says nothing. His eyes are gentle, sorrowful even, and I feel terrible.

"It's fine," I continue. "Things got a little out of hand. We're back to normal now. Restaurant buddies, dorm mates." I stare at the windshield again and try to appear fascinated by the snow, but I can feel him watching me. "Stop looking at me. It's annoying."

"I can't."

"What is that supposed to mean?"

Chris takes an eternity to respond. "I can't stop thinking about you, and I don't know what to do about it."

"What the fuck are you talking about, Chris? I've hardly seen you at all."

"I know. I've been trying to stay away from you. I don't want to lose you, but I don't know that I can get into a relationship with you, either—"

"Chris." I stop him, unsure what I want to say. My hand is still in his. *This*—touching him, being with him—feels impossibly comfortable and right. I put my other hand on top of his and squeeze. Is his a perfect hand? To some, maybe not. Aside from looking a little rough and chapped from the winter cold, the shape of his hand makes me wonder if he broke it as a child and it wasn't reset well. I love this hand. Chris may be imperfect, and he makes mistakes, but I can feel his heart, and I know that he is mine. In what capacity, I don't know, because what I feel for him is complex. It's so easy to be with him and yet also too much. I think I'm starting to understand a little why he ran from me that night.

Still, I want to be with him, in whatever way either of us can tolerate. I don't want to give him up.

"Don't stay away," I finally say calmly. "Don't. We don't have to be boyfriend and girlfriend. We don't have to be defined. We don't have to let anything happen on beds or up against doors. We can just be us. We can just be *this*," I say as I squeeze his hand again.

Chris leans in through the window and holds his cheek to mine as he wraps an arm around my neck and holds me. There are a million things that I want to say to him, and an equal number of things I don't, and I know beyond a shadow of a doubt that he feels the same.

left drowning

FINDING SOLACE

I GLARE AT THE FANTASTICALLY UGLY NEON JESUS
painting that is propped up on top of Estelle's dresser and try to imagine
what it's like to believe that someone is watching out for me, protecting me. It's just not possible for me to believe that there are reasons for
things. I once had faith, and went to church with my family, but now
I don't know what to believe or how to believe. I imagine that anyone
who goes through trauma like I have wonders the same things I do: how
God can exist and allow such awful things to happen. There are no reasons for my parents' death, and that's that. There is nothing like trauma
to make you see the world clearly, and now that I know there is no God,
I cannot go back.

Maybe that's part of why I am so uncomfortable with Estelle's ridiculous Jesus painting. Yes, there is the simple fact that it's goddamn ugly, but mostly it's a reminder of what I have lost and what she still has. Considering that Estelle spends significantly less time in our room than I do, it doesn't seem fair that I am subjected to this piece of trash. Estelle describes the painting as the equivalent of fan fiction. "It's an homage to his character," she said once. "A fanciful play on ideology."

Whatever the fuck it is, I don't like it.

Aside from the unfortunate decoration, Estelle is a great roommate. I even wish she were around more, but she tends to come home late at night. I haven't asked where she's coming from, but it's obvious she's seeing someone. Well, or fucking someone. Since she's made no mention of whoever this guy is, I assume that he is not going to pass the sibling-approval test Chris referred to.

I love how energetic, outspoken, and fun she is, and how she routinely throws barely worn clothing in my direction, claiming the clothes aren't her style. She brings home unusual food from the restaurant, so we always have something to pull from the mini fridge, and because of her relentless pestering, I now own more stylish running gear than I really need. If I'm not careful, I'm going to develop an addiction to online shopping, but Estelle makes browsing through websites fun. It seems that she has money to burn, and although living with her is getting expensive, investing a little in a few pieces of new clothing after years of neglect feels allowed.

But the best thing about having her around is that I have a friend, and friends, I am learning, can change everything. For example, the fact that Thanksgiving is tomorrow and I am happy to be spending it here with the Shepherd siblings instead of going back to my aunt's house.

left drowning

To be honest, I'm especially happy to be spending it with Chris. We'll be getting lots of time together thanks to Eric, who is organizing Thanksgiving dinner, because he paired me up with Chris to complete about six thousand shopping and cooking tasks. Things between us feel comfortable and much less weird since our talk.

And at least one thing is certain: Chris and I are inextricably connected. Do I have factual reasons to know this? Proof? Assurances? No. None.

Some people believe in God; I believe in Chris.

So I am not upset that we're not a couple because, however idiotic it may sound when I tell myself this, I know, *I just know*, that our time will come. But it's not now. For now, we are on hold. And it's not a painful place to be. It's the opposite in fact, because not only do I have him in my life now, I have something to look forward to.

Before I head downstairs to the dorm kitchen, where Chris and I will be baking pies, I decide to make one phone call. James. This will be the first Thanksgiving that I won't see my brother, and while that feels awful, I also think it might be for the best. He texted me last week to tell me that he's going to his girlfriend's house, and I'm relieved that he'll be with someone's family, if not ours. Or what's left of ours. We have no grandparents, no cousins. . . . There is only our aunt, Lisa, and I'm pretty much done with her.

As I dial his number, I vow to rebuild our family, even if it's just me and James. It's not about numbers, it's about quality, and somewhere, in the wake of destruction, we'll recover the relationship that he and I used to have.

He answers on the third ring. "Hey, Blythe."

"Hi." My voice is chipper this time. It's been weeks since we've spoken or communicated beyond short information-only texts and e-mails, and my only goal is to have this call end in something besides tears. "I just wanted to wish you a happy Thanksgiving."

"Thanks. You, too." He does not sound pissy, which is a good start.

"You're going to your girlfriend's house?"

"Yeah. She lives one town over, and her parents invited me since I didn't have anywhere to go."

I take a breath, feeling a wave of guilt even though I know he doesn't mean to bait me. "I'm sorry about that. But it's good you'll have a real house to go to. What's your girlfriend's name again?"

"Angie."

"Right. Angie. Have you met her parents already?"

"No. We've only been dating for a month or whatever. I'm kind of dreading it, but she promises me that they're normal."

"If she's inviting you home, they can't be that bad or she wouldn't let you meet them."

"That's true." He pauses. "Blythe, do you think I'm supposed to wear a suit?"

"I doubt it. Maybe a dress shirt and tie? You better just ask Angie. What if they're all wearing jeans and football jerseys? You don't want to show up in formal wear."

He actually laughs. "True. I'll ask. What are you doing tomorrow?"

"Having dinner with some friends in the dorm. It has a kitchen and a lounge, and we're going to do what we can to make it festive. My friend Eric has a huge menu planned, so we're just going to follow orders and hope we don't get in trouble if we forget to fold the napkins into turkeys or whatever."

"And definitely don't forget to take the paper package of guts out of the turkey," he says.

left drowning

Now I laugh. "Remember how pissed Mom was when Dad did that? And to make matters worse, he cooked it upside down."

"Right, because he said his instincts took over and he was positive it would produce a juicier dinner." I can tell James is smiling, and it's a great feeling.

"I don't recall it tasting any different, do you?"

"No. Although it looked freaky when he brought it to the table."

"And Mom threw a kitchen towel over it so that we wouldn't lose our appetites!"

It's the first time we've reminisced about our parents since they died. This is a small moment, and yet a huge moment.

"James? I wish that Lisa had given us more notice that she was going to be out of town for Thanksgiving." I pause. "I'm pretty pissed."

He perks up. "I know, right? What the hell is wrong with her?"

"I mean, what did she think we were going to do?"

"She didn't think. She never thinks about us."

James and I have never acknowledged what a completely insensitive moron Lisa is. Until now. "Seriously. Did she . . . Did she tell you about the house? Mom and Dad's?" I ask.

"In an e-mail. Can you believe her? What a bitch."

We spend fifteen minutes tearing apart our aunt. It's mean, but awesomely fun because we are on the same side of something.

Then James surprises me with a question. "Are you ready to go back to Mom and Dad's for Christmas? I think it's going to suck."

I'm honestly not sure what to say, but it hits me that while I am motherless, so is James. Lisa has done a shitty job not even trying to fill that role, and it's something that I should do. That I can do. James is only nineteen years old, God damn it, and he's still a kid really.

"No, it's not going to suck. It's going to be the best Christmas we've had since . . ." I suck it up and say it. "Since they died. I'll take us out to get a tree, we'll pull the old decorations out from the attic, and I'll cook up a storm. Santa is going to fill our stockings until they're spilling out onto the floor, and we'll have cocoa and . . . and . . . and I don't know. I'll make weird reindeer appetizers out of marshmallows and pretzel sticks. It can't be how it used to be, so we shouldn't expect it to be. But we'll have something new that is yours and mine. Okay, James? I promise you that it's going to be great." I'm not sure where this whirlwind of determination has come from, but I run with it.

"I don't know." He sounds so sad.

"You won't have to do anything. I'm going to take care of it, and I'm going to make up for the lame job that Lisa has done on every holiday we've spent with her. Now we get to do things our way."

"If you say so." James is skeptical, but I can still hear the teeniest hint of excitement.

There's a knock at my door as it swings open. Chris sees that I'm on the phone and he waves furiously for me to come with him. He's got flour on his sweatshirt and the poor guy looks beyond frazzled.

"Help!" he mouths.

"James, I have to run. There seems to be a pie emergency."

"No problem."

"I'll talk to you soon." I go to hang up but he stops me.

"Hey, Blythe?"

"Yeah?"

"Have a good Thanksgiving."

"You, too, James. Watch out for the bag of guts."

"Will do, sis."

I toss the phone on my bed and head off to bake pies with Chris. I am outrageously happy.

left drowning

It's 11:30 p.m. before we have successfully made all of our assigned desserts. Well, maybe *successfully* isn't exactly the right word. "These look revolting." Chris has his hands on his hips and an extremely dissatisfied look on his face as he surveys our dessert spread. It's true that each pie is either lopsided, slightly charred, or rather grotesquely discolored. The pumpkin pie appears to be all three. "Eric is going to kill us."

"Tough shit. He was asking a lot of two inexperienced bakers working in a bare-bones dorm kitchen." I look down at the food-stained recipe printouts in my hands. "And then tomorrow we're supposed to make four side dishes? I can't even read what these are!"

"Puréed squash, cranberry sauce, sautéed Brussels sprouts, and scalloped potatoes with three cheeses and heavy cream," Chris recites.

I lower the recipes and watch as he continues to glare at the pies. He's just listed the exact four side dishes that my mom used to make at every Thanksgiving. I smile as I realize that Eric is behind this; we'd discussed holiday food last month during one of our study sessions.

"Here's the deal," Chris says. "We'll just dim the lights really low while we eat dessert so no one sees what these look like. It'll be fine."

"It's going to be perfect," I say. "Chris?"

"Yes, ma'am."

"Is it weird not to go home for holidays?"

He turns to me. "No. It's wonderful."

I hate this answer from him. It breaks my heart.

"Don't look at me like that. It's smart to end relationships that are poisonous. It's a good thing. Sometimes you have to cut people out of your life to make things better. So you can move forward. Being here, with my brothers and sister, and you and Zach? This is exactly the kind of Thanksgiving that I'd dreamed of."

Maybe he's right. I certainly feel happier being here than being at Lisa's.

"What about you?" he asks. "You're not going to be with your family. Are you okay?"

"Except for James, I don't have a family."

He steps toward me and swipes a floured finger across my nose. "You do now."

I can't begin to think how to respond to this, so I don't. "You helped plan all of this, too, then? The dinner and stuff?"

"Yeah." He smiles and leans in, putting his hands on my knees, making white handprints on my jeans. "Just because I'm not gay doesn't mean that I can't party-plan." Then he kisses me quickly on the forehead.

Nope, he's definitely not gay. Something I'm happy to attest to.

"I still can't believe Sabin and Estelle got out of helping," I say. "Estelle went out somewhere tonight, and I know that Sabin is at the bars." I take Chris's face in my hands and grin. "I know this because he was relentless in trying to get me to go out with him, but I repeatedly declined because I took my pie-partnership duties with you very seriously."

He reaches over and turns up the volume on the portable speaker that has been blasting his playlist all night.

"Poor baby. Has it been that awful?"

I grin. "You're a nightmare. Hey, we should probably start cleaning up. It's already close to midnight."

I move to slide off the counter and he stops me with his hands moving to my waist. He looks mischievous. "Just one dance."

"Christopher! Look at this mess. I'm tired and we've got so much to do tomorrow, too."

left drowning

"C'mon, Blythe. Dance with me!"

"You're a menace, and I think you're trying to get out of cleaning." But with the goofy look on his face and the way he's shaking his hips at me, I can't resist.

So we dance.

We spin around crazily, we hold tight to one another and sway back and forth, we hold hands and scream out lyrics at the top of our lungs. We stand on the two chairs and lift our arms high while we move to the rhythm.

We don't even think about the dishes for another hour.

When we're finally done cleaning up, we're both exhausted. For once, it actually feels okay to separate from Chris at the dorm stairs and head alone to my room to get some sleep.

The sound of the door shutting wakes me and I glance at the clock: it's 3:26 in the morning. Estelle must really be into this mystery guy of hers. I haven't asked her about him yet. It just feels off-limits for some reason. Maybe it's that I'm still nervous about having a friend. I'm scared to push, unsure of the boundaries in our friendship. I roll over and peek out into the dark room. I just make her out as she strips off her clothes and crawls into bed. I am about to drift off again when I hear her whispering to herself. And I hear the tremble in her voice and the near panic.

"Forgive me my sins, O Lord, forgive me my sins; the sins of my youth, the sins of my age, the sins of my soul, the sins of my body; my idle sins, my serious voluntary sins . . ." Her words bleed together in manic praying, and I am frozen in bed. ". . . I am truly sorry for every sin, mortal and venial, for all the sins of my childhood up to the present hour. I know my sins have wounded Thy Tender Heart, O My Savior; let me be freed from the bonds of evil through the most bitter Passion of My Redeemer. Amen. O My Jesus, forget and forgive what I have been. Amen."

I have no idea what to do. My impulse is to wrap my arms around her, but I think that if she wanted my help, she would have asked. I feel like I am invading her privacy by hearing her prayers, especially since she hasn't invited me into her emotional world. And I know what it's like to want to be alone when you're upset, so I do what I can to block out her words.

I squeeze my eyes shut, but then I hear a familiar phrase that pulls me from the possibility of immediate sleep.

"In the name of the Father, and of the Son, and of the Holy Spirit. Amen."

I roll over quietly. I really don't want to hear this.

"I believe in God, the Father Almighty, Creator of heaven and earth; and in Jesus Christ, His only Son, our Lord; Who was conceived by the Holy Spirit, born of the Virgin Mary . . ."

I pray that Neon Jesus will fly across the room and knock her unconscious.

"Our father, who art in heaven; hallowed by Thy name; Thy kingdom come; Thy will be done on earth as it is in heaven . . ."

These words are recognizable to almost everyone, and I am swept up by their lyrical familiarity and romanticism. The moment is so dramatic I practically expect to hear a Hollywood movie sound track suddenly fill my room.

I hear a small clicking. It's the sound of rosary beads.

"Hail Mary, full of grace, the Lord is with thee . . ."

Suddenly, I am flooded with emotion by Estelle's words, and I miss the hell out of my father. He loved the traditions and the rituals of the

Catholic church. While I never took to Catholicism as he did, I cannot help clinging to Estelle's words, even though her voice is shaking.

"Holy Mary, Mother of God, pray for us sinners, now, and at the hour of our death. Amen."

She starts again, repeating the words over and over, and I am disgusted with myself for finding solace in mouthing the words along with her. Yet it's a few minutes in which I feel close to my father, and I get to have a taste of what it's like to lean on a higher power, to believe someone is watching out for me.

Tomorrow, however, I know I will wake up in more ways than one. I will again be grounded and know that there is no higher power in the real world, because it's a place where there are no good reasons why our souls are ripped.

For now, though, I listen to her prayers. Her voice calms and slows, and she falls asleep halfway through one of her repeated Marys.

I, however, am left awake, wondering what the hell is making her beg for forgiveness.

13

SMASHED UP

THERE IS A GOOD POSSIBILITY THAT I'VE HAD a touch too much wine, but I don't care. I'm of legal drinking age, and if I want to get happily tipsy after Thanksgiving dinner then I will not feel guilty about it. Not now that I've given up the hard-alcohol binge drinking. The wine is enhancing my already good mood, and I take another sip of the chardonnay. It feels just right to be way too full and sitting on the floor of the dorm lounge wrapped in a soft shawl while Chris, who is behind me on the couch, occasionally touches my hair and rubs my shoulders.

Sabin is sitting on top of the half-cleared dinner table where we spent most of our afternoon eating and drinking, and he's got his guitar. For the past few hours we've been yelling out song requests and trying to find something that he doesn't know. And every ten minutes or so, Chris hollers a succession of song titles, "'Freebird'! 'Cat's in the Cradle'! 'Yesterday'! 'Wild World'!" and doesn't stop until I slap his leg enough to shut him up. Fortunately, we seem to be the only students left in the dorm this holiday, so no one else has had to endure our constant noise.

Zach and Eric have been snuggling nonstop all night, and it's pretty damn sweet. They're on the floor, and Zach is sitting in front of Eric, leaning his back into Eric's chest. Eric has his arms wrapped protectively around Zach, and once in a while he leans down and kisses Zach's head or shoulder. It's fucking adorable, and so adorable that I can't even be jealous of what they have. As for what *I* have? I have a room full of people who I didn't have a few months ago. I have more than I could have imagined.

"Well, kids." Estelle gets up from the armchair she's occupied for the past hour. She waves her cell around. It's as if last night's crying and manic praying had never happened. She looks as pulled together as ever.

"I'm headed to my history professor's house. He's invited people who are in town for Thanksgiving over for coffee and dessert."

"Nooooo, don't go!" Sabin takes a swig from his beer. "I was just about to do my rendition of 'November Rain.'"

"In that case, I definitely gotta go." She starts to pull on layers to face the cold.

"Fine, fine. Be that way." He strums the guitar for a second and then lifts his head sharply as a huge grin appears. "But before you abandon us, I have a send-off!" He starts to head for the door to the hall. "Meet me out front on Blakemore Ave. in five minutes." And then he's gone.

"Does he mean outside?" Estelle mock-whines. "Shit, it's cold out! We're into, like, negative numbers!"

"What's he up to?" I ask.

"No idea. It could be anything."

"He's an asshole," Eric grumbles. "But we're still going." He pats Zach's shoulders.

Zach slowly stands before reaching out his hand to pull Eric up. "And then *we* are going home."

Eric looks down to hide his blush. "Everyone bundle up. Hopefully this will be fast."

"If we're going out there, I'm finishing this glass of wine first," Chris says. "Fleece has nothing on alcohol when it comes to staying warm."

I follow Chris's suggestion and finish my wine. "Okay, okay, let's go. The sooner we go, the sooner we can get back to doing nothing. Just as it should be."

Soon we are all assembled on Blakemore Avenue as instructed, shivering and waiting for Sabin. Fifteen minutes go by. The cold is truly painful.

"Where is that drunk bastard?" Chris demands.

"Ha! Look who's talking!" Eric teases. "I think we're all a little drunk."

"Are you drunk enough to give me your coat, because even my tits are freezing," Estelle says. "Pretty sure my nipples could cut glass right—"

"Hey! Hey!" Eric immediately takes off his coat and hands it to her. "If you promise to never again talk about your tits, you can keep this coat forever."

"Aw, thank you, Eric! My savior!" She throws on his coat while he sticks out his tongue.

"Wait, shhhh, listen," Zach says with a slight slur. "Do you hear that?"

left drowning

The unmistakable sound of a guitar echoes around us. We all look up and down the snowy street, but Sabin is nowhere to be found. It is only when he starts yodeling that we collectively realize he is on the roof of the dorm. I look up and cringe. This is not a square, concrete, sterile dorm building from the 1950s, but rather an old architectural wonder, with dramatically steep eaves that project far past the edge of the building, an archaic slate roof, and several balconies. It usually strikes me as beautiful, with the snow-covered peaks and dips. Tonight, with Sabin on top, it just looks dangerous. For the moment, he is safely stationed on a flat area near the third story, but he is eyeing the steep eaves just below him.

"Oh shit," I murmur. "Oh shit."

"What's that in his hand?" Eric asks.

I squint. "I think it's a tray from the cafeteria."

Chris rushes from the sidewalk up the few steps that lead to the dorm's wide walkway. "Sabe? What the fuck are you doing?" he calls up to the roof. "This . . . Dude, this is not a good idea. Whatever you're about to do? No. No way, man."

Sabin yanks the guitar strap from around his neck. "Catch!"

It is not a particularly small miracle that Chris manages to catch the poorly thrown instrument. "Estelle, take this." Chris holds the guitar out without looking away from his brother. "Seriously, Sabin, get the hell back inside."

"I'm going traying! It's going to rock."

"What the fuck is traying?" I ask no one in particular. Nobody says anything. "WHAT THE FUCK IS TRAYING?"

"I assume he's going to sit on that goddamn lunch tray and sled off the roof," Zach says in disbelief.

"No, he is not!" Chris yells.

"Yes, I am, too!" Sabin hollers drunkenly. "Come on up! Come with me! It'll be awesome!"

"No, it's not going to be awesome. You're going to hurt yourself." Chris is overenunciating. "Very, very badly. Irreparably."

This is true. Below Sabin are areas of ground that are either frozen solid or unforgiving concrete. Flying off the roof would certainly send him to the emergency room, if not the morgue.

"Shut your face and get up here, Chris. Don't be such a pussy!"

"I'm a pussy because I don't want to die? Get the hell off there, Sabin!"

"I'm not going to die." He looks pointedly at us and holds his hands out by his side. "I *can't* die. Estelle's precious Jesus won't let me die!" Sabin walks to the edge and peers over as if thoughtfully assessing his chances. As if he is actually calculating the angles and speed ratios and has decided that there is some possibility that he might not shatter every bone in his body upon landing. "Totally doable."

"No, Sabin, no! Not doable! Back up! Back up!" Chris and I are screaming now. Zach and Eric seem too shocked to say anything, and Estelle has launched into incomprehensible praying.

Sabin slaps the tray against the snowy shingles. "Pray, Stellie! Pray to the power of that sweet baby Jesus, and I'll be just fine!"

Estelle stops praying for a moment to yell, "Stop it, Sabin!"

"C'mon, 'Stelle! Our father who art in heaven." Sabin squats down and adjusts the direction of the tray. "Hallowed be thy fucking name!"

He is about to crawl onto the slippery roof when I scream. "Wait! Wait! I'm coming! Don't go yet!"

"Okay! Cool! Hurry up, girl!"

Chris whips around and storms toward me. "What the hell, Blythe? You're sure as fuck not going up there."

left drowning

"If we don't stop him now, he's going to break his neck. I just bought us a few minutes. Come with me."

"Okay. And then what?"

"Well, fuck, Chris, I haven't thought that far ahead. Let's go!"

We run up flights of stairs until we reach the third floor.

"This way," I tell Chris. "He must have climbed from the balcony that's off the upper lounge."

The lounge is dark, and we're lucky that neither of us trips over the furniture in our hurry to reach Sabin. The old French doors to the balcony are open and we run out. The area is enclosed by only a thin, not particularly sturdy-looking iron railing, and Chris tosses the bistro table that's there behind us into the lounge so that we can both stand. To my left is the small flat area where Sabin is standing. The sloped roof in front of him—his goddamn runway—looks perilously steep. I take a second to catch my breath so that I can try and deal with Sabin in a relaxed-sounding manner.

Chris, however, is too pissed off. And scared. "Sabin, man! Get the fuck back over here!"

"There you are!" Sabin turns our way and holds out the tray, which holds what's left of a six-pack. The cans and plastic rings are covered in the snow that has started to fall. "Beverage, anyone?"

"I think we've all had enough," Chris says. "Especially you. Stop screwing around. It's time to come inside."

Sabin just looks past Chris. "Coming, my Blythe?"

I step in front of Chris. My whole body is shivering. "Sabin. Look at me. This is dumb."

He ignores me and throws the beer our way. We let it fly and it lands on the floor of the balcony. "Then I'll go without you." He plants the tray onto the landing and sits down, his legs hanging over onto the icy roof.

"This isn't fucking funny. Please, Sabin."

"Don't you worry, B. Zach and Eric are going to catch me. See?" He points to the lawn just in front of where we are.

Zach and Eric are now holding up a mattress by balancing it on their heads. Or not so much balancing it as they are reeling back and forth while trying to balance it. But the effort is there. Estelle has turned her back, clearly unable to watch.

"Oh God." Chris sounds desperate.

"Sabin, please. Come back inside with me," I plead.

"If you're not coming, I'm flying solo." Sabin inches the tray forward.

"You're going to die!" Chris's voice breaks.

"Don't be so dramatic. I can live through anything. Watch."

"Wait." I throw my legs over the railing and stand a foot away from my stupid, stupid drunk friend.

"No, Blythe!" Chris grabs the back of my jacket and keeps me from going forward. "Don't you dare. Do you understand me? Don't you *fucking* dare."

I turn to him. "I'm fine. Trust me."

"He'll pull you down with him. No."

I remove his grasp on my coat, but he holds my hand tightly in his. "Trust me," I say again. I slowly move out onto the third-story rooftop. I sit down next to Sabin, my right hand still being nearly crushed by Chris's as he leans over the railing. He won't let me go, I know that. "Let's just talk for a second, Sabe. If you still want to tray off here, we will. But first we talk. Deal?"

"Alrighty, B." He puts his arm around me and drops his head onto my shoulder. I'm pretty sure that Chris is on the verge of breaking my

left drowning

hand. God, Sabin is so drunk. I smell beer, for sure, but something else. Bourbon, maybe? I didn't even see him drink that.

"Here's the thing, Sabe. I'm really cold, and I really want to go inside. And I really, really don't want to sled off the roof."

"*Tray*. Tray off the roof," he corrects me.

"I really don't want to tray off the roof," I say matter-of-factly.

"I do," he says.

"I don't want to, sweetheart. I really, really believe that you're going to get smashed up, and if you make me go with you, I'm going to get smashed up also."

"Well, that would suck," he says. "You just got all happy again, didn't you?"

"I did. And I'm not going to be happy if I'm all smashed up."

He sighs into me. "I don't want that either. It's just that . . ."

"What?"

"Sometimes I get so tired. You understand that, don't you?"

"I do. I understand that very well. But right now, we're going to get up and go inside." I nudge his head up so that he can see me smiling at him. I whisper, "I need you, Sabin. I just found you, so you can't do this. I need you to stick around for me."

He nods and whispers back, "You're my best friend."

"You're my best friend, too. I've never asked you to do anything before, but I'm asking now. Come inside with me so that we don't end up in the emergency room. Or worse. I know that you don't want to hurt me."

"Never." He laughs a little. "I'm not Chris."

"Christopher isn't hurting me."

"You sure?"

I nod. "I'm sure. Now let's go." I tug on Chris's hand and he pulls me up. Sabin scoots back and follows me over the railing and back to the safety of the upper-level lounge. The room is freezing from the balcony door being open, and I shut it firmly and lock it while Chris turns on the lights.

Sabin stumbles across the room and lies down on the coffee table while Chris and I collapse onto the couch. Chris takes off my iced-up coat and pulls me in, rubbing my arms and shoulders with his hands, trying to stop my shivering. He has to be just as cold as I am, but he is taking care of me nonetheless.

"That was really dumb, Blythe. But thank you," Chris says. "I don't think he would have listened to me."

"I can hear you!" Sabin shouts from the table.

Zach, Eric, and Estelle fly into the room.

"He's alive!" Eric exclaims. He hiccups while he and Zach grab a seat on the floor.

"Stupid as all hell, but still alive," Estelle confirms. "Now I'm definitely leaving." Even after the drama, Estelle looks perfect, her red dress draping over her body beautifully as she makes her way around the room, kissing each of us good-bye on the cheek. She has shifted from panic prayer mode to typically confident Estelle mode so quickly it's mind-boggling. She gets to Sabin. "I love you. Stop being such a dick."

"Let me walk you?" Eric offers.

"I don't think Zach is letting you out of his sight for ten minutes," she says.

"That's right." Zach tilts his head for a quick kiss from Eric. "But we'll both walk you. You can't go alone."

"I'm fine on my own. My professor is only a block away."

"Stellie, don't go!" Sabin lies back flat on the table and talks to her with his head hanging upside down. "Stay just a little longer!"

"Nope. It's time. See you later, my loves!" Estelle adjusts her giant shoulder bag and steps into the hall, calling to us as she leaves. "I adore you all, even the crazy ones. More than I love turkeys!"

"More than you love vibrators?" Sabin yells after her.

"Ha! No. Never!" she hollers back.

Chris groans. "Jesus, Sabin, shut up!" He takes my feet into his lap and pulls my shoes off so that he can rub my frozen feet.

Sabin giggles. "More than you love Jesus?" he asks loudly. "And his virgin mommy? Bet she had to use a vibrator all the damn time, huh?"

Estelle appears in the doorway. "Fuck you. Watch your fucking mouth." She isn't laughing anymore. "Seriously, fuck you, Sabin."

"Suck it up, sis. Pray to God and maybe I'll find religion, too. Then we can crawl into confession together. A family that repents together, stays together. Right?"

"I do pray for you," she says softly. "For all of you."

"Well, don't!" he snaps. "Keep me out of that horseshit. You're so out of your mind."

"Sabe, leave her alone," Eric says.

"Oh, what the fuck, Eric? Why should I leave her alone? I can't pick on my sister once in a while? Of course I can. I can do whatever I want." His voice is louder now. "Especially when it comes to all that fucking 'Jesus loves me' bullshit."

I can feel Chris's legs stiffen under mine and his hand tightens just a bit on my foot. The tone in the room has shifted. I glance at Zach. We are both in the same position as non–family members, and his discomfort is as palpable as mine must be. Chris is watching Sabin—

waiting—but he doesn't say anything, not even when Sabin launches into a particularly sarcastic delivery of "Jesus Loves the Little Children." His singing is obnoxious and embarrassing, for him and for Estelle.

"Sabin, you better shut your mouth," Eric warns. The only reason he hasn't gotten up is because Zach has a firm grip on his shoulder. "That's enough."

"It's not enough," Sabin spits out. He gets up and cracks open one of the beer cans that he's carried in from the balcony. I hadn't even noticed that he'd taken them inside. He downs half the can and returns to his spot on the table.

We are all quiet while we prepare. It's the eye of the storm, and I am aware that it's going to get worse.

"Ask Blythe if I'm right. She's got to live with that religious nut. Blythe, tell 'em! You don't believe in that shit. Come on, Stellie's a little bonkers, right?"

I say nothing. This is not the Sabin I know, and I don't recognize the surly, nasty attitude that he's throwing out. Although I'm angry, I'm also worried about him. I know that it's just the alcohol talking, or mostly it is, but it's breaking my heart to watch him like this. Estelle hasn't moved from her spot by the doorway, and she looks equally crushed, incapable of defending herself right now.

Sabin looks at me. "You're taking their side on this, too?" he demands.

"Don't answer that," Chris says. "She thinks you're behaving like an asshole."

"Oh, now you're speaking for Blythe? That's fucking rich!"

"I'm not speaking for Blythe. I'm telling you to shut the fuck up and lay off." I can tell how much effort it takes, but he softens his voice

left drowning

as he continues talking. "Sabe. Pull your shit together. You've put us through enough tonight."

Sabin slides off the table and takes another beer. Then he grabs my arm and pulls me from the couch. I wish more than anything that he would pass out, because I don't like who he is now. This is not my friend. This is a drunk, belligerent, disrespectful version of my friend, but I let him take me from my place with Chris because I don't want to do anything to antagonize him further.

"C'mon, B. Tell me that you agree with me. You think Estelle is deluded, right? I mean, there are no guardian angels floating around us, no saints, no all-powerful God. No magical being living in the sky." He wraps an arm around my waist and crushes me against him. Now I'm getting pissed. His hold is too tight and he's hurting me. I know he doesn't know what he's doing, but it doesn't make me any less angry.

I make a sound as he crushes my rib cage, and I push back against him. "Knock it off."

Chris is on his feet in an instant with a firm grasp on Sabin's wrist. I can see that his arm is flexed, but his expression and voice remain calm. "Let her go, Sabe."

With his free hand, Sabin waves the can in the air. "No magical people in the sky, but there are however sinners. Right, everyone?"

"Sabin." Chris is visibly struggling to keep his cool, but he does it. "Get your fucking hands off Blythe. Now." I've never seen Chris like this, with so much rage under the surface. I know he adores his brother, but the cold way he's looking at Sabin right now wrecks me. "I'm warning you."

"Oh, I get it, I get it!" Sabin pulls me in harder. "You're not going to fuck her, but you'll act like she's yours? Pussy."

It feels like it happens out of nowhere. Sabin shoves his mouth roughly against mine, and his tongue gets halfway down my throat before Chris rips him off me. I wipe my mouth with the back of my hand. I am recovering from the caustic taste of beer and bourbon and foolishness as Chris drags Sabin by a fistful of shirt across the room. Chris backs his brother against the wall and holds him there firmly.

Sabin's eyes are red. "There you go, Chris. Let me have it. You know you want to." Chris now has both hands twisted up into Sabin's shirt, and while Sabin may have the size advantage, Chris has the strength advantage. And the clear fury.

"Don't! Chris, please, don't!" As pissed off as I am at Sabin, he's just drunk, and I don't want Chris getting physical like this.

"Blythe, I'm not going to hurt him. I want him to calm the fuck down. Now."

Sabin just won't stop, though. "I'm just sayin', Chris. You've fucked plenty of other girls, but not Blythe? So what the fuck's that about, huh? You don't think she's goddamn amazing? That she's the best thing to ever happen to us? You too good for her? That it?"

The room is dead silent as Chris pulls him forward slightly and then pushes him back against the wall so hard that his head bounces once. I wince at the audible thud, but know as I watch Chris stare into Sabin's eyes that he won't really hurt his brother. Despite the hold he's got on him, Chris shows incredible self-control as he puts his face right to Sabin's and says just loudly enough that I can hear, "No, you stupid fuck. I know that Blythe is *everything*." He pauses. "And *she's* too good for *me*."

I can barely breathe. Nobody moves, nobody speaks.

A few minutes pass while Chris continues to hold Sabin against the wall. "Sabe? Can this be over now?"

left drowning

Finally Sabin's body deflates and he sinks against the wall. He puts a hand on the back of Chris's head. "I'm sorry, man. I'm so sorry. I'm just drunk. I love you."

I see the tension in Chris's shoulders and arms lessen, but he doesn't let him go yet. "I love you, too. Don't be so careless with your life. Or with ours." Chris pats Sabin on the cheek. "Now apologize to Blythe for being a stupid douchebag."

I am in awe of how well Chris has maintained his composure through this, and how he's diffused such a volatile situation. Estelle, Zach, and Eric are frozen still near the door, as if moving an inch might create a new problem.

Sabin rolls his head my way. "Blythe . . ."

He doesn't need to say anything to me. While what has just transpired has scared me to some degree, I know that the flip side of rage is sadness, and that he's feeling something incredibly sad tonight. I don't know what it's about, but I do know that Chris went easy on Sabin and that there has to be more to this story. So while I'm pissed at Sabin, I mostly feel worried and protective of him. Besides, the absolute remorse on Sabin's face says it all. I know how it feels when I'm not myself, when everything that I've pushed down gets twisted and crazy and resurfaces in the most destructive way possible. I can give Sabin more than leeway because I know him, and I know his heart. "It's okay."

"No," he says, sounding more sober than he has all night. "No, it's not. I'm a prick."

"You are. But it's going to be okay. You went into the deep end of the ocean. I know what that's like. But now we're both back." I cross the room to be by Sabin's side. "Let him go, Chris."

Chris looks at me for a moment and then at Sabin. "Are you done?" he asks softly. "Did you get it all out?"

"Yeah."

Chris continues to keep his voice level, almost like a parent talking to a misbehaving child. "If I let you go, and you make one wrong move, I'll have to—"

Sabin throws his hands up in surrender. "I swear to God."

"How about you not mention God again for a few minutes?" Chris says, a touch of a smile on his lips. When Chris releases him and backs off to stand with the others near the door, I wrap my arms around Sabin's shoulders and hug him. I hold him tightly, wanting nothing more than to take care of this drunk, messed-up boy.

"Don't hug me," he says, his arms resting at his side. "I'm a bastard."

"You're not a bastard. Look, I know what it's like to want to lash out. I've been there."

Sabin shrugs.

"So hug me back," I say.

And then he hugs me back and he feels like Sabin again. He feels like part of me.

I hear Chris talking softly to Estelle, and I look up from Sabin's embrace. "It's over," I hear him say. "Please don't be upset. Everything is fine; no one got hurt. No one was *going* to get hurt. I wasn't going to let that happen. Do you hear me?"

She looks blankly at him, but her eyes are rimmed with tears.

Chris keeps talking. "I wasn't going to hit him. You know that, right? I would never do that."

I turn Sabin so that he can see Estelle's broken expression. "Go tell her it's over. But just let her have her God. I don't care if you don't like it. It's important to her. Let her have what she needs. Estelle never pushes her beliefs on you. She never tells you that you're going to hell for not believing in God."

left drowning

"I know."

Sabin is worn out. I can see it in the way he moves to her. She brushes past Chris and flies into Sabin's arms. "I'm so sorry. This is my fault, Sabe."

"Never. You didn't cause this. I'm so sorry, baby girl. With everything that I am—although that may not seem like much now—but with everything that I am, I promise this will never happen again." Estelle nearly disappears in his big arms. "You keep your faith. Always. I won't ever try to shoot it down again. On my life."

"I'm tired now." She has wilted into him, and he has found the strength to hold her up. "I want to go to sleep. You'll stay with me?"

"Anything you want."

"Chris, too," she adds. "Everyone."

"Of course," Chris says.

The six of us leave the battle scene and start to cross the hall into my and Estelle's room.

"So," Eric says in an inappropriately casual voice, "we may need to discuss your mattress situation, Chris."

Chris stops in his tracks. "What?"

"It might be a little . . . damp."

"Possibly frozen," Zach adds.

Chris just shakes his head.

Eric staggers ahead into the room, dragging Zach behind him. "Hey, next time ask someone else to catch the roof surfer."

"Trayer!" Sabin yells. "I'm a trayer!"

14

BREATHING UNDER WATER

THE SUN HAS BARELY STARTED RISING WHEN I wake up. I must have been exhausted to be able to fall asleep sitting up. Except for the fact that my legs are aching from the weight of Sabin's head in my lap, I'm comfortable enough leaning into a pillow with my back against the wall. I had the good sense to change out of my holiday dress clothes and into sweats and an old shirt, so that helps. Sabe is still lightly snoring, and I gently smooth his hair away from his face as he takes a deep breath and snuggles into me, tucking his arms under my legs. Eric and Zach are unmoving, entwined next to us under the blanket that I'd tossed over them. Finally I have a use for this large futon: nursing the wounded back to health.

I rub Sabin's back. His T-shirt is drenched in sweat but I touch him without caring. I want him to feel, even in sleep, that I am crazy about him. That I am unfailingly devoted to him.

Maybe someone else would be too disgusted with everything that he did last night to be near him, but I'm not. I know that he should never have touched me the way that he did. I hate that he forced that kiss on me and that he violated the safe friendship we have, but I forgive him. Easily. The way that he lashed out, the way he did what he could to push me—push all of us—away was a test. He was trying to prove that we would leave him.

None of us will do that. That's why we are all here together in this room—because you don't run after devastation. You stay and hold one another close. At least, that's what you're supposed to do, I'm learning.

I kiss my fingertips and touch them to his forehead before wiping the clammy sweat from his brow. My phone vibrates next to me. Funny how I keep it close to me at all times as though I am always waiting for . . . I don't know what. Something. I take it from the bed and read the text.

Good morning, sunshine.

I look to Estelle's bed. Chris is sitting up as I am, with Estelle sleeping across his lap. He is caring for her the way that I'm caring for Sabin. He looks as wiped out as I surely do, but he also looks peaceful. I give him a small wave. He gets that adorable half smile that I love so much and sends me another text.

Sorry about last night. Probably not the way to finish a holiday.

I write back. *Ending the day with a giant fight? It's a classic. Well done to all of us.*

He shakes his head as he types. *I'm sorry. For so many things.*

It takes me a minute to respond to this. *You only have one thing to be sorry for*, I write back. I pause before I finish my thought, and I know he is watching me. *Don't ever say that I'm too good for you. Say, "Not now." Say, "Maybe never." But don't ever say that shit again.*

I meet his eyes and wait until the smile reappears and he mouths *okay* to me.

Despite the nature of last night's mess, one thing has become crystal clear to me overnight: I have never felt as close to anyone as I do to Chris. It is not from the amount of time we have spent together, but from the strength of the unquestionable bond we share.

Gently, I move Sabin off my lap and ease my body between his and the Zach/Eric lump. I take my robe, a towel, a change of clothes, and my bath basket. I motion to Chris and, although he looks questionably at me, he eases out from under Estelle, setting her head on a pillow.

Wordlessly, he follows me down the hall and around the corner to the bathroom. I leave the lights off and hang my towel on the hook outside of the shower stalls and set the basket on the floor of the shower. I turn the water on and then step into him.

It doesn't matter that we both are covered in the stench of last night's war. He holds me, his hands cradling my waist while I tuck my arms against his chest and rest my head against him.

"If anything had happened to you last night . . ." Chris does not move, he just keeps me in his arms, protected.

"Nothing was going to happen. You were there."

We stand together in the mist that emanates from the shower. The wine is out of my system, my thoughts are clear, and I am hit with the enormity of the impact this family is having in my life. They, and especially Chris, are saving me. Or teaching me to save myself. He is my port

left drowning

in the storm, and that's why I feel comfortable with what I'm going to do. Chris is going to have to be strong, but I have hope that the story I'm about to tell him will help me, free me even. He is the one person with whom I can remember what I have forgotten.

I pull from his arms just a bit. "I want to tell you about the fire. About how my parents died. And I need to . . . to wash it away while I tell it."

He rests his head on top of mine. "Blythe. This is what you want?"

"I have to get this out. If I can tell someone, maybe . . ."

"I understand," he says.

"You're the only person I can do this with."

"If you're sure."

"I am. Are you? You have to be sure, too. I'm going to have a meltdown. I know that, so I need to know that you can . . . that you can tolerate this. I'm asking a lot."

"Anything you need."

The clearest memories of the fire that I've ever had happened while I was with Chris, the day I met him at the lake. Before that, I'd only had flashes of images, but images without a sequence. I hope that telling my story to him, with him, will help me put together the pieces. Remember a more complete version. If I can get this, maybe I can heal.

I start to slip my shirt over my head, but Chris takes over before it's off. Because of this, I know that he is really going to be *with* me and not just act as a witness. Together we push down my sweatpants, and I step out of them. I may be standing in front of him in only my bra and underwear, but I'm not self-conscious at all. This isn't about sex or lust. It's about closeness, and safety, and purging myself of the night when my life fell to shit.

I push the shower curtain aside and start to step in. I can't look at him now.

"You'll stay?"

"Always," he says.

"You don't have to say anything. Just stay."

"I'm not leaving you."

He leans one hand against the tile outside of the shower as I move under the water with my back to him. I hear the sound of the shower rings as they slide back, closing me in. I feel myself shutting down, something that I need to do if I'm going to start this story.

I put my face under the showerhead and loosen my hair from my ponytail. I wait until I am drenched, until the little clothing I'm wearing is clinging to my skin.

I turn around so my back is to the water and, speaking very slowly, start.

"It's a really simple story. I don't know why I've never told it. Maybe there was no one to tell. I don't even remember all of it. Is that normal? The days right before and after are gone. And what I do have from that night is patchy and messy." I place one hand on the wall next to me because I can feel that I am already getting unsteady. "It was summer, and we were all at a vacation house on the ocean for a couple of weeks. My parents and my brother and I. Mom and Dad had just bought a house about an hour away, where we were going to spend summers. The owners were still in that house, though, so we had to rent this other place for a little while. Pretty cool that my parents could take summers off work, right? We went boating, and swimming, and fishing. We played all those stupid board games that you find in summerhouses. Sorry, and Scrabble, and that shit. I hate those games, but they're fun with the right people,

left drowning

and my family was the 'right people.' James and I would swing in the hammock on the porch and read thrillers out loud to each other, seeing who could give the most dramatic delivery." I sigh. "Sometimes we'd all go clamming at low tide.

"The reason we were at that house is my fault." This is the first of my confessions. "I chose it. You know how lots of vacation houses have silly names, like . . . Oh, I don't know. The Captain's Lodge, or Rising Tide, or whatever. I liked the name of the house. For the life of me, I can't fucking remember what it was. I've tried and tried because I feel like that's important to know, but the name won't come back to me. I'm sure I could find out easily enough, but I don't want to be told. I should know it.

"I do know that I chose the house from a list my parents printed out. It was an old house. Wood everywhere. Gorgeous, knotty wood on the floors and the walls. Beams that ran across the ceilings. A fireplace downstairs. James and I had really nice small rooms on the first floor right across the hall from each other. The beds had awesome carved headboards and big quilts. The master bedroom was upstairs on the back side of the house, and it had a view of the trees and the water. I'm sure it was . . ." My arms are trembling now, and I lean my head against the tile for more support. "The house had a special feel to it. Everything felt perfect that summer. Too perfect.

"I can see now that the house was probably not very well maintained, and it apparently wasn't up to any kinds of safety codes. The irony is that because of that neglect the house had character. I guess that's what I found romantic—that it was this classic-looking beach house off in the woods, near the water, and pretty much isolated. It wasn't easy to get to. To get there, you had to drive down a skinny dirt road that wound over bumpy terrain and was hardly the width of one car. Our house was the last one on this poor excuse for a road, but that was good because it was really private and quiet. Anyway, we were there because of the choice that I made, and because it was more affordable than the new house James wanted to rent. He didn't hold that against me, though. Even when we got there and found out the hot water heater was crappy and there was no dishwasher or washing machine. The freezer barely worked so we kept a cooler out on the deck, and every day we'd add another bag of ice to it.

"None of us cared about living like that, though. We all thought it was fun. But we should have stayed at the house James had picked out.

Next confession. "One afternoon—*the* afternoon—James and I went out together to get seafood because we wanted to make our parents dinner. You know, lobsters, steamers, mussels, the works. I don't remember the first part of that day, for some reason. It's like it didn't happen, just like pieces of the other days around the fire are also missing. It bothers me that I don't have the memories. They seem meaningful in some way; I feel it, even though that makes no sense. But . . . Anyway, I know that I went out with my brother. I remember that James wanted to drive. He didn't have his license or even his permit, but he was such a charmer that I caved and let him drive. It's fun to teach someone how to drive, but he was the worst driver ever. He kept grinding the gears and really fucked up my parents' car, because after we'd bought out our favorite seafood shack, the car died on the dirt road before we got to the house. It made a totally shittastic noise and just stopped. I'm sure there was probably something else wrong with it already, but James's driving really finished it off. I should have driven because then the car would not have been blocking the road. That might have helped things in the end."

left drowning

I rub my hands over my arms and shoulders, feeling a chill despite the warmth of the shower.

"So we left the car where it was and came home and had a spectacular dinner with my parents. The smell of everything boiling in the pots was so good. That salty, sweet ocean smell that fills the house. I love that. And we said good night normally. Just, you know, 'Good night. Love you.' Very casual and ordinary, done without any real thought." I am trembling as my voice raises. "Because who the fucking hell says good night to her parents thinking she should say something meaningful because they might be burned to all shit later that night? I didn't know! I didn't know!"

I hit my fist against the wall and start to cry.

"I'm right here, Blythe." Chris says. His voice is steady, gentle. "Do you want to stop?"

He pulls me back enough that I am stabilized again. "No." I want to keep going. I can talk through tears. I know how to do that well.

"That night it was cold, I remember, and my parents lit a fire in the woodstove in their room upstairs. The pipe was no good. The metal . . ." I am breathing hard, starting to gasp for air. "There was a crack in the metal pipe. I don't know what it's called. That black metal tube that is supposed to make woodstoves safe. But it was cracked and the heat from the fire wasn't contained.

"Know what most of the house was insulated with? What was inside the walls? Newspaper. Fucking newspaper. Who in God's name does that?

"When I woke up, my room was filled with smoke. It was so dark, and I could hardly see so I didn't get what was happening at first. The smell. Oh, the smell. It filled my mouth . . . and swamped my lungs in seconds." I turn my body so that my face is in the water and I grab the shower handle. I hold my breath because now I am remembering that I couldn't breathe then, so I feel like I shouldn't breathe now. I wait until I am light-headed before my instincts win and I take in air. "I turned on my cell so that I could see . . . and it . . . threw blue light into the smoke, and I could see through the haze to the door. Nothing looked right. The hall had even more smoke than my room, and I could feel the heat."

It's as if I am back there in the hall, with the crackling sounds, and the atrocious smell, and the belief that death is closing in. I have always remembered my fear, but I have doubted before whether it was justified. The details that are flooding me now let me know I was right.

"I couldn't think logically, but I could feel terror. I could . . . smell it. I couldn't have gone into the living room if I'd wanted to because . . . because the smoke was too thick that way. It was happening too fast, and I couldn't make it slow down so that I could think. No smoke alarms were going off, so I couldn't understand how there could be a fire. It seems stupid but I wondered if it was something else. Like a bomb. I couldn't make sense of it. Honestly, I don't remember deciding what to do. I just moved. I didn't even scream. I don't think . . . I don't think that I made any sound at all." I'm choking now as the words tumble out. "I had my hand over my mouth. So dumb. That wasn't going to help. But I left my room because I had to get to James. That was the only clear thought I had. It wasn't even really a thought. It was a . . . a drive. I kicked my foot out and got his door open. He was still in bed, nearly unconscious. I couldn't get him to move. I may have . . . I think that I yelled at him, but I'm not sure. James wouldn't get up. He just *wouldn't* get up. He was so heavy, and I wasn't strong enough. But I tried. God, I tried with everything I had in me, and then somehow I had him half off the bed, and then I saw the fire."

left drowning

I can feel my pulse starting to pound and my anxiety escalate as the trauma sears through me again in a fresh, torturous way. Part of me understands that I am in a shower, in a full-blown panic. That I'm having some sort of quickly escalating anxiety episode. But I cannot stop it, and I don't want to. I want to be telling this nightmare and getting it out of me. I barely recognize my own voice as I sputter and cough out the garbled words.

"The color is bouncing off the wall in the hall . . . and I know, I know . . . I know it is coming for us."

Chris rips open the shower curtain and catches me with one arm as I drop. There is so much steam in the shower now that I can barely see as he turns the shower handle. "Too hot, baby," he says with more control and calm than the situation warrants.

It takes me a minute to understand that we are now sitting on the floor of the shower. He is behind me. I know the feel of his chest against my back, and part of me is comforted even while most of me is spinning out of control. He reaches up and lowers the water temperature more. I look down and see that my stomach, my thighs, my arms are scarlet. I have nearly scalded my whole body with hot water.

"Fuck, Blythe," Chris murmurs. I hear fear in his voice, but he doesn't let me go. He pulls my head back from the stream of water and pushes the hair from my eyes. I am sobbing now, and he lets me cry.

"I'm here, and I've got you." Then a few minutes later, when my crying has not lessened, "I think you should stop. You've told me enough for now."

Even though I am drowning in water and fire right now, I let out a loud protest and shake my head back and forth so hard that he agrees to let me finish.

"You have to promise me you'll breathe."

"I . . . can't." I *can't* breathe, I can't even see properly. The only thing that I can focus on is the blood that I know is coming. And the screaming.

"Yes, you can. And you will." This is not a suggestion. It's a deal breaker. "Breathe with me."

I am struggling terrifically for air. Because there is none. All I can taste is smoke.

"Feel me." He inhales, and his chest presses into me. "Breathe," he tells me. "Breathe with me."

I feel the rise and fall of his chest, and I breathe as he does. His arms are around me, but he's gentle, careful not to add to my suffocation. It is only now that I notice he is still in his clothes, his jeans now waterlogged and nearly black.

I keep breathing.

"There you go. Good girl."

Slowly, my body cools down. But my mind is still there in the heat and the smoke. I am going to get through this, because even in the state I am in, I can feel how important this is for me.

"I see the fire and I know I'm not strong enough to move James very far by myself when he's so out of it. But I have to. I can't even open the window. It's jammed. Everything in the house is broken, and suddenly that matters. It's not fun anymore. Because I can't get the fucking window open . . . Oh God, Chris, I can't open the window. There's a light on the table next to the bed, and I take it and smash the shit out of the window. And I'm bleeding. My arm is pouring out blood, and for this one second I think that is good because it means I am alive. I am still real."

"It's not happening now. Blythe, you're here with me."

I see that I have started telling this story in the present tense, but I cannot stop.

left drowning

"I can feel the cold air hit me and it means freedom, but there's no time because it's coming for us. It's coming for us." I hear Chris inhale and exhale loudly in my ear, reminding me to breathe. To live through this.

So I do.

"I take the quilt from his bed. It's one of those patchwork quilts, and I'm seeing all the colors and patterns. And there are pictures. These stupid pictures that make me so angry. How can I be looking at fabric animals, and trees, and flowers when I am bleeding and James can't fucking move and we are going to die because I'm not strong enough?"

Chris takes my clenched hands into his, and I dig my fingers into his skin.

Now another confession. Or, rather, a series of them. "I spend too much time looking at this quilt because it's so normal looking while everything else is not normal. But I toss it into the window to cover the glass. I don't do a good job. I don't pay attention. James is so heavy, and I don't know how but I manage to kneel down next to the bed and I pull him onto my back. I get us to the window, and I have to push my brother through. That's when he really wakes up, and he wakes up . . . he wakes up screaming. I'm hurting him so much. Too much. He's stuck on something and I can't fucking get him out. I have to because the fire is almost on us. I don't look behind me because then I'll really know just how close it is. James is hanging out the window, and so I just . . . push him as hard as I can.

"And the sound he makes . . . the sound . . ." I am sobbing hard again now. It's as though James is right here, and I am hurting him all over. "Chris, it's too hot. I'm too hot. Make it stop."

I am escalating again, faster than I can manage. My legs are quivering, my whole body starting to shake. Chris reaches up and slams the faucet so that the water is as cold as he can get it. He moves his hands to my legs, trying to hold me steady, and I do my best to focus on the feel of him against my skin. The cold water is pouring over us, but it's not enough to put out the fire. I close my eyes.

"His leg is stuck in the window. On a big shard of glass. I push James's body out, and I can feel the rip. Oh, I can feel that I'm . . . that . . . I am tearing him apart, but I don't know what else to do and there is no one to help me. I have never been this alone. I just push as hard as I can and then finally, he is through. Outside, I hear him screaming and coughing. The noise is more than I can stand, and I almost don't go out the window myself because I don't want to get closer to that sound. But then I see the fire. Without even turning my head, I can see the fire that is going to engulf me. It has chased me, and it's going to get me. So I get out. Somehow I get out, and I fall . . . I fall into his blood. My brother's blood . . . is . . . everywhere."

"Jesus, Blythe." Chris runs his hands up and down my legs, then up to my arms, reminding me that I am here with him. That I am not in that house, I am not drenched in blood.

"I crawl closer and drag him away from the burning house. The screaming does not end. It just doesn't end. I take him as far as I can, and I have to stop and wipe my hands on my shirt because . . . because I can't hold on to him. My hands are covered in blood. My whole body seems to be covered in blood. I don't know if it's his or mine, but it is all over us and my hands are too slippery to hold him." I shiver against Chris now.

"Do you want the water warmer?" he whispers.

I nod over and over.

"I keep wiping my hands, but I can't get the blood off, and it's impossible to get us away from the house fast enough. Far enough. I'm not going to be able to move James and we are going to die because now

left drowning

the smoke is going to kill us." My voice is broken with terror. "You have to get the blood off me. Then I can help him. You have to get the blood off." I lunge for my bottle of soap, but I'm shaking so much that it's impossible for me to open it.

Chris takes the bottle from my hand and pours soap into his.

"Get it off me! Get it off me!" I am panicked and out of my mind. I know that. "Please, Chris."

He washes my palms and fingers first—so that I can save James—and doesn't stop until my shaking begins to lessen. His hands go everywhere, covering my body with soap, and I watch while he washes invisible blood from my skin. As I lean to the side and dry heave, Chris's hands don't leave my shoulders. I reach for the walls and, with his help, weakly push myself to a stand. "My hair. There is blood in my hair," I tell him sobbing. My throat is sore and my stomach still rolling.

"I do it. I think that I wipe my hands off enough, and then I get James down the dirt road to the car and turn around. I see the house. It's just . . . kindling that is going to be gone in seconds. I can't believe how fast it's burning." Now my memories yield perhaps the worst confession. "And it is only now that the sirens start. And it is only now that I think about my parents."

My knees give out and Chris catches me yet again. He turns me to him, and for the first time since this started, I look at him. I am back in the here and now. I am not there anymore. I don't know which is worse.

"Why, Chris? Why didn't I think about my parents until then? I forgot them. I fucking forgot them!" The absolute atrocity of this consumes me. My eyes ache and the tears are stinging and painful, but they don't stop. "What the fuck is wrong with me? How did I forget them?" I am pounding my hands into his chest.

He wraps his hands around my wrists and holds me still so that I'll hear him. "You didn't forget them. You didn't forget them, Blythe."

He's right.

I didn't forget them.

I can't say it, but he does. "You knew they were dead. When you went for James, you knew they were already dead. The fire was that bad."

"Yes." Later, when I can talk again, when I am buried into the wet shirt that covers his chest and the crying has subsided, I tell him the end. Drained and exhausted, I can now finish this story more calmly because I have no hysteria left to give. "I went back to the house anyway. I left James bleeding in the dirt by the car, and I went back. I remembered that there was a ladder by the side of the house. I found it and stood it up."

I feel his hands against my head as he starts to wash my hair. He is gentle, but he makes sure to get out the imaginary blood because he knows that I need it gone.

"Because my left arm was so fucked up, I couldn't get the ladder to extend at first. Then finally I made it work, and I walked up to the house. It was just . . . it was all flames. But I had it in my head that I'd just . . . what? Climb up and tell my parents to jump out to safety? I wasn't thinking. I just kept moving. So I found a section of the house on the first floor, under one of the windows to their bedroom, where there weren't any flames, and the house still looked like a house. I leaned the ladder against it. I started climbing up, and the metal was heating up under my hands, so that just made me climb faster. I don't remember where I was looking. If I was looking up to their room, or at my feet that were somehow moving, or at the ground. My vision was messed up. Probably from the smoke. I think that I only got up a few rungs of the ladder. Couldn't have been more than eight steps up. I found out later that I

left drowning

had stopped moving. I was just standing on the ladder while the fire was working its way down to me."

I can see again. I feel like me again.

I almost manage a smile. "And then he saved my life."

"A firefighter showed up," Chris says. He tips my head back and rinses the shampoo.

"No," I say. "He wasn't a firefighter. From what I understand, because we were in the middle of nowhere, and the roads there were such a nightmare, it took forever for the trucks to get to us. They had to park at the top of the dirt road and send a water truck of some sort down to the house. And James and I had left the car blocking the road, and the EMTs had to get James out of the way before they could move the car. I remember hearing a huge crash. I didn't know it at the time, but they drove the water truck into the car and pushed it the rest of the way down the road. It would have saved time if I hadn't let James drive that day. The car wouldn't have blocked their way. Maybe something would have been different."

"No," Chris tells me. "The fire was moving too fast, wasn't it?"

"I'm not sure."

"Yes, you are. Think, Blythe. You said it yourself. The house was basically a premade bonfire waiting for a spark. The house was virtually gone when you woke up."

I nod cautiously.

"There was nothing you could have done that would have made them get to you faster."

I nod again.

"Do you believe that?" he asks.

I'm not sure, so I tell the one part of this story that I cling to and that

I have always remembered well. "I was on the ladder when I felt this huge arm fly around my waist. He lifted me so effortlessly . . . and then threw us both onto the ground. I landed hard on top of him, and I saw the ladder fall forward into the fire as the side of the house collapsed." I can breathe freely now as I recount the only moment of salvation in the otherwise unrelenting tragedy. "He's the only reason that I'm alive. He wasn't a firefighter. Just some guy in regular clothes. Probably renting one of the houses near ours."

I don't tell Chris about how that man's face is embedded in my memory. The small scar above his eyebrow, the gray around his hairline, and the sharp jawline that added to his overwhelming aura of fortitude. Nor how this man scooped me up from the ground and ran with me in his powerful arms, taking me away from hell. About how I didn't take my eyes off him while I continued to cough and reach for air as he got me to the ambulance. And how he stopped me from kicking and fighting the medics when I became wild to know if James was dead or alive, and helped me to calm down and breath into the oxygen mask after telling me that James was on his way to the hospital. That I'd see James there.

These are details that I keep to myself.

"Someone came to help me," I say. "I wasn't alone. Even in the chaos of the sirens and shouting, I could easily hear my savior as he told me that I was safe. He said to me, *You are safe, sweet girl.* Over and over he said that. You are safe, you are safe, you are safe, sweet girl. Twenty times he told me that. I counted. *Finally*, I wasn't alone anymore. Ironic, though, because after that night, I became lonelier than I could have imagined. Everybody left me. All my friends, my parents' friends, nobody knew what to do or how to act around me, and so they left. But I never wanted to die. Not that night, not even after. That one man, that heroic man, saved me."

left drowning

Chris smoothes his hands over my shoulders and down my arms. Then he puts a finger under my chin and lifts my face to his. "And so he saved me, too."

For just a moment, he brushes his lips against mine. I stand on my tiptoes and throw my arms around his neck, surprised that I have the strength left to hold him this tightly. I don't know how to thank him for what he just did for me, for what he let me unleash, so I just hold him.

I think he knows what this means to me.

"You were very brave," Chris says. "That day and today. And you *are* safe, sweet girl."

15

THE ILLUSORY POWER
OF BLACK FRIDAY

MY DORM ROOM IS PERFECTLY QUIET WHEN I slip back in after the shower. Sabin is flat on his stomach with his arms and legs spread out, hogging more than his share of my futon. Estelle, Zach, and Eric are also still asleep. I am still unnerved from the shower and glad to have silence, but I also want to revel in the absolute relief I feel now that I've purged myself of that fire story. Later I'll have to examine every detail, but for now I want to take the high and run with it because I've had too much angst for today.

I settle in next to Sabin, and when he lets out a loud morning yawn, I clamp a hand down over his mouth. "Shhh!"

"What time is it?" he whispers.

I lean down and put my mouth by his ear. "Still early." He starts to snore and I have to stifle a giggle. "Sabin, Sabin, Sabin!" I pat his shoulders.

He rouses slightly. "What is it, baby?"

"It's Black Friday."

"Oh."

"Wanna go buy an unnecessarily big TV?"

"Totally." He rolls over and beckons, so I crawl onto him and pin him down by putting my knees on either side of his belly. Sabin rubs his eyes and then blinks up at me. His voice is scratchy and raw, but he once again sounds like the boy I know and love. "Can we get one of those breakfast station thingies, too?"

"I don't know what a breakfast station thingy is."

"You know. It's a combo toaster, coffeemaker whatchamahoozey with a teeny fold-down skillet." He yawns again. "For half a strip of bacon and one small fried egg. A quail egg or somethin'."

"Yes, we can get one of those."

"And maybe a pair of roller skates?"

"If it's a good bargain, yes."

"Awesome. Let's go."

He sits up, pulls me closer so I'm grabbing onto him like a koala baby, and scoots us to the end of the futon.

"Chris's room," I direct him. "He's making coffee to go."

"Yes, ma'am." He carries me easily, opening the door with one hand and holding me with the other.

He takes us down the hall, with me plastered to his chest and my arms and legs wrapped around him. I rub my nose against his. "It's gonna be a really giant television, okay?"

He rubs my back. "Obscenely so."

We get to Chris's door and Sabin pauses before he turns the knob. "I'm so sorry. Last night was fucked up. Really fucked up. I love you, B."

I am not going to cry again today. I'm not. "I love you, too," I tell him.

An hour or so later, after stopping at a diner for breakfast, Chris, Sabin, and I pile back into the truck. I feel more than ready to shop. After what I just went through, and what I put Chris through, something more mindless seems direly necessary.

Sabin throws himself into the small back cab and lies down, giving me the front passenger seat.

"Which mall are we going to?" I ask. Chris pulls out of the parking lot and drives for a minute. "I was thinking the one in Reinhardt."

I look at him. "Isn't that, like, two hours away?"

"Yeah." He takes a right turn and heads toward the highway. "It is."

"Why that one?"

He shrugs. "Do you have anything else to do today?"

I smile. "No."

"Good. I thought we could just drive."

Sabin, who I'm guessing is horribly hungover, falls asleep the minute we hit the highway. I suppose that I should be exhausted, too, but I don't feel it. All I feel is such a shocking level of tranquillity that I can't imagine sleeping right now because I want to enjoy this new feeling.

Chris turns up the radio and then takes my hand as he settles in for the drive. We say nothing for the first hour. Occasionally he drops my hand to change the music, but then immediately takes it back in his. Perhaps I should find this confusing, given that we are not anything other

left drowning

than friends. Friends don't go around holding hands all the time. I mean, it's not like Estelle and I sit around our room holding hands while we do homework. I wonder whether I was wrong thinking that we are meant to be more. Then I decide to focus on what I know for sure: that I have found a friend, this spectacular boy, who has saved me from drowning.

Chris turns down the radio. "Blythe?"

"Yeah?"

"Whatever happened to the summerhouse that your parents bought? The one you never got to stay at?"

It seems like such a funny question to me, maybe because I haven't thought about it in so long.

"Oh. Well, James and I own it, I guess. The last I heard, it was pretty much shut down and a maintenance guy checks in on it a few times a year. My aunt has been paying the taxes and stuff from our account."

"You haven't been to it since that summer?"

"No. It . . . This is going to sound crazy . . . but it's never occurred to me. It wasn't even officially ours yet when my parents died. They'd bought it but we'd only walked through it, we'd never moved in."

"But you haven't sold it."

"No, I haven't."

"How long has it been? Four years?"

"Four years last July."

"July?" Chris squints into the bright sunlight. "Huh."

"What?"

"Nothing. Just . . . It's nothing. Well, maybe you'll go to the house one day."

"Maybe."

For a moment he takes his hand from mine and moves his fingers over my forearm. "How badly were you hurt? You said your arm was bleeding a lot, and with all the smoke . . . Were you in the hospital long?"

I like that he's not afraid to ask me more about that night. "I was treated for smoke inhalation, but it wasn't too bad. My arm was . . . messy. No permanent injury except for the scar, of course. We were not exactly in the big city at a top hospital. I was stitched up and otherwise put back together, but James needed more help than I did."

"James? So he was really hurt," Chris says.

"Yes. He severed a vein—or, I guess, I severed his vein—and some muscle, which is why there was so much blood." Even though I've just relived the trauma of that night a matter of hours ago—and I now have new, sharp, graphic memories—the clarity and full understanding of what happened makes this easier to talk about. I have the complete story and the complete truth, and that is already freeing me. "They were concerned about shock because of all the blood loss."

"You said that he hates you because of that night. Why?"

"So many reasons. He nearly bled to death and was in the hospital for weeks. Before, he'd been a serious soccer player. Incredibly talented, and it seemed clear that he'd go on to play professionally."

"So after the fire, your brother's soccer career was blown, I assume."

"Yes. Months of physical therapy. Months of pain. Some muscle damage. He was devastated. He was the one who was good at something, not me. I was never good at anything. I don't have a . . . a special skill or talent. An injury like his wouldn't have been as big a deal for me." I realize it feels so good to talk about it. I've spent four years having half-conversations with myself, and now I get to have them with someone else. It's a relief because there are no longer secrets. "So he lost his parents and his potentially amazing future in soccer. He thought that I was stupid and careless in getting him out of the house."

left drowning

"That's not fair."

"No, maybe not, but he wasn't that coherent for most of it, so I don't think he can understand. He thinks he would have had the sense to get us out safely. All he remembers is that I fucked up in every capacity, and he cannot forgive me."

"It's probably easier to blame you, because then there is somebody to blame."

"He's welcome to blame God," I say, half joking. "If he still went to church, our priest might insist that he forgive me because that's what a good Catholic should do. 'Forgive us our trespasses as we forgive those who trespass against us.'"

"You grew up Catholic, too?"

I nod. "Well, my dad was Catholic, and so we all went to church mostly to keep him happy. James and I never took it all that seriously, but . . . I guess there were pieces of it that we liked. Mom was more agnostic than I think my father knew," I say, laughing. "She was famous for flashing major eye rolls to me and James just before Communion. Dad caught her once, and she pawned it off as being irritated by an especially dry Communion wafer. She and I secretly shared a wish that they'd instead feed us small bites of the delicious bread from the French bakery down the road."

Chris laughs. "Very sensible. So you hated every minute?"

"Sort of. I guess I liked the idea that . . . well, that there might be some kind of larger meaning to life or whatever. My mother was into that. She had a nonreligious spiritual side to her, if that makes any sense. She believed in the idea of fate and destiny. An interconnectedness and purpose in life." I fidget with the zipper on my jacket. "Do you believe in that?"

"Not at all," he says immediately. "Estelle was hooked from the first time she went to church. Which was mostly after my mother died, by the way. My father took us on holidays and whatnot, but Estelle made me take her every Sunday. I'd wait outside. Here's the truth. We want to read too much into life because it's convenient. Or fun. But there's no imaginary, invisible man in the sky who makes things happen. There is no magical reason that we're dealt what we're dealt. Sabin was being a bastard last night, but he was telling the truth." Chris has the same unromantic view of the world that I do. I suspect that neither of us wants a predictable march through life that includes things like marriage, kids, and a white picket fence. We both have histories that preclude wanting to seek out tradition.

"Take this man who brought you off the ladder," Chris continues. "I know you well enough to say that you don't think he was sent by God to save you."

"No. He wasn't. I don't know who he was, and I have never seen him since that night, but it was him, not God or any other . . . illusory power . . . who tore me away from that fire. I give credit where credit is due. One human being made a choice, he acted, and I owe him my life. No god killed my parents, nearly killed James, and spared me. I know that, and I can't go back and believe in things that I used to believe in . . . or that I used to want to believe in. I don't know how much faith I had to lose that night, but whatever I had is gone now." I take an incredibly refreshing deep breath. "And you understand that."

"I do."

I put my hand on top of Chris's so that I am holding his between mine and look at him while he focuses on the road. "We want what's real. Heroes are real."

"Some," he concedes, "but not all."

"What do you mean?"

"I'm sure many people would consider my father a hero, but—"

"But not you," I finish for him.

"No. Never me. And that, Blythe," he says without taking his eyes off the road, "is reality. What is also reality is that I don't have to see him again. I can make that choice."

"What does your father do?"

"He's an artist. All sorts of mediums. Sculpture, painting, you name it. The house was always filled with materials. Paint, plaster, sheets of metal. Wire. Lots of copper wire."

Chris tightens his grip on my hand. I turn to face him and rest my leg on the cushioned bench seat. "What about winter break? If you don't go home, what do you do? Thanksgiving is one thing, but you can't stay on campus over winter break."

He checks the backseat quickly and then says in a low voice, "Hawaii. But don't tell anyone. They don't know. It's our new family tradition to go away for the month. Last year I rented us a place in Huntington Beach. I don't tell them where we're going until we get to the airport."

"Oh my God, I love it. You guys are going to have a blast. Sounds kind of expensive, though."

"I . . . I have access to money. My mother had money. A substantial amount. And her will, unbeknownst to my father, left all of her money to her children. I'm in charge of the trust." He pauses. "What about you? What are your plans for break?"

"Just me and James. This year we're going to the house we grew up in, not my aunt's, like we always have. Kind of the first time we'll be there in a long time. It's going to be . . . weird."

There is a deep roaring grumble from the backseat. "Where is my ginormous TV? Where is it? I need me some big plasma love."

I smile. Sabin is awake. "We'll be there soon."

"HERE WE COME, STORE OF THE GIANT TVS!" he screams, planting a hand on top of Chris's head and then mine and ruffling our hair. He leaves one hand resting on Chris's shoulder as he sits back. "It's a good day, isn't it?"

"Yes," Chris and I say.

When we get to the mall, we fight our way through the crowd of frenzied shoppers to reach the department store. Sabin disappears into the mob while Chris and I spend twenty minutes assessing the television options.

"Which one do you like?" Chris asks.

"The black one with the big screen."

He slaps my arm. "You've narrowed it down to twenty."

"Oh, I don't know. They all look the same to me." I look around at the array of sets. "It just needs to work."

"That's an excellent quality to look for in a TV."

Now I slap his arm. "You pick. Don't zero out my bank account, but pick the most awesome one or there's going to be hell to pay. I'm going to check on Sabin."

I locate him, not surprisingly, in the small appliance section. When he sees me coming, he joyfully holds up a box and yells, "See? I told ya! Coffee, toast, eggs, and bacon! All at once! It's a miracle!"

I laugh. "I'm very glad you found what your heart desires. Let this be my gift to you because I could never pick out such a lovely, er"—I look at the box again—"baby-blue gadget."

"It's not a gadget. It's a 'breakfast station'," he corrects me.

"I would love to buy you this breakfast station."

"Fine. But in return, I'm buying you some DVDs to go along with your new television." He puts his hand on my back and guides me to the movie section. "Let's see . . . We'll start with *Blue Crush*." Sabin starts

left drowning

piling discs into his arms. "And then *50 First Dates*. Oooooh! *Lilo &
Stitch*! How about *Pearl Harbor*?" He waves the movie at me and winks.

"Kind of a random selection." I stare at the movies until it clicks.
It's not a random selection at all. All of those movies have one thing in
common. Hawaii. "Oh, God damn it, you were awake in the car, weren't
you?"

Sabin starts to dance idiotically in the aisle. "We're goin' to Hawaii!
Oh yes, we are! Gonna be some hula girls and some mahi-mahi dinners!
Swimming and snorkeling—"

"Shhhh! Stop it! You're not supposed to know!" I look around to
make sure Chris isn't nearby. "Don't tell him you heard anything, okay?
He's really excited to surprise you."

"Okay, okay. I promise. Not a word." He turns serious for a minute. "I do have some words for *you*, though."

I frown. "Shoot."

"Chris is smart, but he doesn't know everything."

"What do you mean?"

"Look, Blythe, last night you told me to let Estelle have her God,
to believe in what she needed to." He sighs. "You have to do the same.
If you believe in . . ." He looks around the chaotic store and starts over.
"I didn't hear the whole story, but I don't have to know details to realize
that you've been through some shit, and you have every right to hold
tight to whatever gets you through the night. Know what I mean, sugar?
Maybe you believe that coincidences aren't coincidences. Maybe you
have your own version of a higher power, or you trust in the belief that
there are connections among seemingly disconnected parts of the uni-
verse. Maybe you have a spiritual side that has nothing to do with God
or religion, one that's just your own."

"No." I shake my head. "I don't."

"I think you do. Don't let Chris talk you out of something that's real to you. He's brilliant, and beautiful, and about as perfect as they come, but that doesn't make him right about everything. Hell, even though I freaked out on Estelle, I don't know there isn't something else. You don't know that, and even Chris doesn't know that. There's nothing wrong with that. We don't have to know everything. If you believe in fate and some kind of meaning and sense in this fucked-up world, then believe with abandon, love. Enjoy it."

For a minute, despite the sound of the loudspeaker sales announcements and the nonstop chatter of shoppers, everything seems quiet. It is just me and Sabin in this huge store, and I'm overwhelmed at how well he's tapped into my internal battle. My secret wish to believe in fate, spirituality, or *something* so I don't have to exist with only the cold certainty I feel that there is nothing bigger than random chance. Yet Sabin's words have somehow alleviated the pain I feel over the discord, and for a moment I wonder if it's okay to be undecided. Or maybe to even hope for *something*.

Chris appears. "All set."

I break away from Sabin's stare. "What's the damage?" I ask.

"Nothing. You're all set. We can pull the truck around to the back and they'll load it in for us."

It takes me a second to understand what he's telling me. "You bought me a ginormous TV?"

"And we're going to Hawaii?" Sabin starts jumping up and down and tossing movies at us.

Chris just stands there, grinning.

16

THE OLD AND THE NEW

OUTSIDE IN THE FREEZING COLD, I TRY TO
pace myself on the last run I'll be doing in Wisconsin this year. Tomorrow morning, December 21, I take a flight home. By the late afternoon, I'll be back in the house that I grew up in. James comes in on the twenty-third, so I'll have two days entirely alone. But I am determined not to *feel* alone.

I'm not sure where I'll run at home, and it's making me anxious. If I get lucky, we won't have snow, and it'll just be the cold temperatures that I have to deal with. I'm used to those from running here, and I actually like it now that I have the right running gear. My dependency on running is undeniable, and I know that my workouts are going to suffer over break. The next playlist starts, and I smile. It's a new one from Chris, and it makes this run easy. More than easy; exhilarating.

After, I shower and pack. Estelle is gone—again—so I set her Christmas present on her bed so that I don't forget to give it to her before I leave. I have no idea if I'll see her tonight or even tomorrow morning. As far as I know, none of her siblings know anything about this boyfriend of hers. I certainly wish that I didn't.

I had the unfortunate experience of seeing her with him yesterday, and if I'd finished my anthropology paper just a few minutes earlier, I would not have been in the dark corridor of the department building just before it closed for the afternoon, thick paper in hand, cursing my professor for not accepting digital copies. But I was. When I rounded the corner to my professor's hall, I saw them through the windows of the door that led to the back stairwell. Even with all of the self-pleasuring time I'm afforded with Estelle out of the room, I can't say that I've ever fantasized about watching my roommate have sex with someone.

Especially not a professor.

It does, at least, explain why she doesn't talk about him. I'm guessing that Estelle's God does not endorse fucking your professor. I recognized the man she was screwing because he'd filled in for my own professor one day, and I'd been fascinated by the way he had thumped the desk and then immediately snapped his fingers every time he wanted to emphasize a certain point. I sincerely hope that Estelle does not have to tolerate that habit when they fuck. Like, does he have an orgasm and then do the old thump-and-snap to underscore the point? Luckily, I don't stay long enough to find out, and manage to deliver my paper and get the hell out of there without being noticed. Unfortunately, I am stuck with the visual of Estelle vigorously humping the guy.

Distracting myself, though, is easy enough now that it's the day

left drowning

before my departure. I want James to come home to a fully decorated house, so I've been keeping a running list of things to do and buy. I've ordered him dozens of presents online and done my best to time their delivery for after I'm home and before James is. Wrapping his gifts alone will take hours, because I want them to be perfect. Aunt Lisa was a complete disaster when it came to gift giving, and I will not miss forcing a smile after opening my annual gift card to the Olive Garden or something dull like a set of twin sheets.

When my suitcase is packed, I stop by Chris's room to give him his present.

He opens his door wearing a Grinch T-shirt. "Bah humbug!"

"Ditto," I say. "But I'm here to give you a little present anyway."

"If it's not high-end electronic equipment, I don't want it."

I hand him a gift bag. "Okay, then. It's high-end electronic equipment."

"Yippee!" He sits down on the bed and shakes the bag. "Ah, I'm pretty sure this is a special gizmo for shrinking down ginormous televisions that have taken over your room. Right?"

I glance over to where the Black Friday flat screen he bought for me occupies nearly his entire desk.

"I think that you secretly love having this in your room, and that when Sabin and I are not here you watch giant-scale porn."

"Obviously. But I'd still like to have desk space for the rare occasions when I'm not watching porn. And, hey!" he says with exaggerated annoyance. "Estelle came over last week and watched *What You Need to Know about Roman Catholicism*. That's your fault."

I grin. "Sorry about that. Now you know why I wanted the television in here. Besides, the only way I could at all comfortably accept that you paid for it is to make sure it's half yours. Now open your present. I have to go double-check that I packed everything and go to bed. I have a six a.m. flight."

He takes the wrapping off the square box and shakes it again, listening to it rattle. "I think it's broken. You better return it," he teases.

"It is not broken. Now open it!"

He reads the card. *So you'll always have what you need.* I wiggle my toes inside my shoes, slightly nervous that this might be corny, but he empties the contents of the box into his hand and smiles at the silver disks. "Skipping stones." He rubs one with his fingers and then pretends to throw it.

"That's why there are twenty," I say, laughing. "I assume you'll throw a few in the lake. Or all of them. Maybe they're for making wishes."

"I'm not throwing these away on a ridiculous whim." He looks up at me from his spot on the bed, and we're quiet for a moment. "These are really awesome, Blythe. Thank you."

"I wanted you to open them on Christmas, but I didn't think it'd be nice to make you pack them. They're kind of heavy."

"Speaking of which," he says as he reaches under his bed. "This you can't open until Christmas. It's packed well and not heavy, so it goes home with you. And no peeking."

"God, Chris, you didn't have to get me anything!" I gesture to the monstrosity on his desk.

"That was a Black Friday present. This is a Christmas present. It's nothing crazy, and I don't know why I picked this out, but . . . It's random. It just made me think of you for some reason. You'll probably hate it."

"I'm not going to hate it."

left drowning

"No peeking until Christmas. Promise?"

"I promise." The present is wrapped in deep blue paper with a dark green ribbon. *The colors of the Atlantic Ocean*, I think. I'm dying to know what it is, and I immediately try to calculate how many hours are left until Christmas, but I'm not that good at mental math. "What time is your flight tomorrow?" I ask.

"Noon."

"You probably have to pack still and stuff, huh? I should get going and get some sleep." I hate good-byes. And I'm out of practice because I've had virtually no one to say good-bye to for so long.

Things haven't felt awkward with Chris in a while, but we're not going to see each other for over three weeks, and . . . I don't like that. In the scheme of things, it's not that long, but time moves differently in our insulated college life, I think. This break will feel interminable.

"Hey, do you want me to give you a lift to the airport?" he asks.

"Thanks, but like I said, it's a six a.m. flight to Logan. I don't think you want to get up at three thirty."

"Bet you don't, either."

"Not really, but I wanted to have the whole day there to get stuff ready for James."

"Sounds to me like you'd be better off staying awake all night."

"That sounds boring."

He smiles. "Want company?"

"You don't want to do that!" I protest.

He props up pillows and pats the bed. "Sure I do. Come on. I'll make you a French press coffee and we'll watch a movie. I'll even heat some milk for you in my frother."

I cross my arms. "Extra froth and no porn?"

"'Extra froth' and 'no porn' do not belong in the same sentence." He tosses a pillow at me. "But if that's what you want. Weirdo. Grab a seat."

Man, I'm going to miss him.

James is having one of his friends pick him up at the airport tonight, and I'm disappointed. I guess that I had some wistful vision of us reuniting at baggage claim, complete with tear-filled greetings and excessive hugging. The good thing is that I've had some time to adjust my expectations and am prepared to go with whatever homecoming attitude he brings. It's unrealistic to expect that coming into this familiar house that holds so many old memories of our parents will be easy. This is not a situation that lends itself to a comfortable holiday.

I've spent a number of hours outside the house going food shopping and doing other holiday errands, but I refuse to be driven out of my house because of memories and because of my emotional reactions to even small things. Like, that the hum of the fridge is still exactly the same, and that creates the expectation that there will be accompanying sounds: my father's shoes slapping across the tile floor, my mother groaning as she can't get the kitchen radio to pick up the station that she wants. . . . Sounds of normalcy and happiness.

With one hand, I stir the pot of spaghetti sauce that is simmering on the stove, and with the other hand I hold an invitation, staring at the cursive lettering. It's an invitation from my parents' old friends Lani and Tim Sturgeon, who have asked me and James to their Christmas Eve party.

I'm going to accept.

This feels like a spectacularly bold move, and I know that's completely silly. People RSVP to invitations all the time. I, however, do not.

left drowning

But I dial their number anyway with my free hand, using the other to keep stirring the sauce. My family spent many dinners and even a few weekend vacations with the Sturgeons, and they knew our family well.

Lani answers and is unable to disguise her surprise that it's me. "Oh, Blythe McGuire! It's so good to hear from you. Tim and I think about you often."

"You do?" I blurt out. "That's . . . that's so nice. Um, I was just calling to say that James and I would love to come over on Christmas Eve if it's not too late to reply."

"We would be *thrilled* to see you," she says. "I'm really excited that you two are coming."

"Well, thank you so much. I guess we'll see you—"

"Blythe?"

"Yes?"

There is an uncomfortable moment of silence, and I dread what she is going to say next.

"How are you?" she asks.

"Fine, fine." I blather on about college courses for a few minutes.

"I'm glad to hear you're doing all right. We never heard from you after . . . after your parents died. I know it was such a chaotic time then, and later your aunt assured us that you were both doing as well as could be expected, and that you were busy with school and moving on. And we didn't know if you'd want to hear from us or not. I mean, we were your parents' friends, after all, and you probably had your own friends to lean on. After the funeral service, Tim and I almost picked up the phone so many times, but we didn't want to intrude or . . ." Lani fumbles for words. "We didn't want to make things worse. If seeing us would have made it harder on you, we would have felt terrible. I hope you didn't think that we didn't care. Or that we *don't* care. We loved your parents so much, Blythe. And we love you and James." I hear her voice crack and am moved beyond words. Somebody did and does care about us. "But you're happy now?"

I am nodding and smiling and furiously stirring the pot on the stove. It takes me a moment to be able to answer her. "I am. It's been . . ." I am trying to think how to phrase it. I want to be honest. "It's been a very, very hard time, and I've struggled a lot, but this year things are finally turning around. I have good friends now, and that makes my world bright again. I've missed you, also. It's going to be just great to see you."

"Wonderful. Tim will be delighted to hear you're coming. Oh, and Nichole Rains will be here with her parents. You two were friends in high school, weren't you?"

"We were. It will be good to see her."

"Excellent. We had dinner at her parents' house last week, and she was asking about you."

"She was?" I'm surprised.

"Absolutely. She said that you had sort of fallen off the map after graduation, and she was really hoping to reconnect with you."

Flabbergasted does not begin to describe how I feel, but I manage to thank Lani again for the invitation. My plan was to force myself to go and simply get through the party. Instead, I'm realizing, this might actually be nice.

I turn down the heat on the sauce and reexamine the apple pie that I baked. The pie is cookbook-photo-worthy, and I nearly text Chris a picture of it with a note saying that he was clearly the downfall of the Thanksgiving pies. But I don't.

I go to the living room. It looks as though Christmas vomited all over the room, but I wanted to use every single decoration that had been stored

left drowning

in the six boxes in the attic. I'd forgotten that my mother had a thing for old-fashioned Santas, and there are all sorts of St. Nicholas items displayed around the room. It borders on creepy, but I think I've pulled it off by covering the room in white twinkle lights. Those do a lot to offset the tackiness. A lot of decorative accessories in the house were tucked away for the renters' sake, but after I took out the holiday stuff, I retrieved the dishes and bedding and such that James and I are used to. I've already unpacked the boxes of stuff that Lisa unceremoniously moved here from her house, and it's nice to see our familiar bedding. The relief that she is out of town is immense, and I'm convinced that seeing her would undo the tone that I'm hoping to set for this time with James.

I've been torn, because as much as I want this house to feel the same as it used to, I also want to make it feel fresh, so I've been trying to mix in the old with the new. All the decorating, unpacking, shopping, and general fussing I've been doing has been good for me. Even though I've teared up a few times, I can feel a level of competence and independence growing.

I am proud of myself.

The tree looks crazy. It's absolutely covered in ornaments. So much so that there is barely any green from the branches visible, but I think it's damn awesome. I've arranged and rearranged James's presents a hundred times and moved his stocking from one part of the mantel to another over and over, even though I'm quite sure that he's not going to walk in here and have some kind of meltdown because his stocking should have been three inches to the left, or one of his presents is at an improper angle.

I snatch the Kindle that I treated myself to for Christmas and occupy my busy mind with news stories and downloading books. Without a social life here, I'll certainly have plenty of time to read over break. I already miss the Shepherd crew, but I am going to lean on myself and feel good about it.

I am ten chapters into my book when I hear the front door being unlocked. It's amazing somehow that we both still have our house keys. I force myself to stay on the couch because I know that the last thing I should do is swoop over to James and make a scene.

My brother practically falls into the living room, weighed down by three mammoth duffel bags. He lets them fall to the floor and stands up. "Hey," he says.

I take him in. He looks the same as he did four and a half months ago—I know that rationally—but at the same time, he looks even more incredible. I see the little kid who let me stand on the back of his tricycle, the one who used to beg me to throw him from the dock into the ocean, and the one who blew us all away with his incredible athletic prowess and the equal level of modesty that went along with that.

As I look at him, though, for a moment I also see the boy who is lying in a pool of blood outside a burning house. But I will not go there now.

"Hey, back." I set down my Kindle and focus on how healthy and handsome he looks. He's let his light-brown hair grow out a bit and it suits him, although I nonetheless have the maternal instinct to brush it off his face so that I can see his blue eyes. The sleek brown leather coat and jeans he has on hug his frame, and I can see that he is in as good shape as ever. "How was your flight? No delays out of Boulder?"

"No, it was all fine. Except that I'm starving. Should we order something?" He stands in the center of the room with his hands in his pockets.

"No, I've got dinner on the stove." I eye his luggage. "Laundry?"

"Oh. Yeah. I'll start it tomorrow."

left drowning

I walk over to his bags, and my feet sink reassuringly into the carpet in just the way they always have. "No problem. I got it. You want to shower or anything before we eat?"

"That . . . would be good. Thanks." Now that I am near him, he gives me a half hug as I'm bending down to pick up a bag. "Holy shit, Blythe!"

"What?" I ask, somewhat alarmed.

"You look . . . really good. God, you're so skinny." He pushes me away and assesses me. "Wait. Are you okay?"

I smile softly. "I'm fine. I've been running, so I've lost some weight."

"You totally have. And you're sort of muscly, and toned, and shit. But it's more than that. Did you change your hair or something? And you're kind of . . . I don't know. Glowy."

"I can assure you that I'm not pregnant, if that's what you mean."

He laughs. God, I've missed that laugh. "I didn't mean it like that. You look good. Really . . . pretty."

It's a bit unnerving how surprised he sounds. I don't think I'm any particular beauty now, so I must have been pretty awful looking these past few years. "I'm going to start a load. Towels are in the bathroom for you, and there are clothes from stupid Lisa's on your bed. No rush. We can eat whenever you want."

James looks sort of dumbfounded. Exactly what I was hoping for. Admittedly, I am showing off a bit. *Look at me! I'm functional! And not pudgy!* It's important to me that James sees that I am trying.

"Yeah, okay. I won't take long."

We eat dinner and I ask him a hundred questions about school, about his girlfriend, about music he's listening to. Anything that I can think of. I want to know my brother again, but I try to keep the conversation casual. Not once do I mention anything that could conceivably be construed as depressive. James is—I can hardly believe it—responsive. He even asks me about my life. It occurs to me in a rather schmaltzy manner that he may have been "saved by a good woman." This girlfriend of his is probably showing him love and stability, both of which he needs and both of which I have not been able to give him.

Until now.

The next evening we go to Lani and Tim's party. Lani hugs me so tightly that I nearly lose my breath, and it's wonderful. James flirts, I can't help noticing, with anyone vaguely close to his age, and the girls love it. I eat fancy hors d'oeuvres and drink one glass of champagne. I sing wretched, awful Christmas carols at the top of my lungs. I speak to my high school pal Nichole for about thirty minutes. There is no discussion of dead parents or my catatonic state during our senior year of high school, and we exchange phone numbers. Next summer, after graduation, she is planning on interning at a Boston-based online magazine that reports on all things New England and thinks I should try for a position as well.

The night is pretty fucking magical.

I'm very aware of how well I am operating in situations that I would have been incapable of broaching even last summer. Chris, Sabin, Eric, and Estelle have rescued me, and I can't fathom how I can ever begin to repay them.

James acts like he hates it, but I make him get into bed before midnight because when we were growing up, we were required to be in bed while it was still Christmas Eve and not one minute into Christmas. It was some weird ritual that my parents had. He demands to know why I am not in bed, too.

left drowning

"Because I am an elf, dummy. And elves must work late into the evening and do secret . . . elf crap or whatever. Now go to sleep!" I hear him try to hide a giggle as I leave.

I putz around the living room some more. James's stocking is bursting, absolutely bursting, when I finish filling it, and then I head into the laundry room to throw in another round of his laundry. The second half of the duffel's contents that I load into the washer smells just as disgusting as one would expect a college boy's to. I also have the gross experience of finding a box of condoms in his bag. *Awesome. My little brother has had sex before I have.* Should I have some kind of sex talk with him? Ick. Probably not.

But maybe.

Before I go to bed, there is one thing that I want to do. I kneel in front of the Christmas tree and snoop around. James has left me a few presents under the tree, which I find incredibly thoughtful. Actually, more than a few, I notice. Huh. Usually he gets me a shirt from his college and one or two other small things. And I have presents from Eric, Estelle, and Sabin, too. This is so much more than I need right now.

However, that does not stop me from finding the blue box with the green ribbon from Chris. I want to open this alone. I'm sure that he has not gifted me anything inappropriate that would embarrass me in front of James, but I still want to be alone for this. There is a small envelope attached to the box with a card. I hesitate to open it, which is stupid because it's not as though Chris will have written some dramatic and romantic confession of the heart on a two-by-two-inch card. And not that I want that anyway.

The card actually is a confession of sorts. It says: *This belongs to you. I have no idea why. I'm weird.* I laugh out loud. Inside the box is a mass of tissue paper and Bubble Wrap, and it takes a few minutes of unwrapping to find what's inside.

I don't know why this belongs to me either, but I agree that it does. Chris has given me a beautiful porcelain sea urchin. The main color of the shell is the palest green, nearly white, with darker green and white dots that line and texture the piece where the spines would have fallen off. They tickle my hand as I gently touch its exterior.

I love it. I love it more than anyone should love a porcelain sea urchin, and I don't care that my adoration for this little thing doesn't make sense. I set it on the floor in front of me, lie down on my stomach, and prop my chin in my hands. For twenty minutes I stare at it.

This is, and will always be, the most spectacular present I'll ever receive.

left drowning

BLAME(LESS)

CHRISTMAS MORNING IS GREAT. I KEEP US MOVING
so that there is not much time to overthink how fucked up the day is, and
how inexcusably awful it is that we are alone on such a major holiday.
I blast music and giggle to myself when the radio station plays Michael
Bublé, and we open presents and eat an enormous breakfast. James gives
me presents that do not include any college sweatshirts, and I suspect
that his girlfriend helped him pick out the perfume, fancy makeup, and
shimmery scarf. I like her even more. He seems to really love the clothes,
gift cards, overly expensive headphones, and new phone that I got for
him, and it is great to see him happy.

Estelle got me an utterly gorgeous deep purple off-the-shoulder top and a designer handbag, and the gift bag from Sabin holds a beautiful silver cuff bracelet. Eric outdid himself by giving me my pretend genie wishes: a basket of small stuffed-animal alpacas, a can of whipped cream, and huge gel inserts that I could stick into my bra to achieve triple-D breasts. I have to explain the odd collection to James, who seems momentarily concerned about this new group I am hanging out with.

James and I watch action movies and stuff ourselves silly. It is a goddamn great day.

While my brother spends a lot of his vacation out with his high school friends, I spend a lot of time dealing with online banking and bill-paying arrangements. I want to take over all of the stuff that Lisa has been doing, something that I should have done the day that I turned twenty-one and could legally manage all of our finances. It's a monstrous amount of paperwork and playing phone tag with our lawyer and accountant, but I straighten out some incredibly boring property issues and make irritatingly grown-up financial decisions. I make arrangements for the house to be maintained while James and I are back at school, and I get in touch with the property manager who has been overseeing the house in Maine and making sure it doesn't topple into the ocean. I confirm with him that, no, I do not want to rent it out.

Every phone call sucks to all hell, but I get shit accomplished, and I feel in control.

The most important thing that I do is send an e-mail. I write Annie, my mom's best friend, who soldiered through her own grief to take care of me and James during the weeks after the fire. I track her down on the internet and write her an eight-paragraph letter. It takes me three hours to find the words to tell her that I royally fucked up, that I miss her and need her. I do what I can to explain my pain and my healing (or lack thereof) over the years. Aside from Chris, there's nobody I've opened up

left drowning

to like this, and the risk feels immense. But like one that's worth taking.

There are frequent texts and pictures from Sabin, and even a video of the four of them waving and yelling hellos at me from a Hawaiian beach, and the occasional text from Chris to see how I am, but I am careful not to let myself obsess over my communication with them. This is my time to myself, and time to be with James, and I'm thrilled that we've made it two and a half weeks without a scene.

And then we have a shitty conversation, James and I.

To be fair, it is what I thought I wanted; an honest exchange.

And it fucking hurts, and it fucking sucks.

Yet it's necessary.

James is sitting in the corner of the sectional in the living room, watching television, and he interrupts my reading. "Blythe?"

"One sec." I hold up a finger. I'm totally involved in this book, and he probably wants a ride somewhere.

"Blythe," he says more insistently.

I look up and see that James's eyes are red and watery.

Oh my God. My heart sinks. He's miserable. I thought that we were doing well, and that I'd set up this break to be as easy as possible, but I can see suddenly that I've failed.

He begins talking, dumping onto me the truths that, so far, he has never shared. "It's so hard to be here. In this house, especially like this with the damn holidays and all, and not have them here. It's just that . . . everything feels so fresh since this is our first time back, and it's too much. It's too much. I feel like they just died yesterday." My brother bursts into tears, and I'm completely taken aback. I don't know if I should go sit next to him and comfort him or not. "I want them back," he says.

"I know. Me, too."

James struggles to get these next words out. "I want them back so much that, Blythe, I'd make the worst deal possible."

He's made a huge confession. I know exactly what he is thinking, and I don't want him to have to say it. I've had the same unbearable thought myself, and I know how it feeds self-hatred. I don't want that for my brother, so I say out loud what must burden him to the core. "You'd trade me to have one of them back."

He completely breaks down. This is new because I've always been the one in pieces, and James has been the calm, collected, smart one. Now I have to step up.

"James, it's all right. I will not let you feel bad for wanting them back. If I could give you that, I would. No matter what the cost."

"I'm so sorry, I'm so sorry," he says, fully crying now.

"I know that you blame me for that night. For why we were there, for how I . . ." I have to compose myself to continue. "For how I hurt you."

"No, you don't understand."

My brother has tears flowing down his cheeks. I hate this. "I can take it, James. I blame myself, too. The sound of your screaming will haunt me forever. Do you know how often I've gone over that night in my head and envisioned how I would do it differently? How I would have woken up at the first hint of smoke? Or that I would have checked to make sure that I'd knocked out every shard of glass from that window? I go back even further, to when I picked that rental house. I should have let you pick the house. *Everything.* I would change everything. But no matter what you want to throw at me, I'm not leaving you, James. Ever. So you be as mad at me as you need to, and I will still never leave you, and I'll never stop loving you. You are my brother forever."

left drowning

James is too upset to speak, so I continue.

"I understand. This is . . . part of what we have to go through. What's happening right now. I believe that this is going to get better. I know that I've been out of it and useless for so long, but I'm back. And I'm not Mom. I know that. You should have a mom and dad, and you were unfairly robbed of that. It's not easy for anyone to lose a parent, but you lost both when you were still a kid. I can't make that shit go away, but I am going to be here to help if you'll let me."

He's rubbing his eyes and sniffling, and I get up from my seat and sit next to him. I start to put my arm around him, but he collapses into my lap.

"I did something bad, Blythe," he says through his crying. "You're not going to want to be around me if I tell you." James is like a little kid right now, bawling and clinging to me.

I can't imagine what he's talking about, but he clearly needs to get something else off his chest. As I rub his back I think how foreign it is for us to touch each other, but I'm glad that he's letting me comfort him. "There's nothing you can say that would do that."

He can't even look at me as his garbled words come out. "I could have played soccer. I wasn't hurt the way you thought."

I freeze. "What . . . what do you mean?"

He keeps hiding his face. "I told everyone that my leg was too damaged for me to play anymore because I didn't want to. I couldn't. Soccer didn't mean shit to me after, but everyone wanted me to be this big soccer star. I just didn't care. Except for the scar, my leg is fine."

My brother's leg is fine.

The ramifications of what he is telling me hit me. I have spent four years blaming myself, *hating* myself, for taking away a huge piece of

James's future. Soccer was something that I believed could have been a salvation for him in a horrible time, and now I find out he didn't even want it. Yet he let me take responsibility for destroying what little he had left.

I keep my voice level because I don't want him to know how furious I am. "Why didn't you tell anyone that you could play? That you were pretending?"

"Because . . . because everyone expected me to want to . . . I don't know . . . prove how tough I was in the face of such shit. What a great story, right? Local boy goes on to triumph in the face of tragedy? And I didn't have the heart to do it."

"Who else knew you were fine?" I ask.

He shrugs and wipes his nose. "Just the doctors. I mean, the coach never made me prove that I couldn't play. I just said there was too much muscle damage and pain for me to get back to anywhere close to what I was."

I nod, trying to process what he's told me. I am seething, absolutely filled with rage for what he's done to me, and yet . . . I know how easy it is to go crazy when your parents burn to death one floor above you. Chris was right when said that it was easier for James to blame me for everything. If I'd had someone other than myself to blame, I might have taken advantage of it. And my brother was only fifteen, he was just a kid. Fuck, he's still just a kid in a lot of ways.

I say the one thing that I know to be true. "It must have been hard for you to tell me the truth." And then I have to ask him, "Why now? Why are you telling me now?"

"Because . . . because you've been so nice to me. I think that before, when you were so messed up, it was easier to trick myself into thinking

left drowning

it was true. That my lie was actually true and that you deserved all the blame because you were so awful to be around. The way you were acting made everything so hard."

I love James, but I fucking despise him right now. He used my grief and my depression as an excuse to perpetuate a lie that hugely contributed to my miserable state.

"You're going to hate me forever," he says.

"No, James. I don't hate you." I move my hand on his back again. As much as I am confused and out-of-my-mind angry, he has still done something brave by telling me this.

"I'm really, really sorry. It was really fucking dumb of me, and I wasn't thinking. I was just so mad about everything, and it snowballed, and I didn't know how to get out of the lie, and . . ."

I shut my eyes and continue to rub his back. In my head, I am screaming, *You son of a bitch! You fucking little shit!* Instead, I think about how Chris managed that Thanksgiving fiasco with Sabin, how he was able to handle his brother so coolly when he probably wanted to throttle him. No good would come from screaming, so I speak calmly. "I understand. I know what it's like to get stuck."

I am holding back tears, for him and for me. James is in horrible pain, again, and now so am I, and I'm stuck parenting my brother when I could really use a little fucking comforting myself. Life is not fair, but it is what we have to deal with. And we are going to deal with it so that we can live. No, so that we can *thrive*.

"Why does it still hurt so much?" he asks. "Why can't we just move on and deal?"

"I know. We've been grieving for more than four years, but not grieving well. And now, it seems, it's time."

There is no set pattern to grief, despite what every stupid psych text has told me. There is no time frame that dictates when and how you'll feel what you feel. You just get to deal with hell however, and whenever, it hits you.

"We're going to get through this," I tell him.

"It's so hard to be home," he says. "It's too hard."

I picture Chris helping me to breathe.

I stroke my brother's hair and think for a few minutes. Finally I ask, "Do you want to go back to school a little early? Do you have someone you could stay with?"

He nods and wipes his eyes again.

"I'll change your plane ticket. It's not a problem."

"Are you mad that I want to leave?"

"Of course not. School is where you're probably the most comfortable, and you should be wherever will help. I know this house doesn't feel like home."

"I'm so sorry," he tells me again. "I'm going to make this up to you. I don't deserve how nice you've been or now nice you are being now. I ruined everything."

"It's all right." In disbelief over what has just transpired between us, I drop my head back on the couch. "We're going to be okay, you and me. One day, we're going to be okay."

But we are not okay now.

left drowning

18

HIM AND EVERYTHING ABOUT HIM

THE FLIGHT BACK TO SCHOOL FEELS INTERMINABLE.
I wish the Boston-to-Madison trip could happen in an instant because I just want to be back in my dorm. The weather does miraculously cooperate, though, so at least I am not made to suffer through countless delays that end in a cancellation. By the time I land, I am nearly desperate to get to Matthews. Because I have no one to pick me up, I accept that I'll have to pay a small fortune for a cab to deposit me back at school.

James left Boston yesterday, the day after our talk, and I took one day to shut down the house before I caught my flight. I didn't bolt, though. Returning to school is not about running away. Being in my parents' house for that long was hard, especially coupled with James's revelation. It's going to take time to deal with my brother's lie and what it did to me. There's no way to fix things between us overnight, or even in the next few months. I'm going with the assumption that I'll forgive him when I'm ready. I feel good because I made major progress in more ways than one over break, but it was time to go. Had I stayed any longer, I could have undone the good things, the "successes" that I can add to my mental list. They are hard won, and I am not giving them up.

Only when the cab is a few miles from the dorm do I realize something. Something crucial. *I cannot fucking get into the dorm.* It won't reopen for another week. How could I be so dumb? Last year I heard someone in one of my classes bitching about getting locked out when he came back early because Matthews temporarily changes the locks or something, so I know that my key won't work.

I direct the cabdriver back to downtown Madison while I do a fast search on my phone for a hotel. Fuck it. I'm going to stay in the nicest, most expensive hotel I can find for the next week. No homework or trekking across a frozen campus—instead, lots of bubble baths and room service. After filtering my search results by price, highest to lowest, I call the first one, the Madison Grand Hotel and Suites, and book a room. Technically, I book a suite.

Despite the rather generic name, the Madison Grand is indeed grand, and the staff is extremely gracious and professional as they check me into my room, asking about my day of travel, whether I'm hungry, whether there is anything else they can get me. Something to eat? Extra pillows? Towels? Dry-cleaning? I'm sure they are thrilled to have a six-day suite booking at this dull time of year, and I laugh as I acknowledge to myself that I enjoy how they fuss over me. Hotel staff are not supposed to be substitutes for parental love, but I'll take what I can get. I

left drowning

need pampering, and if I want to imagine their concern for my needs is the equivalent of parental caretaking, I will.

After my bags are delivered to my suite, I unpack almost everything. I hate living out of suitcases, and this suite is going to be my home for six days. The dark espresso furniture is modern and sleek, and the massive window overlooks the sparkling lights of the city.

In the bathroom there's a whirlpool tub with shutters that unfold to overlook the bedroom, allowing for a view through the suite's windows of the night sky. After a raid on the vanity basket of high-end products that will surely cost me plenty, I run a warm bath and soak for twenty minutes, trying not to think of anything but the sensation of the water. I shave everything that should be shaved, plus a little more, and wrap my hair in some weird mud product that is supposed to enhance the shine. Later, I rinse off and refill the bath with clean water and turn on the jets. Holy crap, this is awesome.

The swirling water dances over my skin, dances *everywhere*, and before I know it, my hand is between my legs. The chaos and emotion of my trip home weren't exactly conducive to arousal, but clearly my body is needing to compensate for that down time. This tub could hold another five people, but I'd settle for just one more. I'm aroused enough, and I could probably make myself come, but I take away my hand after a few minutes. There is nothing particularly interesting about this for me right now.

It is not *my* touch that I want.

I know I shouldn't fantasize about Chris, but I can't help it. Giving in to my ache, my fingers move between my legs once again. My brain starts running a movie reel of what Chris and I could do together, how I would touch him, how he would sound and move. I brace my foot against the side of the tub as I shove a finger inside myself. Flashbacks of

Chris doing this to me heighten the feeling, and I move faster. It's easy to conjure up exactly what he did to me against the door to my room, exactly how he affected me. I remember his sound, his touch, and every graphic, perfect word that he said to me. I think about his hand between my legs, how he got me so totally wet, how I could feel his hard cock press against me when he held me tight . . . I imagine what it'd be like to feel him inside me, how he might feel and sound and move . . . What he might say to me. . . .

I stop my hand. God, what is wrong with me? I'm momentarily surprised that I'm thinking in such a raw, graphic way, but I remember the way Chris dirty-talked his way through making me come so hard in my room and realize that side of him seems to have rubbed off on me. Maybe it's no surprise I'm thinking in X-rated terms now.

Fuck. Fuck!

I take my hand away in irritation. I don't want to come by myself. It's not enough anymore. The fact is that I am a senior in college, and I want to have sex. To be more accurate, I want to get fucked until I can't see straight. *Classy*, I think. But that's what I want. Unfortunately for me, that is not going to happen right now.

I stand up and check the vanity basket again to see what other products I can smear on myself. The foot scrub could be appealing, except that I hate the smell of fake raspberries, so I investigate further. There is, of all things, a vibrator in a discreet sealed box nestled in with the bath salts. I don't pick it up—I'm not after that kind of touch, either. The pack of condoms and lube in there seem to be laughing at me. I scowl at them, hurl both through the open shutters, and watch them land them on the bed. Then I grab a nice innocent jar of salt scrub. This is not going anywhere erotic.

left drowning

Later, after I've dried my hair and thrown on comfy black leggings and a snug camisole tank top, I order a huge dinner. There is no point in getting dressed up, and I'm happy to be wearing clothes I can stretch in. My muscles still feel limber because I was able to get a temporary membership to a gym back home, so all of my hard work wasn't undone over break. As I reach for my toes, I am happy to notice that my flexibility continues to get better every week. By the time my food arrives, I am stretched out for no good reason.

I dim the lights, take the first of my dishes, fettuccine Alfredo, to the big armchair, and stare out at Madison while I pick at my food. Now that I have three extraordinarily fattening entrees in the room, I'm not hungry. What I am is worked up and cranky and sexually frustrated. I sigh at the picturesque view out the window. The downtown city lights shine brightly, particularly the capitol building, which is encased in a luminescent white glow.

After a few more bites, and a good gulp of the room-temperature gin and tonic that I mixed for myself, I roll the cart into the hallway, catching someone from room service as he leaves another room. I take a silver bucket from the table and head for the ice machine near the elevator. Might as well continue raiding the minibar.

Just as I turn the corner back to my room, I see him coming out of a room at the far end of the hall.

Chris is walking toward me, strolling casually down the hall with his hands in his jeans pockets. I'm unable to move until he finally looks up and sees me.

"Well, hey, you," he says with a smile. He is tanned and excruciatingly gorgeous, and I nearly faint. "What are you doing here?"

My chest is probably visibly heaving. I drop the bucket and walk quickly toward him. He's got to see how I am looking at him, how I am essentially in heat. Chris meets me halfway, and I grab a fistful of his T-shirt in my hand and pull him in tight. I lift my mouth up close to his. "I need you," I say, each word deliberate and loaded. I'm not sure, but I may have actually growled.

I keep him close as I back up and lead him to my door.

"Blythe, what are you doing? I thought we agreed that we weren't . . ." But his hands are on my waist, then under the top of my leggings, and he is following my steps without any protest.

I smile. "Shut up." I reach behind me and wave my key card. The second I hear the door unlock, I slam down on the handle and take us into my room.

Now it's his turn up against a wall.

His mouth tastes like orange soda, which I find spectacularly adorable, and I kiss him long and hard. And not because I like orange soda. My hands are practically clawing through his hair and over his chest.

I can tell that Chris is surprised by how aggressive I am, but I don't really care. And he gets over it quickly, because as I continue to kiss him, his hands move over me. He's digging his fingers under my ass and lifting me up and against him. Already we are moving together in a way that we haven't before, even that night in my room. Despite our height difference, we fit perfectly, and feeling him press his hips into me makes my ache for him climb. Even through his jeans, I can feel how hard he is.

As I continue to kiss him, I find his waistband and yank his shirt out until I can touch his abs and stroke his lower back. I grab his ass hard and then come back to the front of his jeans, stroking him with one hand and undoing his belt with the other. He gasps and leans his head against the wall. "Blythe," he whispers into my mouth.

left drowning

I breathe in my name from his lips. "Yeah?" I say back, unable to hold back a smile.

"I don't know if this is smart," he says, yet his hands are now over my breasts, getting my nipples hard.

"I think it's brilliantly smart," I manage.

"But we can't . . . get involved. I told you, I'm not boyfriend material."

"I know." I rub my hand against the front of his jeans a little harder.

"We're friends. I don't want to screw this up."

"Me neither. We won't."

"You're just saying that now, but later it could feel different."

"I'm a big girl, and I know what I want." And I do. I don't know where my confidence with him has come from, but I've got it.

"You know how much I care about you, but it's just more than I—"

"Christopher." I interrupt him and pull back until I am looking him directly in the eyes. While I appreciate his checking to make sure that I'm cognizant of what I'm doing, I also know that he is as ready for this as I am. "I don't want you to be my boyfriend." I unzip his pants. "I want you to fuck me."

He is breathing hard, and it takes him a moment to speak. "Are you sure?"

"Yes."

He looks at me with heat in his eyes now. "I can do that."

"Good."

He moves fluidly to help me get him out of his unzipped jeans, and I place my hand over the front of his blue boxer briefs. He groans and touches his hands lightly to the side of my head as I kneel in front of him and graze my lips against the fabric. I always thought maybe I'd feel tentative during my first blow job because it would be new to me, but instead, I want him and everything about him immediately. I slide a hand between his legs and move it far back until I have his ass in my hand. I pull him against my mouth, aware that he can feel the heat from my breath. I can't wait any longer. With the other hand, I pull down the front of his boxers and immediately touch my tongue to him. My need for him is powerful, urgent, and I feel delirious that I am finally getting to touch Chris in the way that I want. I lick his entire length.

Chris lets out a sound. "God, Blythe . . ."

I pull his briefs all the way down and start to sweep my tongue slowly over him. Fuck, he feels so good on my lips. Every taste of him makes me want more. When I move up a bit and then wrap my lips around him, Chris groans loudly. Now I know why he wanted to hear me, to know what I sound like, because listening to him is incredible. I take him deeper into my mouth and then pull back again. Slowly I find a rhythm that seems to work for both of us. I have a moment of wondering if I'm doing this right, and then I let that worry fall away. It's a blow job, not rocket science. I could care less about rocket science. What I do care about is that the noises Chris is making are pure pleasure. I circle my hand around the base of his cock and slide up and down with my mouth. The way he sounds and the soft touch of his fingers in my hair makes me crazy. As much as I'm dying to make him come like this, it's not what I want most right now, so I stop as soon as I feel like he might be too close.

I pull down his pants and briefs all the way and stand back up while he steps out of them. Chris wraps his arms around me and draws me in. Our kissing is heated and rushed now, our roaming hands not able to get enough of each other. He barely gets me out of my leggings and underwear before he lifts me up, and I wrap my legs around his waist.

left drowning

He walks us a matter of feet away, and I swipe the box of condoms that I'd conveniently tossed on the bed after my failed masturbation attempt.

"Thank God," Chris says as he takes the box from me and then sets me on top of the dresser.

He puts his hands over my breasts—just roughly enough that I can feel how much he wants me—and I lean back on my hands. He looks fucking amazing right now, still half dressed in his navy T-shirt and pinching my nipples through my tank. I have to shut my eyes for a second when he runs the shaft of his cock up and down between my legs.

Yeah, we're not going to need the lube from the vanity. I'm definitely wet.

I can't take it anymore. I feel like I've been waiting an eternity for this. "You have to fuck me," I pant. "You have to. I have to feel you inside me."

Chris kisses me again, then says, "And *I* have to be inside you."

The sound of the foil tearing turns out to be incredibly hot because it means that I'm about to get what I want. And watching him put on the condom and prepare to fuck me is even hotter.

He pulls me to the edge of the dresser, and I have the brief thought that this dresser was clearly designed for the two of us because he is perfectly positioned to enter me. His mouth is on my neck, kissing me hard, and his hands run up and down the outside of my thighs. Our pace is manic, we're unable to slow down, and I don't want to.

"Your body is fucking perfect," he whispers. "You are so beautiful."

He steps closer, and I whimper as I feel him brush against me. "Chris, please."

"This is what you want?" he asks while he kneads his hands into my back. "I want you to be sure."

I take his head in my hands and make him look at me. "I am."

He gives me the hottest look I've ever seen in my life. "God, I want you so much."

"Show me," I pant as I wrap my legs around him.

We're looking at each other as the head of his cock moves into me.

I'm so worked up and so frantic, but then he holds still. "Oh God, please don't stop," I beg.

He puts his hand on the side of my face. "Baby, breathe for me. I don't want to hurt you at all."

He's right. I am inadvertently holding my breath, and my whole body is tight with eagerness. I nod and make the lower half of my body, at least, relax. I look at Chris and nod again. As I exhale, he eases a little farther inside me, and it's all I can do not to lose my mind. He's barely moving, and I can tell he's concerned about being gentle. But I'm not. I lean back more and lift up my hips so that I take him in farther. There is some piece of me that is aware this does hurt, but mostly all I feel is that I want more. When I put my foot on the dresser and lift up higher, Chris gasps and bites his lip as he moves deeper into me. We hold still just for a second and watch each other, both of us breathing hard and trying to control ourselves. But then I tell him, "More. I want more."

He smiles and leans into me. "You're all right?"

I lower and lift up again as my answer.

"Whatever you want, baby." When he puts an arm around my lower back, pulling me close and pushing himself deep inside me, I groan so loudly that I'm pretty sure I've caused him hearing loss. I love the feel of his hand on my back, the way he's supporting my body as he moves out and then enters me again.

"Jesus, you are so hot," he breathes.

I move my hands to his hips and lift my mouth to his. It's so hard to speak now, but I tell him, "Then fuck me harder." After having lived so

left drowning

long without the desire for touch, for sensation of any kind really, I'm finally compensating. I want to feel him as completely as possible. I kiss him once and pull on his waist to press myself against him so that he is all the way inside me.

Chris starts to slide in and out a little faster, staying deep when he goes in and then pulling out almost entirely. Each time he enters me sets off another wave of my hunger for him. I feel absolutely out of control, but for once it's in the best way possible because it's the most natural sense of exhilaration I've ever had.

Just when I am really starting to feel sore, he slows and changes the tone of our lovemaking. He embraces me tightly, and we kiss until we are drowning in each other and cannot breathe. Chris keeps me close but starts to rock his hips just a bit, grinding into me, staying deep and showing me an entirely different experience. The way his cock is moving inside me . . . Oh God, this could be addictive. We move rhythmically and intensely, glued to each other. Then I understand something: this is why they say that people become one.

He's breathing hard into my ear, and by the rasp in his voice as he says my name, I know that it's my turn to get to listen to him come. He drops one hand from my back to steady himself on the dresser as he moves faster and harder, building to his orgasm. His grip on my back gets stronger, and he pulls me as close to him as possible. I am transfixed by the way he starts to groan and slow down, thrusting involuntarily as shudders overtake him.

His mouth is on my neck, his tongue soft and beautiful as he kisses me everywhere he can reach. Then one hand cradles my face while his lips find mine, and he is sensual, and soft, and slow as we come back down.

We linger, sharing the moment, until he slowly pulls out but does not take his hands from me. "God, I'm sorry. Are you okay? Did I hurt you? I just . . . Fuck, I just couldn't stop. I've never . . . been like that." Hearing him struggle for words is awesome. "So . . . lost in it."

He starts kissing me again, and I groan as he moves his tongue against mine.

Finally we come up for air. "Yes, I'm more than okay. That was . . . amazing."

He shakes his head a bit. "This was not at all how I envisioned you losing your virginity."

I tip my head to the side and smile. "Oh, I see. So you *envisioned* me losing my virginity?"

"Well, I mean . . . "

"And did *you* happen to be a part of this vision?"

"Um . . . I might have, uh, thought about . . ." He clears his throat. "Obviously we have a certain chemistry, and . . ."

I put him out of his misery and kiss him again. "I am not complaining at all. Did you think I'd want flowers scattered on the bed and candles everywhere?"

Chris traces his finger across my lips. "No, but this was maybe a little rushed. I should have been . . . more careful with you."

"You gave me exactly what I wanted."

He lowers his head to my shoulder and pulls aside the thin strap of my top with his teeth. "No, I was too out of control."

I shiver as he teases my skin with his tongue. "You don't like being out of control, do you?" I murmur.

He laughs lightly. "Not really."

"Well, I liked it."

He laughs again. "I'm glad."

left drowning

Something occurs to me. Something not sexy at all. "Oh hell. I'm not bleeding, am I?"

Chris takes half a step back, and he rolls his eyes when I hold up his chin so that he can't look. I peek down and then touch my hand to myself. "Thank God."

"No?" he asks and immediately steps closer to me and nuzzles my neck.

"No. Then I really would have had to tip the housekeeper big."

"You're going to have to tip her big anyway, I think."

There! I knew we could fuck and not be weird about it. We're still us. I tangle my fingers in his hair. "Hey, Chris?"

"Mmm?"

I feel his teeth graze my shoulder again, and it takes me a second to ask him what I wanted. "What the hell are you doing back in Madison? Hawaii sounded like it was going great."

"Oh. That. Don't tell Sabin that I told you this. He has a court date, so we'd planned on being back now."

"What the hell? For what?'

"That idiot got himself a DUI last summer. He'd be really embarrassed if you knew, so don't say anything."

"I won't. He's not going to jail or anything, is he?" I am momentarily pulled from my postsex bliss, and I'm worried.

"No, no. Nothing like that. I promise. He hasn't been able to drive since then, though."

Now that Chris says this, I realize that I've never seen Sabin drive. It's always been Chris, Estelle, or Eric.

His hands are drifting over me, and even this light contact between us is already arousing me again more than I can believe.

A small sound escapes my lips. I can't help it. The feel of his touch melts me.

"And what are you doing here?" he asks.

"Just . . . I had enough time at home."

He frowns. "You all right?"

"Yes. It was mostly really good. But some shit went down with James and . . . I'll tell you about it later. Everything is going to be fine, though."

He relaxes. "Good." Chris's hand on the back of my thigh is going to make me explode. He's quiet for a moment as he nuzzles into me. "I still think that I have to make this up to you. We need to go slower. A lot slower."

He lifts me up into his arms and moves us to the bed, setting me down gently. I stare in near awe while he pulls off his shirt. He is so fucking beautiful. His ripped chest is tan and even more mesmerizing than the last time I'd seen him without a shirt. "You ready?" His flirtatious smile kills me.

Unable to answer him, I nod.

I put my hands around his neck and watch while he moves on top of me. "I have a lot of other things to do to you, but first I need to be inside you the way I should have been the first time." He takes his cock in his hand and rubs it against me. I am still soaked from coming, and he covers himself in my wetness. We both groan softly while he does this, and when he touches himself to my clit, I gasp.

I can't reach that box of condoms fast enough.

When we're safe, he lifts his chest over mine, holding himself up on his forearms. Chris looks at me as reaches between us and starts to gradually move the tip of his cock into me. I immediately go from highly

left drowning

aroused to completely crazed and put my hands on his lower back to pull him in harder.

"Uh-uh, baby." Chris shakes his head and raises my hands next to my head. He entwines our fingers. "We're going to go slow, like it or not."

I squirm under him, lifting up my chest in frustration, and he smiles but spreads his legs enough to lock me into place. He waits me out. Theoretically, I love the idea of going slow, but I'm still starved for intensity. If I could move, I'd be fucking the daylights out of him already. What I don't know yet is that he's going to give me the intensity I want *and* go slow.

He slides in just a bit more. And then he pulls out. And then he pushes in even more and holds himself there. Chris slips a hand under my lower back and keeps it against me as he eases his cock all the way inside me. He's making me moan again, and I'm getting louder by the second. Just as I'm about to grab his waist and pull him against me, he holds himself up on his elbow as he begins to fuck me slowly.

I start to get lost in him, and soon I'm drifting into the rhythm, instinctually tilting my hips to meet his. I feel him caress my breast and kiss my cheek. He makes love to me without hurrying, without rushing anything. The hand underneath me lifts my body up to meet his, and I begin to lose all sense of time. All I can do is drown in the experience, helpless in a wonderful way.

Then he's talking to me again. I'd never thought I'd be so into that, but hearing his voice seems to up the intensity of what he's doing. "You're incredible. God, you have my cock so hard."

I groan and begin moving my hips faster, and Chris pushes up onto both hands now. He stays deep inside me and rubs his body against me.

I instinctually squeeze my muscles to tighten around him, making him catch his breath. He lifts up a little higher, just enough so that his cock presses up, hitting a spot that causes me to tremble. So he starts fucking me just a little bit harder . . . just a little bit faster. The slight edge of pain doesn't bother me at all because he has tapped into my built-up need for pleasure, and that overtakes everything. Now he's getting louder, too, and listening to him makes me absolutely crazy. I am writhing under him, my sounds getting more and more desperate while he brings me closer and closer to coming.

And as he talks to me, I start to come. "You feel so fucking good. Do you know how many times I've thought about this? The way you would feel, the way you would make me feel . . . What it would do to me to be inside you. How you would move against me."

I close my eyes and drift.

"Yes, there you go." The seductive edge in his voice rocks me. "I can feel how tight your pussy is now. How close you are. Come on, Blythe, let me hear you . . ."

I stay in that heightened state for a moment before my whole body starts to throb under him, and then I'm making all kinds of noise and saying his name over and over.

This is a euphoria that I've never imagined. That I never knew was possible.

When I've regained some level of coherence, Chris kisses me again. I can't get enough of his mouth against mine, and I put my hands on the side of his face, holding him while I start to choose our pace with my hips. I feel his muscles clench and he drops down against me and goes harder. He's gotten me so wet, and he moves easily in and out.

I tell him not to stop.

left drowning

I tell him how he's made me feel, and how completely I want him. I tell him to come for me.

And feeling him tense up just before he does is possibly the best thing in the world. I hold Chris tightly as I move my hips back and forth to try and give him the same level of ecstasy that he gave me. I raise my legs up around him and make him go faster, bringing him to orgasm. Chris makes it so easy for me to respond, to move with him and for him. I love how it feels as he pounds against me while he comes. There is nothing better. And I know that he must be coming hard because he thrusts into me over and over, until he is almost spent. And just before he's done, he is kissing me again, and I get to feel his breath in mine while he finishes.

Overwhelmed. I am entirely overwhelmed by him and by being with him.

Eventually he moves from on top of me and lies back on the bed, pulling me to nestle into the crook of his arm. He kisses the top of my head while he drifts his fingers across my back. Neither of us can talk. I cannot believe how good he has made me feel. I just can't. I mean, the first night that I have sex and . . . that? He's clearly some kind of sex god.

I mold my body to his, feeling intoxicated by the amount of pleasure the last hours have provided.

"You're still okay, right?" he asks me.

"Of course."

"You sore?"

I shrug.

"Yes?"

"A little," I admit. "But I like it."

He laughs. "You do? Why is that?"

I move on top and sit up while I straddle him. I grin. "Because it means fantastic things just happened."

"I'm glad you think they were fantastic." He looks just as happy as I do. He takes a deep breath. "Look, I know this is a stupid, corny thing to say, but . . . Blythe, it means a lot to me that I'm the first guy you've been with."

Chris draws his hands over my breasts, touching me so tenderly and exquisitely that I can't believe how fortunate I am to have my first time be with someone whom I trust so completely with my body. With all that I am. "It means a lot to *me* that you're the first guy I've been with."

His hands go down the length of my torso, over the curve of my hips, and across the top of my thigh. "Your body . . . ," he starts. "Your body is just rockin'."

Now he's embarrassing me. I wasn't the slightest bit uncomfortable having him do significantly more intimate things than pay me a compliment, but he's being ridiculous. "Stop it."

"Seriously. I mean, I'd love your body no matter what, but I have to admit that running has made you even more . . ." His gaze follows the path of his hands as they travel over me, and I have to look away. "Look at you. These legs, and this waist." His hands sneak under me. "And this gorgeous ass."

"Chris . . ."

"It's true." He sits up, puts a hand on the back of my neck and strokes my cheek with his thumb, and then rolls a lock of my hair over his finger. "And these beautiful curls . . . Face it. You're gorgeous."

"You're a dope." I squeeze his arm and touch his perfect chest. "And look who's talking. You're a block of muscle." Then he lets me move my fingers over his face while I take in how extraordinary he is. "These stunning green eyes, and this disgustingly perfect masculine jawline."

left drowning

"Now *you're* being a dope."

I lean in and rub my nose against his. "And this adorable nose."

"Now you've lost it." I can tell he doesn't like his crooked nose, but he kisses me anyway. "Hey, Blythe?"

"Yeah?"

"We're good, you and me? This doesn't feel, you know, weird to you, does it?"

"No, it doesn't. We're completely good. I know what this is, and what this isn't, just like you do."

He nods, and we're quiet for a minute. "Since we're going to be in this hotel for a few more days, maybe we could . . ."

"Yes. I think we definitely could." Thank God. I'm not done with him by a landslide. I still have a lot of catching up to do.

"What are we going to tell them?" he asks with a smile.

"Your family?'

"Yup."

"I have no idea. That we're going to fuck each other's brains out for a few days and that they can just deal with it?"

"That may be more descriptive than they'll need."

"Or we can tell them nothing and hope they don't walk in on us."

"I like the sound of that." He tickles me under the arms and tosses me onto the bed. "But first, we need food. I was on my way to dinner when . . . You know."

"When I assaulted you in the hallway?"

"Yes, exactly." He grabs my hand and pulls me out of bed. Chris throws on his jeans and grabs the room service menu before he starts to lead me to the couch that overlooks the city.

"Hold on, I'm grabbing a robe."

"No! No clothes!"

I laugh but go to the bathroom and retrieve the soft white robe that is hanging there for guests. I shut the bifold doors by the tub. I may have just done a lot of things with Chris that I've never done with anyone else, but I don't plan on having him watch me pee be the next one.

By the time I'm out of the bathroom, Chris is sitting on the edge of the oversize chair and ordering food for us. I sit down behind him, clasp my hands together over his stomach, and lean my head against his back. I listen to the rumble of his deep voice as he orders. He looks back and I nod that the order is fine. I'm starving now. "Yeah, charge it to room 2021," he says and hangs up. "Dinner's on me."

"Chris, you don't have to do that."

I bring my right hand to his back as he hangs up, and I pull away to admire again how toned and strong he is. And while he is these things, he is also vulnerable like we all are, proven by the two significant scars on his back. A broken line that starts from just below his left shoulder and ends midway down the right side of his back, a space of probably four inches or so between them. I don't really know if this is really one scar or two. I remember how he threw a shirt on by the lake, and suspect now that he was covering his scars the way I often cover my own. I realize that even though Chris and I have been plenty naked with each other, this is the first time I've seen or touched his scars, almost as if my hands had knew where not to go while we were intimate. The texture is familiar to me because his scars feel like mine. He stiffens slightly as I touch his skin, and I understand this all too well. I tighten my hold around his waist, letting him know this is not a big deal.

He takes a deep breath. "Sorry. I totally forgot. That probably sounds crazy."

left drowning

"There's nothing to be sorry for. You know that." I pat my left hand against his stomach, reminding him that I really do understand.

I'm still touching his scars. For some reason this is not a question that I want to ask, but I do anyway. "How did you get these?"

He takes my left hand in his and looks out at the view. The buildings are lit up and showing us a deep blue night sky. "Ugh, a skiing accident when I was a kid. The tips of skis are sharper than you think."

I cringe. "Ow."

"Ow, indeed." As he pulls me onto his lap, he nods to the window. "Stellar view, huh?"

I look at him. "It certainly is."

He smiles. "And this chair is very comfortable." Chris moves his hand inside my robe, just under my breast.

"It is."

"And that couch just screams possibilities, doesn't it." Now he has my nipple between his fingers.

The surge of desire that moves through me leaves me nearly incapacitated.

"After dinner, though. We need fuel." Chris parts my robe more and leans in to sweep his tongue over my breast. "Sound good to you?"

I can only nod weakly in response. It may be the middle of the night, but I am wide awake.

BELONGING

WAKING UP WITH CHRIS'S MOUTH BETWEEN MY LEGS, his tongue working against me hard, and finding that I'm halfway to orgasm is not a bad start to the day. At all. When he first went down on me last night, I thought that I might absolutely combust. That first touch of his mouth to my clit was more than I could have imagined, and apparently he likes this as much as I do since he's doing a damn spectacular job of hitting all the right places with all the right rhythms. Chris can read my body with shocking clarity.

He spreads me apart with his fingers and covers me with his mouth as he sucks on me slowly. I reach down and put my hand on his head and lift myself into him.

He pulls away slightly so that his mouth is barely touching my body, and he starts to kiss me lightly, just barely letting his lips brush against me. I run my hands through my hair as he parts me open again and traces his tongue over my clit. I'm moving against his mouth now as he puts his hands under me, squeezing me softly and letting his fingers wander. He lifts his tongue and moves down, pushing it inside me for a minute before moving even lower. I spread my legs apart more. I'm breathing hard, practically panting, and I can feel my orgasm coming.

I move to put myself in his mouth again. "You ready?" he asks, and takes my moaning as a yes. "Good. Because I can't wait any longer to taste you while you come."

Those words alone almost do the trick.

His tongue is on me again and he drives his fingers deep inside me, hard. My muscles tighten, and I can barely breathe. His mouth and hand are moving perfectly, bringing me closer and closer to the edge, and he's got total control over me now. It feels like forever that he keeps me on that delicious brink of ecstasy that he gives me just before I come. This? This I cannot do to myself. And then Chris moves just a little faster until I explode. He lightens the pressure as I start to throb against his mouth. I can't believe how hard I'm coming, how much I'm trembling, how loud I am. He lifts his mouth and gently rubs me with his fingers, making sure I get to enjoy this fully.

And although I've just had the most incredible, satisfying orgasm, and I can hardly see straight, I want more.

I'm still dizzy and breathing hard when he kisses his way up my body. "You and your pussy are fucking delicious."

"Wait . . ." I'm still half asleep, but I'm alert enough to realize that he's fully dressed. "Why are there clothes? Stop it with all the clothes-wearing nonsense."

He kisses me again. "I have to go. I'll be back later this afternoon."

"Sabin?" I ask.

"Yeah. Dinner at seven tonight, okay?" He pauses. "So I'll be here at five."

I smile. "Five is good. Hope things go well today."

"Go back to sleep, sweet girl." He pulls the comforter over me and kisses me on the cheek.

I sleep until after one in the afternoon. Getting laid until all hours of the night is evidently exhausting. After I shower and get dressed, I text James. I'm not ready to fake a friendly chat, but I don't want to cut off communication with him. Housekeeping knocks on the door, and I decide that if ever a room needed cleaning, it's this one.

Besides, I'm starving. The hotel lounge has a nice lunch menu, so I head down there and inhale a sandwich and then ask for the largest cappuccino they'll make me. Then I order another one.

I've only been awake for a short time, but I check the time because I cannot wait until five o'clock. It's impossible to stop smiling like an idiot, so I hold my phone in front of me to give anyone nearby the impression that I am wildly amused by some stupid regretsy post.

An e-mail comes through. One I've been hoping for. Annie has written me back. A long, thoughtful, amazing response to mine. She is heartbreakingly understanding, and not only does she not blame me for pushing her away, but she even confesses that to some degree what I did was a relief. I remind her of my mom in the same way that *she* reminds *me* of my mom. We can recover from that, though, she says. She promises. Annie insists that we talk on the phone—soon if I'm up for it, but later if that's what I need.

I'm tempted to call her right then, but I decide to move slowly. My e-mail reply to her is full of relief, and joy, and assurances that I will call soon. And I will.

left drowning

I look around the hotel lounge. Spending money on this place is obscene and unnecessary. Normally I am not a particularly self-indulgent person, and if I hadn't run into Chris here, I suspect that I would have moved myself to a much cheaper place after a few nights, when the amount of money I was wasting hit me. As it is, I am going to make peace with spoiling myself this week. Not everyone has the opportunity to escape into a hotel fantasy life for a week, and I am grateful that I can do this for myself. Especially at a place like this. The Madison Grand is very modern, but still cozy and comfortable, and there's something sexy about it. Of course, everything seems sexy to me right now. I check out the potted tree a few feet away. Okay, good, I do not find the tree sexy at all, so I have not entirely gone off the deep end.

I can hardly believe how good last night was. I knew Chris and I had a certain energy together, or whatever, but I could never have imagined it would be the way it was. He is thorough and disciplined, but apparently also capable of losing control in a way that drives me insane. And the way he balances complete tenderness and care with that rough, dirty edge . . . It's just damn hot. I'm aware that I was more than ready to have sex, but Chris seems to elicit a side of me that I didn't know I had.

I guess when I imagined losing my virginity, I thought it would have a specific beginning and end; that I'd have sex one time and that would be that. Instead, losing my virginity to Chris led to a long night of sex so good that I never could have dreamed it up before. My craving for physical contact, for complete sensory inundation, feels endless right now. I wasn't aware that my body could be so awake. Chris ignited this in me with his first touch, back when he taught me to skip stones, and he's been bringing me back to life ever since.

Best of all, I don't feel uncomfortable about what we've done. I'm not a gooey, lovesick mess. I feel something for Chris that I can't even define. Having sex for the first time hasn't changed what I feel, and hasn't created something that didn't already exist. What we did last night, what we're going to do tonight, is just another part of us being together. The idea of Chris as my "boyfriend" still sounds totally ludicrous. Boyfriends are about dates, and silly anniversaries, and crap like that. I can't help feeling like becoming boyfriend and girlfriend would trivialize whatever is between us. If Chris and I ever do *really* get together, it's not going to be trivial. It's going to be the love affair to end all love affairs. It's obvious that what we've been having is hotel-only sex, but I'm not worried about what happens when we go back to school. We're solidly part of each other's lives, and that's not going to change when we leave the hotel.

And for now, he is giving me exactly what I want, and I hope that I'm giving him at least a fraction of the physical fulfillment that I've had. I am saturated with the need to bring him to the edge of insanity the way he did for me. It amazes me that with Chris, I have such a sense of confidence and security despite my inexperience. I would do anything with him.

I make a stop at the drugstore across the street and load up on condoms before I head back to my room. God, yesterday I thought I knew what "feeling edgy" meant, but today is the real deal. All I want to hear is the sound of Chris knocking on my door so I can get my hands on him before dinner. Of course, I am dying to see Sabin, Estelle, and Eric tonight. I really do miss the hell out of them, especially my Sabin. It will take all my control not to yell at him for being irresponsible and stupid enough to drive drunk. What a dumb college-boy thing to do. He definitely deserves to be in deep shit for that, but I don't want his life to be ruined, so I hope that court went as well as possible today.

I get a text from Chris at four thirty, telling me that things with

Sabin are not too bad, and he'll fill me in later. He hasn't told the others that I'm in town yet, so we'll surprise them. Oh, and we're all going somewhere nice for dinner, so I should dress up.

Well, shit! I fly over to the closet and pull open the doors, stripping down to my underwear as I scan my closet. I need Estelle. It takes me twenty minutes to decide on a sleeveless black sheath dress that falls mid-thigh and tall black boots, both of which Estelle made me order from one of her favorite online stores. As I lay it out on the bed, it occurs to me that I really miss Estelle, and not just for her fashion sense. The truth is that we're not exactly close in the sense of trading intimate secrets or engaging in stereotypical girl talk. I doubt she'll ever talk to me about banging her professor, and I won't talk to her about sleeping with her brother. Obviously. Yet despite the general lack of emotional sharing between us, I know undoubtedly that our friendship means the world to both of us. I scrounge through my drawstring bag of jewelry and pick out the silver cuff bracelet that Sabin gave me and a silver beaded choker that I'm hoping matches.

I look the outfit over and decide it seems like a safe bet. The fact that it's a sleeveless dress and I'm not bothered makes me happy. Chris has had his hands and eyes on every inch of me, including my scar, and nothing freaks him out. We're both beat up in different ways, and it doesn't change anything.

The knock on the door electrifies me. I open the door wearing a black bra and underwear and silently thank Estelle for her insistence that I quit wearing ugly cotton crap sold in three-pack boxes.

"Holy hell," Chris says slowly.

"Hi, honey. How was court?"

"I don't even remember now." He steps in, slips his hand around my waist, and pulls me in. "I think there was a judge there. It was someone robed. Could have been a monk." Chris runs his hand down my front. As if I'm not already intoxicated by him, his sex appeal just soared up even more because he's dressed up like I've never seen him. It's not like he's in a full suit or anything, but compared to his usual college-casual look, the slick black blazer and white dress shirt he's wearing are pretty damn hot. He does, of course, still have on jeans, but he's traded his favorite sneakers for black shoes. But while I'm loving the look, my main impulse is to strip it off him.

I pull myself together enough to ask, "Did the judge happen to say anything important? You know, about your brother's fate?"

"Ah, how quickly you forget." His hand covers my breast and he tightens his hold for a brief moment. "I don't believe in fate."

"So you don't believe that you're fated to come repeatedly tonight?"

"That's not fate. That's just fact." He kneels in front of me and presses his mouth over my underwear. "And we're both going to come repeatedly tonight. I have spent the entire day thinking about how good you taste." The back of his hand runs gently over me. "I didn't hurt you last night, did I?"

"No," I murmur.

"Or very, very early this morning?"

"Definitely not."

He leans forward on his knees and kisses me. "You're not sore?"

"Not much." I allow myself this white lie.

"In that case, there will be even more coming tonight."

I reach behind me to steady myself on the wall. I try to focus for one more moment before my ability to think clearly totally collapses. "And what about Sabin?"

"I have no idea what his plans are for tonight."

left drowning

"Very funny."

"Probation, license suspension, and he'll be writing a big check."

I inhale sharply when Chris follows the line of my underwear with one finger. "Could be . . . worse." My voice is shaky and I can feel my skin heat up. For an all-too-short time, he touches under my underwear slowly and carefully. I am beyond worked up and wet within seconds.

Chris stands up and kisses me on the cheek. " You should get dressed. We gotta go." I can feel him smiling against me.

"What? You said dinner was at seven."

"I lied. We're meeting earlier because Sabin wants to go to some play."

I really shouldn't have a tantrum because that would be tacky and pathetic. But I still give him a look that says I might kill him.

"I'm not going with them," he reassures me.

"What reason did you give?"

He grabs my ass with both hands. "I said that I couldn't be out late because I had to come back here and fuck you until you pass out."

"Christopher!" I laugh. "You did no such thing."

"No. I still haven't even told them you're back, so they're going to flip. They missed you. Especially Sabin."

"I missed them, too." I start to slip from his arms. "For the record, I do think you're an asshole for teasing me."

I sit on the edge of the bed and start to put on my black nylons. Chris folds his arms and leans against the wall, watching me, studying the way I move. While I'm completely comfortable with him in almost every way, it's making me nervous to have his eyes on me so intently. But I can tell that he likes this, so I take my time getting dressed, doing what I can to draw it out. By the time I slip on the second high-heeled black leather boot, Chris looks like he's about to attack me. *Damn, Estelle is good.*

After I slide the dress over my head, I cross the floor slowly and turn my back to him. "Zip me?" I lift my hair.

"Of course." He's clearly trying to torture me because he smoothes his hands over my entire upper body before zipping my dress in the slowest possible manner.

I tilt my head back and lean into him. "Chris . . ."

"We have to go or we'll be late."

I hate him right now. I hate that he has the self-control to get us out of the room, because I can damn well feel how turned on he is.

"Dinner better be really fucking good," I say.

Chris drives us to the restaurant in his truck. We haven't said it out loud, but it's pretty obvious that we've agreed not to go out of our way to let on that our only real plans for the rest of the week are to have sex with each other.

The restaurant is modern and dimly lit with blue starburst lights. Sabin, Estelle, and Eric are seated at a large semicircle booth, and Sabin flies out of his seat when he sees me.

"Lady Blythe McGuire!" He rushes over to me and lifts me into the air in a hug. "I missed the hell out of you. What are you doing here?" He sets me down and holds me by the shoulders. "Wait. Is everything all right? You okay?"

"I'm fine. I just came back early and ran into Chris. Apparently the Shepherds and I have excellent taste in hotels."

He hugs me again. "C'mon. I'll buy you a drink."

He scoots me into the booth first so that I'm next to Eric, who hugs me, and Estelle on his other side air-kisses me. I love that we are in this fancy restaurant and Sabin has on his cowboy hat. Chris sits next to his sister and takes a sip from her water glass. Everyone is tan and radiant looking, and I am blissfully happy because I am back where I belong.

"Our girl has returned early," Sabin announces, "so now we have someone we are not related to who we can play with! Chris has been sick of us since New Year's Eve, but I know you can counteract how boring we are. Right, Chris? Blythe is a lot more entertaining than us."

I have to bite my cheek so that I don't burst out laughing. I can't even look at Chris.

"None of you are in the least bit boring," I say. "You guys must have had an amazing trip. So tell me all the details! How was Hawaii?"

"Full of spectacular hard-bodied men," Estelle says dreamily. She is, as usual, in full makeup and beautifully dressed in a taupe sweater that looks like cashmere.

Eric rolls his eyes. "That's true. There were also *other* incredible views, though."

I listen to them gush about the plush condo Chris rented for them, the impeccable beaches, the day hikes they took, and Chris and Sabin's disastrous attempts to learn to surf.

"It's true," Chris says. "We sucked. I don't think either of us stayed up on the board for more than two seconds."

"It was still fun, though, right, Chris?" I love how Sabin looks at his brother. I think back to the fight on Thanksgiving night and how that could have ripped a family apart, or at the very least caused serious tears, but the adoration in Sabin's eyes is unmistakable. He clearly looks up to Chris in so many ways, and I wish that James had a fraction of those same feelings for me. One day, one day. Maybe.

"Hey, we went back and surfed again the next day, didn't we?" Chris gets a spark in his eyes. "You know, Blythe, there are really so many things that I want to do again . . ." He sighs dramatically, and I resist kicking him under the table. Then he raises his glass to Sabin's and nods in Eric's direction. "And I'd like to give you two credit for your waterskiing success."

Eric sighs. "Man, I could do that every day. Blythe, you would love it. Have you ever tried?"

I shake my head. "Nope. I've done a little sailing, but that's it. Oh, and I can row a rowboat like nobody's business."

"Very impressive," Estelle says, smiling. "I could sit in a rowboat and bark orders while a half-naked Hawaiian boy rows us to a deserted beach."

"That's enough out of you, young lady!" Sabin jokes. "My sister is not to be thinking anything indecent about boys. Not until you're forty, Estelle."

"Fine, fine. Blythe, have you enjoyed any new and exciting physical activities we should know about since we last saw you?"

I'm never going to make it through this dinner.

"Yes, tell us." Chris jumps in. "Any new hobbies you've added to your repertoire?"

I clear my throat. "I think that I've got all I can handle as it is."

"Yeah, so how's the running going?" Eric asks.

He and I talk together for a bit, and he tries to entice me to enter one of the spring races in Madison. "You could totally do it! A 5K? 10K?"

"A 10K!" I nearly shriek. "I can't do that, Eric."

"We'll see," he says.

Dinner is nonstop conversation and delicious food. I eat ceviche out of a martini glass and devour my scallop entree, which comes with so many components I can hardly identify what I'm eating. But every-

left drowning

thing is outstanding. Eric feeds me a forkful of his polenta with basil and cream, and I can't help groaning over how good it is. I also can't help noticing with satisfaction that Chris shifts in his seat when I do so.

When they ask me about my trip home, I'm surprised to find myself giving more details than I would have expected. I even tell them about going to the Christmas Eve party at Lani and Tim's and talking to Nichole about applying for an internship after graduation.

"Are you definitely going back to Massachusetts after graduation?" Estelle asks. "We'll miss the fuck out of you if you do."

Sabin throws his arm over my shoulder. "We would miss you, but this sounds like it could be cool. Besides, if it's a magazine, maybe they have travel features, and you'd actually, you know, travel. To Hawaii! And need an assistant to carry your suitcases!"

"I'm sure you know just the person for the job." It hits me that I only have four months left at Matthews before graduation. "I don't know. A lot can happen in a few months."

"A lot can happen in a few hours," Chris adds all too casually. He takes the olive from his martini and winks at me as he pops it in his mouth. Relentless. He is relentless.

I cock my head and glare at him. "Are we getting dessert? I love dessert. Sabe, want to share something with me? I think I saw a cranberry torte thing that looked good. And coffee. Espresso, maybe."

"Yeah," Chris says under his breath, "Blythe's definitely going to need an espresso."

I clear my throat. "So, the torte?"

"Oh, I'm in! I love me some torte," Sabin says as he rubs his belly. "What is a torte exactly? Why isn't it a tart? Is a torte a subcategory of tarts? Why don't all tarts taste tart?"

"Can we still order it even if we can't classify it?" I ask.

"Definitely. Hey, B., do you want to come to the show we're seeing tonight? I can probably get you a ticket still."

"No! No, she can't," Chris says all too quickly.

Sabin frowns.

"I mean, Blythe was saying on the way here that she's exhausted from her trip. You know, holiday nonsense and all."

"Oh hell," Sabin says under his breath. "No way. No, no, no."

I glare at Chris again. He smiles at me and shrugs.

Estelle and Eric are busy scrolling through pictures on their phones and deciding which ones of Eric are the best to send to Zach, and they don't notice anything.

When the bill comes, Chris refuses to take any money, which irritates me, but I'm not surprised. He does enjoy caretaking.

Sabin claps his hands together. "All right, little siblings. We have to run if we're going to make the show. And Chris and Blythe need to get to the hotel so that they can get back to fucking each other to all hell."

"Oh Jesus, Sabin!" Chris tosses up his hands.

"What in the world is going on?" Eric says. He and Estelle have finally looked up from his phone.

I can't even look at Estelle because she's got the most satisfied grin on her face. "Well, fuckin' finally, am I right?"

This is humiliating.

Sabin wraps his arms around my head, covering my face so that I can't even see, and fakes a soft sob. "My innocent little friend has been violated! Sullied!" He tickles me, and I nearly crash into Eric laughing.

When we all say good night, Eric lets our hug linger for a moment. I realize that he had very little visible reaction to Sabin's outburst, and I wonder if he disapproves. I brush it off for now.

left drowning

After we say good-bye to the three in the parking lot, Chris and I climb back in his truck. After just a few minutes of watching him drive, I can't take it anymore. Just looking at his hands on the steering wheel is turning me on. God, I love his hands. The way he moves, the way his fingers find every spot on my body that gets me hot, the way he intuitively knows when to be gentle and slow . . . and when to push harder against me, to be strong and firm. Those hands do incredible things to me, and they've made me greedy and needy.

I run my fingers through his dark hair and scratch my nails down the back of his neck. I can't go another second without Chris touching me. I lift up slightly, hike up my dress, and slip my nylons down. I put one foot up on the dashboard. I lean back and open my legs before I take his hand in mine. I push my underwear to the side and set his hand on me.

"Put your fingers inside me," I say. "Please." I can barely talk.

"Like this?" he asks teasingly.

Very slowly, he eases one finger in. I close my eyes and put my hands up to my head. I can feel how ridiculously wet I am already, and he's not even moving his hand. He's just holding his finger inside me.

"Christopher, please," I beg.

"Oh, you mean like this?" He briefly takes away his hand and then pushes hard against me, shoving two fingers deep inside. I moan, and he starts moving in and out, slowly and firmly. I have no idea how he can do this and drive, but he doesn't take his eyes off the road.

"Is that what you wanted?" he asks.

I nod.

"And what about this?" I feel his fingers pull out and run over me a few times before he settles on my clit. "Did you want this, too?"

I moan as he starts to brush a finger over me. He presses a little harder, and I start gasping. The truck stops, but he leaves it running. Thank God we're back at the hotel in the dark underground parking lot. Chris leans over to kiss me and switch hands, this time yanking my underwear down hard before rubbing me again. His tongue is in my mouth, and I think about how incredible it will feel later when he goes down on me.

I can't believe that I'm going to come already, but his fingers are on just the right place.

However, I still plan on giving him crap for earlier.

I pull my lips away. "I'm still pissed at you," I whisper.

He smiles at me and pushes his fingers back inside me. "I can tell."

I whimper and start breathing harder, and my hands are gripping the back of the seat. He's moving steadily inside and against me, and I come hard. If it didn't feel so fucking good, I might be embarrassed at how loud I am. As it is, I couldn't care less. My whole body shudders under his touch.

"I'm going to take you up to my room now and continue apologizing for not fucking you before dinner."

"Yeah?"

"You good with that idea?" he murmurs while he kisses my neck.

"Mmmhmmm. And you can also apologize for baiting Sabin the way you did."

His tongue is slick on my skin, and the throbbing between my legs is relentless. "I did nothing of the sort."

Now I can't help laughing. "Yes, you did. You were like a dog pissing on a tree, marking your territory."

"You don't look anything like a tree."

"I'm flattered. But that was not nice, what you did. And it was

left drowning

unnecessary." I push him up so that he'll pay attention for a second. "Sabin is my friend, that's it."

He smiles. "I know that. I was being an ass. So now I really have some more apologizing to do, huh?"

Somehow we make it up to his hotel room. I hear him throw his wallet from his pocket into the room, and then he's behind me, grinding against me. Listening to me get off has made him completely hard. His breath is hot on my neck while his hands unzip my dress and then find the hem, lifting it up over my head. I can feel how much he wants me now. I kick off my boots and he takes hold of the top of my nylons and underwear and kneels as he pulls them down. I feel him lick the curve under my ass as he helps me out of my clothes, and then he reaches up to unhook my bra.

REFLECTION

OUR FIVE DAYS AT THE HOTEL PASS INSANELY
quickly, and before I feel ready, it's our last night together. The next day
we'll be returning to campus. This will be over. I know that we're not
done and that there will be more to us, but for the moment, this time at
the hotel with him is all I am ready to handle. Even so, I'm a bit shaken
by how much I am dreading separating from him, even in just the physical capacity. Our friendship is solid and unwavering, I am sure, but I'm
still edgy at the thought of this ending.

Virtually all that Chris and I have done over at the hotel is make
love. Or fuck. Whatever. We've gone slow and gentle, we've gone hard
and rough. We've traded power back and forth. Sometimes he leads me,
defining what we do, how we do it, and what the mood is. Sometimes I

do. I have been relishing the chance to be in control, to make decisions for myself, to take what I need, and to give to someone else. So I am sore, very much so, and my entire body hurts, but in the most amazing way. My ability to connect physically, to feel sexual and sensual, is undeniable now. Chris has given that to me.

We've been in bed all day. I think both of us are conscious of the ticking clock. His brothers and sister stopped calling, and texting, and banging on the door two days ago.

Chris leans over me, kissing my chest and my stomach.

"How can you be this good?" I whisper. "It's impossible."

"If I'm good at all, it's because of you. Because I want to give you everything."

He lowers his kisses and bends up my legs. I know what he's about to do, and I'm dying to let him do it, but there's something I want first.

I move between his legs and take his cock in my hand. He is so hard, so perfect. I start moving slowly and then lean over and begin to slide him into my mouth. I keep my fingers around the base and press my tongue against him as I take him in fully. The taste of him is extraordinary. The taste is mine. When he's wet and slick, I tighten my lips and begin to move up and down, doing what I've gotten good at over the past few days.

Chris groans loudly. "Fuck, your mouth is so hot. God . . ."

Hearing him say this makes me move faster. Tonight I'm going to make him come in my mouth. It's something that we haven't done completely yet because the lure of having sex has always taken over, but right now I desperately want this. I'm moving my hand up and down in rhythm with my mouth as he shifts under me, and I love how it feels to blow him. Soon his hands are in my hair and his breathing quickens.

"I can't last like this, Blythe. You're too good. . . . God, you're too good."

I don't need him to last because there is no way that I'm letting him stop me this time. And I know for sure that this isn't going to put him out of commission for the night. I start sucking on him faster, harder. I couldn't stop even if I wanted to.

His hands are tight in my hair now, moving up and down with my head, and I can tell by the sounds he's making that I have him on that same edge where he puts me. I slow down a bit to keep him there because I want him blind with pleasure.

I love it. I love making Chris feel like this. I feel him clench his muscles as he pushes a little farther into my mouth. Then he is saying my name, and I taste him, I drink him in, totally turned on and high from being able to satisfy him like this. When his groaning has subsided, when he's fully done, I kiss my way breathlessly up his muscled chest, and before I even reach his mouth, he flips me onto my back and starts kissing my neck.

"That was . . ." I feel him shake his head. "There are no words."

His tongue makes its way over my body. He moves his lips across my inner thigh, and I can feel my legs start to shake because I know what his tongue is about to do to me. "I love making love to you," he tells me. "Your body feels so damn good." Then his mouth is between my legs. I reach down to find his hands, and I take them in mine. I close my eyes while he does what he does so well.

Every little touch of his lips, his fingers, his tongue . . . Everything he does makes me want more of him. Just when I'm getting close, he stops and pulls away. Chris sits back on his legs and sets my hands on my own body. He watches while he moves my hands for me, over my stomach and my breasts, tracing the path that he kissed moments ago. Then he puts my own hands between my legs. I rub a finger against myself while Chris takes a condom from the bedside table. He moves one hand to put the tip of his cock against me and puts the other hand back over mine so that he can feel me make myself come. Which I do. Or, rather, we do. And just when I start, just at that moment when I feel everything begin to release, he slides inside. He leans over me now, moving his hips just slightly while I tighten around him over and over. As loud as I've been tonight, I can't make a sound now. Feeling him inside me like this consumes me.

I tuck up my knees and pull him deep into me. He lifts up just enough so that we can look at each other. "God, Blythe," is all he can manage to say.

He looks more lost in this—maybe in me—than he has until now, and it's momentarily disarming. But I want to try something, so I lift up my leg and push against him, cuing us to roll over so that I can be on top. Another thing that we haven't gotten around to trying yet.

I lean over him, barely moving. It's like the first time all over again: tight, and intense, and amazing. More than that, I am overwhelmed by how connected we are to each other, and how perfect this is. It's almost totally dark in the room, but the light from the city is enough to cast a glow over us. Chris is still, letting me move tentatively as I get used to how this feels. His fingers run lightly over my back, down my ass, and across the back of my thighs. The way he caresses my breasts is tender and loving, and I'm pretty sure that I could stay like this forever. So I take my time.

Because I can't get enough of watching him, I try sitting straight up so that I can look into his eyes while I start to grind more confidently. Even though we're moving slowly, he can hardly speak. "Blythe." The way that he says my name this time is different, more loaded.

He holds his hands up for me and I put my palms flat against his, our fingers pressed together. We cannot take our eyes off each other. I lean on him for support while I start to rock my hips back and forth, and the intensity grows fast. I just need a little more . . .

"Come for me. I want to watch you come." Chris doesn't even sound like himself. He is practically begging me, his voice desperate and full of emotion. "Please. Oh God, Blythe . . . I need you, I need you."

He bends his arms so that I tilt forward just a hint. And that's what does it. Chris intertwines our fingers and lets me brace my weight on him as he moves with me, both of us working to rub my clit against his body.

I don't want this moment or this night to end. What I'm feeling is more than just sexual arousal. I am shaking from the intensity we share, and I'm hyperaware of how bonded we are to each other. I don't even know what to make of this experience except that I feel connected to Chris, to everything about him, through to my core. It is terrifying and wonderful.

I can feel my orgasm start, and the sensation is so intense that it's nearly enough to make me cry. I let it wash over me while I writhe against him like I'm never going to see him again. Then his hold on my hands tightens, and I force myself to keep my eyes open so that I look down and watch him come under me. He is breathtaking as he does so, staggeringly gorgeous.

My entire body is trembling when I fall against him. I cannot kiss him soon enough, and his lips stay against mine for . . . I don't know how long.

We kiss forever.

He runs his hands through my hair, and we stay like this, as one, for a long time. Too long.

left drowning

And then I realize what has happened between us tonight.

We just fell in love.

I am not confusing sex with love. Unfortunately.

Because this is not what I want, and it's not what he wants. Not yet. We're not ready.

This love will wait. It has to.

There is something else that I know for sure, and I'm not sure how to feel about it. I have the thought calmly and sanely. It's not a hysterical reaction to my first-ever sexual experience, it's just my truth.

I will never sleep with anyone besides Christopher Shepherd.

We lie in bed, silent and wrapped up in each other for a long time. Then Chris gently lifts me from him. "Bathe with me?" he asks.

"Of course."

He turns on the light over the vanity and leaves the overhead one off. I get to have my tub for two, just like I wanted. But I am melancholy now. Part of that may be because I am worn out both physically and emotionally, and part of it is something else. He runs the water and holds my hand, helping me in. His hand stays on mine as he sits and brings me in front of him. The only noise comes from the tap that cascades water down the side of the tub. I lie in his arms silently while the bath fills. His hands trickle over my arms and my breasts. This time, though, his touch isn't just sexual. It's more than that.

I close my eyes and let myself be held and . . . and loved. Later, he sits me up and very, very slowly washes my body and my hair.

This time there is no imaginary blood and no screaming.

"Christopher," I murmur.

He moves a soapy hand over my shoulder and murmurs back, "You're the only person who calls me that. I like it."

When he's done, I pull the drain and watch the water empty. I turn around and kiss him softly before I slide behind him and refill the tub. I run my hands over the muscles in his arms and his back. His skin is slick with water and my hands glide easily over his body. And over his scars.

While the tub refills, I kiss his back and massage his shoulders, savoring every moment that I have with him.

I trace his broken scar with my fingertips over and over. And I think. And then I understand—I see—something. His skiing-accident explanation? I've given the same lie when asked.

Chris drops his head down. He can sense that I know.

Finally, I say what I don't want to, but what needs to be said.

"This wasn't an accident, was it?"

He doesn't answer me right away. I cup water in my hands and drop it over his skin. I watch the drops roll across his body, and I wait.

"No, it wasn't an accident," he finally says. "Not really."

And with those words, my heart shatters.

His father was a much meaner son of a bitch than anyone has told me.

I keep dousing him with water, almost ritualistically, until he turns and pulls me firmly into his lap and takes me in his arms. I stroke the back of his neck with my hand, maybe to comfort him, maybe to comfort me. No matter what I may be screaming in my head, I will stay calm for him. I know all the things not to say, but I don't know any of the things *to* say.

"I'm okay, Blythe," he whispers. "I'm okay. It's over."

I nod.

"Do you hear me? I'm safe."

I nod again.

"Sabin, and Estelle, and Eric? They're safe, too."

I don't want to let go of him, but I want out of this tub and back

left drowning

in our bed, where we are protected and shielded from everything. He stands with me and steps out, supporting me around the waist with his hands as I step over the edge of the tub. I can't stand to have him even a foot away from me, and I wrap my left arm under his and my right goes over his shoulder. I lock my hands together and set my cheek against his strong arm. I look in the mirror at the two of us. Our reflection in the mirror is poignant because I don't know when I'll see us like this again.

And then I see something that I can't make sense of. I study the reflection while I cling to Chris. What I am looking at is not possible.

The scar on my forearm sits perfectly between the two that angle across his back. My scar fills in, it *completes*, his. As if we are an exact match . . . as if we are . . .

This is crazy.

I cannot show this to Chris. We don't believe in fate, or destiny, or coincidences . . . or whatever the hell this is. We don't believe in the unexplainable, and this is unexplainable.

And yet, I believe.

I start to shiver. Chris breaks our hold to get a towel, and he shrouds me in the thick white terry cloth. "You're cold, baby. Here." As he dries my shoulders, I move my hands to his face and hold him. His green eyes are dark tonight, more muted than usual. He is tired, I can see that. But effortlessly, with one arm behind my back and the other under my legs, he lifts me and carries me into the moonlit bedroom, and we make love over and over again for one last night.

It is hours later that we fall asleep with me enclosed in his arms.

When I wake in the morning, he is gone.

In my hand is one of the silver skipping stones that I gave him. There is a folded note, too, that reads, *So that you always have what you need.*

21

HARD TO HOLD

LATE FEBRUARY BRINGS BRUTALLY COLD WEATHER and even blizzards. It's always like this, but I'm more aware of the bitter cold this year, not to mention the never-ending snow and ice, because of how it impacts my running. The indoor track is virtually empty on this Saturday afternoon, exactly how I prefer it. My guess is that almost nobody else wanted to brave the storm that hit today to walk across campus to the gym. It's that bad out. But it's half the reason that I'm here. The dorm feels claustrophobic to me today, so I had to get out. It probably took me as long to bundle up in protective clothing as it will to complete my run.

There is one other girl on the track with me, and a few guys lifting in the weight room. The glass wall to the room affords me an easy view when I run past, and I spot Chris when I run by. We don't usually overlap because I often run in the early morning and he usually works out in the late afternoon, but today I've spent most of the day finishing schoolwork.

He waves as I near the weight room on this lap, and I wave back. He's got on a tight blue nylon shirt and black shorts, and I can't help slowing my pace a little as I take him in. Knowing what is under that shirt and shorts is distracting. I look away and turn up the volume on my music. The most recent playlist from Chris blasts loudly in my ears, and I refocus on my run. The timer that I've set reads sixty-three minutes. Another twelve and I'll stop. I know that I'm still not very fast, which is why I make myself run for so long, so I push hard for the last few laps until my legs and my lungs are burning.

After a cooldown walk and a shower, I stand in my bra and underwear in front of the locker room mirror and dry my hair. Usually I throw my curls in a ponytail, but today I'll turn into a walking icicle if I go outside without drying it. As I run the brush through my hair and work the blow dryer on high heat, I am noticing the scar on my left forearm more than usual. It's not that I'm self-conscious or embarrassed about it again, but I'm more . . . I don't know what I am. Confused. Bewildered. I haven't told Chris how our scars match up. I can't begin to make sense of it.

I halfway want to tell Chris about it, but I'm afraid he'll be dismissive. For me, there is meaning in how we fit together, there has to be—but I know he won't see it the same way. Estelle would make too much of it. Sabin would get it. But Chris? No. Besides, the reentry back to school after our days in the hotel was hard enough, and there is no reason to complicate what is over for now. It's not the right time to talk about scars, mine or Chris's. And I don't need details to know the profound significance of Chris's scars, physical and emotional. What may have happened to him, and to Estelle, Eric, and Sabin, is more than I can stand. But I don't know the story yet, and imagining details is not smart. I need facts, but I have an unwavering respect for privacy, so I will not ask about this.

It's taken us a little time to find our footing again with each other, and some of that struggle is probably from the fact that Sabin, Eric, and Estelle make no secret of staring back and forth between us at every given opportunity, waiting to see what might happen. I don't know about Chris, but I haven't talked about our time together with any of them. I don't want to talk about it, and luckily, none of them has asked me directly. What went on between me and Chris is ours and ours alone. I can't even tell Sabin, and I tell him everything else. I've listened to his many one-night stand stories, but I will never talk to him about the hotel.

But despite the curious stares from the Shepherd siblings, Chris and I are now finally back to normal. Well, whatever is "normal" is for us. We joke and hang out, we study together sometimes. It's easier in a group because there's less opportunity for any loaded eye contact. I try not to touch him much because the electricity that I still feel from any brush of his skin—or, hell, the fabric of his clothing—can make me catch my breath. I've accepted that the heat between us is just a part of who we are. But that doesn't make it any easier when I'm trying to pay attention to Dostoyevsky and feel him put a hand on my shoulder to ask if I want a cup of coffee. Because then all I can think about is how that hand can move so skillfully over my breasts, between my legs . . . So, that's challenging. But we have not so much as kissed since that last night

left drowning

in the hotel. As much as I wouldn't mind a repeat of a number of things, we are in a good place with each other. Being on hold is not an unhappy place to be.

Just as I finish layering on my clothing, down parka, and hat, I get a text from Sabin saying that I should come meet them at the union. *Of course I will*, I text back. I'm relishing our time together, knowing that graduation is nearing every day. I'm getting closer to applying for the internship that my old friend Nichole Rains talked to me about back in Boston. The reality is that I need to make plans for after graduation, and those plans have to include going home: I need to build a home base for James. I *want* to be there, I do, but I also am not ready to leave this group of friends. To leave Chris. He has no firm idea about what he's going to do after graduation, either, but I suspect that he'll stay in the Madison area and get a job of some kind. After the summer, though, both of us could theoretically be free to go anywhere.

As I swing open the door from the gymnasium, I am hit with blizzardy snow. Just before the door blows back into me, Chris puts his hand out and stops it from smacking me in the face.

"My hero!" I clasp my hands together and bat my eyes.

"Damn straight." Chris grins. "You going back to the dorm?"

"Student union. Sabin said they're all there. Want to come?" I have to yell through the wind to be heard. It's dark, and I'm already fantasizing about having a giant cup of cocoa with whipped cream.

"Definitely."

I groan and lean forward, covering my face with my hands, as a howling wind whips over us. "Motherfuck!"

Chris laughs and throws his arm over my shoulders. "Suck it up. Only another month or so of this."

It feels good to have this happen, because while I don't necessarily want to throw him down in the snow and screw him, I do like the closeness between us, so I lean into him while we walk. We make our way through the stormy weather, each of us nearly taking a spill on different ice patches, and I cheer when we tumble into the overheated student union relatively unscathed. "Heat! Thank God!" I sigh happily.

I scan the room, excited to see all the Shepherds, and Zach, too, whose company I've really been enjoying lately. He's genuine, and fun, and passionate, especially about Eric. He's also . . .well, Zach is normal. He's got nice parents who live in the suburbs of Minnesota, and the fact that he's gay has never caused the slightest issue for them. Zach is so devoid of emotional baggage that it's a joy to hang out with him. He's also a great companion because he gets statistics—and we're in the same class this semester. Having him hold my hand through it is amazing, since I seem to have zero grasp on anything mathematical. Mostly, though, my academic performance is soaring. My adviser, Tracey, actually dropped me an e-mail to say that she's been watching my grades since our meeting last fall, and she's impressed, which makes me happy.

Chris yanks off my hat and shakes it at me, throwing snow in my face. I laugh and chase him over to the table where Eric, Zach, Estelle, and Sabin are sitting. Chris flops into a chair, and I clap my snowy mittens over him to repay the favor, but I jump into Sabin's lap before he can retaliate again.

"Sabin! Help!" I squeal.

"You're freezing and wet!" Sabin complains, but he lets me stay where I am anyway, even helping me take off my coat. I love the lap spot that he always provides. Sabe is like an inappropriate Santa Claus. "Look at your cheeks! You've probably got frostbite." He puts his hands on my face and tries to warm me up. But then he's rubbing crazily and smooshing my face while I try to get away.

"Boys are impossible." Estelle stares into a compact as she reapplies lipstick. "Leave her alone, you two, because payback is a bitch. Blythe and I will get you when you least expect it."

Sabin takes his hands from my face. "Okay, okay, I know better than to mess with that tag team."

He is super scruffy today, even for Sabin, and while I am finding his squishy lap very comfortable to sit on, he has definitely been gaining weight. I can't resist, so I poke him in the belly. "Might want to come to the gym with me or your brother once in a while."

The table lets out a collective, "Ohhhhhh!" and I get another face squish.

"Sabe, seriously," Eric says. "The belly is really getting out of hand."

"Yeah, come lift with me at least," Chris offers. "Or go run around the track a few times."

Sabin rolls me into him, stands with me holding him like a koala baby, and shakes my backside to the table, making me laugh again. "Why? So I can have an ass like Blythe's?"

"In your dreams you'd have an ass like Blythe's." Chris winks at me. Another group "Ohhhhhh!"

Sabin sets me down on the ground. "Okay, okay. I hear you. You think I'm fat and disgusting." He fakes a sob. "That calls for hot chocolate. Blythe, come with me. I'm so out of shape that I may need assistance walking the distance from here to the counter."

"Consider me a human cane," I say.

As I walk by Chris, I mess up his hair and he smacks me on the ass.

"See, Sabe? HARD AS A ROCK!" he yells as we walk away.

I just shake my head and keep walking.

"You two aren't . . . you know . . . again, are you?" Sabe nudges me with his elbow. "I kinda thought that Chris . . ."

"What?"

"Nothin'," he says and looks ahead.

"No, we're just friends. It's good, really," I promise him.

The line at the café takes forever. It seems half the campus is holed up here during the storm. We're just collecting the drinks we've ordered for the table when Zach catches up with us at the counter.

"Hey!" Zach leans a hand against the wall. "I'm really hungry. Do you guys want something? I was thinking we could take a couple pizzas back to my room?"

"My fat belly and I always want pizza. Totally good idea," Sabin says.

"Sure, let me just warm up before I go out again." I am still shivering when I take two steaming cups from the counter.

"Aw, let's just get them now and head over. I'm, like, really, really hungry." Zach bounces in front of us while we start back to the tables.

"Dude, what the hell? We'll eat pizza in a little bit. The lady is still currently an iceberg. Calm down." Sabin frowns at him.

Then Zach stops walking. He's less bouncy now. "Sabe . . ." He tips his head back just the slightest bit. "It's just that . . ." Zach looks at me.

"Oh fuck," Sabin says under his breath.

I follow Sabin's gaze. Immediately I know that this is the moment I will remember as the first time I felt very real and very painful heartbreak.

Everyone is still sitting in their seats at the table, but there is now someone else there, too. She is standing behind Chris, her hands rubbing his shoulders. For a second, I try to tell myself that I'm seeing something other than what I am. But when she tilts his head back and kisses him on the mouth briefly, there is no point. He does do a quick scan for me, but he doesn't spot me through the crowd. I can tell he's uncomfortable, but I don't give a shit.

"Blythe." Zach touches my arm.

"Who is she?" I ask softly.

Neither of them says anything. I turn my back on the view. I cannot look at this.

Sabin turns and throws the cups from his hands into the trash can. He takes the two I am holding and does the same. "Zach, get her coat. Let's go."

I look at Sabin. "Who is she, Sabin? Who is she?"

"Don't cry," he says. "Please don't cry."

"I'm not going to cry, I just want to know who the *fuck* she is."

Sabin starts walking me to the door, and his hand on my back is the only reason I am able to find the exit. "Just hold on, baby girl."

He tries to get me to wait in the entryway, under the blasting heaters, but I push into the snowstorm. Better to freeze out here than share the air in there with her. "Jesus, Blythe! Stop!"

I am running through the snow, with Sabin falling farther behind with each step. I want my room, my bed. I want away. Zach appears and forces my hat on my head and my coat over my shoulders while Sabin swears up and down. When we get to my dorm, I shake off my coat, locate my key in the pocket, and fumble hopelessly with the lock. Sabin tries to take it from me, but I shove his arm away. "I can open the fucking door by myself!"

It takes a minute, but I do. They follow me silently to my room, and I can practically hear them flinch when I hurl the keys across the room and they hit the wall. I sit on the bed and take off my sopping wet shoes. Then I throw them one at a time at the same wall.

"You could have at least aimed for Neon Jesus," Sabin whispers.

"Shut up. You're lucky my hands are empty now." I take a deep breath. "Sorry."

"Don't be sorry. Throw whatever you want," he says.

Zach sits down next to me, and Sabin squats in front of me. I can't look at either of them.

"Will you two just go, please?"

"No," Zach says. "We're not leaving."

"Please go. I'm embarrassed enough." I look at Sabin. "Please, Sabin." The more I talk, the more difficult it is to control my voice. I do not want to fall apart.

Neither of them say anything for a minute, and I'm hoping they'll give up.

"Blythe, I'm so sorry." Sabin takes my hand.

I look up at him and feel my eyes sting. *Fuck.* "How long?"

The pause before he answers me is excruciating. "Since a few weeks . . . after."

"A few weeks after we got back to school?" I wipe my face with my sweatshirt. "Have you known the whole time?"

"B., we didn't know how to tell you . . ."

"No, no, it's okay." I shake my head. "And it's fine. *I'm* fine. Really." I stand up and step around Sabin. I locate my sneakers and calmly go and set them on the heater, keeping my back to the boys as I look out the window and start babbling. "These are going to take forever to dry out. I might have to use my backup pair if I want to run tomorrow morning. I'll have to get up early because I still don't have

left drowning

that statistics stuff down, and I also have about a million chapters left to read for lit class. Actually, I should get to sleep if I'm going to get up early."

"It's six o'clock," Zach points out.

We're all quiet again, until I finally turn around and crumble.

"Sabe . . ."

My friend lets me fall into his arms, and he strokes my hair and tells me over and over that it's going to be all right. "She's just some stupid girl, Blythe. She's not you."

"He doesn't want me." I keep my face pressed into him, hiding my eyes under the flap of his leather jacket. "But I can't be upset, because we agreed we weren't going to be anything else. I just thought that later . . . we would. I'm just so messed up still."

"Chris is the one who is messed up." Sabin holds me tighter. He is my rock right now.

"He said . . . he said he didn't want a girlfriend. Sabin, that's what he said." I lift my head, and Sabin rubs his thumbs under my eyes. "She's not just some girl. She's his girlfriend, isn't she?"

He doesn't need to answer me.

I step away and go to the sink to wash my face. "What's her name?"

"Jennifer."

"I assume she's nice?"

They don't say anything.

I throw water over my eyes and pat my face dry with a towel. My bed is screaming my name, so I crawl past Zach and lie down. "You can say she's nice. It's okay."

Zach lies down next to me. "She's fine. There's nothing particularly wrong with her."

"There is too something wrong with her." Sabin lies down on my other side. "She's boring as shit."

Zach laughs. "Well, there is that."

"Good." I sniff and stare at the ceiling. "Why didn't you tell me? Why didn't Chris tell me? Don't answer that. I know why. Because you all think that I'm so fucking fragile, and I'll come completely unglued again."

"No. Because we were hoping she wouldn't be around for very long," Sabin says.

"But she's still around." I fight back tears. "Is he sleeping with her? Forget it. I don't want to know. It's none of my business anyway."

"He's not, if that's any comfort," Sabin says quickly. "This dumb thing between them isn't going anywhere, B. It's not. She's not enough for him."

"Neither was I."

"No, no, sweetie. Don't you get it? You were too much for him." I realize that Sabin has said exactly what Chris said that night in my room when he left so suddenly.

"I was fine. I swear to God I was. I wasn't ready for anything either, but I didn't think that . . ." I don't even know how to finish this sentence.

Sabin does. "That he'd run out and do something so stupid and thoughtless." He scratches his unshaven face and smiles at me. "I'm telling you, I *promise* you, this won't last. It's not like he's going to get married or anything."

There is a knock at the door, and my stomach knots. "No," I whisper adamantly. "No." I do not want to see Chris now.

Sabin nods. "I got it." He's off the bed in a flash. The last thing I hear him say as he storms out into the hallway and slams the door behind him is "Are you fucking kidding me, Chris? C'mon, man, you gotta get the hell out of here. Give her a goddamn minute, okay?"

I hear their footsteps retreat down the hall. The room feels emptier without Sabin in it.

I don't cry again, which is good. "Zach . . ."

"I know. This was not supposed to happen."

"No. It wasn't."

I'm so stupid. I guess that it *was* really just sex between us. The friendship part, I know that was real, but the other stuff? I must have been the only one who felt it. There is no deeper connection between us, no larger reason for our scars, no epic romance that has yet to unfold.

Except I don't believe that. I should, based on what Chris is doing, but I don't. My heart is screaming something else. Maybe that's wishful thinking.

Zach sits up and looks around the empty room. "Take it from someone who is also in love with a Shepherd brother. They are easy boys to fall in love with, but hard to really, *really* hold on to."

"Eric adores you."

Zach nods. "And Chris adores you. That's easy to see. He does. But people like Eric and Chris? Having a relationship, trusting in that? It's a lot harder for them than it is for most of us. You can imagine, I think, Blythe. Chris just wants safe and easy right now. It's because he loves the hell out of you that he's running."

I think about Chris's scars and what kind of harm could have possibly caused them. And I say something that makes me sick to my stomach. "I think Chris got the worst of it."

"Yes," Zach says. "I think you're right."

22

ONE FOR NO, TWO FOR YES

LATE MARCH SUCKS. THE ONLY GOOD THING IS that my preferred running weather is finally here, because the daytime temps are sometimes reaching the mid-fifties. Being able to run outside again is a godsend. That said, I'm not fucking happy. No, I'm not in the depressive fog that fell over me after the incident at the union, but I'm not exactly cheerful, either. I miss the hell out of Chris.

Sabin was wrong. Chris is still with Jennifer, and I do everything that I can to avoid him and especially to avoid seeing them together. It's as though we got divorced and have shared custody of his siblings and Zach. We just can't be around each other. I'm sure it's made him uncomfortable the few times that we've all been together because I can't act like nothing is wrong. It takes all my energy to smile and make friendly chitchat. I chose not to sit with him and the others at Sabin's play last week. It was too hard. The best I can say is that so far I have managed to avoid being introduced to her. As far as she knows, I probably don't exist, and I prefer it that way. I keep as far away from Jennifer as possible. Even from a distance, though, I know that she's pretty, but not too pretty, which makes things worse. I can't even tell myself that he's just fucking some hot piece of ass in a meaningless college-boy kind of way.

I don't discuss the Chris-Jennifer situation with anyone. Estelle is praying for me, and for me and Chris, and while I was tempted to roll my eyes when she told me, I couldn't. It's not often that Estelle is straightforwardly sincere. The boys don't broach the issue with me. There's really nothing to say. Sabin hovers more than he needs to, but I appreciate it.

I take comfort in the fact that none of them seem particularly enthused by Chris's new relationship. I gather they are polite, but they don't include her in their group. Eric conceded that she doesn't fit the way that I do. Or did, I guess. The short period of time that I had with all of them, when things felt perfect and safe, is over. It's not the same now that Chris and I are barely speaking.

Despite my earlier insistence that I wasn't ready for something serious with Chris, I'm not showing signs of being the opposite of that with other guys. I never feel like flirting with anyone, and I haven't even gone on any dates. I am more social than I've been before while attending Matthews, meaning that I actually talk to other people and study with small groups outside of the Shepherd crew, but I am not attracted to anyone. I wasn't ready for Chris, but what's clear now is that I don't want anyone else. For him, that's obviously not the case.

After Sabin turned Chris away from my door right after the episode at the union, Chris tried talking to me one more time. He came to my room, and I opened the door, but before he could even say a word, I shut it in his face. I don't hate him, I never could, but I sure as shit don't want to talk to him. It's brutal to go from what we had to this. My heart fucking hurts all the time. Although I want him back with me, I am not going to throw myself at him, or beg, or otherwise make an ass out of myself.

At least planning for graduation is offering some distraction. Annie is coming to Madison for the ceremony, and I cannot wait. Not only that, but I asked her if she would help me move back to Boston and stay with me for a while. I thought she'd turn down such an enormous request, but to my surprise she jumped at the chance. Her marriage broke up a few years ago, she has no children, and she said this is the perfect reason to take a much-needed break. She's stopped practicing as an attorney full-time and instead does a lot of consulting from her Chicago home, so it's fairly easy for her to travel when she wants. The truth is that I'm going to need help leaving Matthews and settling in back home, and I'm proud that I got myself to directly ask for help. Annie is proof that sometimes relationships can fall apart and be rebuilt, so I cling to that.

And I run. Every day, no matter how much I don't want to, I run because of that hope.

I am barely past campus grounds on my Saturday-morning run when my feelings start to boil over.

Fuck everything.

I am going to run until I puke.

I am going to get that magazine internship that I applied for.

I am going to hang out with Nichole this summer.

I am going to let Annie mother the shit out of me.

I am going to ask—no, insist— that James come to my graduation.

left drowning

Chris can go fuck himself.

Naturally, it's at this moment that Chris's truck turns the corner and pulls alongside me. I glance to my left as Estelle waves from the passenger seat. I avoid looking at Chris. I don't realize that Sabin and Eric are riding in the bed of the truck, sitting on milk crates, until Sabin yells to me. Chris drives ahead so that I am running behind the truck.

Sabin sticks out his tongue at me and grins. I stick out my tongue back, but I am not in a smiling mood. I wait for Chris to step on the gas and put distance between us, but Sabin slaps the side of the truck. "Slow down, Chris! We got ourselves a live one!" He lifts his guitar and rests it on his knee while he strums and looks at me.

I give him the nastiest look possible. My music is not up loud enough to block out his booming voice, and I promise myself that from now on I will crank the shit out of my playlists.

Eric is yelling at me, but his voice doesn't have nearly the obnoxious power Sabin's does. I remove my earphones. "What are you guys doing? I'm kind of busy."

"I know." Eric leans in and says something to Sabe and then he holds up his arm and points to his watch.

"What?" I really wish they'd get the fuck out of here.

Sabin keeps strumming his guitar. "Eric tells me that you're training for a half marathon."

"No, I am not." Eric is going to be in deep shit. Yes, he brought up the idea of a 10K, but that's only a little over six miles. I cannot run a half marathon. That's over thirteen fucking miles.

"I told them that you could run a half marathon at a standard marathon-qualifying time!" Eric shouts. His unreasonable exuberance grates on me. "One hour and twenty-seven minutes."

Sabin leans off the side of the truck bed and calls out to Chris. "Stay with her, Chris. We're going to clock her mileage."

"Go to hell!" Not only can I not run a half marathon, but I am obviously not ever going to run a full marathon. I can't stop myself from glancing at Chris in the driver-side mirror. We make eye contact for a fraction of a second, and even that is more than I can take. I put my earphones back in and jack up the volume. I refuse to have a yelling conversation with these lunatics, and I'm not in the mood to run behind the truck. And what are they all doing out so early in the morning together anyway? Damn bad luck for me that they happened to find me.

Unless Eric organized this. Damn him.

I keep my head down and do what I can to ignore them until they go away. What I'm not prepared for is that Eric seems to know my route, so just before I make a turn, I see him yell up to Chris, directing him where to go. Although I hate deviating from my routine, when we hit the end of the road that leads to the lake, I go right instead of left. Chris has already gone left, so I'm free.

Until I hear his truck peel back a few yards before he bangs out a U-turn.

"Fucking asshole," I mutter. I keep my eyes on the road and just run, not even flinching when his truck pulls in front of me again. Sabin and Eric are cheering and clapping, and I can't help but crack a smile. They are ridiculous. I give in and accept that they are here for the duration of my run. At least I don't have Chris in that truck bed facing me, too. Presumably his eyes are on the road. Eventually I circle back and pick up my favorite route.

Goddamn if Chris doesn't keep the truck fifteen feet in front of me at all times, even waving the occasional car to go by us. I feel incredibly

left drowning

stupid, but I maintain my normal pace. Twenty minutes later, out of the corner of my eye, I catch Zach waving wildly to signal me. I look up and see him shaking his head. He cups his hands and yells at me.

Annoyed, I take out my earphones again. "What?" I yell, not hiding my aggravation.

"You're too slow," he calls out. "You're way, way too slow."

"Too slow for what?"

"If you're going to run this half marathon, you better hurry up."

"I told you I'm slow! Stop saying the word *marathon*! Go away."

Back to the music. But my fucking phone is dead. I can't believe this. This has never happened. I have never run without music, and I can't. Without the sound and the mood . . . Music blocks out everything: ankle pain, shaky legs, the cold, and most importantly, it prevents my mind from taking over. I start to walk. Within seconds Sabin is banging on the truck again, and Chris screeches to a halt.

"What are you doing?" Sabin looks unreasonably upset.

I catch my breath and hold up my phone. "Dead."

He holds his hands out at his sides. "So what? Just run, baby!"

I can hear Chris all too well when he leans out the window. He looks right at me. "She can't run without music."

I hate that he knows me this well. I fucking hate it. And I fucking hate how much it hurts to look at him.

And then there is music blaring from his truck. I'm going to murder him. I walk faster and reach the back of the truck. "Can you please go home now, all of you, and leave me the fuck alone?" My voice is cracking and my throat is tight.

Estelle rolls down her window, too, and seats herself on the door frame, her feet in the car and her upper body hanging out the side, to watch me. "Come on, Blythe. Run." The truck moves ahead again.

"Blythe, run, damn it," Sabin insists. "Please. You can do this. It's only . . . What? How many miles left, Chris?"

Chris holds out three fingers and then two. Three point two miles. He's been clocking me.

I start running. He's playing the first playlist that he ever sent me.

Eric hollers to be heard over the music. "You're running a nine-and-a-half-minute mile. You need to be doing an eight-point-five-minute mile at the very slowest, just to catch up."

I'm pretty sure that I can go the distance, but I don't think I can make the time. I'm a slower runner than even I thought. I've never paid attention to distance or pace before, but I do know that by picking up my pace by a full minute is going to be tough, so I'm really going to have to sprint. But, shit, I didn't know that I could run over ten miles at all, nor that I have been doing it frequently. Now they're asking me to finish this half marathon.

Sabin and Eric shut up and let me run. Chris holds out his hand and flashes me two fingers as I run through the playlist that first kept me from walking. Last September feels like eons ago. I nod back and immediately hate myself for acknowledging him, for responding to the natural way in which we communicate.

"Faster, B. You have to run faster!" Sabin calls out.

My legs are burning. I'm not made to sprint like this, and it hurts.

"Look at me," he says.

So I do. He spends so much time goofing around that moments when Sabin is *real* totally get me. I push a little more, and Sabin starts strumming his guitar along with the music. We must look like fools, but now I'm curious to see if I can make this time.

left drowning

"Attagirl!" Eric claps.

Sabin is playing along to a song that I always run hard to. It's one of those songs that would make me cry if I had any extra breath left to give. Even with the music loud, I can hear Sabin singing to me, so I focus on the back of the truck and push myself.

The music changes again. It's this song by The Lumineers that I love—that Chris knows I love—and I can see him tapping his hand along with the music.

Fuck him.

I'm about out of stamina. It'd be impossible for me to finish at this pace.

"No way, Blythe!" Sabin looks pissed. He can see I'm weakening. "You are not stopping now."

I just can't. I can feel my legs slowing despite my efforts. I'm burned out.

"I thought you were a fighter, B.!" Sabin yells. "You're not gonna fight for what you want, is that it? Stop being such a pussy. You want your man? He's right here." Sabin stands up and beckons me with his hands, then points behind him and gives me a taunting half smile. "Are you going to let him get away? After all this, you're not going to just fucking give up, are you? Run a little faster, and you might get him."

Sabin's being a goddamn asshole. I hope he falls over while standing up on the moving truck. I hold up my middle finger.

"Oh yeah? A *fuck-you*? Good to see there's a little fight there after all. You better go after what you want. What's *yours*. He's right there, Blythe. He's right fucking there! Go get him."

I hold up both middle fingers.

"Oooooh, my feisty girl is back! Maybe you'll run a little faster now." Even with the music at high volume, and Estelle and Eric singing and slamming their hands on the car to the beat, I can hear Sabin clear as a bell. So I know that Chris can hear him, too. "So what's it gonna be? Are you gonna fight? Are you gonna win?" Sabin is full-on screaming at me now. "One *fuck-you* for no, two for yes. Do you want him, Blythe? Do you want him enough? Do you fucking *love* him enough?"

I hate Sabin right now, but I am running harder and stronger than I ever have.

And I hold up two middle fingers. Of course I love Chris enough.

Sabin grins and winks.

My emotions are raw now, and against my will I look in the driver's mirror. Chris is watching, mouthing, *Come on, come on* . . . His face is serious, nervous almost, and his piercing eyes are glued to me. Soon I don't hear the music, I don't hear Sabin screaming at me or my feet slamming into the concrete. I hear nothing but air and see nothing but Christopher. He wants this for me. It's because of him that I have any capacity to power ahead in this run. I do want him, and I do love him. I would lay down my life for his, and what enrages me is that I fucking know he would do the same for me. If I can run fast enough, far enough . . . If I can run through the heartbreak . . .

Eric starts clapping, and I know that I've hit the distance. I slow to a walk, pulling my eyes from Chris's. I have to stop and put my hands on my knees. I can barely catch my breath. The truck stops and Sabin hops over the back. The music turns off, and all I hear is my struggle for air. "You did it, kiddo! That was awesome. Get in, and we'll drive you back."

My breathing slows enough that I can talk, but not enough to completely stifle the choke in my voice. I stand up and put my hands on my waist. It's a battle to get my words out. "You're a son of a bitch, Sabin. I love you, and I will always love you, but don't ever fucking do that to me again."

"Blythe . . ."

"I'm not kidding. I know what you were trying to do, but it's over for him. It will never be over for me, but it's over for him. I don't need the extra humiliation, I don't need him hearing all of that, and I don't need to fall apart again. So fuck you for pulling that shit." I drop my hands to my knees again. I feel like I'm going to throw up. "Fuck you."

Sabe steps in closer and puts his hand on my back. "I'm sorry."

I nod. "I know."

"It can't be over." He sounds as sad as I am.

"But it is."

Now Sabin's voice cracks. "Why . . . why didn't he choose you?"

I hear Zach's words in my head. I tell Sabin, "He wants to hide, and I can't take that from him."

I look up at Chris in the driver-side mirror for a minute. For a moment I think he's going to get out of the car, but he doesn't. I turn around and walk away.

I am miles from the dorm, but I'll walk it alone.

23

THE MOST HOLLOW VICTORY

SITTING IN AN UPSCALE MADISON RESTAURANT WITH Annie, James, and Sabin hardly seems real. But it is. Annie looks exactly the same, and I admire her as she sits across the dinner table from me. She's let her straight brown hair grow to midway down her back, and she compulsively tucks it behind one ear every few minutes, just as she always has. Her brown eyes are just as expressive as I remember, and she still has the ability to say a thousand words with one eyebrow arch. Seeing her is exactly what I need right now. To some degree, she will always remind me of the torturous aftermath of my parents' death, but I'm ready to move past that. She is full of smiles and exuberance, and we do not talk about my parents or the fire. We focus instead on the future, since that's all I want to think about right now.

Sabin has, of course, charmed the absolute shit out of her. While the biker jacket is still on, surprisingly he is wearing a button-down shirt and dress pants. It's an odd combination, but Sabin is a bit of an odd combination, so this suits him.

Annie refills her wineglass and holds up the bottle with a questioning look. "More?"

I shake my head. "No, I want to be clearheaded for graduation tomorrow."

"Then I'll toast to your magazine internship on my own. I'm so proud! It's much more exciting than my boring lawyer work, although at least I'm happier telecommuting. What will you be doing for the summer, Sabin?" Annie asks, turning to him. "You'll be a senior next year, right? Big year ahead."

"I'm going to stay here in Madison, and do some performances with a community theater. They've got a great summer lineup, and I'm preparing to dazzle the city's entire female population. So sorry you won't be here for that, Ms. Annie." He is an incorrigible flirt.

"I'm sorry, too." There goes the eyebrow. "And your brothers and sister? What are they doing?"

"Eric is staying in town, too, and working at a bank. Sounds noxiously boring to me, but he likes that sort of stuff. And he's going to blog for the theater company I'm with, so that'll be cool. Estelle will be smelling feet all summer at some super fancy shoe store and still working at the restaurant where she waitresses near campus."

"Hey, Sabe." I want to cut him off before he mentions Chris. "I've always wondered why she worked there. I mean, not to be weird, but it doesn't seem like she needs the money."

He smiles. "No, it's not for the money. It's because of Anya."

"The older lady who owns the place? With the bun?"

"Yeah." He smiles lightly. "Estelle's not much for seeking out an obvious mother substitute, but I think Anya's got that grandmother feel. It's something. We don't . . ." He waves his hand around. "We don't have grandparents. We don't have uncles and aunts and cousins. It's just us." He looks at Annie. "No, no, do not make that sad face, beautiful Annie! My personality more than compensates for our scant selection of relatives! Besides, we now have the hot cousin in the mix." He nods at me, and I laugh. "Tell me what your plans are. Lots of bikini wearing for you, I hope, Annie?"

Annie looks at me. "He's a good one, this guy, huh?"

"Beyond good," I assure her.

"I think we've got our summer plans down, and I believe they involve kicking things off with a Cape Cod trip."

"I think that sounds perfect. What do you think?" I turn to my brother.

Having James here is amazing, and we feel more like we used to than I could have hoped. I've learned that if I use time intelligently, it can actually do a lot to fix wounds. When I finally asked him to come to graduation, I wasn't sure what he would say. I hadn't exactly been overly warm toward him since Christmas, but he'd handled it well because he knew that I deserved his patience. As much as I can be, I am over his lying about his injury. There wasn't really anything specific we had to talk about. It just took time for me to let what came out of Christmas break settle. We can't change the past and the choices that we've made. Besides, I have an opportunity to have a real relationship with him, and I've decided that I don't want to miss it. What I do miss is the fun that we used to have together, so we're getting that back no matter what.

"I think *three* weeks on the Cape sounds even better than two, don't you?" James smiles broadly and nudges me.

"Yes, I do." I nudge him back.

James put his arm over my shoulder and pulls me in while we blink pleadingly at Annie. "It sounds fun, doesn't it? Three whole weeks to splash in the ocean, roll in the sand, fish off the boat?"

"You are still expected to find a job, you know, young man." Annie looks pointedly at James, but still smiles.

"I'm quite sure that three weeks of decompression would totally rejuvenate his desire to seek employment. Right, James?"

He nods seriously. "Absolutely."

Annie laughs. "You two fools are lucky that I've had so much wine, because I totally agree. Let's do it!" She fishes her phone from her purse. "I'm going to call my friend who's letting us use her house, but I think it'll be fine. She's going to be away for another few weeks anyway." She gets up from the table and touches James on the arm. "Walk with me outside. I can tell these two need a minute."

I have no idea what she's talking about, so I turn to Sabin. He is visibly teary. "Oh my God, Sabe. Don't. No crying, okay?" I put my hand over his giant hand and squeeze. "What is it?"

"It's . . . weird to watch you with James."

"What do you mean?"

"Well . . . the way he . . . put his arm over your shoulder just now. That's *my* thing with you." He shrugs.

I smile. "Well, my, my, Sabin Shepherd, are you jealous?"

"Fuck, yes, I am. But I'm happy for you. You have a family back now."

"You listen to me, all right? Listen," I say firmly. "You are my family. From the minute that you stole my coffee, you were my family. That's for always. I will always need you no matter how close James and I ever get. All four of you, you have changed my life."

"Shit, I'm going to miss you." He can't look at me, and that's probably for the best.

I give in and let my eyes fill. There is going to be a lot of crying this weekend. That's unavoidable. "This is going to be a hard good-bye," I say.

"Yes, it is." He takes my wineglass, fills it, and drinks half the glass. "But I know it's not your hardest."

"No, you're wrong. This one is different, but it's just as hard." I get up from my chair and take my favorite spot in his lap. I won't get to have his big arms around me anytime that I want after this. What I am losing is starting to seem like too much now, and I don't know how to deal with it. "You'll come visit me, you promised."

He hugs me and nods into my neck, and I bury my face into him. "Yeah, I will. And maybe you'll come out here, too? We could have a Thanksgiving do-over?"

"I can't come for a holiday. Not if—"

"I know. Not if Chris is here."

I relax into Sabin's comfort. I know that I'm going to need it in a minute. In the way that Chris was able to stabilize me in the past, Sabin is going to have to stabilize me now, because I'm about to ask him what I don't want to hear, but what I need to hear. "Chris is staying in town, isn't he?"

Sabin pauses and then nods again. "Yeah, sweetie."

"And there's more, isn't there?"

"There is."

I don't say anything for a minute. "They're sleeping together, aren't they?"

"Oh, I have no idea. But, Blythe . . ." He starts to say something else and then stops.

left drowning

"What are you talking about?" And then I know. The horrible understanding falls into place for me. He doesn't have to tell me because I know. I can feel it. "Oh God, Sabin, no." I shut my eyes and let the tears fall. I hold on tightly. It's worse than I thought. "Please tell me no. He can't do this."

"I'm so sorry. I'm so, so sorry. I didn't know how to tell you."

"When?"

"Not until next June."

Chris is getting married.

The phrase repeats in my head until it seems like I'm shouting it at myself. I feel numb. How is this possible? I thought he was just like me.

I thought the only marriage proposal he'd ever make would be a drunk one, on a rooftop, holding a wedge of lime.

I thought neither of us would ever chase after tradition for the sake of tradition.

I thought our being together would be a slow build.

I thought we would find our way into a love with no return.

I thought that we were an absolute.

I was horribly, horribly wrong.

Sabin rubs my back and lets my tears fall over his jacket. "Maybe you can stop him."

"No, I can't. Even if I could, I don't want to have to stop him."

I am numb as we wrap up the evening. By the time I'm back in my dorm room, I've decided that I want away from Matthews, away from Chris, and away from all the pain that's here. If I can just get through the next thirty-six hours, I'll be fine. I will. I can do this.

It's just fucking heartbreak, that's all.

Determined to avoid acting pitiful, I take my dirty clothes down to the laundry room in the dorm basement and load them into the machines. I sit on the hard counter and stare at the wash cycle. *Spin.* Yeah, I am definitely spinning. The room is empty except for me, and it's probably the quietest place on campus, since everyone else is out partying before graduation tomorrow. One in the morning is not a popular time to go stain-free apparently, but that's good because I don't want to see anyone. That's why I'm here. I couldn't give a shit about going home with dirty laundry, but sitting in my room with all its packed-up boxes is depressing. I already miss Neon Jesus.

Of all the people who I do not want to see, Chris tops the list. So when he walks into the laundry room, I immediately white-knuckle the edge of the countertop.

He sets his laundry on top of a washer. "Hey."

"Hey."

Chris leans against the machine. As much as I don't want to look at him, I can't help myself. Maybe it's only been a few months that we've been distant, but it seems an eternity since I've had the opportunity, forced or not, to see how painfully intoxicating he is. It perplexes me that he isn't hounded by women at every turn, because he's that intensely attractive to me. I don't notice anyone else. Even the resentment and bitterness at the forefront of my thinking cannot put a dent in how desirable he is to me in every way.

This is one of the last times that I'll see him, I realize. I won't get to see him brush his black hair away from those green eyes, I won't get to see how his shirts always cling so perfectly to his body, and I won't be on the receiving end of that half smile that infuses my world with so much.

We sit there for a long time; the background noise from the machines is the only thing protecting us at all from the paralyzing tension between us.

left drowning

Finally he breaks the silence. "I talked to Sabin." He blows the hair from his eyes. "He told you."

"I don't want to discuss it."

"Blythe . . ."

"No. No, shut up, Chris." I feel myself shift gears to a place where I cannot control my rage and my pain. "Just shut the fuck up. Did you think that I'd congratulate you? Yeah, I'm supposed to, I know that. How can I? Jesus, Christopher. What have you done? My, God, what have you done to us?"

"I was going to tell you myself, but—"

"But what?" I slide from the counter and continue to explode. "Who the *fuck* decides to get married after a few months? At our age? There is so much time left to decide . . . to make these kinds of promises later. Why now? Chris, why now? You didn't even want a girlfriend, much less a wife! And . . . and . . . and now you're engaged? Why didn't you just tell me that you didn't want me? That would have been fair. This? This shit is not fair. You know goddamn well how I feel about you, Christopher."

He doesn't take his eyes from me, and he lets me unleash all of my hurt.

"Does this all make me sick? Yes. Does the thought of you touching her the way you touched me fucking tear me apart? Yes. But, for the record, am I jealous? No. This is not jealousy. I don't want what you have with her. I would never want something like that with you. And fuck you, no, I'm not going to say her fucking name." I am crying freely now with no pretense that I can hold it together. "I want what we started to have. What we *could* have. I mean, am I crazy? Did I really make that all up?" I look at him and shake my head. I start to calm down because I recognize something in him. Something I saw during our last night at the hotel. "No. I didn't. I can see that . . . I know you, Chris, and I know that you felt what I did, didn't you?"

He doesn't say anything. He doesn't have to.

I'm right. He fell for me as I fell for him. It's a fucking hollow victory if ever there was one.

"But I can't hate you, because you saved me. Without you, I'd still be a walking zombie. Being with you let me . . ." I look around the room, trying to figure out a way to say what I want. Wading through words in my emotional state is nearly impossible. I have next to no idea if I'm making any sense, if I'm reaching him in any capacity, but I need to empty myself of this so that I can go on. "Being with you let me feel, feel *everything*, and I needed that. I remembered better with you, I healed better with you, and you made . . . you made everything real."

I stop. Now I really understand.

"And that's why you can't ever be with me, isn't it? I make everything too real for you. She doesn't do that. She lets you push away what you want to forget. She makes it safe in the way that you need it to be. You clearly need to trick yourself into . . . I don't know . . ." I am trying so hard not to go to pieces, but it's a losing battle. "You need to feel *normal*, whatever that means. Lying to yourself? It's like what James did. It will catch up with you. It will. I wish I could hate you, because that would be easier. But I can't, because now I understand that you have to do whatever you can to get through . . . through whatever happened. Even though I don't know exactly what that is."

He cuts me off. "That doesn't matter. That part of my life is over. I will *not* look back." Although his voice is firm, he is infuriatingly as calm as ever, while I am anything but.

"See? That's exactly what I mean. You *feel* with me, the same way that

left drowning

I do with you. I don't know why that is, but it's true. From the moment I saw you by the lake, you did something to me. You . . . moved me. And when you put your hands on me that day, you infiltrated every part of who I am, and we belonged to each other. Whether you want that or not. And when we were . . . when you and I were in bed, Chris . . . that last night . . . I could feel you, everything about you. That's what you don't want. I get how it feels like it's too much. I couldn't handle it then either, but I was willing to wait. We shouldn't have slept together. It was the worst thing we could have done. That's my fault, though. I take that responsibility."

Now he is upset. Now his eyes are red. But he doesn't break down the way I have because his protective walls are thick. "Don't you dare say we shouldn't have slept together, Blythe. Don't you dare."

I ignore him. "But if attaching yourself to her is what you need—if she's what you need—to be okay, then I would never try to take that from you."

He speaks softly, and each word stings to all hell. "She *is* what I need. We're compatible, and it's good for me. It's what I can handle."

"Compatible? Is that all you're looking for in life? You don't sound even like you're following your heart."

"Not every choice has to be governed by emotion."

I wipe my eyes. Chris takes a step toward me, but I put out my hands and stop him.

"No, don't touch me. I can't take it. Please. I just can't. I'm not going to see you again, I know that, but I can't say good-bye to you. How can I?" I am so consumed with sadness, I can barely see, and I let my words and my tears flow freely. "How can I possibly say good-bye to the person I am so hopelessly, deeply, and permanently in love with? Because

I love you, Chris. I do. I will always be in love with you, even though you'll never love me back. You have been my sanctuary this year. You saved me. Do you know that? You saved me. And I wish that you would let me save you." I don't want him to have the chance to say anything else. I can't bear any more of this. I walk to the door. "I really thought good things were coming for us, Chris. I believed. The irony here is that when you saved me, you made me strong enough so that I won't go back to the dark world I used to live in. Even though you just ripped out my heart. Chris. Oh God, Chris."

Despite whatever else has happened in my life, I have never felt this type of loss. I look at him for what feels like the last time. "You are the great love of my life that I'm never going to have."

left drowning

24

STRONG ENOUGH

IT'S GRADUATION DAY. THIS IS A HARD DAY
for so many reasons, but it is also a glorious one. I have started to
rebuild my life. I have Annie and James, I have an internship, and I
have a house to live in. I have a lot more than most people. Best of all,
I still have Sabin, Estelle, Eric, and Zach. It's going to be a horrible
transition to not have their near-constant presence in my daily life. I've
come to depend on them all so much, and I'll have to remind myself
that while I am losing them in some ways, I am holding on to them in
so many others.

The Chris situation is entirely different, and it will make staying in
touch with the others harder. I wish I could keep them separate from

him in my thoughts, but it's impossible. I'll just have to do my best.

During the ceremony, my eyes feel heavy. Sleep was more than elusive last night and I am exhausted, but I make sure to pay attention to every detail so that I don't forget anything. I listen to the speeches, to the music, and to the roar of the crowd. I talk to the graduates on either side of me, grateful that, thanks to alphabetical seating, Chris is nowhere in my sight. When it's my turn to cross the stage and take my diploma, I can hear my friends screaming and cheering for me. I turn and see Sabin standing on a chair and waving like crazy. As I'm walking down the aisle to return to my seat, a hand reaches out and touches my robe. My academic adviser, Tracey.

Impulsively, I throw my arms around her. "I did it."

"Yes, you did. I've been watching you. Three-point-eight GPA this semester? Not shabby at all. You look wonderful. Good for you, sweetheart. Now, go. Enjoy your day." She smiles broadly and pushes me back into the crowd.

I barely look when Christopher graduates, realizing this is it. Our time is up. We won't have a good-bye, because that would be intolerable.

I watch in awe when the air above me fills with graduation caps, representations of our collective accomplishment that soar over us. It might have happened late in the game, but I have to admit, it's great feeling part of something larger. Being able to fit into a world outside of myself is more rewarding than I could have dreamed. While I don't know what I'm going to do with my life exactly, where I might be in five or ten years, I am better positioned to figure that out than I was at the start of senior year. The depression that swallowed me back then is nearly incomprehensible now. I won't go back there no matter what. My life has taken a drastic turn in the right direction.

left drowning

The downfall of shaking depression, though, is that I feel the let-downs harder.

Later that evening, I have dinner with Annie and James, and Annie gives me a top-of-the-line laptop as a graduation present. I insist that it's way too much, but she in turn insists that she has no children of her own so the least I can do is let her spoil me when she wants to. I agree to the emotional spoiling, but the financial is less easy, although I am very grateful for the new computer. James shyly gives me a pair of earrings. He's concerned that I won't like them because, since he and his girlfriend are no longer together, he had to pick them out on his own. I adore them. The three of us are going to be a good team, I know that, but I'll miss the Shepherd crowd. The inevitable distance between us has already arrived.

Returning to my dorm room for the evening is brutal. Nearly everything of mine is gone from the room except for my suitcases and futon. Chris is going to help Estelle move my bed into storage after I'm gone tomorrow morning, and she'll have it for the fall semester of her junior year. Sabin has his license back, and he's going to drive me to the airport, where I'll meet Annie and James. I can't think of anyone better to send me off than my first friend here.

Just as I'm getting flooded with loneliness, the door flies open and Estelle, Eric, and Zach barrel in.

"You're here!" Estelle says happily. "I was afraid Sabin had you off partying your last night away."

"Nope. Low-key tonight. I don't need a hangover for the flight."

"You ready?" Eric asks.

I shake my head. "No. I don't know . . . Maybe. "

We are all looking at one another, knowing this will be the last time we'll be together like this. Yes, we'll see one another again, but it won't be the same. Things are going to change. They already have. I hate good-byes, I really do. I've never had to deal with them in this way, and there are no right words that I can think of to tell them how much they mean to me.

"Let's not draw this out," I finally say. "This is going to suck, so let's get it over with."

"Short and sweet?" Zach offers.

"Yes," I say. "Make it quick."

Zach steps in and hugs me. "I know how much you're hurting. You're tough, though, and it's going to be all right." He kisses me on the cheek and then goes to leave. "I'll be outside."

"Bye, Zach." I wave. I won't allow more tears.

Estelle reaches into her giant purse that is barely containing the mess of stuff she is carrying around. She hands me a wrapped present. "This is from us. *All* of us."

"Oh, you guys didn't have to get me anything."

"You just graduated from college. Of course we did. This is a big day, and we're proud of you." Eric sighs. "We love you so much."

I unwrap the box and have to bite my cheek so that I don't burst into tears.

"This . . . this was our mother's," Eric says shakily. "She wore this necklace all the time. She had a letter charm for each of our names. C, S, E, and E. And we got you a B. You're one of us. No matter what."

Estelle groans. "He means no matter what kind of stupid asshole Chris is."

"Estelle!" Eric snaps.

"It's true and you know it. Someone has to say it out loud. Blythe, we think he's making a huge fucking mistake." She takes the silver necklace with the small charms from my hand and turns me around. "It should be you. We won't say that to him, and we will be as decent as possible about it, but none of us are the least bit happy."

I lift my hair while she does the clasp. Although I don't want any of them thinking badly of Chris or disapproving of his choices, I can't help but feel flattered. She turns me around again. "There. It looks perfect on you." She looks at my expression and clamps a hand over my mouth. "Stop it. Don't say thank you to us. This is us thanking *you*. I'm going to take my hand away, and you're not going to say it, agreed?"

I nod and she drops her hand.

Eric clears his throat. "I'm . . . I'm gonna go after Zach. He's leaving tomorrow, too, so . . ."

"I understand," I say.

Another good-bye. Another hug. "Love you."

"Love you, too," I tell him.

He holds me for a long time and then leaves before either of us loses it. He doesn't have to say anything else to me.

Estelle is next. My roommate and my tough-as-shit friend.

She takes a deep breath. "Okay. I'm going out for the night, as I'm sure you guessed."

I smile.

"I know that you know. So thank you for not blabbing to my brothers. They'd freak. I appreciate your discretion."

"You'd do the same for me."

"Blythe, listen. This mess with Chris? It sucks. It really sucks." She reaches out and touches my necklace for a moment. "Our mother would have loved you. I don't even remember that much about her. Just bits and pieces, but I remember how it felt to be around her, you know? And I'm sure that she would be goddamn ape-shit crazy for you. Just like we all are."

I can't talk, so Estelle continues.

"All of us, Blythe. I hate everybody, and even I'm fucking nuts about you. You're a cool shit. Chris is so out of his mind that he can't see what's right in front of him. He's going to regret this. He's going to fucking regret it because you're going to go off and find someone else, someone smarter than Chris. And I'll try to be happy for you when you do, even though I don't want you with anyone else besides my stupid, blind, stubborn brother."

"Oh, Estelle . . ." I know what she's trying to do, but I don't have that kind of hope right now. "There won't be anyone else."

"Don't say that, Blythe. Don't sit around waiting for him. That's not fair to you."

I know she's right, but it's too soon for me to even consider love after Chris. I'm still in too deep.

"I'm not a hugger, but I'm going to hug you anyway." She smiles at me, but she looks like she's fighting as hard as I am not to cry.

"Okay, I'm ready. Bring it." I force a smile back and hold out my arms.

She squeezes me hard. "I'm going to miss the fucking fuck out of you."

I laugh. "And I'm going to miss the fucking fuck out of you, too."

"And I'll video chat the holy shit out of you all the time."

"And I'll love it. Just no vibrators on-screen, okay?"

"God, you really are a bitch after all." She gives me one last squeeze and blows me a kiss as she leaves.

left drowning

For one brief moment, she drops the hard edge. It not what she says, but the tone in her voice and softness in her face. She looks like a little kid, and that hurts to all hell. "I know that I'll never have another mom, and I know that you're way too young for me to look at that way, but . . ." She taps her stiletto heel. "There's something about you. I will never for a second forget that I had the best fucking roommate anyone could ever ask for."

~~~~~~~

At one fifteen in the morning, he shows up at my door. I know it's him just by the rhythm of his knock. I'm too tired to care that I'm in a ragged shirt and underwear, and I stumble through the dark.

I open the door and step aside, but Chris stays where he is, hands in his pockets and his eyes to the ground. He's not here for a good reason, that much I can feel.

"Are you looking for Estelle? She's not here."

He just shakes his head.

"Chris?" Something is wrong. Any animosity I have dissipates immediately. I take him by the arm and lead him through the dark. "What is it?"

He sits next to me on the bed, silent. I give him time because I can tell this is hard for him. Chris doesn't seem like himself, and he's worrying me. I take his hand. "Tell me."

"My father had a heart attack. It was bad."

"Oh God, Chris."

He lies down as though he doesn't have the strength to sit any longer, and I move with him, keeping his hand in mine. He immediately rolls into me, silently asking me to hold him. And I do.

"Are you okay?" I ask.

"No." He whispers and presses his cheek into my chest. "I'm not okay because he's not dead."

It takes me a second to understand what he has just said to me. The tragedy of it. I have no idea how to respond to this.

"Why didn't he die? Why didn't he die?" Chris grabs on to my arms so that I hold him closer. "Why wasn't I strong enough?"

"Strong enough for what?"

"Why wasn't I strong enough to kill him myself?"

"Oh, Chris . . ." What in God's name has Chris suffered through? I can feel him crying in my arms. How in the hell can I protect him from this? There is no way.

"I wasn't strong enough to kill him, and I'm not strong enough to be with you."

I shut my eyes, and for the next hour I keep him in whatever safety my embrace can provide.

We don't move, we don't talk.

We just cry. And breathe.

Later he pulls away slightly and looks at me through the dark. "I'm sorry about last night."

"Don't be." I stroke my thumbs under his eyes and wipe away tears. "I said a lot of things that I shouldn't have."

"I'm not strong enough to be with you. I love you, sweet girl. Of *course* I love you. So much. But I still can't do this. You were right. What you said about me."

"It's okay. I understand."

Chris moves and leans his chest over mine. It's hard not to cry when he kisses me, because we are kissing for the last time. So I drown in him, wanting to commit his taste and his feel to memory so that I will always

left drowning

have that. His tongue moves slowly, his lips delicately covering mine as we take in every detail of each other. Our hands stay clasped together, never parting.

He only says one thing to me as we kiss our way through the night. "You said something last night that was completely wrong. Sleeping together was not a mistake. Blythe. I could never touch anyone the way that I touch you. And I will never regret falling in love with you. Don't forget that."

And this is how we say good-bye.

25

BEGIN AGAIN

ESTELLE MAKES GOOD ON HER PROMISE TO VIDEO-chat the shit out of me, and Sabin calls even more often. It's a good thing, because it's been a long, quiet year since I left Matthews, in which I've somehow managed to play successfully at being a grown-up. In the fall, I got a job—at the same magazine where I did my summer internship. I live in my parents' house and keep up the yard and the bills. I haven't become an incredibly fast runner, but I keep at it, unflagging. I even adopted a dog from the local animal-rescue shelter that I named Jonah, and with whom I am totally in love. One look at the dog, and there was no choice. He is a fucking German shepherd, for Christ's sake. I couldn't go home alone.

It's May now, and unseasonably warm, and when Jonah and I come in from our Saturday-afternoon run, we're both thirsty as hell. As I'm downing my water, the phone rings. It's my old pal Nichole, who has turned out to be a great friend since I arrived back in Boston. Although she never stops trying to get me to go out and meet guys.

"You sure you don't want to come out with us tonight after dinner? I'm meeting up with Stephanie and Abbi. Remember you met them last fall?"

I half smile at her persistence. "You're sweet, but you know how I am."

My friend sighs. "Oh, Blythe."

"What?"

"You still miss him."

"Nichole, we've been over this."

"Honey." She sounds like a seasoned advice-giving pro. "He's getting married in a few weeks."

I touch my fingertips to the necklace with all of our initials and sit down at the dining-room table, holding the phone. "I know."

"You're still not showing up?"

"I wasn't invited. It's a family-only ceremony. Somewhere in Newburyport, I hear."

"I know you weren't invited, but you could still show up." She claps her hands. "To break up the wedding!"

"Absolutely not," I say again.

"Newburyport is only an hour away. A nice drive north . . ."

Her singsong voice is not swaying me in the least. "No. I'm not going for any reason."

"Why the hell is he getting married in your territory? There should be some kind of rule about him not crossing into Massachusetts."

"I guess the girl he's marrying used to spend family vacations in northeast Massachusetts and loves the coast or whatever."

"I think it's shitty."

"Join the club. Anyway, it doesn't matter. James is coming home soon, and he and I are leaving for Maine the day before the wedding. Being in another state seems like a good idea."

"So you're not even going to see the rest of his siblings? I know how much you miss those guys."

Now it's my turn to sigh, because I do miss them. Terribly. Sabin came to visit me twice this year. I celebrated my twenty-third birthday with his bear hugs and one too many cocktails. We manage to have a friendship that allows us not to talk about Chris, for which I am grateful. Our relationship can survive on its own. I've always known that intellectually, but it's been good to see it in practice. This is true with Eric and Estelle, also, and I owe Estelle a video call tonight, actually.

"No, I won't see them this trip. I don't really want to be around them right after the wedding. It'd be too weird. Trying not to talk about everything."

"So you know where and when the ceremony is?"

"Yeah, Sabin let it slip. He's driving me crazy. I wanted to know as little as possible, but he's been trying to bait me the way you are. So stop saying words like *ceremony* and *wedding*."

"Chris wants you to stop the wedding, Blythe. He's making sure you know about it."

"No. He got engaged, he's been with her all year, he could've ended things anytime he wanted to. He has to make his own decisions. This is not going to play out with me busting up the wedding, and Chris and I getting a happily-ever-after."

"Maybe when the wedding is over . . . Maybe that will help you move on."

I nod. "Maybe. I don't know. Nichole, I know you think that I'm crazy. I might be. I should be over him by now, but I'm not. It's not a choice. I can't help it. It's not like I'm pining away or crying all the time. I'm not *waiting* for him."

"I know you're not. But I wish you'd dated someone else this year. Anyone else! But I get it. I think I'm jealous of that kind of love. It's what people dream about."

I groan. "Yes, it's incredibly fulfilling."

She snorts. "That's not what I mean. The ability to feel so deeply for someone. That says something about you."

"Yes, that I'm a moron."

"Noooooo. It says that you listen to your heart."

"My heart is a stupid asshole." Nichole laughs and then says she has to get off the phone to meet her friends for cocktails. I really am happy to stay at home instead.

I have plenty to think about and plan for with James coming home so soon. He and I are debating whether or not to sell the Massachusetts house. It's too big for me to live in alone all year, but we are both attached to it, of course.

One decision we *have* made is to go up to the house that my parents bought in Bar Harbor, Maine. The house we have not been to since they purchased it five years ago. In lieu of James getting a job this summer, I've agreed to let him head up the repair work that invariably will need to be done on the house. The construction job he found last summer seemed to inspire him, and he's been studying architecture at school. He seems truly excited to fix up the place. As for me, I think three months by the ocean with my brother is going to be good. For some people, the plan might seem like a strange choice for a girl in her early twenties, but I don't seem to want what most people my age do.

Anyway, there's plenty to do in Bar Harbor. It's an idyllic small town on Mt. Desert Island, which is technically not an actual island, since it's connected to the mainland by a thin strip of land. It's home to Acadia National Park, and James and I are planning on doing plenty of hiking and exploring with Jonah. The two of us are in a significantly stronger place in our relationship, but this summer together will solidify the progress we've made.

After I take a long, hot shower, I have a glass of wine. By the time I get around to video-calling Estelle, I'm well into my second glass, which at this point is a lot for me.

I curl up on the couch with my glass and laugh when Estelle answers my call with a jovial "Blythe! Blythe! Blythe!" and an excessively wiggly dance that she performs in her dorm room. She was smart enough to snag herself a single this year. I'm not sure anyone else could put up with her the way I did. Or love her as I did and still do.

"How are you, crazy?" I raise my glass to her. "Happy Saturday!"

"And a happy Saturday to you! School is out in a few days. I cannot wait!" I suspect that Estelle has been drinking already, too, given the volume at which she is speaking.

"Tell me everything." I sit back and let her fill me in on how she is wrapping up the year. I know that she and the professor stopped seeing each other last fall, and she seems to have been bouncing from guy to guy since then. I have yet to hear about the same guy more than once, but I'm holding out hope. Eric and Zach are still together, and they're planning on spending the summer together in Madison, and Sabin will be doing local theater stuff again.

left drowning

"Oh, and did I tell you about Sabin?" Estelle leans into the camera until I can practically see up her nose.

I laugh. "No, what?"

"Do you remember that Chrystle girl from last year?"

"Sure. He hooked up with her again?"

She holds up two fingers. "Her and her roommate, Maryse. Together." She collapses into giggles.

"Oh God, gross! Estelle! I don't want to hear those details! Yuck. I can't think about Sabin like that!"

"Roommates, of all things! How cliché! You didn't see us hooking up with a guy together, right? I mean, I wouldn't be able to look at you the next day. Not that you're not super crazy hot and all that, but . . . And there's the fact that you've hooked up with my brother, which would up the creep factor." She claps her hand over her mouth. "Oh shit. I'm sorry."

"Estelle, it's fine. Stop."

"Fucking hell, Blythe. I shouldn't have brought him up. I'm a tactless bitch."

"Just touch your hand to Neon Jesus, and all will be forgiven."

"Hold on!" Estelle bounces up, and I hear her shoes clack on the floor as she walks to the painting that hangs behind her. She reaches up and pats Neon Jesus on his head. "I'm sorry! Did you hear me? I'm sorry!" Her cropped shirt lifts as she reaches up. I know the camera image is not perfect, but I swear I see a bruise that wraps over her hip bone. I forget it about as soon as Estelle's face comes careening back into the screen because she startles the shit out of me, and I almost spill my wine. "N. J. says I'm forgiven."

I wave a hand. "There's not really anything to be forgiven for."

"Hey, B.?"

"Yeah?"

"You all right?"

I nod. It takes me a second to ask what I do. "What about Chris? Is he okay? He's . . . he's still happy, right?"

"I don't know how to answer that. He's fine, I guess. He acts fine, but I think he's different. He's . . . I don't know. He's a little boring, to be honest."

"What? Chris is not boring, that's ridiculous."

"He is. We all think he's a little dull now." There's a knock at her door. "I gotta go, love."

"Okay. Have fun. Hey, 'Stelle?"

"Yeah."

"Call me when it's over. Not until then. We'll just have to avoid talking about it. Tell Sabin and Eric. Please. It'll be easier after."

"Understood. Be brave." She kisses her fingers and blows me a kiss. "Miss you, you fucker."

"Miss you, too, you fucker."

I shut the screen. The next time I talk to her, Chris will be married. Maybe then I will really believe that it's over between us.

I am the queen of wishful thinking.

left drowning

REGROUP

"DID YOU REMEMBER THE BUG SPRAY?"

"I think they sell bug spray in Maine," I tell my brother. "Besides, I have packed everything that I can think of. The car is full. If we forgot anything, we'll buy it in Ellsworth. Relax." I reach into the backseat of the SUV and pat Jonah. This dog is the reason that I bought such a big vehicle, but without it, we might not have had room to cram the car with all of our summer supplies. Jonah pants excitedly at me. "I know. James is going to drive us crazy."

"How about liquor? Do they sell that there?" James takes the familiar route to 95N. We'll take this highway through Massachusetts and then all the way north to Bar Harbor, Maine.

"Very funny."

"Seriously, my dear sister, what's with all the travel-size liquor bottles?"

"So what? I had an impulse purchase at the liquor store. You're driving, I thought I'd have a drink." I pour the mini gin into my half-emptied bottle of lukewarm tonic water and take a straw from my purse.

"Yeah, or ten, from the looks of it."

"We have to drive right past Newburyport. I could use a little liquid courage."

He pats my shoulder. "Fair enough." James does not know the whole story, but he knows enough to understand that I do not want to drive through the town where Chris is getting married. And on the *day* that he is getting married. "Look, Blythe, I'm sorry that I got food poisoning and was sick all day yesterday. I know you wanted to leave then, but I can assure you that I would not have been a good travel companion. I'm sorry."

"I know, I know. It's not your fault. I just want to get out of Massachusetts as quickly as possible."

"This really sucks. I'm sorry."

I turn up the radio. "Just don't get pulled over."

"I don't plan to."

"What I'm doing is illegal and stupid. So don't ever drink in a car."

"I don't plan to."

"And you shouldn't be driving with a passenger who is drinking."

"I know that!"

"I'm just sayin'."

I sink into my seat and suck on the straw. It'll be an hour before we hit the scene of the crime, so to speak, and I might just be good and drunk by then.

"James?" I take another sip.

left drowning

"Yup?"

I slide on my sunglasses and look out the window. I have dealt with a lot of shit head-on over this past year, and I'm not going to apologize for needing to run now. Getting away from home, hiding out in Maine for the summer . . . I deserve this. As for getting drunk on the day of Chris's wedding? It is what it is.

"James, I'm going to get really shit-faced, okay?"

"Have at it. I'm here."

I love James. I mean, I really, really love him. And I *like* him. He's letting me lean on him now, and it helps me feel less alone in my grief over this fucking Christopher Shepherd situation. If I can make it through stupid Newburyport without having some sort of psychiatric episode, then this summer will be really awesome.

My parents would be proud that we are off to Bar Harbor together. I shake open the map of Mt. Desert Island and look at the red circle where our house is. Neither of us remembers too much about it because we only walked though it for a few minutes five years ago. It appears that our house overlooks Frenchman Bay, which I think sounds rather elegant.

James lets me play the music I want as the empty bottles start to accumulate. Every song that I choose is one of my Chris songs, and I can feel that I am drunkenly spiraling into an abyss of heartache. Heartache and anger. *I mean, married? Fucking married?* What a stupid, absolutely stupid and irresponsible thing to do. I get that Chris needed to establish a safe, easy relationship, one that wasn't going to challenge him or bring his past to the surface. His father must have done a fucking number on him, on all of them, and on Chris especially. But Chris is smart, in control, and capable of so much more than a superficial relationship. He deserves better, whether that is with me or not.

I wish I knew more about his father, but it's a topic that has clear boundaries. I have never spoken to Sabin or the others about it beyond a few sentences here and there. The work that they've done to move on, to build successful lives, is commendable, and dredging up memories they want to forget is not my place. Chris has made it clear to me that he's okay, that he has left that part of his life in the past. The Shepherds are a dynamic, loyal, vivacious family. They all know how to love. I see that in how they love one another and how they love me. So why wasn't Chris able to give me more?

I suck down the last of my drink as an early sign for the Newburyport exit flashes before me. It's only a quarter mile away, and we're hurtling toward it.

"Take the exit! Take the exit!" I yell.

"Blythe. That's not a good idea."

"Yes!" I slap the dashboard. "Do it."

"Yeah, that sounds smart. This is going to go really, really well."

"Hey! I may be loaded, but I can still understand sarcasm. I'm not kidding. Take me to this fucking ceremony by the sea so I can tell Chris . . . just, lots of things. I'll think of them."

"Oh God. Here we go." James veers the car to the right, cutting off a van, and we soar off the highway. A quick search on my phone pulls up the location where the ceremony is taking place. I roll down the window and sense that we're in beach territory now. The air smells different, the greenery is different. Everything is different, and everything hurts.

I am not exactly slurring, but I'm close. "Take a right here. And then go straight to the end of the road. The piece-of-crap mansion is going to be there."

"I wish no one had told you the location or date. Or anything about this."

"Yeah? Well, me, too, but they're all big blabbermouths."

We drive past an SUV that is parked at the start of the pebbled road that leads to the large and elegant yellow home. The scene of the crime, as far as I'm concerned. It's quiet here today, with only a few cars pulled up out front. James pulls over halfway to the house but keeps the car running. I'm sure he's hoping that my impending diatribe will be short. "I really don't think you should go in. This is close enough," he says.

"I'm not going to vandalize the place. Jeez." Although the idea of egging it is not a bad one. If I had eggs. I stare at the house. Fine, I admit, it's beautiful. So to compensate I holler, "Look at that stupid wrap-around porch with a view of the ocean. And the stupid floral garlands hanging there. Honestly! The place is wretched!" I check my watch. Thirty minutes until the wedding. "I bet everyone is gonna stand out-side there." I point to a grassy area that overlooks the water. "Chris must hate all this clichéd crap. Absolutely loathe it! There will probably be some schmaltzy harp music, and poetry readings, and a grand ol' speech from her father about eternal love and taking care of his daughter. I will never have harps and poetry and fathers. I will never have eternal love because it's all bullshit. I don't get to have that."

"You shouldn't be here. Seeing this," James says. "Don't do this to yourself." He squints. "What's up with this place, though? You said the wedding was supposed to be small, but how come there are no other cars in the lot?"

"Don't know, don't care. What's important is that I'm gonna move on to rum now," I announce as I mix up rum and fruit punch in a thermos. "How disgusting does that sound, huh? Rum. I hate rum. Nobody should like rum. The only time rum should be consumed is at a tropical resort. And then you have to have those asshole little umbrellas and mini plastic swords that hold fucking fruit chunks. Wait. Do we have any swords?"

"I can't say for sure, but I'd be surprised if we did."

"I swear to God that we have swords." I open the car door. "James, we do! I bought some at the supermarket because I thought it'd be funny to make drinks together and sit outside at the house. I mean, we're going to have a lot of work to do there, right? So we'll need beverages. And swords can double as appetizer holder-y things because food always tastes better on a stick." Holding my thermos, I stumble to the back of the SUV and lift open the hatch. "Seriously. Swords for all!" I start rooting through bags. I know that I packed a bunch of grocery stuff in a blue duffel. My search yields the bag, and I begin to root through it wildly.

James stops the ignition, comes out of the car, and starts repacking everything that I've removed.

"AHA! I HAVE LOCATED THE SWORDS!" I scream triumphantly. I hold up the ziplock bag of multicolored drink accessories.

James laughs. "Feel better?"

"I feel zillions better. Now I can drink some rum. And prepare my disruptive speech. Should I start with how the bride is boring and useless, or how I think *he's* an idiot and a pussy?"

"Wow. Both, you know, really good options. Let's think for a minute."

As I am in the process of struggling to open the bag, which in my opinion, is intricately sealed in a mind-boggling way, I hear loud whooping and cheering from behind me. I turn around and watch as a small group of people runs in our direction at top speed.

"James?"

left drowning

"Yeah?" He is standing with his hands on his hips, looking at what I'm looking at.

"Am I a little drunk, or are there some people running?"

"You are definitely a little drunk. And there are people running. Or maybe skipping?"

I lift up my sunglasses. "Fancy runners. Maybe I should wear a tuxedo when I go running. Then maybe I'll run fast like they do."

"Yes, probably." He sighs. "Hey, wait a minute. Isn't that . . . Sabin?"

"Oh. No, that person is running too fast to be Sabin. Sabin's belly is too big."

But as they get closer, I see that, in fact, Sabin is leading Eric, Zach, Chris, and Estelle in a high-speed race. Even in her long, fitted purple dress and heels, Estelle keeps up with them. "Thank God!" she is hollering over and over.

I lean against the open trunk and drop some swords into my thermos while I watch dumbfounded as they run past us. I am clearly hammered out of my mind.

I look at James. "What the fuck is happening?"

He shakes his head.

I hear a "Holy shit!" and a moment later Sabin is standing in front of me. He is sweating in his suit, even with his tie off and draped around his neck and the top buttons of his shirt undone. There is more hollering, and then Estelle, Zach, Eric, and finally Chris are lined up behind the car. I blink a few times.

I lean in and whisper in James's ear. "I think you need to take me to the emergency room because I am hallucinating."

"Blythe!" Sabin bear-hugs me, and I spill rum punch down his back.

"Would you like a mini plastic sword?" I ask.

"I would! I would!" He lifts me up, and I am eye level with Chris.

Chris is handsome beyond words. Flushed cheeks, bright eyes, and a smile that nearly makes me weep. When Sabin finally puts me down, I shuffle backward until I am sitting on the bumper in front of the luggage. I get hugs from the group, except from Chris, who stays awkwardly where he is. I hear James introducing himself to everyone but Sabin, who he's already met a few times. I am too busy trying to get my eyes to transmit information properly to my brain to deal with normal social graces.

"What are you doing here?" Estelle asks, her eyes shining with excitement. "I can't believe this!"

I start giggling and can't stop. James is rolling his eyes and finally answers for me. "We're heading up to our parents' vacation house for the summer. We made a . . . pit stop. Um, to say congratulations."

"Noooooo." I sneer at my brother. "That is entirely inaccurate." I point at Chris. "I totally did not want to come to your horrible wedding, but I felt an obligation to tell you what an ass you are, and that you should definitely, definitely not be getting married. Under any circumstances. But now you look so cute and everything in your suit, and that makes me feel awful." I assess the others. "Actually, all of you look cute. But Chris looks the cutest. You, my friend, look like a fucking god in that tuxedo."

Chris smiles at me. "Are you drunk?"

"Yes, I'm fucking drunk," I snarl at him. "Why wouldn't I be drunk? Everyone gets drunk at a wedding. Especially your wedding. So screw this. Go off and get married. Have fun. I hope the appetizers give you food poisoning."

Sabin laughs and takes the thermos from my hand. "Now things are really getting fun."

"We can toast to you just graduating. Oh. Happy graduation! Yay!"

left drowning

I then lean forward with a wobble. "Watch out. There are mini plastic swords floating in there."

He takes a swig. "They add a nice flavor."

"I know, right? I think it's the green ones that do that. Green swords have superpowers."

James clears his throat. "I'm sorry. I tried to tell her this wasn't a good idea."

"That's correct!" I shout. "He did. He did do that." I hiccup violently. "But now I recognize that it's stupendously tasteless and tacky to break up a wedding." I turn to my brother. "James. Psst! James. I'm feeling very embarrassed. I'd like to depart this venue."

"We're going to get on the road," he tells the group. "So very sorry about this. Really."

"There was no wedding," Eric says quickly. "It's not going to happen."

"What?" This information does, in fact, reach my brain.

"She never showed up. In fact, Chris almost didn't show up! She called him and they talked and decided not to get married." Eric is doing a shitty job hiding his happiness.

"She said that she knows he doesn't love her. And she's been banging Jim Lancaster for the past six months." Estelle can hardly talk fast enough to get the words out. "Supposedly she was holding out on sex until she was married, but obviously that wasn't exactly the case, and she's been fucking this guy's brains out."

"Estelle!" Chris clamps a hand to his forehead.

"Well, it's true. Good thing you weren't fucking her, or she might've thought you actually loved her."

"Seriously? The details are not necessary." Chris is quite clearly mortified.

"Wait a minute. What? I like details. The details are fascinating." I start laughing again. The alcohol is really doing a number on me. "You haven't . . . I mean, all year . . . Like, *nothing* between you and her?"

"Tell her the rest," Estelle says smugly.

Chris looks embarrassed. "Not now, okay?"

We are interrupted by barking from the car. "Ohmigod. Jonah!"

"You have a dog?" Zach asks.

"I do indeed have a dog. And he's awwwwwesome. You have to meet him." I shuffle to the side door and let him out. Jonah jumps up and licks my face and then bounds over to meet the new people. Sabin is immediately taken with Jonah and kneels down to pet him.

"So, you're going up to the house? The one you've never been to?" Sabe asks us.

"Yes, we are. We are going to fix it up. Okay, fine, James is going to fix it up, and I am going to serve cocktails with swords."

"When you sober up, I'm sure you'll help me." James has the tolerance of a saint today.

"Maybe. Or maybe I will just stab you with mini swords and make you work faster."

Sabin stands up and looks at James. "Sounds like it could be a lot to take on." He pauses and flashes his best Sabin grin. "Want some help?"

I look at Sabin and realize he might be serious. He's crazy like that. James doesn't know him well enough to realize that this proposal he's making has legs.

"You feel bad for me," James says, with a good-natured smile. Then he gestures at me. "You've noticed that my future assistant seems unreliable."

"I'm not joking," says Sabin. "I'm totally serious." He gives each of his siblings a long, slow, searching look. "Let's all go!"

left drowning

"Sabin, you can't just invite us up to their house," Chris protests. "Stop being crazy."

"Of course I can. We're family. Right, Blythe?"

"Yes!" Estelle claps her hands. "Let's do it! Summer with the McGuires!"

"Estelle!" Chris glares at her.

"You're serious!" A big smile spreads across James's face. "Sure, why not? Come up for the summer. All of you. It'll be a blast!" James is barreling ahead with plans that I am too dizzy to keep up with.

"What are you doing? They probably have shit to do, James," I point out with a definite slur. "You know, like normal people. Jobs and whatnot. Plans!" I wave my arms around chaotically.

"Well, Sabin did get dumped by the theater," Estelle announces. "So he's free."

Chris frowns. "What do you mean, he got dumped? Sabin?"

"Oh, those assholes. I showed up late for a couple things, and they wigged out."

"Were you planning on telling me about this?" Chris is not happy.

"Maybe, maybe not." Sabin twirls around ridiculously. "Depends on how much of a prick you're going to be about it. Let's focus on the positive here. Now we've got a summer vacation with our best girl and her debonair brother!"

"This is impulsive and intrusive, and we're not doing it." Chris puts his hands in his pockets.

"It's not like you have anything to do," Estelle says rather snidely. "What's-her-face is going to move her shit out of your apartment by herself, and you don't have a job anyway. You were just going to be honeymooning and then looking for a job after. C'mon. We've got the goddamn money, let's be honest. I want to have some fucking fun!"

I notice that she and James have made undeniable eye contact. Great. This could be interesting, if my brother can keep up with her.

Everyone stares at Chris while he fidgets. "You guys, they don't want us crashing—"

"Chris." I look at him. There is no question. Especially in my drunken state, there is no possibility that I could refuse this opportunity to regroup with the people I care most about. Bullshit between me and Chris aside, this is right. "Get in the car."

He steps closer and takes me by the arm, walking me away from the group. I trip over the gravel on the driveway a few times, but at least I don't totally wipeout.

"What's the problem?" I ask, slurring just a little bit. "I heard you've been a little boring lately. Why not try something unexpected? This could be fun."

"Let's just think for a minute, okay? Try to sober up for one minute. This is nuts."

"So what? We're all a little nuts."

"You and I haven't talked in a year. Not since that night."

"I know. I loved that night. And I hated that night."

Chris meets my eyes. "I know." He holds the hair back from his face and sighs. "What are you really doing here, Blythe?"

"The better question is, what are *you* doing here?"

He smiles at me. "Fair enough. I was here about to make a huge mistake."

"Tell me why it was a mistake."

He looks away, taking his time before he speaks. "Because I'm not in love with her. I told her that today when we talked. She . . . she doesn't have hold of my heart."

Neither of us says anything.

Alcohol makes this easier. "I didn't want you to get married. At all. I really didn't, Chris."

We step in to each other, and I lean against his chest while he holds me delicately. Oh God, he feels so good. I am reeling to feel him so close.

"Were you going to break up the wedding?" he asks with a hint of amusement.

"Maybe." Now I'm embarrassed. "Maybe not. I don't know."

"I missed you, Blythe. Jesus, I missed the hell out of you." He tightens his hold on me. "I don't want to be away from you, not again, but this summer vacation idea is ridiculous. We can't just all blow off life and congregate for the summer. Who does that?"

"We do. You said it once. 'What's a little risk now and then?'"

"You remember everything, don't you?"

"I do."

He strokes my back while he thinks, and while I silently will him not to let go.

Finally, after what seems like forever, he shouts to the group. "Okay, people!" I wait, wondering what his final decision will be. He pulls me tighter and yells, "Let's do it!"

"Hot damn!" screams Sabin, who whoops and runs straight to us. He grabs Chris by the face, and plants a slurpy kiss on his brother's cheek. "Not getting married is the smartest thing you ever did. But you have to ride next to the smelly drunk girl. Shotgun!"

Things move surprisingly fast once the decision is made. James and I trail the Shepherd siblings back to their hotel, and within minutes they're back outside, dragging down their suitcases. Of course, Estelle's is impressively large. Clearly I'm still drunk, but as we pull out of the hotel parking lot, I feel dizzy, and not just from the drinks. It has only taken twenty minutes for the entire course of my summer to change dramatically. Not just mine, either—every one of us is taking this leap together.

I'm happy that Sabin and Chris decided to pile into the car with me and James. Sabin is up front, and I am in the middle seat in the back, with Jonah's front half on my legs and Chris on the other side of me. Eric has good company with Estelle and Zach in the other car. He's trailing us, driving the big Volvo SUV that was Estelle's birthday present this year, after Chris apparently freaked out and decided her sedan wasn't safe enough to drive in the Wisconsin snowstorms.

As naturally as breathing, Chris puts his arm over my shoulders. I slump into him and rest my hand in his lap. He folds our hands together and kisses the top of my head. I close my eyes. The alcohol is probably making this reunion seem falsely normal. Maybe I am too foggy to realize how weird this is. I recognize that we have careened into very new territory, obviously, yet being with him is what I have wanted more than anything, so it feels somehow right. At the moment, I don't care what this is or what it might become. Above everything else, I have my friends back.

Sabin still has possession of my thermos, and I hear him rattling through my bag of little bottles. "Where are we going, by the way? I don't even know where this house of yours is."

James changes the radio station. "Bar Harbor. It's about five hours from here."

I feel Chris tense. "We're going to Maine?"

"It's okay, Chris." Sabin's voice is reassuring. "We're going to be far north. Don't stress."

I rub my face against Chris's chest. "Why?"

He rubs his thumb over the top of my hand. After Sabin turns up the radio, and he and James are engaged in conversation, Chris tips his head down to mine. "We lived in Maine for a while. I wasn't planning on going back again."

Hearing this makes me realize how many details of our lives Chris and I have never shared with each other. There are huge gaps in the basic information I know about him. In retrospect, there are reasons for these gaps. "I'm sorry. I didn't know."

"The fire was in Maine?" he confirms.

"Yes."

"For some reason, I always assumed you'd been vacationing with your parents in Massachusetts. The Cape, I imagined. This is the first time that you'll be there since? And you can deal with it?"

"Yes. I can do this. It's going to be easier now." I hold his hand tighter. "How could I not know you're from Maine?"

"We did live all over, and we were only there for about four years. Nowhere near Bar Harbor, though." He reaches the hand from my shoulder to scratch Jonah's ears. "Good dog, huh?"

"He is."

"A sweet boy for my sweet girl."

I close my eyes again and rest against Chris. I absolutely adore him. "I'm kinda drunk, and I have to go to sleep, but first I have to tell you a secret."

I feel him laugh lightly. "Okay, go."

"You can't tell anybody."

"I promise."

"I tried to run a marathon this year. Actually two."

"Yeah? That's amazing."

"I said *tried*. I can't do it. I can do a half marathon, but not a whole fucking one. I tried one outside of Boston last October and one in Virginia in March. I wanted to qualify for the Boston Marathon. That's the one I want, and I can't get it. I suck."

"You don't suck. I think you're amazing for even trying."

"I can't do the speed, I can't do the distance. I'm not cut out to be a runner. I make myself get out there anyway, but I'm no good."

Chris smoothes back my hair. "You're more than good."

"Don't tell anyone. It's embarrassing."

"I won't tell."

"And another thing. I'm glad you didn't get married. Even though part of me understood, I am mad at you, and I think you're a dick, but I'm still glad that there was no wedding. But I'm sorry if you're upset and if today was supposed to be a good thing for you."

"I'm relieved."

"If I weren't so boozed to the nines, I'd think of something smarter to say." I inhale deeply. "I missed you. I should be embarrassed to tell you that, but I don't care. I missed you so much, Chris."

"I missed you, too, Blythe. Get some sleep."

I touch my fingers to the necklace of silver letters that rests against the top of my chest. "This is all sorts of fucked up."

"I know, baby. I know. But the best kind of fucked up."

left drowning

FROM ANY DISTANCE

"WHAT DO YOU MEAN, THERE ISN'T A STARBUCKS in Ellsworth?" I feel like I might cry. I have a headache, and I am completely weirded out that we're arriving by caravan into Bar Harbor. I rub my eyes and yawn.

Ellsworth is the last substantial town before Mt. Desert Island, where Bar Harbor reigns as one of Maine's most coveted vacation spots. The town has plenty of shops with everything we might need, but the prices are outrageous. That's why we stop and load up on groceries and general house supplies in Ellsworth. I'm sure we look like a weird motley crew with everyone except James and me in formal wear.

As we drive out of Ellsworth with the shopping done, I realize that I'm a little nervous about what state the house is going to be in. Last week, I'd ordered sheets, towels, pots and pans, general kitchen supplies, and all that boring but essential stuff, and had them shipped to the house. The caretaker was kind enough to make sure everything arrived. As for actual furnishings, they came with the house, and I just hope that nothing is moth-infested and gross.

"If I don't get a coffee soon, there is a good chance that I'll die."

"They had coffee brewed at the market," James points out.

"Not that shit! Real coffee." I am battling a hangover. Or I may still be tipsy.

Sabin reaches back and pats my knee. "A coffee you will have."

"A strong one, right?"

"The strongest. I got you a bag of Colombian roast at the store, and Chris found a French press at the other place. According to the map, we'll be at the house in twenty-five minutes. Chris? You're in charge of coffee distribution when we get there."

"Absolutely."

"I think we're going to have to make a second trip back to Ellsworth later today or tomorrow," I say, feeling my nerves go on even higher alert. There is so much to do. "The house is probably a dump after all this time."

"Hey, B., relax. We're here to help." I have missed how Sabin takes care of me. "You have nothing to worry about. It's a big deal to go to this house. We get that. For real. And we're honored that you let us crash the party. We'll make as many car trips back and forth as you want until you have everything that you need for the house."

"Of course we will," Chris adds. "Anything you guys need."

I feel better. It *is* a big deal to see the house again. "James? You all right?"

"I am. I want to be here. And we've got backup now." He high-fives Sabin. I like how these two have buddied up.

I agree. We have the best backup possible.

left drowning

I bounce my foot nonstop as we get closer, and Jonah pants out the window while I stroke his fur obsessively. Ellsworth's chain stores have disappeared, and greenery takes over as we climb a hill. As Sabin relays directions to James, I am surprised to feel a smile overtake me. From the road that leads to the house—our house—I catch glimpses of the dark blue ocean through the trees. We are close. I don't know if I'm remembering or if I just feel it. James takes us down a hill, closer to the water, then takes a sharp right, and we go down a long driveway that lands us by a substantial lawn. I look to the right at our house.

It's beat up. It needs a serious paint job. White chips are practically flaking off in the wind. The lawn has been mowed, but the overgrowth around the back of the house is going to be a big project. The deck off the front needs major work.

To me, however, the house is spectacularly beautiful.

I let Jonah out and follow as he leads the way. I am in a daze, and it's not from the leftover alcohol that is surely still running through my system.

I remember. I run ahead a bit. Leafy tree branches hang over the land in front of the house, but I know that to the left is a wooden staircase that leads to another grassy area, and past that is the rocky bit of shore that is ours. Chris catches up to me.

"You okay?"

I nod. The concern in his voice is unnecessary. "I remember this, Chris. I haven't until now. The days before and after the fire? I told you I don't remember them. All this? The house? It was blank. We'd been up here just a few days before . . . But I'm starting to remember this house at least. Wait. The living room. It has cathedral ceilings and a fireplace with a stone hearth. Tons of big windows. And there is a staircase there to the second floor." My memories are spilling out. "Next to it is the dining room with sliding glass doors to a porch. The kitchen is huge. I mean, huge. Like maybe this place used to be a . . . a bed and breakfast or something. My mother said . . . She said something about having friends up to visit when we were here. How we could have as many people as we wanted with all the room. Upstairs is a long hallway lined with bedrooms. I don't know how many. I can't remember that. And down by the water? A long skinny dock that leads to a square platform dock. It had a small boat tied to it. A kayak . . . " I shake my head. "No, no, a canoe, maybe. I'm not sure."

"That's all right." Chris is smiling at me, and he gestures to the house. "Well, go find out."

I call for Jonah and he immediately returns to me, his tail thumping against my legs. I hear the others behind us, and then James is next to me. "Holy shit, Blythe," he says. He is as stunned as I am. "The house is so big." He takes my hand. "I didn't remember it being this big."

"Me neither."

"Go inside," Eric prods. "Check it all out."

I turn to James, and he gives me a look that tells me he agrees with what I'm about to say.

"We're all going in together."

Sabin's hand is on my shoulder. "Don't you think you two should do this alone?"

"No. This is for all of us."

~~~~~

It takes that entire first month for me to feel like the house is in acceptable shape. The furnishings that came with it are outdated, but they fit the feel of a summer vacation home. I can't imagine this old house filled with a bunch of sleek modern shit from Crate and Barrel. It is supposed to have the mismatched chairs and a lumpy sofa. The dining room has a

left drowning

long wooden farmer's table with exactly enough room for all of us to sit comfortably on the benches, worn soft over time. I'm grateful I thought ahead to order so much online, because the kitchen is filled with essentials and we have all-new sheets and towels.

There are six modestly sized bedrooms upstairs. Eric and Zach are in one room, and the rest of us in our own rooms. Although I suspect that Estelle and James are sharing on occasion. I'm pretending that their overt flirtation is nothing more than innocent fun, but the floor in the upstairs hallway creaks loudly, and I hear doors open and close at odd hours. The rooms all have sturdy-enough platform beds, and I've replaced a few of the more saggy mattresses with thicker versions made of memory foam. So far I have not actually heard beds squeaking, and I am grateful. We salvaged a number of old quilts, although it took a few rounds through the washing machine for me to feel as though they were hygienic enough to sleep under. General dusting, vacuuming, scouring, and polishing have made a world of difference. The house feels warm and alive. James has started ripping up linoleum on one of the bathrooms and tiling it himself, and I'm very impressed with what he knows how to do.

While James and Estelle may be room hopping, Chris and I have stayed in separate rooms. We are affectionate, regularly touching each other in passing, even snuggling on the couch by the fire at the end of the day. We started a routine where he reads aloud to me from old paperbacks at night, and there is something incredibly intimate about it. Yet we haven't even kissed. We are coupled up, that is clear, but we haven't acted on it. Chris hasn't actually tried to get things going, but that's because I haven't let him. I know how he moves, how he sounds, how he breathes when he's about to move in. I haven't let it happen because . . . well, because he was supposed to get married less than a month ago. Because

I'm scared. But I let him hold me in his arms, I let him stroke my hair, and I let him watch me. And he watches me all the time. I love the feel of his eyes on me, the way he takes me in, and the way the hint of a smile crosses his face when he knows that I've caught him.

Of course, I watch him, too. He, and James, and Sabin have been painting the outside of the house, and watching Chris shirtless on the ladder while he works on my house is undeniably hot. I'm glad he doesn't hide his scar from anyone. James did give me a questioning look, but I just shook my head. Sometimes I take a break from what I'm doing and sit on the lawn under the guise of supervising. I used to yell out, "You missed a spot!" every few minutes just to piss them off, but after all three of them tackled me with dripping paintbrushes last week, I stopped. I'm still washing paint from my hair.

I notice one thing in particular about the painting process: how Chris subtly discourages Sabin from working on a ladder. He frequently redirects Sabin to the lower windows, to the porch, and to the siding that he can reach from the ground. He has the same unspoken concern that I do. Sabin is drinking too much. We all drink, yes, and I'm no exception, but Sabin is consistently drinking during the day. I know that he's just staying around the house, and we've got a fun party atmosphere going on, but his drinking has a different edge to it. He's been in a great mood, though, so it's not like it's causing trouble. Yet.

It's an unusually warm Saturday almost four weeks from the day we arrived when I take my first swim alone. We usually go down to the ocean as a group, but for some reason, after my early evening run on this particular day, I want time alone.

The water is absolutely frigid when I jump in, and I'll be lucky to finish more than just a few laps, but the shock of the cold and subsequent rush of adrenaline is amazing. I'm a competent swimmer, and I

left drowning

stay fairly close to the shore, but when I look up, I notice that Chris is watching me. He never gets in the water, and I wish I knew why. But he always wears his suit anyway and keeps one eye on me at all times. I get the feeling he's standing guard over me, making sure that I am safe.

It's around seven, I'm guessing, and the light is beautiful, with the sun just thinking about descending for the night. I keep swimming, and every time I lift my head from the water to breathe, I see Chris's figure on the shore. I would know him from any distance. I swim the crawl in long, slow strokes.

I would know him from any distance. I'm confused as to why this phrase recurs to me obsessively as I finish my quick laps. I'm convinced that I'm missing something in this thought, but I don't know what.

I lift myself onto the end of the dock, emerging from the water chilled to the core but energized all the same. I take my towel and wrap it around me, taking in the scene on the lawn ahead of me. Sabin is fiddling with perfecting the outdoor lights as Jonah sits poised by his side. Estelle and Zach are having some sort of wild dance-off on top of the picnic table; James pulls himself away from staring entranced at my former roommate to throw another log into the fire pit. Zach and James spent an afternoon last week making it, and now we have a great spot to hang out after dark. Chris is standing on the rocky shore, a few yards from the start of the long dock. I start the walk over the weathered wood.

"Good night for a fire," I say. The music blaring from the outdoor speakers and the group's noise make me have to raise my voice.

Chris doesn't answer me, although he follows me with his eyes as I approach him.

"Chris?"

He is staring intensely at me. "Yeah."

"You all right?"

"Yes, I'm fine. It's just that you look cold."

"I am. I'm going to take a hot shower." I gesture behind me. The outdoor shower is probably my favorite thing here. Before coming here, I'd never showered outside, but there's nothing like it. It took three rounds of scrubbing the wood walls with bleach and then going over them with a coat of sealer to make the shower feel truly clean, but now the roomy enclosure is heaven.

I start to walk ahead, but then turn back. "Hey, Chris? I need to ask you something."

"Anything."

"Are you worried about Sabin at all?"

"What do you mean?"

"He's . . . he's been drinking a lot."

"Yeah." Chris sighs. "I know."

"So are you concerned?"

He shrugs. "I think he's just a little lonely. You know, for female companionship. He loves it here, obviously, but it's not the college scene that he's used to. He wants to go out tonight and pick up a tourist."

"Okay. If that's all you think it is."

He takes a step into me. "Don't frown. I don't like to see you unhappy." He touches my face for a second.

Without warning, the energy and the sexual tension between us erupt and eclipse the background noise.

"I missed you," he says. "I don't know how to tell you how much."

It's not just what he says, but the way he looks. I take his hand, and walk him to the shower. He steps in behind me and shuts the door. Immediately, his hands touch the top of mine, and the back of his fingers glide up my arms, making me shiver.

"Still cold?" he whispers.

left drowning

I turn around and shake my head. We lift his sweatshirt over his head so that he is in his swimsuit, too. I put my hand on his chest and push him to the bench that runs against one side of the shower. "Sit," I tell him.

The music and laughter from the others fill the air, and we laugh when Sabin yells, "What do you mean, we're out of graham crackers? How are we supposed to make s'mores?"

I turn on the faucet and stand under the hot water while Chris watches me. Moving slowly, I take my time, wanting him to be sure. There is no way we can take this step and not have it mean something. Plus, I don't mind teasing him because fair is fair. I've spent the past month enduring his running around the property in shorts and nothing else. He's even more toned and strong now than he was in college. All the hikes that we've done on Cadillac Mountain combined with the laboring on the house have cut more lines into his body. Just because I haven't thrown myself at him doesn't mean that I haven't noticed. I rest my foot next to him and cover my leg with shaving cream. I shave more slowly than necessary, and Chris doesn't look away for even a fraction of a second. When he slides his palm up my leg, I let him get as far as midthigh before I remove his hand and step back under the water. "You're killing me," he says.

"Good." I wash my hair, arching my back and lifting my ass in his direction. When I inch a soapy hand under the top of my suit, he practically growls.

Chris reaches for me. "Come here, beautiful. I can't keep my hands off you any longer." I allow him to pull me in, and I straddle him, sitting up so that I can look at the person who I have ached over for all these months. Getting to feel his body underneath me again is electrifying. I run my fingers through his hair, and he does the same as I let my head fall back. He caresses my back and arms, moving to my waist, up the front of my suit and over my breasts. I move my hips slightly against him, feeling him get hard, while my fingers graze over his chest. For a while, we do nothing but touch each other like this, gently and slowly, starting to explore each other again.

"Chris?"

"Yeah, baby?" He places a finger on my face and traces it over my jaw, down my neck, distracting me from what I want to ask.

"You really haven't . . . since us? With anyone else? With her?"

He smiles softly. "No."

"Why? From what I've heard, you used to"—I smile flirtatiously—"get around enough." I touch my fingers teasingly to his lips, and he sucks on them. The shock that tears through me at the feel of his mouth makes me inhale sharply. "You seem to like sex enough."

"I certainly do like sex enough. And . . . yeah, I guess that I used to be more like Sabin, but I was glad to have an excuse not to." He brings his mouth close to mine. "Because after you? After you it was different."

"So," I whisper, "it's been a long time."

"You're really going to drive this point home, aren't you?" He tickles my waist and I squirm.

"Yes. I like that you haven't been with anyone else. I think it's weird, and I'm massively surprised, but I like it." He doesn't say anything, so I answer his unasked question. "I haven't either."

Chris pulls me in. "Oh God, I was hoping you'd say that. I've missed the hell out of you. The thought of you with someone else . . . It's been excruciating. I know that's not fair because of . . . well, for so many reasons. But to think someone else might have his hands on you, touching you, turning you on. Fuck, it drove me crazy."

And then he kisses me. I hadn't forgotten how it feels to kiss him,

left drowning

but I am still thrown into a whirlwind of lust and love when his tongue enters my mouth. Within seconds I am grinding against him. The kissing—God, the kissing alone—could make me come.

We don't stop for air until the change in music reminds me that we are really not alone here.

"We should stop." I close my eyes as his hand slips under my bathing suit and covers my breast. "Chris, everyone is here." But now I'm starting to grind into him.

"I know that." Chris moves his hand between my legs, and I clamp down on his shoulders, already desperate. "But you don't think you're getting out of this shower until I make you come, do you?"

I groan as he gets under my suit and presses his thumb against me. With the way he works his touch so perfectly in response to my body, it's no wonder I could never want anyone but him giving me this. The pressure he uses is precise, and in only seconds I am intensely heated. It has been way too long since I've had this kind of physical release, and I know I don't have the ability or the desire to delay this. My orgasm swells fast, overwhelmingly fast, and I start to pant in his ear as I rock against his hand, his hard cock underneath me enhancing my longing for him.

"Shhhh. Quiet, love," he reminds me, and I do what I can to control my noise. Chris moves continually against my clit, and when he feels my body at its height, his own breathing changes. "That's what I want. Yes, come for me, Blythe," he whispers. "Fuck, yeah. Come . . ."

The wave of pleasure crashes into me, and I can't win against the sound that erupts from deep within me. Chris covers my mouth with his and drinks in the near scream that I release. The way he cradles me while I come is incomparable. He's sweet and protective. I can still entrust my body to him. Whether the same goes for my heart is a question that will have to be answered with time.

Before I've started to recover, I am already breathlessly asking him what I'm scared to. "What are we doing? What are you doing?"

"Loving you," he says simply. "If you'll let me."

"Always. God, always."

He lifts me up and walks us through the water spray until my back is flat against the wall. I can't pull together any coherent thoughts. All I can do is try and take in what is happening between us. His tongue and lips race hungrily over my skin while his fingers start to slip off the straps of my suit. Just as I cover his cock with my hand, Sabin's booming voice yells out, "Where in the goddamn hell are Blythe and Chris?"

Chris drops his head to my shoulder and laughs, and I cringe at the sound of heels clicking against the walkway. Estelle wears her heels even on the rough terrain around here. She bangs on the door and yells, "They're fucking in the shower! Thank you, Lord!" Then her heels continue down the walkway while a collective round of applause echoes into the now-dark sky.

"Congratulations! But hurry it up, kids! Dinner is almost ready! And we're hitting the bars after this!"

"Leave them alone!" Zach shouts crankily. "At least somebody's fucking."

Chris lifts up. "We're not fucking!" he hollers. Then he looks at me and winks before he adds loudly, "Not yet!"

"Well, I've been getting laid! I've been getting laid!" Estelle announces this news with an all-too-cheery tone.

I rest my head against the wall. "Oh no. Oh no."

Chris laughs. "It's not that bad. I think they could be good together."

left drowning

"Your sister and my brother? That is . . . creepy and gross."

"It's harmless. A summer fling."

"Is that what—"

"No," he stops me quickly. "That's not what this is."

I relax a bit as he rubs my shoulders. "We should probably, you know, dry off."

"Yes. For now. Besides, I don't want this first time to be as rushed as our last first time." He kisses me softly. "We're going to have slow, meticulous, exhaustive, fantastic lovemaking."

I smile. "And hot and dirty?"

"That's my girl."

I turn off the shower. "You and I have spent a lot of time together in water," I say.

"We have." Chris retrieves the towels that are hanging over the top of the wall and hands one to me.

"It's funny." I think for a bit as I dry off my hair. "You almost never walk out on the dock and you never go in the ocean. You did the first day I met you, though. Remember? You waded into the lake. But you hardly even get your feet wet now."

"You're right. I don't."

"And . . . ?"

He hesitates. "I have a love-hate relationship with water."

He has just voiced something that I've thought about myself many times. I take his towel and wrap it around his neck. He looks sad now.

"When you're ready, you can tell me about that."

He nods.

"Whatever you want to tell me, it's going to be okay. You're not going to scare me off. I promise you."

"You say that now." He rubs a hand over his eyes. "You say that now."

"I'll say that forever." I hug him tightly. For the first time in a year and a half, I slide my left arm to the place on his back, the place where we fit so incomprehensibly perfectly. "I know what it's like when we're together. I don't know why that is, but even here it's happening. It's because you were with me that I remembered this house before we went inside."

"Blythe, I think that's a little far-fetched, don't you?"

"Christopher, listen to me." I put my hands on either side of his head so that he can't turn away. I want him to really hear this. "When we are together, the world gets sharper, the past becomes unobstructed, and . . . the floodgates open. You can't pretend that didn't happen to me; you saw me reconstruct the fire from memories that I didn't know I had. It'll happen to you, too. You'll reconstruct your own fire."

"Now *you* listen to *me*. The *future* is sharper and unobstructed. That's how the floodgates are opening."

"Either way, I won't leave. We ran away from each other before. Mostly, you ran. I'm ready for this now. Are you?"

"To move ahead with you? Yes." He swipes his tongue over my mouth and whispers in my ear. "To take you to bed forever? Yes. To make you come in my mouth, to feel you writhe under me while I slide my cock inside you? Yes. To listen to you scream and beg me to stop because I can't get enough of you? Absolutely. Am I ready to focus on giving you levels of pleasure that you've never even dreamed about? Yeah. I'm ready."

I laugh. "That's not what I meant."

"I know what you meant." He holds me against him. "I'm here."

left drowning

28

REACHING

I ONLY HAVE ON A T-SHIRT, NO UNDERWEAR, but Chris is fully dressed. We're in my bed, and I'm sitting between his legs with my back resting against his chest and my legs draped over his. The room is dark, but the television is on because some movie that Chris is obsessed with just started. We've been sitting this way for the last half hour since we got into bed not long after dinner. There's just enough light from the flickering screen for me to watch his hand. He's lightly moving his palm over my thigh, up and down, his hand just next to but never touching between my legs. He's already been doing this to me for a while. Too long. And with the way we're sitting, I can't get my hand on his cock. Which I want more than anything.

For the past month we've been screwing our brains out. And making love. And then screwing our brains out again. I'm concerned that I've become some kind of deranged sex addict. The good news is that we seem to be able to leave the bedroom long enough to scrounge for survival items, like food. And lube and condoms. There was the one time that Chris made Sabin go to the store and throw the box up to us through the window, but mostly we've done our own errands. We've given up trying to be quiet, although we sometimes replace our noise with loud music. Our other housemates seem to have developed a high tolerance for our noise level. The downside is that I'm not in much of a position to complain about the noise that Estelle and James make at night. And admittedly, they are sort of cute together. It's funny to see my brother fussing over a girl the way he tends to Estelle, and it's even funnier to see her let him, but they genuinely seem to care about each other. As for me, I am so completely in love that it feels like nothing else matters.

I turn my head a little to the side and feel Chris softly kiss the top of my head while his hand keeps teasing me with his soft strokes. Then he finally puts his hand between my legs, and I shudder. All he has to do is touch me once like this and my mind starts swimming. I picture us hot and fucking hard. . . . I think about how his cock feels as he drives into me over and over. . . . I want that heated moment just before he comes, when I'm grabbing onto him and we're both gasping and moaning. It's like I have a reel of porn of the two of us that plays over in my head. Flashes of what we've done. What else we might do.

Because he's so good—so perfect—he makes me greedy and impatient. Maybe if he fucked me a few hundred more times it might be easier for me to stay in the slower moments. But even then . . .

But right now my endgame involves sweat, and cum, and plenty of

left drowning

noise, and I want to get there. I curl my hips up to push against his hand, but he pulls away a bit. Chris leans his head down and whispers to me slowly, "Don't move yet."

I drop my hips back down and try to relax into him. But then he puts his hand back where I want it, cupping my pussy and staying there. He says something that I don't understand . . . and I realize that he's talking about the movie. I don't even remember the name of this film that he loves so much, but clearly he wants to watch it until it's over. Which will take another hour, at least. *Great.* I decide that I better slow myself down, because he is going to make me wait for this interminable hour to pass before he gives me what I want.

But I can wait, I can calm down. I think.

I put my hand in his free one and squeeze tightly. He squeezes back. Finally he touches one finger to my clit, just for a second, and then takes it away. He does this again. And then again. I try to distract myself so I don't scream by counting every time he touches me. He can't do this forever, right? I get to twenty and give up, letting him do what he's going to do. Then finally he starts to stroke where I want ever so slowly and gently, and I love this. It's simultaneously hot and soothing, and he lulls me into a place where I'm not so rushed. Where I just want to stay like this.

He uses his whole hand, brushing against me again and again. His fingers touch everywhere lightly, never staying in one spot for more than a moment. And because he's obviously trying to drive me insane, he every once in a while laughs at the movie we're watching. He asks me something about the plot, and I realize I have no response because I can't pay attention to anything except how he makes me feel.

Finally, unable to stop myself, I lean to the side and turn my mouth up to his and kiss him. God, he's just a delicious kisser. I can't get over it. I feel his tongue against mine while we kiss, teasing, and soft, and endless. Then he moves his mouth away and leans back as he takes my nipples between his fingers.

Now he's done it. Just when he had me in a slow rhythm, my heart rate is back up, and I desperately need him. This drives me crazy, having him play with me like this, rolling my nipples between his fingers, pinching me, pulling . . .

"You have to fuck me, Chris."

"Not until you're dripping wet," he whispers back.

"I am, I promise you."

"I'll check."

He takes a hand out from under my shirt and moves it between my legs. My breathing gets ragged as his finger moves inside me and then pulls back to glide across my clit.

"I told you I was wet," I say.

So far his hands have moved slowly tonight, as though every goddamn touch has been calculated to keep me below that line where my orgasm starts building, that frustration level just before I'll scream. So when he takes his finger from me and pushes it deep inside me, I can't help but groan and push back against him. He pulls out and then slides two fingers in. I dig my hands into his legs as I arch my back.

"Don't move yet, Blythe. I'm not done checking."

Now he's just fucking with me.

He presses his hand tightly against me and flexes his fingers back and forth a few times, getting me hotter and even more impatient. But then he takes away his hand and moves back up to my breast. "You're definitely wet," he tells me. "But you're not as wet as I want you."

left drowning

I groan again. He's got to be kidding me. I can feel how wet his fingers are as he rubs them across my nipple.

"Besides, the movie's not over yet." I can tell he's trying not to laugh.

God, I hate him sometimes. He's a control freak who gets off on exactly when and how I come, but giving to me is what arouses him. I'm still teaching him that his pleasure is just as important to me. It's harder for him to surrender to me the way that I do to him. He's learning, but for now, I'm going to let him play this game.

I'm whimpering, and I check the clock. Fuck. It's ten forty. Surely this favorite movie of his won't end until eleven. I can do this for another twenty minutes, right? I can take it. Except that his grip on my breasts and my nipples is tighter, a little more urgent. He knows how to give me the mix of pleasure and slight pain that I love, and I can feel him breathing harder in my ear because he loves what he's doing to me. Chris shifts his hips, and I feel his cock against my body. I close my eyes. I swear to God that I could probably come like this.

One hand goes back where I want it. He starts working my clit between two fingers, and every few seconds he pinches me lightly, tugs a little. I look down. I want to see him do this. I want to watch how he can make me so deliriously turned on.

"You have the best fucking pussy," Chris says. "You know that? You do. And I promise I'm going to make you come so hard."

This he doesn't need to tell me, because I know he will. He always does.

"You're starting to get there, aren't you?"

"Yes." God, the sound of his voice is making me squirm, but at least he's letting me move now.

"You can't think about anything else now, can you?"

I shake my head. "No."

"You can't think about anything else but how it will feel when I make you come."

"Chris, please . . ."

"How you'll tense up, how your whole body will shake, how you'll say my name. How you'll beg me to do it again. You can't stop thinking about it, can you?"

"No."

"You just need a little more, baby, don't you?"

I nod.

"A little faster, a little harder?" He knows damn well this is what I need, but he likes keeping me on this edge.

"Chris, you have to fuck me." I'm panting now. "You have to fuck me."

"You think you're wet enough for me now?"

I laugh a little. "Check."

He takes away his hands so that he can move out from under me. I lean back, holding myself up on my arms so that I can watch him again. I want his clothes off. I want his body against mine. I want to feel him, and hear him, and taste him.

But he kneels next to me and spreads my legs open. Now his fingers disappear inside me again. "You're almost where I want you."

I drop onto my back and put my hands in my hair. God, he's driving me fucking crazy. His fingers are still inside me and he leans in over his hand, holding his mouth just above me, letting his breath blow over me and making me shudder.

"Chris . . . Yeah . . . God, Chris . . . Please."

left drowning

He licks my clit. Once. "You do have the best pussy," he tells me again. I can't hear that enough. And then he waits a moment. I squeeze around his fingers, reminding him what I can do to his cock. He leans in closer and puts his lips around me, sucking me gently. I put a hand on the back of his head. I feel his tongue start to press against me, and I pull him in tighter. He starts to move his fingers just a little faster . . . In and out, back and forth. When he rubs his teeth against my clit, I groan loudly.

That's it. I'm getting him naked now, even if it means he has to stop touching me for a minute. I reach over and grab at his shirt and get him to lift up. I stay on the bed, my legs spread, and watch hungrily as he yanks his shirt over his head and undoes his pants.

He may love my pussy, but I love his cock just as much. "I promise you, I'm dripping wet now," I tell him.

He crawls between my legs and shoves his hands under my ass. "Not that I don't trust you, but . . ." He pushes his tongue inside, tasting me, smelling me, breathing me in.

I push my feet hard into the bed. "Jesus Christ . . ."

Then he raises up his body, moving his chest against mine, and kisses me. I can taste myself on his tongue, and I feel his cock brush over me. "Wet enough for you?" I ask.

He pushes up onto his arms and smiles. "You're drenched."

"So you have to fuck me now." I sound pathetic. I know that. But I can't help the whimpering tone in my voice.

"Yes," he says. "I'm gonna fuck you now."

He lifts off me and kneels, sitting back on his knees, watching me as he presses his cock up against my pussy. The seconds it takes him to put on a condom feel like hours. But then he rubs his cock over me and slowly starts to ease in. He pulls back just a bit and then moves in a little more.

"Chris . . . Chris . . ." Looking up at him while he kneels between my legs is unbelievable.

Chris looks at me and winks as he licks his fingers and presses them to my clit. It's a hot fucking move, and he knows it. I smile at him. He fucks me a little bit faster. Not hard, not deep, but faster. I need that friction, that speed. He's got me figured out, and he knows how to make me come.

I'm starting to tense up. . . . I'm getting close. . . . God, I'm so close. . . .

I can't stop saying his name.

I love how he looks when I'm like this. How it makes him so fucking hot to get me off. It's exactly how I feel before he comes.

He is so hard, and his breathing is picking up. "I want you to come, Blythe. I want you to come. Baby, tell me when you're ready." His voice is husky, and raw, and full of need.

He keeps fucking me like this and rubbing his hand against me until my breathing gets labored and I push his hands away. Because as much as I enjoy this touch, right now I don't need it. I just need that perfect cock of his. "I'm almost there. . . ." Talking is nearly impossible.

He drops down, holding himself up, and drives into me, deeply. He fucks me faster now, just barely pulling out but grinding into me hard. He's rubbing against me every time he moves, but that's not what's getting me to the brink. It's how his cock is moving, how he's lifting inside me.

I can barely breathe or think, but I say two words to him. "Don't. Come."

left drowning

"I won't," he promises. I tighten around him, and he knows by the way I sound that I'm just about there. "Yeah, Blythe, come for me," he's saying, talking me through it.

"Come for me. . . . Your pussy is so fucking hot. . . . I feel how wet you are, how tight you are. . . . Let me hear you."

I take his shoulders and dig my nails in. He listens to me groan as my orgasm starts.

I'm grabbing him so hard that I can't believe I'm not drawing blood. My whole body spasms, I feel myself detonate around his cock over and over as pleasure flows through me. Fuck, he is so good. I cry out again and again with each wave. When I start to slow down, I murmur through my panting, "Don't stop. Go slow, but don't stop . . . Please."

I'm still coming, and I pull him in closer. Chris put his hands underneath my body, holding me, cradling me. Every few seconds, I shake again. He rubs into me hard, making sure I come until I can't anymore. Until I'm totally spent.

I wrap my legs around his waist and lift into him. And now he's the one saying my name over and over. Hearing me come like that has gotten him close. Closer than I want.

"No," I tell him. "Don't you dare come yet. I need you to keep fucking me."

I've learned that sometimes this is what I want after I come—I want to get fucked long and hard. While I am crazy about the times we have gentle, tender lovemaking, I'm equally aroused by the grittier, dirtier side of sex. Fortunately, so is Chris, and likely even more so than I am.

Maybe it's not fair to ask him to wait, especially after what he just did for me. But it *is* his fault for being so indescribably good and for making me want as much as I do from him.

"Blythe, I don't think I can wait." He's still grinding into me.

"Yes, you can."

I love this part: the power exchange.

Sometimes he's in charge, sometimes I'm in charge. We've started to share this power more equally, trading it back and forth, often over and over in one night. And then there are times when there is no power game, when we do everything together, we feel everything together, we come together. I'm going to need that again. Later tonight.

But for now, I need him to do what I want.

I push him up hard and he stops moving.

"Think about whatever you want. Painting the house. Doing the dishes after Zach made that gnarly batch of chili." I smile. "I don't care what you have to do. Think about whatever you have to, but don't stop fucking me. I need you, Chris."

Chris shuts his eyes for a minute. I love watching him focus like this. I can feel the shift in his body, the ability to control himself reappearing. He pulls out farther now and fucks me like I want. Slow and steady and deep. I look down and watch his cock thrust smoothly in and out, slamming into me over and over. I'm even wetter now after coming, and this can't be making things any easier for him. But somehow he is able to last for me.

I can still feel the end of my orgasm, how sensitive I am, how I throb each time Chris enters me. I pull him in faster. Rougher. I love when he holds himself up on his hands, angles his body against me. I tuck in my knees. "Harder," I tell him. "Harder." He gives me what I want. He's completely immersed in me now, I can tell. He can keep going.

I put my hands on his chest. He's starting to sweat, which turns me on even more. "Yes, Chris." He fucks me for what feels like forever, but I can't get enough. I push his chest up higher, and he sits back so that he's kneeling again, his hands holding my legs.

We watch how deep his cock goes inside me like this, how hot it looks, how good we look fucking.

"Blythe." He can barely talk, but he looks at me. "Fuck, I love your pussy."

I smile again. I can toy with him, too. "I know."

Over the past month, Chris has empowered me in ways he probably wasn't planning on. I can be bold and insistent, and, like right now, even a little self-satisfied. He's learning to let me play with my power, just as I let him. On the flip side, I can be vulnerable and honest with him to a degree I never imagined. In bed and out. I can be everything with him and for him.

Right now, Chris is on that pleasure edge, and I can't make him wait any longer. "I'm going to make you come now," I say. "As hard as you made me come."

I slide my legs out from between us, and he drops his weight onto me. I tighten around him and rock my hips hard. I put my hands on his ass and pull him in, over and over, getting him louder and closer. "I want you to come *on* me. Let me feel it."

His body starts to stiffen as he pulls out and gets the condom off fast. He rubs himself over my body until he shakes hard against my stomach, and then I feel him come on my chest as he groans my name. He sounds and feels unbelievable.

Chris puts his hand over mine and moves it across my stomach to my breasts. I love this. While he catches his breath, he looks between us and watches as I rub the wetness over my nipples. He kisses me now and lowers his body to rest on mine. I want to stay like this—with Chris pressed against me, kissing me, tasting me—until we can fuck again.

I kiss the sweat from his shoulders and neck. "You were born to fuck me, Christopher Shepherd."

He tucks my hair behind my ears and kisses me softly. "I was also born to love you."

Later, Chris falls asleep and I watch him breathing peacefully. We have been drowning in each other. In beautiful ways, yes. But I know there are other reasons for this intensity. Chris is escaping, running from his own hell, and I am enabling that because I don't want to lose him. I can't.

But I also know that we can't stay like this forever. I have to get back to pitching more articles for the magazine where I used to work in Boston. They're not paying me much for my freelance writing, but I want to stay in their good graces. Chris and I haven't talked yet about what we might do when summer ends. Estelle, Eric, Zach, and James have to go back to school, and surely Sabin will want to get out of the Bar Harbor area soon, since there's not a particularly hot theater scene here.

At some point, I'll have to get back to Massachusetts. James and I have made the decision to sell our parents' house near Boston. The truth is that we've overspent fixing up the house here on Frenchman Bay, but we both agreed that the investment is worth it. This place now feels more like home to us. I'm not sure if I could live here year-round, but the idea certainly has its appeal. It would be incredibly quiet during the long off-season when the tourist crowds disappear, but I might very well like that.

But tonight we aren't going anywhere. So I watch Chris sleep, and I wait for the fear to hit him. I'm scared to get up for a glass of water because I don't want him to be alone when the dreams crash over him. He sleeps on

left drowning

his stomach, his hands up by his head, his breathing deep and even. For now.

Every night there is a point when Chris reaches for me in his sleep. But he doesn't reach for me just out of affection. He reaches for me for protection and for comfort. Over the past few weeks he's had nightmares, although he never confirms them for me in the morning. He sleeps through the dreams, even when his body flinches, sometimes thrashes, and he panics and sweats. But he always reaches for me. I whisper to him that he's safe, that my sweet boy is safe, and I wrap my whole body over him and will him to feel the intensity of my love and my belief in him.

Why is he having these nightmares so vividly now? I don't know for sure, but I believe it's being back in Maine, the place that he never wanted to come back to. Then there's our proximity to the water. The way Chris looks out at the Atlantic haunts me. I see his deep love for the ocean, but I also see his conflicted feelings and the fragility that he hides so well. The justification he gives for never swimming is that the water is too cold. But I know that's not the whole story, since physically, Chris could tolerate the cold. It relates to what he told me about having a love/hate relationship with water. It's the *hate* part that terrifies me. I have the same thing because of my association between the house fire and the ocean, but I have been using the ocean to help me heal.

Here's the other thing about his nightmares: I think they are unleashed by being with me. I know it. Our connection elicits the past and the truth from each of us. He thinks that's crazy, but I don't. It defies my lack of belief in God and fate, but I know this to be an absolute and unexplainable truth.

I admire Chris for how his strength never falters, but I also look for the times when he is vulnerable, because I like taking care of him. So far these moments have come when he is asleep or during certain moments when we are making love. Otherwise, he tries to shield me from what he sees as weaknesses, the things he thinks I don't want to see. What he doesn't understand is that seeing him with his guard down is what I am ultimately after, however afraid of it I am. It will show me that he has let me into his heart in a consequential, profound way, and it means that we have a chance at longevity. Of course, as much as I want his walls to come down, I don't know what it will look like when they crash.

But I can feel it coming. Chris hasn't said anything to me yet, but I know without a doubt that we won't be able to hide from what is tormenting him. I haven't wanted to think too much about what exactly his childhood was made of—what it was like for Sabin, Estelle, and Eric, too—and his insistence on looking solely at the present and the future has distracted me from looking at his past. But as much respect as I have for his privacy, it's getting harder for me to ignore the fact that he will not be able to run from his own memories forever. I can recognize trauma in another person because I have experienced my own, and to see it in Chris is slowly torturing me.

I feel it brewing furiously beneath the surface of our love: the looming promise of an inevitable, destructive storm.

I hope he will reach for me then.

I am going to fight with everything that I am to save him and to save us, but I won't be able to do it alone.

The room is dark, and I hear a light rain start outside. I lie on my side and press my body against him with some faint hope that I can shield him from the haunting internal terror. My arm gravitates to his back, and I rest my scar between his two, forming the solid line. I want more than anything for the power of us together to be stronger than the power of the damage.

If I still believed in God, in *anything*, I would be praying.

left drowning

JULY TWENTY-FIRST

CHRIS TAKES THE HIT TO THE BACK OF HIS HEAD WITH AS LITTLE
defiance as a teenage boy can. Defending himself, talking back,
usually doesn't go over well. Not that anything goes over well
when his father is like this, but shielding his body or mouthing
off can easily lead his father to turn on one of the younger
kids instead. It has been three days since the latest episode
began, and if history repeats itself, this should be the last day.
It hasn't been this bad in a long time.

Months sometimes go by with nothing. A quiet house, a
semblance of normalcy—albeit a cold, intimidating household—and then, as if out of nowhere, it starts. Sometimes
a clear bad mood triggers it, sometimes his father's manic
elation over whatever art piece he is working on ends in an
abrupt downward spiral. The unpredictability is the worst
part. Not knowing when it's coming, when the rage and need

for control will start, is perhaps worse than when the fire finally ignites. The waiting, the fear that an explosion can happen at any time, that's what is most terrifying.

Well, maybe not the most terrifying. But there is a certain ironic release of tension when his father finally lashes out, because at least then the anticipation is over, and there is something clear to deal with. To endure.

All Chris has to do is get through the day. Unfortunately, it is only late morning, so he has a number of hours ahead of him. As long as he keeps his brothers and sister from witnessing whatever happens, he'll consider today a victory. That's one of the things that he occupies his mind with during these times; strategizing how to keep them from getting hurt and from seeing as little as possible. And he thinks about the future and how this present hell is not forever.

It's just pain.

All he has to do is breathe through it.

Chris is going to get them all out. He and his brothers and sister are unfairly alone in this, so Chris will protect them until they all leave for college. No one would believe them about what goes on in this house because his father is so fucking idolized around here. The hugely successful artist who bravely soldiered on after his wife's death and raised four children on his own? The man who is routinely hailed for his dedication to his volunteer work? Who makes large donations to his church? He couldn't possibly be such a fucking crazy asshole.

A number of years ago when he was in middle school, Chris made an attempt to get help after one particularly awful night.

left drowning

The night that his father seated them all at the dining room table and demanded that Chris lay his hand flat on the table. His father spent the next hour alternately holding a heavy rubber mallet two feet above Chris's hand and then pacing the room, laughing and talking about building strength of character, teaching them to feel no fear. He talked about the respect that he deserved after all his success. Chris only heard pieces of it, never really made sense of the words, because the sound of fear that ran through his own head masked whatever crazy stuff his father was preaching. Chris tried hard not to flinch when his father pretended that he was going to slam the mallet down on his hand. He didn't want to scare Estelle, Eric, and Sabin more than they already were. He wanted to be strong for them, and he tried to reason that his father often enjoyed delivering hours of terrifying threats that usually didn't pan out. For him, instilling fear was sometimes enough.

Still, Chris's determination to hold still faltered. He couldn't help it. After one of the fake swing, when his father landed the mallet two inches from his hand and Chris automatically pulled away, Estelle and Eric both screamed and ran from the table. They were caught on the second floor of the house, where their father spent twenty minutes tying the twins to the banister rungs where they had an eagle-eye view of the table. Chris can still see the wire being formed into intricate twists and knots, like samples of their father's sculpture, but perversely showcased around their wrists and their necks. Leaving was not an option, and shutting their eyes was not allowed. Sabin and Chris never broke eye contact while Sabin's hands were bound behind him, securing him to his chair. Sabin's expression was worse than the twins' tears, Chris thought. The look of heartbreaking sympathy for how much more Chris endured cut the deepest. Sabin didn't get half of what Chris did, mostly because Chris needed him to keep the twins away from harm, and it was usually easy enough to get his father to direct all of his attention to Chris. He was the oldest, he could take it better. Keeping their father away from Eric and Estelle was often doable. Chris just had to bait him by saying something along the lines of, "You're going to work the little kids over? What? You can't deal with me? I'm the one you want." He couldn't always protect Sabin, but he tried because Sabe was more fragile than he was.

So that night wore on.

The threat of the mallet continued until Chris finally yelled, "Just do it!" knowing what this would earn him, but also knowing that his shout would end this episode. It would be the grand finale. It was the type of climax their father fed off, and delivering it would at least make the torture stop. "Do it!" Chris screamed again.

And his father did, pounding the mallet onto Chris's hand, then tossing it aside and retreating to his expansive studio on the opposite side of the house. The pain was shocking, but as soon as his father was gone, Chris got up from the table. It took a while to find something to cut the wire and free the others, and he assured them repeatedly that he was okay. Yes, his knuckle was probably broken, but he would be fine. Sabin wrapped up his hand tightly with a bandage and homemade splint and got him two bags of ice to try to cut through the pain and swelling.

left drowning

The next Sunday, Chris took Estelle to church as he always did. They got there early so Chris could talk to the priest. He showed the man his hand, tried to explain. It backfired. At that day's sermon, the priest lectured the congregation on lying and sinning in general, and made a point to say that lying—especially about one's father—was most certainly a sin. Chris understood what the priest was saying: After everything their father had done to support the church financially, this was how his children were repaying him? With lies because they were ungrateful troublemakers? Chris realized that nobody was going to save them. There were rarely physical marks to show, anyway, this broken hand being one of the exceptions. In this small town, there were few ways, if any, to combat their father's public image.

After the church episode, Chris and Sabin talked it over and agreed: they shouldn't try for help. Besides, even if help came, it would mean they would be split up. Who would take four children? And older children at that? No one. That's who.

And they refused to be separated. That would be worse than this life. Together they could stand, divided they would fall.

Now that Chris is well past middle school, and fully grown, he has more self-control than he did during that episode with the mallet years ago. That self-control is what allows him to absorb his father's blow without comment when a second hard hit lands on the side of his head. It's not as blinding as the first. The repeated direct physical hits are unusual. And scary. Chris recovers quickly and continues moving the concrete and stone blocks from one side of the studio to the other. The underside of his hands is red and raw, and his legs and back hurt, but he is going to be fine. The lashes on the back of his legs sting something awful, but that's what happens when you stumble, crack the corner of a stone block that could have been used as part of a multimedia art piece, and then get lashed with a piece of plastic cord. Who knew plastic could hurt so fucking much? It's like that rubber mallet. It was just rubber, right? But his middle knuckle still shows the effects.

Chris drank a ton of water and ate well last night and this morning because he knew he would need to stay hydrated and need as much energy as he could find. He is seventeen years old, going into his senior year of high school, and he is strong, he reasons to himself. Mentally and physically. He can let this crazy bastard do what he needs to because there is no other choice. So when his father announced after breakfast that "it's time to get to work," Chris felt as prepared as he could be.

Rote, exhausting, pointless tasks are his father's preferred method of torture. Long hours prove a capacity for physical endurance, or so he says. The lashes and knocking Chris around are not typical, though. This could be a very bad day, Chris knows, but he finds comfort in his belief that the others will not be touched. His father's attention will be only on him today, he can feel that.

So far it's been three hours, hardly a record. Eventually, this will end.

When the heavy blocks have been moved to his father's incomprehensible degree of satisfaction, Chris is instructed to put his back flat against the wall and kneel with his arms out. Most importantly, he is to watch while his father continues

left drowning

to design the nine-foot-tall metal sculpture that occupies the center of the room. He is to watch while the artist lights the blowtorch, and while he passes far too close to his eldest son. The heat from the flame can be felt with too much clarity, and Chris repeatedly tells himself that his father would not actually burn him. It's the game that the artist likes, the taunting and the terrorizing. The utter exhaustion he causes. The breaking.

But I will not break, Chris screams in his head.

It's been a while since Chris has had to prove his stamina like this, and he curses himself for having slacked off on working out. He is already worn out from the past few days, and his legs are shaking as a searing ache runs through his quads. Eventually his father has him stand up fully and raise his arms out to the side. The smell in the room is noxious, chemicals and burning metal. It's adding to his queasiness. His arms are past the point of hurting. They tremble, but Chris will not let them drop, especially not while his father still holds that blowtorch. There are risks worth taking and risks not worth taking.

Chris is not sure how long he spends in the studio with his father, but his vision is blurred as he is led out of the room, so he knows it has been a long time. That first hit to the head was probably harder than he realized. He is taken out of the house, and across the property. He is given instructions and then kicked in the direction of the ocean. It is when his father kicks him that Chris hears a small sound that is cut short. Before his father has a chance to make sense of the noise, to understand what it is or where it came from, Chris distracts him. He turns boldly to his father and finds the courage to mouth off. "What the hell is the point of this?" He earns a third hit to the head and double the task ahead of him. He has also spared the others. Getting caught hiding in a tree could be very bad for his siblings.

Before he returns to his madness in the studio, Chris's father reminds him that he will be watching periodically. There will be no rest and no varying from the routine.

Chris walks ahead, relieved to be on his own for the rest of the afternoon, despite what he still has to do. He looks up into the tree and manages a smile. "It's all right." Chris knows it's not all right that he is almost seeing double, but that will pass.

"Chris?" Sabin is crouched on a large branch against the trunk of the tree, and he has a firm hold on Eric and Estelle, both of whom look ungodly confused and terrified. The twins are not that little anymore, they are in middle school now, but they are not used to this. Chris and Sabin have protected them too much, so when they do see the truth, they freak.

"It's okay, Sabin. He's gone. I'm going down to the beach for a while. Why don't you take Eric and Estelle to the movies? And dinner. Just grab your bikes and get out of here. Come back later tonight."

"I'm not just going to leave—"

"Sabin, don't! It's not that bad this time. I promise you."

Sabin pauses. "You sure? I don't have a good feeling."

"It's almost over. Go on. I don't want you guys around, or I'll just worry. Please take them out of here. For me, okay?" He turns for the beach before his brother can protest.

"Chris!"

left drowning

"What, Sabe?"

"Take this." Sabin tosses down a red baseball hat. "For the sun."

"Thanks, bro. Now go!"

"And here!"

Sabin drops two bananas into Chris's outstretched hands. "Sorry. I didn't think to grab anything else."

"It's all right, buddy. Thank you."

"Shitting rainbows," Sabin says.

"Shitting rainbows," Chris agrees.

Chris hesitates before putting on the hat. His father sent him out here in cargo shorts, and no shoes or shirt. He'll notice the hat for sure if he checks on Chris, but whether he'll care or not is unknown. There are no guarantees, no rules. Chris decides it's worth the risk; the sun is glaring today.

Chris scarfs down the bananas and then takes the two metal buckets from their spot on the boulder and begins. He starts at one end of the rocky shore, trudging through the heavy sand of low tide and into the salty water. The sting from the lashes on his legs is infuriating. This is a shitty enough day, and it would be slightly more manageable without the added pain. He berates himself for cracking that concrete block. He is strong enough not to have stumbled. Chris fills both buckets and walks to the other side of the shore where his father's property ends, and dumps them out. He reloads and repeats the walk. This might not be so bad. Despite the circumstances, Chris loves the ocean. The smell, the sound, the view. It's sensory overload, and it might help divert his mind, let him dream and fantasize about the good things that might come in the future. After this, everything will be exceptionally wonderful.

The first hour is tolerable. The salt water eventually feels soothing on his legs, and it's probably good for cleaning his wounds. Plus, it's helping to keep him cool on this hot July day. The water, despite providing the problematic weight in his already tired hands, is also his ally. He and the ocean are partners in this hideous day. It is not the water's fault that Chris is suffering.

The second hour is tougher because his body is already so worn out. The past three days have been filled with grueling tasks, belittling comments, and threats about what will happen to the others should Chris fail at what is expected of him. As easy as it would be to let his mind take him somewhere else, into an imaginary world where this is not happening to him, he refuses to go that route. Escaping, blocking this out, will make him insane, he's sure of that. Reality is crucial, he believes. Prayer will get him no relief. Begging the sky for a miracle won't work. Chris is able to handle what his father throws at him, and he will just continue as he always has, shielding the other kids. The truth is that the gaps between his father's episodes have gotten greater and greater over the years. It's not as though every day in the house is filled with gruesome beatings. Save for a handful of physical incidents over the years, it's all just a mind-fuck, and Chris will not let that drown him. He's done everything that he can think of to take care of his brothers and sister, and he's done a damn good job, too. Chris can't exactly replace their mother, but he cooks, helps them all with homework, and does the laundry when his father lapses.

left drowning

He even walks Estelle to that church she insists on attending.

It's during the third hour of this increasingly strenuous task that his resolve starts to crack. There is no part of his body or mind that does not hurt to all hell. It's just water, it's just water. How can carrying water be so bad? It can't. Just breathe into it. Breathe into it and keep going. But every step becomes more burdensome, the act of pulling his feet from the sand more and more grueling. Every muscle in his arms feels like it's going to tear each time he lifts up a new bucket of water. But if he stops, it will be worse.

He should have killed his father. He still could. He could kill him in his sleep with one of the hunting rifles in the house. Or he could poison his food. Maybe he'll do that. For a moment Chris fantasizes about actually doing this, but despite all the reasons it would be justified, he knows that he isn't capable and that it's not right. And that having a dead father is a sure way to guarantee separating the kids.

He holds tightly to the vague plan in his head, which is merely that there is a future outside of this house. He will get his siblings to that future no matter what.

As his arms fatigue even more, the buckets drop down in his arms. He must make a conscious effort to keep his arms bent so that he doesn't keep battering his thighs with the weight. Chris keeps a steady pace, though, because if his father should choose to look out from the upper windows of their sprawling house and see imperfection, one of the kids will pay the price later. As he mulls over the idiocy in perfecting such a meaningless task, he trips and spills half a bucket of water. Panic grips him, but he continues on.

Sweat drips from his upper body. Chris can feel the sun-burn on his shoulders and back. It's going to make sleeping tonight terrible, but he should be exhausted enough that nothing will keep him awake. Still he feels near to fainting. If he doesn't take a quick break, he's not going to make it. His father is going to ring a bell from the deck to signal when he can stop, but that won't be for hours, he's sure of that. Chris turns to the trees and looks to the upper deck of the house by his father's studio. If he's checking on Chris, he would probably be looking from there. He leans his head to the side to look past one large branch of a tree, and seeing no one, he drops the buckets and leans over, placing his hands on his knees while he dry-heaves. Damn it. He needs water badly. Man, what he'd give for just a little water. Chris turns and wades into the ocean up to his mid-calves. As tempting as it is to gulp down ocean water, he's not that dumb. He shakes his head. No, he'll just make himself sicker.

Maybe he has no future after all. Maybe none of them do. Maybe the four of them are already broken beyond repair. Can they really have any sort of life after this? Probably not.

Chris looks out where the ocean meets the sky. He could swim to another shore, run off, and never come back. He con-templates the idea of immediate freedom. Maybe he really should swim out there and never come back. Give himself over to the dark water of the Atlantic. But he would never leave his siblings. Never.

Suddenly, Chris realizes that he is making eye contact with someone. She stands on a floating dock in the cove and looks back at him.

left drowning

She is beautiful. He can't even see her clearly because of the distance, but he can feel her beauty. He guesses that she is around his age. She probably has a wonderful, normal life, the way every teenager should. Exhaustion, sadness, and despair overtake him.

The girl gives him a small wave, and he waves back. He knows that he shouldn't do this because his father might flip, but he can't help himself. He is drawn to her. Wait, does he know her? No, that's not it. Yet there is a familiarity about her presence.

She cups her hands to her mouth and yells across the water. "Hi."

"Hi, back!" Chris replies.

"Are you . . . okay?"

Chris drops his hands onto his hips and looks away. Shit, she's been watching him. He must look crazy. "Yes, I'm fine."

"What are you doing? With the buckets. Are you in training for something?"

Chris can't help but laugh. It isn't a bad thought. Maybe he could pretend he is conditioning himself for a triathlon or something. Instead he is training for survival. "Sort of."

The girl calls out over the lapping water, insisting that he needs a T-shirt because he has a horrible sunburn. She pushes him to at least go get a shirt. Her yelling could be echoing up to the house, Chris realizes, and he glances back to make sure that his father isn't coming. She refuses to take no for an answer, and when she starts to untie her rowboat from the dock so that she can come to him, Chris immediately yells, "No! Don't do that!" If she comes to the shore and he is seen talking with her . . . God, he doesn't know what would happen. He checks behind him again. Still safe. He feels awful yelling at her like this. She is kind. She knows something is wrong, he can tell, but he doesn't want her worrying about him. "Just . . . No. I'm sorry. I'm so sorry."

Chris and the girl stand silently until he suddenly feels that they understand each other. He can't explain his situation to her, and now she all at once seems to accept that. Chris struggles to fight back tears while they maintain eye contact. Perhaps it's because he needs something to hold on to, needs someone, but he is convinced that she is the reason he is not dropping to his knees and surrendering. This girl, he is sure, is his salvation, and he can practically hear the strength that she is sending him, the exact unspoken words that she hurls over the water. I'm here. I'm right here.

Part of him wishes she would leave. Stop looking at him. No good can come of this, he knows. But Chris can't bring himself to ignore her, or be rude, or do more to push her away than he already has. When he tells her that he has to keep going, he can see her thinking, pondering what his actions mean. She knows he is in trouble, Chris can tell.

"I have to keep going," he says desperately.

"I'm going to stay with you," she tells him.

These are the kindest words Chris has ever heard, and it's all he can do to answer her. "Thank you."

He refills the buckets of water, walking them from one side of the shore to the other, emptying and refilling them. He treks endlessly through the mud, his feet often digging into shell

left drowning

shards. He recognizes that physically, he is near collapse. Mentally, too. She is the reason he can continue. He pauses once, noticing something in one of his buckets. A sea urchin. He is reminded how much life is out there in the ocean, in the rest of the world, all of it waiting for him. Maybe even she could be waiting for him. Who knows? But only if he can just do this. He takes the little green creature out gently and walks a few feet deeper into the water, letting it float to the bottom. With the current, maybe it will find its way to her.

Chris looks to her as he walks, nodding a bit. She is now in her bathing suit, having tied her red shirt to a life vest. Wait, what is she doing? Chris is moved beyond words when he understands.

"The tide is coming in," she calls.

He watches as the current carries the life vest to shore. When it is close enough, he stops walking and puts down the buckets. Because his fingers tremble so horribly, it seems to take forever to undo the knots. She made sure they were tight enough so that the water bottle, in particular, would reach him. The red T-shirt that she has sent him feels like heaven when he puts it on, the cold fabric cooling off his shoulders and protecting him from further sun exposure. He glances at the house, and then he downs the bottle of water, raising it to her when he's done.

He looks down at the shirt as it drips water over him. Matthews College. He doesn't know where this school is, but it's immediately clear to him that he will go there. All of them will go there. There will be college, and family, and joy. It's a *goal, it's a future. It's a goddamn plan. He smiles for a moment. Maybe he will even get the girl.*

He will not fucking break. His father will not ruin him. Any of them.

Her voice sails to him once more. "I'm not leaving you."

The sound penetrates to his core. He feels partnership, and love, and he realizes that he must be delirious because what he thinks so vividly is, She is the past, and the present, and the future. She is through, and over, and under. *He knows this is inexplicable nonsense, but he lets her presence comfort him. So few things are comforting. She sits on the dock, unmoving, for the next hour and a half.*

She is his rock and the reason that he is able keep moving until he finally hears the bell ring from the house. Tapping into his last reservoir of strength, Chris throws the buckets as hard as he can against a group of boulders near the shore. He did it. This bullshit, abusive task is done, and he made it. He paces back and forth for a minute, enjoying the brief high from completion. His arms are lighter now because he doesn't have to carry the weight of the ocean, and he turns to the girl, the incredible girl who has held him up for hours, and he raises both hands into the air, his palms held high, fingers spread.

She raises hers, too, and they reach out as though they are touching palm to palm. Her fingers fold as if they are falling between his, and Chris makes the same motion. She has become part of him, this girl, and he lowers his hands to rest over his heart. He will keep her there always.

left drowning

29

BECAUSE OF, IN SPITE OF

WHEN I WAKE UP, IT'S COOL AND CLEAR, WITH A BIT OF
fog floating over the water. This is August on the coast of Maine: the
opposite of Boston, where it can be so oppressively humid in late summer.

Sneaking out of bed without waking Chris, I make coffee and take
it out front, where I gaze out at the beautiful coastline and warm my
hands on my steaming mug.

Despite the gorgeous weather and the scenery, though, I can't shake
the feeling of dread that weighs on me. Maybe it's just that I'm tired.
Chris will probably tell me later that he slept through the night, but in
fact, his sleep was severely disturbed. I know that he had nightmares,

and I barely slept because of his thrashing and because of my worry. Chris is asleep now, though.

James and Estelle are entwined in the hammock that hangs between two trees on the far side of the lawn. I smile. They must have slept out here last night. I like seeing my brother taking care of her. Well, as much as Estelle will allow anyone to take care of her. He's doting and affectionate without being pathetic.

I read the news on my Kindle for half an hour before James appears. He looks like hell.

"You need a coffee, huh?" I ask.

"Yeah. Thanks." He pulls a sweatshirt over his head and sits down in the wicker chair across from me. When he rests his elbows on his knees and puts his head in his hands, I realize that something is very wrong.

I go to the kitchen and take my time making him a double espresso. Everything has been going so well, so James's obvious stress concerns me. I think I was right: I am going to have to brace myself for this day. When I return, he is sitting up again, but his expression concerns me.

"Blythe, I need your help."

I sit. "Anything. What's going on?"

He looks away. "I don't even know how to say this . . . I don't know what to do or why . . ."

"Is it Estelle?"

"This is really uncomfortable."

"It's okay, James. You can tell me anything."

He starts talking, but he still can't look at me. "I really care about her, you know? I do. I think she's fantastic. Sure, she's got this kind of tough exterior and all, but she's super sweet, too. She's smart, and funny, and wild." He pauses. "It's the wild part that . . . It's not right, Blythe."

left drowning

"Honey, I don't understand." He's getting visibly upset, so I move and kneel next to him. "What do you mean?"

"In . . . in bed."

"Oh." I can see why this is uncomfortable for him.

"I don't want to talk about this, but I have to, Blythe."

"I'm here. You can tell me."

"Look, I know some people like . . . rough sex, or whatever, right?"

"Um, sure." He's right, this is not a talk I want to have with him, but I keep at it. "And she wants that. From you."

He nods.

"And you don't want that," I say.

He shrugs. "See, I kind of did. I mean, a little rough. Like, there's fun wild and then . . . there's not fun."

I shake my head. "What do you mean by 'not fun'?"

"She wants me to . . . hurt her. It's been building. It started with smaller stuff, stuff that was okay, and I guess some of that was fine with me, but she's asking for more and more. And it's freaking me out. We've been fighting because I can't do what she's asking." He takes a deep breath, and his eyes fill with tears as he finally looks at me. "Blythe, last night, she asked me to hit her. Hard. Jesus, she wanted me to leave bruises, and she was crying and begging me to . . . She was freaking out on me. I've never seen her like that. Or anyone like that. I can't do that to her. I *won't* do that. I couldn't hurt her. Ever."

"Oh my God, James." I am so taken aback that I don't know what to say yet, but I throw my arms around him and hug him close.

"Why would she ask me to do that?" He puts a hand on my arm and squeezes. "Do I seem like some guy who would do that to a woman? Is that it? Is there something wrong with me? We were outside, in the yard, and she . . . God, she was trying to get me to shove her around and shit. She started yelling at me, saying that other guys have given her what she wants, and maybe she'll have to go find someone else. She said that maybe I'm too . . . naive, or whatever. Too inexperienced for her. What she wants, though? That's not right, is it? I can't do it, and I don't understand why she'd want me to. I really like her, Blythe, I do, but I don't get this, and it's scaring me. What am I supposed—"

Chris's voice is shaking as he interrupts us. "James?"

I turn to him. His expression is pure disbelief, but I am less surprised. I remember the bruise that I saw on Estelle's hip when were on video chat. And I remember her crying in our dorm room. *Repenting*.

James looks panicked. "Chris, I swear to God, I didn't—"

"I know you didn't. I know you wouldn't." He crosses the porch and drops onto the wicker sofa. "You didn't do anything wrong. This is not your fault. At all." He rubs his hand over his face. What a thing to wake up to. "Blythe? Do you mind if I talk to James for a few minutes?"

"Of course not. I'll be in the kitchen."

I walk into the house through the living room and notice Zach crashed out on the couch. Eric must have been snoring loudly, because the old couch is certainly not comfortable. I spend two hours in the kitchen, cleaning, planning dinners for the next few days, fussing around. I don't want to talk to anybody right now, so I'm glad to be left alone in here. Later, Zach pops in for coffee, but he's exceptionally sullen and quiet, and he lets me chop vegetables for the grill in peace.

James and I go downtown for lunch. He doesn't want to talk about Estelle anymore, and neither do I. My brother is obviously terribly embarrassed, which I get, so I don't press him on the issue, but he looks better as the afternoon goes on. Being with me seems to help him, so

left drowning

that is a good thing. Just as we finish lunch, I get a text from Chris. He is taking Estelle to Seal Cove, and asks if he can take Jonah. I tell him of course. Jonah loves that trip. Chris and I have been there a few times. It's a magical walk down a mossy, rocky path to the cove, and on lucky days, you arrive at the beach to see tons of seals sunning themselves on the rocks. I hope today is a lucky day.

But I know that it's starting. The storm. The one in the increasingly dark sky and the one on the ground.

James and I take one of the touristy boat rides through the harbor. He is one of the volunteers who helps raise the giant red sails. Despite what has happened with Estelle, he is able to smile into the bits of filtered sun that hit his face as he pulls on the thick rope that soon flaps loudly in the wind. I am very lucky to have him back in my life. I take a video of him with my phone and then have him pose with the ship's mascot, an enormous black Newfoundland.

I want to delay going back to the house, so I persuade James to walk through busy downtown Bar Harbor. We get ice cream and browse in the bookstore. I buy him some clothes for school from one of the sporting goods stores, even though he insists it isn't necessary. After we've exhausted the hilly streets and nearly every store, James stops me. "Blythe. I want to go back. I need to see Estelle. Make sure she's okay."

"Of course." So I take us home.

I pull the car up to the house and put it in park, but James doesn't move to get out. "She's probably angry at me for telling."

"No, she won't be. You did exactly the right thing. Did it help to talk to Chris?"

"Yeah. I still don't understand, but he made me feel better. Do you get it? Why she would . . . you know, want that?"

"I'm afraid I might, James." I hand him the keys. "Take Estelle out for dinner or something if you want. I'm going to find Chris."

But I don't have to find him, because I know where he'll be. And I'm right. I walk slowly across the upper lawn, down the wooden stairs to the lower yard, and then to the beach and the long dock that stretches into the ocean. Chris is sitting on the end, his feet hanging over the edge, and Sabin is lying down behind him holding a beer can with one hand and petting Jonah with the other. My dog seems to be on high alert, panting and thumping his tail as he looks around.

"C'mere, Jonah." I clap my hands, and he races down the dock to greet me. I kneel down and scratch the scruff of his neck. "You watching over the boys? Huh? Yeah?" He bounds away and plants himself back next to Sabin.

I step over Sabin, who appears to be sleeping, take off my shoes, and sit next to Chris. He puts his arm around me and kisses me. "Hey." He sounds as tired as he looks.

"Hey. How are you? And how's Estelle?"

He sighs. "I don't know how to answer you."

"Blythe, Blythe, Blythe!" Sabin thumps the deck with his hand, and I turn around. He is drunk. Really drunk.

I glance at Chris. "I know," he says. "I know."

"Hi, Sabe." I lean back and rest my head on his stomach.

"Where you been today? I missed you, B."

"Out with James."

"Oh. First I thought you and Chris were locked up in your room again. I mean, Jesus, you two are like rabbits. It's never just you and me anymore. But then he came back and you stayed away."

"I'm sorry. We'll do something tomorrow. Just the two of us." I don't want to have any kind of conversation with him. I can tell he's way too

left drowning

drunk to make any sense, and if I say the wrong thing, he could get irritable. "Promise."

"Okay, B." He pats my head. "It's just that I miss you, and you're missing everything."

"What am I missing?" I ask lazily. I love Sabin, I do, but I wish he'd go to his room and sleep this off. I want to talk to Chris alone.

"Like, did you even know that Zach and Eric broke up last night? Huh?"

I sit up. "Chris, did you know this?"

"No. Sabin, what the fuck are you talking about? They couldn't have broken up."

Sabin laughs. "Jesus, you two are so fucking out of it. You haven't noticed anything wrong? The fighting? The snarky comments?"

Chris and I really have been in our own world.

"Zach's been on the couch for two weeks. According to him," Sabin starts as he heaves himself up and slouches forward, "they've never even slept together. Can you believe that shit? I mean, they sleep in the same bed, but that's it."

"What?" This surprises me. They are so affectionate and loving in public. "That's why they broke up? That doesn't sound like Zach."

"No, dummy." Sabin finishes his beer. "Eric broke up with him. He says that Zach wants too much of a commitment or whatever. But the good news is that now maybe I'll have someone to hang out with. Someone who's not all coupled up and shit." He reaches for Jonah. "I do have this guy, though. Right, buddy?" He lets Jonah lick his face while he pats him.

Chris is frozen. Estelle is asking my brother to smack her around, Eric just broke up with his long-term boyfriend, and Sabin is, once again, incredibly drunk. Sabin babbles incoherently to Jonah while Chris stares out at the ocean.

"Everyone is crumbling," he says softly so that Sabin can't hear. "I can't believe this. They're crumbling, do you see it?" Chris gets up, walks around Sabin, and hops off the deck to the sand.

I watch him as he searches the beach. He's looking for stones. It takes a while, but eventually his pockets are full and he starts skipping them across the surface of the ocean. He works his way up and down the beach, and he wades through the water to stand in front of me. Chris looks incredibly sad today. I kiss him and then nudge him to turn around and sit in front of me so that I can rub his shoulders. The tension he carries is enormous.

Sabin is still playing with Jonah, stroking his fur. "Hey, Chris?" Sabin is slurring something fierce now. "Do you remember . . . ," he starts. "Do you fucking remember those two dogs that our father used to have?"

Chris tenses noticeably. "Sabin . . ."

"I'd totally forgotten until now. Remember? He was such a fucking bastard. Do you remember? He had two dogs for a while, right? And I remember this one time . . . Christ, what a sick asshole . . . he put their food dishes on the floor and he hit 'em with something while they ate." He closes his eyes and pulls Jonah in close. "I don't get why they kept eating. I mean, there's our father, hitting 'em with a . . . with a . . . what was it? A belt?"

"Sabin, stop."

"No, c'mon, Chris. I'd forgotten about this until now. What was it? Must have been a belt."

The man I love hangs his head. "No. No, it wasn't a belt." I stop rubbing his shoulders and quickly pull him in so that my arms are around

left drowning

him. He reaches for my hand. "It was a switch. He'd made it from the willow tree in the yard."

"Right. That willow tree." Sabin laughs, and it is one of the worst sounds I've ever heard. "A switch. Yeah, so he's yelling about what fucked-up animals they are, and every once in a while, he'd let them have it. For nothing." Sabin leans his head against Jonah. "No one's gonna hurt you, boy. Jesus, Chris. Those poor fuckin' dogs." Sabin lays back down on his side. "Shitting rainbows," he says with a laugh and then immediately passes out.

Jonah curls up protectively next to him. "He's okay, Jonah. He's okay," I try to reassure all of us.

"No, he's not okay, and you know it."

Chris takes a stone from his pocket and hurls it while I hold him. He throws another. "The thing is, Blythe? My father never had dogs." He throws again. "He had me. And he had Sabin."

Inside, I explode. I rage. I cannot begin to process what he has just said because the ramifications are enormous. I'd known, I'd *felt*, that it would be bad. Very bad. But not like this. The scope, the vast depth, of their father's madness is something that I cannot begin to take in. This is a man I will forever feel only vehement disgust and hatred for. What he has done to the people I love most in this world . . . It is incomprehensible.

For an entire hour, we don't talk. The sky, however, speaks to us in distant rumbles of thunder. Chris shivers. I keep him as close to me as possible, and we just watch the tide come in. I let the tears cover my cheeks and fall to his shoulders because it would be impossible not to cry, but I don't melt down in front of him. I can't because he isn't.

He slides off the dock and collects stones again. It's a routine that will ground him, I know. "It wasn't constant, and it wasn't usually like . . . what Sabin just told you," he says from the shore. "We went to school, played sports, had friends. But then that would change. We . . . or I, mostly . . . weren't hurt all that often. Months at a time would go by where things were normal enough. Six, eight months of near-total normalcy. Sometimes a whole year. But when it happened, it wasn't usually about . . . direct hits. It was usually about stamina, endurance. Wearing me down. Sometimes wearing *us* down." He is incredibly rational now, overly logical about this. It's his protection.

It takes another twenty minutes of silence and stone collecting until he is ready to tell me what it was like to grow up with a monster for a father. As I hear details of how the people I love were brutalized in ways that I could never have imagined, I move next to Sabin and run my hands over his arms, then lifting up his shirt, looking for scars that maybe I never noticed. While I don't find any, I am not reassured. I take in what Chris tells me with as little visible reaction as possible. I need to be brave for him, as he has been brave all his life.

"My father was very sick," Chris says. "Psychotic, to some degree, probably. He built up my body and tried to tear apart my mind."

"But you're still here."

"I am."

"And Estelle, Eric, and Sabin, they're here also."

"I thought that I'd protected them enough. Estelle thinks God protected her. After everything I did, she fucking believes God is the reason our father never touched her."

"But you're the reason."

"Yes, but now I see that I didn't protect her. I stopped him from going into her room one night, and I paid the price the next day, but

left drowning

even though he never got into her room, I still failed. I failed them totally."

"Oh, Chris, no. You didn't fail. How could you have protected them? You were a kid. This shit isn't supposed to happen. But I know you, and I know that you did more than anyone could have. Than anyone should have to do."

"I thought they'd all be okay, Blythe." The mix of desperation and anger in his tone is awful. "I thought that . . . we would get out, and it would be over. But look at them. They're all a mess, aren't they? I fucked up."

"No, no you did not. Christopher. They love you, and they are devoted to you. Always. I knew that the minute I saw you with them."

"Oh Jesus, Blythe, come on. Look at Estelle. She's sucked your brother into this mess now, too. This is my fault. I should have gotten us away from my father whatever the cost. I thought being torn apart from each other would be the worst thing. I was horribly wrong."

"It is not your fault that your father was out of his mind. That he hurt all of you. Maybe he didn't touch them the way he did you, but they . . . saw."

"Yes. They did."

"Can you imagine the guilt they carry? Not only the terror, but the guilt?"

Chris shakes his head. "For what?"

"Because they couldn't protect you the way you protected them. They didn't share everything that you went through."

He wipes his eyes and turns in to me. "I thought because he never went after her or Eric that they would be all right. She's certainly not all right. And even Eric. Breaking up with Zach, not being able to sleep with him? That's because of this. And Sabin. God, Sabin . . . We're all irreparably broken."

Chris and I sit facing each other, my legs over his.

"You are *not* broken. I love you," I tell him.

"You only think you do. You don't know everything."

"I will love you no matter what."

"We'll see."

"Nothing, nothing will ever change how much I love you."

"My back. Those scars? Do you want to hear about that?" He's daring me to listen, perhaps threatening me with the truth.

I can hear this because I can do anything for him. "If you want to tell me, yes."

With his head buried against me, he talks in a whisper and tells me about the night that his father nearly killed him.

"You know how you don't remember some of the days around the fire? It's the same for me with the night I got these scars. I don't know exactly what happened before or after. I vaguely remember exhausting work with no point, and threats. Endless threats. I think he had me move . . . I don't know . . . blocks of some kind in his art studio. That was his style. He liked to torture me by giving me unbearably heavy things to hold, and making me stand still with them for hours. I think this type of thing went on for days during this episode. All I know is by the time evening arrived, I was tapped. I was so weak by then. He'd left us alone that night. Gone out and wasn't home when we went to bed. I know we had dinner. Or I think we did. I don't know. I don't remember that part."

"That's okay."

"Then it was late. After midnight, I'm sure. He pulled me from my

left drowning

bed. Grabbed me by the neck and dragged me down the stairs. Something about how a New York gallery was backing out of a deal. They'd commissioned a bunch of pieces, and . . . He wasn't making any sense. The house was dark, and he kept bumping me into walls and furniture while he pulled me. The next thing I knew, my head was in the toilet. Underwater. He held me down, and I just wasn't strong enough to fight back. Then he'd pull me up for a second, explain that we were a drain on him and that's why his work was suffering. He'd make us move again. A new location would help. My head would go under the water. Over and over. At first, I thought he would just let up quickly and leave me there. I couldn't breathe, but I was sure that he would stop, and I could go back to bed. All I wanted was to go back to my room."

I inhale and exhale deeply so that Chris will breathe with me. And he does.

"He didn't stop, though. He just kept going and going. I had this belief in a future and in escape, but the longer it went on, the less I believed. I started to fight him, but there was nothing left in me. And then he held me down harder, and I knew he wasn't going to let me up again. That I was going to die. I was . . . very sure of that. I was going to die, and that was that. I don't even think that was his intention. I think it would have been an accident. He couldn't have wanted a dead kid on his hands, right? It wasn't planned. He was just completely crazed.

"And then I heard this weird sound; even as I was drowning and dying, the sound came through to me. Suddenly his hands were off me, but it still took me a second to push myself out of the water. Then I understood what the sound was. His fucking volunteer's pager was going off. That always trumped everything. So he turned it off, and he just left me there while he drove away."

"I was coughing and trying to get air. I just wanted to get back to bed, so I crawled out of the bathroom to the bottom of the staircase. I reached up for the railing and walked about five or six steps up. Then I got too dizzy. I just couldn't stand. I still couldn't breathe."

I inhale deeply again, reminding him that right now he does have air. "Of course you couldn't. Nobody could have."

He is still talking in a whisper, so softly that I have to strain to hear him. Like a little kid telling a secret that he isn't supposed to. "I started to fall backward down the stairs. I managed to stay upright, but I couldn't really figure out my footing . . . So when I hit the landing I just stumbled hard across the floor. Because I couldn't see, and I couldn't get my balance . . . I was so disoriented. That's when I crashed into the glass display case. It was this giant floor-to-ceiling monstrosity that my father had built to keep a bunch of my mother's things in. She had china and these silly little glass animals that she loved. That's what I fell into, and the entire thing shattered around me.

"It must have made a hell of a noise because Sabin woke up, and you know how nothing wakes him. Apparently I passed out for a few minutes, not long. When I came to, the lights were on, and he was crying and fishing me out of the glass. I kept telling him that I was going to be okay. But I didn't know how much blood there was yet. He got me upstairs to our bathroom and pulled out glass from me for half an hour. When I fell, I must have . . . ripped open my back on something. Maybe glass, maybe one of the metal shelves. I don't know. Sabin wanted to take me to the emergency room, but I wouldn't let him. Because you know what was crazy? There was something good about what happened. I mean, really, really good. I knew that it was over. Nothing would happen again. My father

left drowning

didn't want to get caught, and he'd get caught. This had gone too far. It was too . . . visible. I just suddenly wasn't afraid anymore.

"Sabin stopped the bleeding by putting pressure on my back like I asked him. He bandaged me up with piles of gauze and tape. And we left the mess of glass and blood on the floor for my father to clean up. Sabin stayed in my room that night. He stayed up all night, sitting up against my door just to make sure. But I knew it was over, and I knew what to do.

"The week before, I'd found out that when I turned twenty-one I'd be in charge of most of my mother's estate, including the house. I don't like to think that she knew what he was like, but . . . her will gave everything to us. So maybe she knew, and that's why she left me in charge. So I threatened him. If he stayed the hell away from my family—*my family*—I'd let him keep that fucking palatial house that he loved so much. He could keep working, he could keep being the goddamn local volunteer hero, he could keep his image that he valued so much. But he wasn't going to touch any of us again, or I would take it all. Every bit of it.

"That night, after Sabin patched me up, I had him leave a note on top of the broken glass and my blood. It read *No more. Or I take it all.* When we got up the next day, everything had been cleaned up. My father never said anything about it, of course. But after that, all the shit stopped. He wouldn't give up that house, or the studio in it, or my mother's money.

"I went to college nearby for my freshman and sophomore years, and so did Sabin for his freshman year. We didn't want to risk leaving the twins alone with him. Then we all went to Matthews together."

"So that's the night that my father tried to kill me. He would have, too. I'd be dead if it weren't for his pager going off. So there's no God, no divine intervention. Just a page that happened to come through when I needed it the most."

Chris holds me tightly, still not looking at me. "Now you know. Now you know how completely and irreparably broken I am. I may have lived, but I am too damaged for you. I am not the person you think I am or the one you deserve."

Before I can protest, he kisses me. And the longer he kisses me, the more I know that he is trying to say good-bye to me and good-bye to us. Eventually he pulls away.

"I was afraid this would happen. Being with you? It brought everything back, just like you said it would. It makes all of it worse. No, don't look at me like that, Blythe. This is not like what you went through. I told you not to fight your past and to let it into your life because I knew it was something you could deal with. This is different. I can see now that we will never escape this. It was better before when I could hide and just stay with the future. We can't pretend that you don't know this truth, and we can't pretend that this will work between us. I wish that I could be somebody else, but what's happened to me is inextricably part of who I am. Who I will always be. It made me the person who you think you love. And so you love me either because of that or in spite of it. Both of which are unbearable."

30

ONCE BEFORE

ZACH AND I ARE ALONE AT THE HOUSE all night. Both of us are numb. The others have taken Sabin to the emergency room. The minute that Chris finished trying to tell me that we are over, Sabin vomited and started to choke. Chris rolled him over, and when Sabe stopped heaving, he was still unconscious. Chris wouldn't look at me, but adamantly refused to let me go with them. My hope is that Sabin will have his stomach pumped to all hell or something, and he'll be okay. So I stare at my phone, waiting to hear something.

Outside, an earsplitting clap of thunder announces that the storm that's been on the way has arrived, and a hard rain starts to fall. Zach has lit a fire to try to take away the chill, but neither of us can stop shivering. We haven't talked about the implosion of either of our relationships.

The devastation and confusion are too great. Also, the anger. We fall asleep together on the couch.

Zach wakes me early in the morning. He's showered, his hair still wet, and he shakes me hard until I growl at him. I don't want to be awake. I want to disappear. He tells me to get dressed and to meet him in the car.

"What is it? Wait, is it Sabin?" I sit up.

"No. He's okay. I got a text from Estelle. He's going to be fine. Get dressed." He hands me a travel mug of coffee. "We're taking a trip."

"Where are we going?"

"Just get ready."

Thirty minutes later, we are driving out of Bar Harbor. Zach's aviator shades hide his eyes, but I can see determination in his posture and his grip on the steering wheel. He has been unusually curt with me today, but I don't like being kidnapped.

"Zach." I touch his shoulder softly. "Where are we going?"

He clamps his mouth shut and doesn't answer me right away. "You know what I know now, don't you?"

"Yes."

"In fact, you know more. I didn't mean to listen in, but yesterday I heard a bit of a conversation between James and Chris. Estelle? She's . . . There's a lot more isn't there? They're all in deep shit."

"Yes." My voice splinters. "Yes."

"It's much worse than I understood. So much worse."

"I know. I had no idea. Zach, *where* are we going?"

"I don't want to talk. Just let me drive."

I'm exhausted, but I can't rest. I shut my eyes, and I am haunted by Chris's stories. The repeated trauma they faced . . . It's too much. I

left drowning

know how markedly I fell apart after the fire, and this is so much worse. How they have functioned at all, much less seemingly so well until now, is impossible to understand. They are tough, all of them, but as Chris pointed out, they have been damaged profoundly. What Chris had to go through, what he endured . . . What has been done to his body and mind . . . I have graphic images of his childhood that I cannot stop seeing.

I am deeply in love with Chris. He is everything to me. He saved me, and he's not going to let me save him. I don't even know how to process that. I don't know what to do.

"Zach, pull over." I've started to cry now, immediately choking on my sobs. "Pull over."

Zach veers the car off to the side of the highway, and I can barely see as I get the door open and lean against the guardrail. I vomit repeatedly. Zach gets out and comes to stand next to me with his hand on my back while I empty my stomach, coughing and crying.

"I know, Blythe. I know."

"Oh, Zach. No, no, no! Please tell me this didn't happen. Please, I can't stand this. Please, make it go away. Not them. Not Chris. Not Eric and Estelle. God, not Sabin. Not my Sabin. Oh please. I don't want to lose Chris, I don't want to lose him. None of them. We can't let them go."

He hands me a tissue from the car and then takes me in his arms. "I know, sweetheart. They can't . . . they can't tolerate relationships. That's why Chris and Eric are trying to leave us. Our love is too much, and they don't think they deserve it. Or they're afraid it won't last. Or . . . any number of things. Their attachment issues are wholly fucked up. It's not their fault."

We cry together, both of us on the verge of losing the people we are madly in love with, and both of us filled with immeasurable anger and heartbreak.

Zach gets me back into the car and buckles my seat belt for me, as I am too hysterical to do anything but fall apart.

"We need to keep going, Blythe. Let's just keep going."

I can't imagine where Zach is taking us, but at this point, it hardly matters. I cry until I have no tears left.

It takes about two hours of driving, but finally I calm down. I can feel that I am shutting off, as if the depression that Chris helped me chase away is reappearing. It's going to take hold of me, and I don't know if I'll be able to fight it this time. Not without Chris.

I realize that Zach has stopped the car. We are parked on a gravel driveway in a tree-filled area that overlooks a huge contemporary house. The hard angles and sleek design feel cold and stiff. It looks to be three floors, and the view to the ocean must be extraordinary. Even from the car, I can hear the waves hitting the shore. The house is isolated on what appears to be a huge piece of property. There are no other houses in sight.

I wipe my eyes. "Where are we?"

"This is where it all happened."

That's when I understand. We are at their father's house.

"I wish he were dead." His eyes flash. "They wish he were dead. He *deserves* to be dead."

I watch as he seems to shudder with a rage I've never seen in him before. His face is flushed. I know I'm watching a transformation and that it's out of my power to reason with him. I watch as he reaches around to the backseat, his hand fumbling as if for something he's just remembered. Then I see that he's got a hold of a baseball bat.

left drowning

I stare at Zach and feel all my senses come alive. I grab the arm that's not holding the bat with both of my hands.

"Oh Jesus. Fuck, no, Zach! You're out of your mind. This is not the answer."

"It is. You know it is. This son of a bitch is out of his mind. You heard what he did to them! You heard it! He fucking terrorized them. This sick fuck is not going to take anything else from those kids. They all want him gone, you know they do." He pulls his arm from me and gets out of the car, leaving it running. He is gone before I have time to think. I sit unmoving in my seat. I understand what Zach is feeling. Their father's death would bring a degree of peace and justice that nothing else can. But this is crazy. There's some part of me that doesn't believe it is happening. I force myself to breathe. I know I have to move. I should stop this. Or I could let this be over in a few minutes. It's hard to think, and I struggle for too long before I get out of the car.

But the moment I open the door, I start to run down the driveway. Zach has parked a good distance from the house. My feet are pounding and my heart is racing, but I don't know that I'm going to be in time to stop him. I run hard. This is not the answer, and it's not what Chris would want. As I run, I am overwhelmed with a sense of familiarity. The smell, the sound of the water here . . .

I find Zach standing outside the front of the house. An Adirondack chair on the deck faces the ocean, and a man is sleeping in it. A plaid wool blanket covers his lap. I don't even want to look, so I keep my back to the deck. Zach is still holding the bat, but his arm is slack by his side. Thankfully, he can't do it, because I wouldn't be able to stop him.

"Zach, let's go. Now."

"That's him. Look how big he is. How powerful he must have been before he got sick." Tears stream down his face. "How could he have done what he did? How?"

I can't stop myself, and I turn to get a good look. I suddenly want to see the person who has inflicted so much pain. Who does this? Who terrorizes and belittles and scares the shit out of kids? That's not how the world should work.

So I focus on this man who has so viciously tormented people I nearly worship. When I see his face, the shock threatens to drop me to my knees. I walk closer until I am only a few feet from him, and I am sure. I know this man.

The man asleep in the chair in front of me, I have seen him once before. He is a bit grayer now, but I know his strong jawline and the scar above his eyebrow. I know his strength and his heroism. I know how I have idealized him for years, and I know how his image has gotten me though countless nights of my own pain. I know the sound of his voice. *You are safe, you are safe, you are safe, sweet girl.*

I know all of this because the man who tortured the love of my life is the same man who pulled me from the ladder just before it collapsed into the burning house.

left drowning

31
SAVING GRACES

ZACH AND I DON'T TALK FOR MOST OF the ride home. I haven't told him about Chris's father. I just can't. The devastation and confusion are too great. For now, this knowledge is solely mine, and I'm not ready to change that yet. One of the things that I love about Zach is that he respects boundaries the way that I do, so he does not press me despite the obvious fact that I am in shock. I do, however, say firmly, "I can fix this. I can get them back. I just need to think." He doesn't question me, but just nods, continuing to hide behind his sunglasses as we drive. We stop at a convenience store for gas and something to eat. Both of us are sick to our stomachs, but we agree that some food might help. I scan the drink cases, unable to decide—nothing could possibly sit well. Then I smile and reach for an orange soda.

At the house, I walk through the living room past James, Estelle, and Chris, who have returned from the hospital, and go up to my bedroom. I need quiet. I sit on the side of the bed, the bed that I share with Chris, and stare at my reflection in the dresser-top mirror. I can't decide if I still look like a kid or if I look like a woman. I'm at a funny in between stage. Perhaps I should see myself as younger simply due to my age, but what I've been through makes me feel older. It's not an uncomfortable thought, being totally grown up. I like who I am, who I've grown into. Had I not lived through the fire and through the aftermath, I might like myself less. I am affected by my past, just as everyone is, and being able to embrace that centers me. That strength and stability is going to help me today.

What am I going to say to Chris? I've had a long drive to process things, but I'm still missing a piece of our story. I know it. The quilt is cool against my skin when I lie down on the bed, and I tuck my knees up into my chest while I try to digest all that has happened over the past twenty-four hours. Too much. A massive storm of information has engulfed me, as I knew it would. That's how a storm with such power happens; you sense the build and darkness, you prepare as best you can, you do what you can to get through it even as it devastates your entire world. Whatever you do, however much you brace yourself, you will still be caught up in forces that you cannot control. So the question is how to navigate through the chaos. It takes thought, and trust, and serenity.

Later I get up and pace. I'm close. I have the answer right here, if I could just . . . I sit up slowly and look to my dresser. The sea urchin that Chris gave me so long ago sits in the center. I pick it up gently and rub my fingers over it. He said this belonged to me, and I felt that to be true also. Neither of us had a reason, but it simply felt so right that questioning it was not a priority. That's how it has always been with him. The natural, instinctual flow between us has always felt so right. Now I am sensing that our connection is even deeper than I have previously imagined. I start to roll the sea urchin back and forth from one hand to the other. *Think. Think.*

As it turns upside down in my palm, I stop. I'd never noticed the small circular disc on the bottom of the sea urchin. After some gentle prodding, I get it off. The porcelain figure is hollow, and something is stuffed inside, presumably to protect the fragile piece from breaking. I remove a wad of faded red fabric. I put down the sea urchin and hold up the scrap of cotton. I have flashes of memory, sensory input from this small bit of old fabric that triggers emotion and, minutes later, images. Then I know what it is. I know the color and texture very well.

My heart nearly stops.

I squeeze my hand around it as I walk from my room into Chris's. Ignoring my general high regard for privacy, especially Christopher's, I begin frantically rooting through his dresser and his closet. It's got to be here. He must have it.

It is an hour later that Chris appears in the doorway to my room. "Blythe?"

I am sitting on the floor while tears cascade down my cheeks. I am not sad, I am just overwhelmed. I don't know how to explain this to him because I cannot explain it to myself. I look up at the person who I love more than anything in the world.

"Blythe, what are you doing?" He kneels down in front of me.

I can't speak. There is no way to begin.

"Sabin is all right," he says. "He's going to rehab. The hospital staff is very nice here, and they're helping us find a good place. He'd like for you to call him later."

I nod. "Of course. I'm relieved he's okay."

Chris fiddles with his watch so that he doesn't have to look at me. "We're going to pack up today. Probably leave tomorrow."

"No," I say clearly. "No, you're not. You are not ending things between us. You are not ending *us*."

"I need to. I can't do this with you. It's too much." He stands.

"You've said that before, but I'm not going to accept it this time. You don't know what you're saying, and you're not being fair to me."

"Look, the things you think you love about me? You shouldn't. Not really. My . . . past. It's part of me, it affects everything that I do in the most fucked-up way. You think that I'm strong, you love that I take care of you. But I'm only like that because of what happened. I was forced to become bulletproof and competent because I faced complete insanity. That competence and diligence that you get off on is tainted. Jesus, even in bed. You like how I am with you. I'm . . . controlling. I'm in charge a lot. You even said it to me, that I don't like to be out of control. See? How am I supposed to be who you want when you know why I am the way I am? It's not real strength." His voice shakes. "Every part of me is affected. It's why I left you in the first place, why I ran to someone safe. Because you can't possibly deal with what a fucking disaster I'm bound to be. You know all that. So you should know that I'm not good for you, or for anyone. I have done everything wrong so far. Everything. I'll end up destroying you the way I've destroyed everything and everyone. The only smart thing that I can do now is to leave."

"Stop it. Just stop it!" I'm angry now. "Don't you ever talk about yourself like that, and you don't you dare presume to tell me why I love you. Give me more fucking credit than that. You got yourself, and your brothers and sister, through the unimaginable. And you got me through my own nightmare. I love you for so many reasons, but I don't love you because of those reasons. I love you simply because I do. And that's it. That's the only goddamn thing that matters. I love every single part of you. So, no, Christopher, no. We are not over. And I can prove to you why." I stand up, using the bed for support. I am shaky, but I am also clearheaded. "I want to show you something. I need you to trust me. Can you do that? Just for a minute."

Chris looks so tremendously sad, but he nods.

"I'm going to fix this. I'm going to make this okay." I don't know if I'm talking more to him or to myself, but I am trying hard to believe in what I am going to show him and tell him.

I stand him with his back to my dresser. "Just stay there. Don't move." I take the lightweight full-length mirror from the other side of the room and lean it against the bed so that it reflects into the mirror across from it. I stand in front of him and take his face in my hands. I lift up and kiss him softly. He doesn't kiss me back, because, I'm guessing, he feels broken and unworthy of anything even close to love. I can't stand that. As I lift the bottom hem of his shirt up, he tries to stop me, but I brush him away. "Trust me." Chris lets me raise his shirt. I move my left arm under his right and set my forearm on his back, angled up to meet the other hand that goes over his shoulder. "Look in the mirror." I hold him tightly, close my eyes, and wait. "It's okay."

In a few seconds, I feel him tense. His panic sets in. I know how this feels from him because of the many nights that he has awoken me with his nightmares. It was disconcerting for me when I saw this, but for him it is terrifying because it defies how he makes sense of the world. There is no logic or explanation to this, and I know that he's scared.

"Breathe with me, Chris. Breathe." I inhale and exhale. *It's simple. This is how you do it. In and out. Breathe.*

"Blythe, how can . . . No. This can't be real."

"But it is. This is real. *We* are real."

There is disbelief in his words that I know all too well. "We're like . . . puzzle pieces that fit together."

"Yes. Exactly. I first saw this when we were at the hotel. I didn't want to tell you then because I didn't understand it. But I do now." I step out of the way as Chris reaches for his shirt and pulls it quickly over his head.

"How could you possibly understand this? It's just some weird . . . coincidence. It doesn't mean anything. It can't."

"It does. It means everything." I reach behind him and take something from the dresser. I hold up the torn remnants of my red shirt up and rest it against my chest.

"Why do you have that?" He is momentarily angry. "I don't want you touching that."

I step out of his reach. "I know. Because this shirt means something to you, doesn't it?"

He pauses. "Yes. It does. Put it down."

"You don't see it yet. Think, Chris. Remember. Do you remember me?"

His face drains of color, and he starts to shake his head.

"This is my shirt. This is my Matthews shirt."

"No, Blythe. It's not. It belonged to . . . someone else."

"No. I remember that day now," I say gently. "You were the boy

left drowning

on the beach. With the buckets. And I was the girl on the dock. I gave you this."

"No. No, there's some kind of mistake."

I drop the shirt. There is fear in his eyes that I have to get rid of somehow. "I know that this is a lot, but you have to listen to me. Just listen. I saw you, I talked to you, I am the girl who gave you the shirt and water."

He is near tears. "What?"

"You know this. Some part of you remembers. It's why you gave me a piece of my shirt back with my Christmas present. I didn't find it until today. Until it was time."

He sits on the bed. I give him a few minutes to let the memories take over. I've had the entire drive home and time in my room, and I still can't process this. He's in the thick of it.

He looks to my dresser, at the sea urchin. "I must have known. It's why I gave you that. That day on the shore, when my father made me stay out and fill bucket after bucket with water and I thought I would collapse. The day you were there, with me, I found a sea urchin in one of the buckets—"

"And you stopped what he was making you do, and you gently set it back into the water."

"Yes. I did."

"There's more, Chris."

He looks at me and waits.

"That night? Later that night was the fire. And also later that night, your father tried to drown you."

"The same night?"

"Yes. The same night. Our worlds exploded on the same night.

Your father almost killed you, but he didn't. Tell me why again."

"What? Because . . . because his fucking pager went off." Chris puts his hands in his hair. Then he freezes. "No way, Blythe. Don't say it. That is not possible." He is starting to piece it together.

"It is possible. Your father was a volunteer firefighter, wasn't he? His pager went off because of the fire at my house. He is the man who saved my life."

"Oh Jesus, no." Chris walks to the window and keeps his back to me. "Stop this, Blythe. Stop it. This cannot be right."

"There are reasons that we have never talked about certain parts of our life. Neither of us mentioned Maine, and you never told me what your father's volunteer work was . . . Some part of us sensed this. But we weren't ready. We're ready now. We're strong enough."

"It's too much."

"I saw him today. Your father. Zach and I went to see him. Don't worry, he didn't see us. When I saw him, it took me back to the night of the fire. I know your father, Christopher. He is the person who pulled me off the ladder."

I let silence take over for a while. Chris has to figure out how to accept this. If he can.

"My father tried to kill me. And then he saved you."

"Yes."

"There is no way that this happened." He can't stop shaking his head. "This means that your fire saved my life. That your parents' death saved my life. That your depression, your guilt, those years you lost? Everything you suffered through gave me life."

I stand behind Chris but don't touch him yet. "We can't begin to piece this all together in any kind of logical way, but, no that's not what it means. It means

left drowning

that there was a fire that was going to happen no matter what, and my parents were going to die no matter what. But don't you see what else? That night had a purpose. A very good one. To keep us both alive. Maybe it's our connection that protected us. We both could have died that night, but we didn't because of each other. Your father was close to the house, and he got there in time so that I didn't die, and that saved you. I know the irony is incomprehensible. I do. But it's what happened. God, my parents would never have wanted children to go through what you all did. If the fire ended it for you? I know them. I know them *so* well, and they would be grateful to know that something good came from the fire. Our lives and the love we share are the saving graces of that night."

He drops his head, crying now. "That shirt? That really was you. You were on the dock."

"Yes."

"You stayed with me. For hours. You stayed *all day*."

"Of course."

"I was so amazed that you didn't leave."

"I would never leave you, Chris. Even then, when I didn't know you."

"You kept me from falling apart. Not just on the shore. But that night. When I thought . . . when I thought that I was going to drown, I thought about you. How I would never get to meet the girl who stayed with me. The girl who gave me strength. Who helped me plan a future and who got me to Matthews. I think that I must have gone to school there to . . . to find you. I didn't think about it like that until now, but I was looking for you. Focusing on you that night made me hold on longer than I might have. When I couldn't breathe, and I was choking, and dying in the fucking toilet . . . I fought to stay alive because of you. His pager went off, and I felt so guilty being grateful for that because it meant that someone else was in trouble. I didn't want anyone else to be hurt, but . . . I also didn't want to die. When I woke up in glass and covered in my own blood, I thought about you. You were all I had. I've kept your shirt with me since that day because it was all that I had of you. Or so I thought."

Now I press my body to his and wrap my arms around his waist. I lean my head against his back and wipe my eyes on his shirt. "Don't you see, Chris? You and I are supposed to be together. Not because we *have to* be together. There is always a choice. This is not an obligation or a duty. But our lives are entwined, they have been, for good reasons. I've known that from the moment I set eyes on you. It never made sense to me before. How I felt so deeply connected to you before we'd even spoken. But I did, and I do. I have loved you since that day on the dock. Probably even before that. I feel as though I have loved you my entire life. Please, Chris, I'm right here. I will give you everything I have if you'll just let me. I am strong now, and I can handle anything. More than that, I *want* to go through your life with you. I am begging you, Christopher. Begging you with all of my heart. Let me take care of you the way that you have taken care of me."

Chris turns around, wraps me up in his arms, and rests his chin on top of my head.

I hold him tightly. This is terrifying because I don't know if he will take the risk to stay with me. I know he's not one for reaching out for help or love even in better circumstances. I shut my eyes. "You think that I couldn't possibly fall in love with the vulnerable side of you. And you're wrong. I love that part of you, too. Chris, I don't know what I believe in anymore. . . . I know that you don't believe in God, or fate, or anything. If you can just push aside that rational, logical, fucking solidly

left drowning

cognitive piece of your thinking and just *feel*. Listen to your heart. The other shit? It doesn't matter. The past? The horrible nightmare you've been through? We can handle that. We can. We already have, don't you see that? For you, telling me the details of your life seems like something new between us, but I've always known in some ways. Maybe not the specifics, but I've known, and it's never made my total love for you falter one bit. Never."

I'm afraid to stop talking for fear that he will walk away for good, but at some point I have to turn the cards over to him. This could be the end. I may lose the only love of my life. But I have fought for him as hard as I can. It's all that I can do.

"Just feel *me*, Chris, then nothing else matters. Belief in anything is hard, I know. But I am asking you to believe in me and to believe in us the way that I do. Can you do that? Please, Chris, please believe in us."

He steps back and looks at me. His cheeks are damp as he lifts our hands between us so that we are palm to palm. Chris nods and drops his fingers next to mine.

TWENTY, TWENTY-ONE

AT NINE THIRTY THIS MORNING I LEFT HOPKINTON, Massachusetts, and I am now entering the town of Wellesley, somewhere around mile eighteen, I think. I am running the Boston Marathon. Sort of. It's not the real marathon day because I don't want that pressure. Next month, I will stand in Newton and watch the real one as it takes place, and I'll hand out water and orange slices to exhausted runners at the finish line. While I admire those who have the ability to run on race day, it's not for me. I don't like the competition and the crowds. I just want to run the route, and I want to finish. I don't care how long it takes.

The weather is on my side today. This last Wednesday in March is cool and dry. Weather around Boston is very unpredictable, and some marathon days have been dreadfully hot and humid, leaving even well-prepared runners in bad shape. I'd fall apart in shitty weather, so I'm lucky. I've been carb-loading for a few days and I'm hydrated. My sneakers are a reliable pair that I broke in over the past month.

What's working against me? If I continue at the pace I'm at, I'll come in at over five and a half hours. That's a damn ridiculously long time to run, and my stamina is nearly depleted as it is. Yet I can't imagine that I can pick up my pace. Eighteen miles is longer than I've ever run, and I'm hurting like I never have before. Fighting to do something that I'm not meant to do is scary. The fear of failure is scary. The average women's time is closer to four and a half hours, but because I want this so much, I don't give a shit if it takes me nine hours; I just want to finish.

Not only am I a slow runner, but running on an unofficial day means that I have to deal with sidewalks, and cars, and traffic lights.

However, I do have some help with that.

I take a quick glance at Zach, who is driving a few yards ahead of me with the hazards on. I love him for how he's unabashedly blocked intersections and ticked off drivers by trying to keep a clear path for me as often as possible. At this point I'd welcome the excuse to stop at a traffic light, and I groan inwardly every time I hit a green.

My legs are jelly, and I have never been this exhausted in my life. I just can't do it. Accepting defeat is my only option now. I stop running and bend over, shaking my head as I turn off my music. Fuck this. Zach beeps the horn repeatedly, and I shake my head. He backs up and yells out the passenger window to me.

"No way, Blythe. You can do this."

"I can't," I manage. Jonah barks loudly out the window.

"Look ahead. Look up there." He points up the hill. "Look what she did for you!"

Even in my state, I have to laugh. Estelle is just in my sight. She has traded in her usual high-fashion look for sleek neon-pink spandex and matching sneakers.

I restart a slow, painful jog on Commonwealth Avenue to reach her, steeling myself not to think about how far I still have to go, all the way through Wellesley and up Heartbreak Hill in Newton before I can reach the finish line in downtown Boston. She and the others were supposed to meet me at the finish line, but my sagging spirits are lifted.

"What's up, bitch?" she asks as I come to a stop.

"I'm done," I pant.

"No, you're not. I came out here for spring break. I could have been in fucking Barbados or something, you know, but I'm not. Worse, I got all dressed up like an asshole for you, so now put your music back on and just run like I know you can."

"I just can't."

Estelle glares at me and puts my music back on. She grabs my arm and pulls me ahead. I have never seen Estelle do anything resembling exercise, so to see her run is nothing short of amusing. And it gives me the kick I need to keep going.

She's been in therapy since the end of last summer. They all have. And while she and James are not officially together, they are "on hold" the way Chris and I once were. I think they are going to make it, and I've been impressed with my brother's compassion and patience.

Estelle jogs with me for a bit and then blows me a kiss and darts away to join Zach. He beeps the horn again, and Estelle points from the window.

left drowning

I smile again. Now Eric is waiting for me. He's got earphones in, too, and he pumps his arms up and down as I approach. He gives me a nod and then joins me. We run silently. It's always been so easy to be with Eric, and today is no different. Our hours of silent studying together have instilled in us an ability to enjoy a comfortable silence. He's had a hard year, and it was only a month ago that he and Zach got back together.

I stumble over a crack in the pavement, and Eric puts his hand on my back. I am soaked in sweat, and I wipe my forehead with my hand. As much as this run is killing me, I cannot stop. Whatever pain I am feeling is so much less than what my friends have been through, and I have illogically convinced myself that if I can finish this marathon I will be completing some piece of all of our stories. That doing this will secure our healing. It's dumb. But now that I am seeing my friends, I am even more dedicated to finishing.

I brace myself because I have just reached Newton, the most challenging part of this route. It's got four hills, the last of which is my reason for running this race. Heartbreak Hill: the ninety-foot incline that's set between mile twenty and twenty-one. And it's a goddamn bitch. It's where more people quit the race than any other spot. It comes at the worst possible time in the run, when runners who are much stronger than I am give up.

Eric knows where we are. He keeps his hand lightly on my back, and together we run the first hill. When he drops back to join Zach and Estelle, I'm not sure how I am going to go on. I drop my head and consider whether or not this is worth it.

And then someone grabs my hand and runs with me. James. He gave up his spring break to be here with me, too. I'm sure the lure of seeing Estelle was appealing, of course, but my brother loves me. He'll be back with me again in Maine this summer. I don't think that either of us misses our parents' house in Massachusetts that much. It never felt like home without them. The house on Frenchman Bay? That is the family home.

"Thank you for everything, Blythe." He looks straight ahead as he runs. "I've never told you how courageous you were that night of the fire, but you did everything. You saved my life, and I'm sorry that I was so ungrateful. You've done more for me since that night than I deserved. I know that. I love you a lot. I really do."

"I love you, too," I pant. "And I still miss them."

"We always will. But you've made it easier for us. We'll be okay."

The second hill hurts like all hell, but together my brother and I run through our loss. We run through the fire and our parents' death, through his lies, through my coming undone, and through the relationship that we nearly lost. We run through the rebuilding and the survival. James holds my hand tightly, and he wipes his eyes once as we finish this leg.

The third hill. I am at my weakest now. It's my turn to wipe my eyes as James passes me off to Sabin. Sabin will always have a special piece of my heart in a way that nobody else ever could. He's not exactly like a brother, but he's not just a friend. I stop my music and start to say something.

"Don't talk, and don't start crying yet! I'm so proud of you, B. I know you're tired. You're almost there. A little bit more. We can do this."

I nod and let my hand disappear in his.

He has trimmed down a good deal of his waistline this year, and he looks wonderful. And sober. Six months of inpatient rehab and therapy

left drowning

have been intense for him, and I think he's had the hardest time of everyone because he had forgotten the most. Or blocked it out. He was allowed to leave rehab for short periods after the first three months, so I have seen him a few times since last summer, including at Christmas, when he was at my house in Maine. He chopped wood by hand and lugged it into the house, setting it in neat piles by the fireplace. In the evenings he did the dishes and then played his guitar for me. Sabin even spent hours on my computer helping me sort through old family pictures and putting them into an album that we had printed up. I got pretty bored after a few hours, but Sabin thought the pictures of me as a little kid were a riot, and he pestered me for days to wear my hair in pigtails. He was somewhat withdrawn over the fall and winter, quieter than he usually is, but during the past few months he's started to sound more like himself again. Just without the booze. He never stopped being loving, caring, and sweet anytime that I talked to him during this year of recovery, but I'm happy to see that the goofy and loud parts of him are returning.

"Dude, running sucks," he says as we reach the peak of the hill. "You are one tough girl."

I am barely running now, just shuffling really, when we near the base of Heartbreak Hill. "You ready?"

I shake my head. "No. It's too hard. I don't want to do this."

He drags me forward. "Don't stop moving. It's the worst thing you can do. I read that. This is hard, but it's not too hard."

"I can't. Why did I try this?" I pant.

A voice other than Sabin's answers. "Because you believe in this."

I love this voice. It cuts through everything that is hurting and reaches right to my heart.

"Chris, I hurt. Everything hurts." He is next to me, and he grabs my free hand so that I have two of my most adored people on either side of me, holding me up as I run.

"I know, baby. Sabin is right, though. You can do this."

"You'll stay?" I ask. "To the end?"

"Of course."

"I can't do this without you."

"And I can't do this without you. We're going to run Heartbreak Hill together."

"I'm so tired."

"I know. But you have to keep moving. Come on."

Now I turn to look at Chris. As always, he takes my breath away when I see him. We've lived together in Bar Harbor for seven months, but every day I am staggered by the sight of him, and every day I fall more in love.

He hands me a bottle of water and smiles. "Thought I'd return the favor."

I drink a third of the bottle. "I love you."

"I love you, too. So much."

Sabin takes the bottle so that we don't have to carry it and then kisses me on the cheek. "He's got you. You guys can do this. Go! Go! We'll meet you at the finish line." He walks to Chris's truck which Zach has been driving, and hops into the bed. "Go, sweet girl! Run! Both of you!"

Sabin, Estelle, Eric, James, and Zach cheer as Chris and I start to run the hardest hill. The truck lets out a long, loud honk, and they speed along Commonwealth Avenue and head for downtown Boston. I hand Chris the other earbud, and we run to the same song that we listened to

left drowning

like this so long ago in his dorm room at Matthews when he first told me to run through the pain.

Heartbreak Hill is indeed a fucking bitch. The steep incline is cruel and unforgiving at this stage of the run. People say that it's all downhill after this, but it'll still be a hell of a run. Going downhill takes control.

"Slow and steady, sweet girl," Chris says. He keeps my slow pace. He is as strong as ever, but he doesn't make me feel weak. He makes me feel capable despite how I falter in my run.

Chris and I live a quiet life in Bar Harbor. I mean, except for the loud sex. Of which we have plenty. I'm still freelance writing for the magazine, but I'm working on a novel also. This was Chris's idea. I have no idea if it'll go anywhere, but I'm enjoying giving it a try. Chris has immersed himself in Acadia National Park, and he's become quite a good guide, leading us on challenging hikes and day trips. He got a job in the park's administrative office and has surprised himself by getting involved in all the boring details, like the park's budget. We've met some people who live in the area, and occasionally we have another couple over for dinner or go out with friends for an evening. Chris's coworker owns a sailboat and has offered to take us out when the weather warms up a bit.

The winter months there would be considered impossible by some people, but Chris and I don't mind. His truck can drive over nearly any snowfall, and we have a lot of supplies shipped to us. I'm quite happy not to leave the house for days at a time. Jonah keeps me company while I curl up with a blanket and my laptop and write by the fireplace. Our life is blissfully low-key. Except for when James and all the Shepherd siblings come to stay. Then it's the best kind of chaos possible. Christmas was absolutely insane. Annie came out, too, and I think we all want her to adopt us. Except for Sabin, who still flirted with her like only he can. They will all be back out this summer, and James and Sabin have more plans for restoring the house, including sanding the wood floors and redoing the deck. Annie is staying with us for just a week, though. She has a boyfriend now, and they're going to rent a place near us for the summer. She wants to be available for us—or, I'm guessing, keep an eye on us—without having to live with seven recent college grads. I can't blame her.

For months Chris resisted seeing a counselor. When his father died in the late fall, however, I insisted. He wasn't sad about his father dying, but he was less relieved than I think he expected. There are pieces of his past that I cannot help him work through. He does talk to me, but it's going to be a long time before he chooses to share everything. Or maybe he won't share everything, and that's okay, too, but he knows that I am always available. I've gone with him a few times to talk to the counselor. Hearing his stories is hard for me, and I have been battling my own rage and sadness over his childhood. I had amazing parents who died too soon, and he had an abusive, sick father who died too late.

When we are at the midway point of the hill, he wipes tears from my cheeks as we run. This moment is both incredibly painful and equally freeing. He knows how to read my body, and he knows when I'm about to break.

"I am overwhelmingly in love with you," Chris says as he matches my steps. "I've spent most of my life thinking that my father never gave me anything but pain. But that's not true. He did give me something. Someone. You. He gave me you. Last summer, you asked me to believe in us. I don't believe in much, as you know, but I do damn well believe in us. Forever."

left drowning

Reaching the peak of Heartbreak Hill is easy now.

"We'll make it to that finish line, won't we, Blythe?"

"Always."

We run through the remnants of our pain, and more importantly, we run for our present and for our future.

Together we kick heartbreak's ass.

Acknowledgments

WHILE WRITING MAY OFTEN BE A SOLITARY PROCESS, the times when it isn't require a certain strength from those who dare to get involved with a moody, stubborn, exhausted, overcaffeinated author. I owe thanks to so many people.

My associate publisher, Tim Ditlow, believed in *Left Drowning* before knowing what exactly this book would become. An act of faith if ever there was one.

The indescribably talented Kate Chynoweth did the most spectacular editing job any author could dare to hope for, and she brought out the best in me and in this story.

Lots of love to my most tolerant agent, Deborah Schneider, for telling me that I "wowed" her. (I suspect I may have wowed her with chaos, but she's too nice to say so.)

Another round of thanks to Lori Gondelman for proofreading and all-around handholding during the birth of yet another book. Jenny Aspinall, Marlana Grela, and Chrystle Woods all read chapters at various stages and were immeasurably helpful and supportive. Huge thanks to my cheering squad!

Thank you to Karen Lawson for connecting me with the very kind

Dr. Barnett, who explained medical facts in shockingly understandable language.

Julia Clark, assistant chief of the Orland Fire Department, and Michael Ferreira, first lieutenant of the Upper Greenwood Lake Fire Company, both volunteers in Maine, graciously donated their time to walk me through more detail than I knew I would need, but that I demanded anyway. Both of them are amazing, tough, and unspeakably brave. Stay safe, you two.

Andrea DiMella endured emergency phone calls to answer my repeated questions about running. She is an angel. And disgustingly athletic and non-lazy.

Mad love and respect to my father, Carter Umbarger, a most brilliant psychotherapist and even more brilliant father. Thank you for helping these characters stay real. I love you, Daddy. And equal adoration to my mother, Susan Conant, who gets both the blame and the credit for getting me into this business. I am very lucky to have such wonderful parents. Not everyone does.

My readers and bloggers gave me the ability to continue writing. I don't know how to thank them for all the reviews, the enthusiasm, and the humbling love. I lean on them more than they will ever know. Endless gratitude to each of them for sticking with me.

And, oh, my fellow authors. There is no way I could have survived the *Left Drowning* process without them. Endless love, thanks, and admiration to: Michele Scott, for her daily (sometimes hourly) assistance as a friend and talented writer. Tracey Garvis-Graves for her unfailing and powerful championing during my darkest hours. To Andrew Kaufman, because he never failed to holler, "See? Now they're listening to Jessica!" when I needed it the most. To Abbi Glines and Tammara Webber, for being rocks of sanity in a chaotic world. To Colleen Hoover, because sometimes you really do just need some damn flowers. And to Jamie McGuire, for also being a rebel with a cause.

To my twenty: I love all of you, and I would have undoubtedly collapsed without your strength. Fight the good fight, girls. Our power together is immeasurable.

New York Times bestselling author JESSICA PARK mines the territory of love's growing pains with wit, sharp insights, and a discernible heat and heartbeat. Her previous novels include *Flat-Out Love* and *Relatively Famous*, and she authored the e-shorts *What the Kid Says* (Parts 1 and 2) and *Facebooking Rick Springfield*.